DOCTOR WHO

SHORT TRIPS:
THE CENTENARIAN

A Short-Story Anthology
Edited by Ian Farrington

Published by Big Finish Productions Ltd
PO Box 1127
Maidenhead SL6 3LW

www.bigfinish.com

Managing Editor: Jason Haigh-Ellery
Consultant for BBC Worldwide: Justin Richards

ISBN 1-84435-191-2

First published July 2006

Cover art by RED INK 2006
Original sleeve design by Clayton Hickman

The *Centenarian* concept by Ian Farrington and Joseph Lidster
Samson Griffin and Gemma Griffin created by Joseph Lidster and used with kind permission
The Slarvians created by Cavan Scott and Mark Wright and used with kind permission

With thanks to
Claire Bartlett, Nicholas Briggs, Jonathan Clements, Paul Cornell, Mark Coupe, David Davies,
Maureen Davies, Sara Eggen, Nigel Fairs, Jo Goodwright, Chris Green, Dave Hoskin, Alethea Kontis,
Shaun Lyon, Paul McGann, Iain McLaughlin, Stuart Manning, Studio Robb, Denis Steer,
Molly Steer, Steve Tribe, Jennifer Ugarte and, especially, Robert Dick

Typeset in Quadraat

Printed and bound in Great Britain by Biddles Ltd
www.biddles.co.uk

Tuesday 25 December 1990

Linda Grainger opened her eyes and looked at her family. Mum was shouting at Dad, who'd clearly had too much to drink. He was trying to swing her around the living-room floor. Mum stopped shouting and started to laugh. Over on the other sofa, Granddad Edward was quietly snoring, exhausted after, once again, telling everyone his life story...

From *She Won't Be Home* by Joseph Lidster
Short Trips: The History of Christmas (2005)

Prologue

Joseph Lidster

Violet looked up at the White Rabbit and shivered. She clutched her arms protectively across her chest, chilled more by the horrors of the previous night than by the biting mist. All was dark and still. The unseasonal thick fog pierced only by Big Ben's pale white face.

'San Francisco latest!' A young boy's voice echoed down the road as he flogged copies of the *Evening Standard*. Violet remembered what Mr Peake had said about the earthquake. It had been two months ago, but she could still see his face, grey and gaunt, as he'd informed the staff of America's devastation. She looked down the river at the Houses of Parliament, at Big Ben, at all the other still and safe buildings and tried to imagine them crumbling away to nothing. Shaking her head, she turned back to face the old public house. 'She pressed a hand against the damp stone wall and wondered if anything could ever –

A man's hand erupted through the fog and gripped her wrist.

'What are you doing, Violet?'

She stared up at her fiancé. 'Richard! You frightened me!'

He let go of Violet's wrist and smiled. As she looked into his fine face, she again felt an urge to pinch herself. That such a handsome man, indeed a footman, could be interested in her still seemed unbelievable.

'You're late!' she admonished, trying not to smile.

Richard laughed. 'Well, if that doesn't make a change, I don't know what does!'

She grinned. 'I'll forgive you if you buy me a drink.'

'After you,' he said, pushing open the door. 'My darling!'

Violet curtsied then laughed. 'You're such a silly man!'

They walked into the public house, the sudden noise of people threatening to deafen them after the cold silence of outside. Warmed by the open fire, Violet loosened her shawl as Richard pointed her towards a secluded booth. She pushed her way through the carousers and sat down at the empty table. Hearing Richard suddenly laugh out loud, she looked up and watched as he joked with the young barman, Len. Then, remembering why she was here, remembering what had happened, she looked down at the table and nervously ran a fingernail through a groove in the wood. Even here, with him, was she really safe?

'I must stay calm,' she muttered. 'Or he'll just laugh at me.'

'Laugh at you, my dear?' Suddenly, Richard was stood at the table. 'Why ever would I do that?'

'How was Len?' she asked as he sat down across from her. Her fingernail pushed further into the wooden tabletop.

Richard passed over her ale and chuckled. 'Never mind Len. What's this story you've got to tell me?'

Suddenly, she winced as a tiny splinter pricked her finger. A ruby bead of blood began to form under the nail as she pulled her finger out of the wood. Richard reached over, took her wrist and pulled it towards him. Then, he gently placed the finger in his mouth and sucked soothingly. The pain eased as quickly as it had started. Shocked, she pulled the hand away.

'Richard! People will stare!'

He sat back and winked at her mischievously. 'Let them stare!' He laughed, not noticing her rising hysteria.

'If the master and mistress ever found out I was here, I'd be dismissed! Imagine if they found out I was engaged! I'd be on the streets!' Her face began to shake as her eyes filled with tears. 'Richard, I couldn't bear to lose you but I can't think about what would happen if...'

She stopped as he leant forward and took her hand in his.

'Ssh,' he said quietly. 'I hardly think their sort are likely to come here. Violet, what is it? This isn't like you.'

She tried to pull her hand away but he held it firm.

'I...' She paused. 'Something happened last night. Something terrifying and unnatural!'

He gasped, his eyes wide in mock surprise. 'What happened, young Violet?'

'Don't laugh at me!' she cried before leaning forward and lowering her voice. 'The mistress gave birth!'

He leaned further forward, so that their faces were mere inches apart. 'So? Old Mother Grainger finally spewed her spawn!'

Violet's mouth fell open. 'The mistress isn't like that! She's a lovely lady!'

'That hasn't stopped you lying to her about us!' He slouched back and took a swig from his pint. 'Anyway, I'm sure she's perfectly lovely but she's not my sort. I like a girl with more...' He indicated Violet's chest.

'You're horrible, Richard! To talk about my mistress like... well, sometimes I don't know why I agreed to marry you!'

He sighed. 'I'm sorry. So, what happened?'

Violet looked across the bar. Despite the riotous laughter and blazing fire, she trembled. Shadows flickered across her face as she turned back to her smiling fiancé.

'The mistress was attacked!' She took a quick sip of ale before continuing at a whisper. 'She was attacked by the Devil!'

Yesterday morning, Mr Peake gathered us all together in the kitchen. He told us that some very important people would be attending the master's birthday party so we'd all have to be especially diligent in our duties. He doesn't tolerate anything other than the highest of standards, doesn't Mr Peake.

Anyway, the mistress had arranged the party as a surprise as she had hoped to lift the master's spirits. He'd been in a foul mood for some time now. So, as Mr Peake instructed, we spent the day cleaning and sweeping and furiously working to prepare everything. The food arrived at midday and I swear I have never seen such a huge ham! It was a struggle for Mrs Best to find a platter big enough! I spent the afternoon polishing the finest cutlery and then, at six o'clock, the first guests started to arrive.

The poor mistress got into quite a stir, I can tell you. The lady has been with child for eight months now and I don't think she'd realised how hard it would be for her. Richard, you wouldn't believe who was there! Lord Greystone, General Kirby and his wife, Lady Louisa and Mr Pollard, Dr Hallis, a group of young gentlemen I didn't recognise and… and Sir George Steer.

Everything seemed to be going so well. The guests were entertained – shockingly, some were quite tipsy – the table was set and we were all being, as Mr Peake had requested, 'especially diligent'.

And then, the master arrived home.

His face was redder than I have ever seen it. I swear it was like a big dark tomato! When Mr Peake opened the front door for him, the master stormed in and actually threw his coat at him! Mr Peake, though, is the finest butler. He calmly hung the coat and asked the master if he would like a drink preparing. The master shouted something about 'that socialist idiot Hardie' and barged right past Mr Peake! He nearly knocked him over!

I was quite scared as I could see that he was heading to the drawing room. I ran up to him and tried to warn him about the party. I know it isn't my place but I suspected that he wouldn't appreciate the surprise. Not in the mood he was in. He looked down at me and shouted!

'What is it, girl?'

He's never spoken to me like that before and I was desperately trying to think of something to say when, before I could speak, we heard one of the guests laugh out loud. The master pushed past me and flung open the drawing room door. The guests were all so stunned that they forgot to say 'surprise'.

Anyway, the mistress quickly walked over to him and took his hand. She kissed him on the cheek and wished him a happy birthday and… his face changed. I know that, despite all their recent arguments, they really do love each other and just one kiss from her was able to lighten his mood considerably. Indeed, he actually started to laugh! Then, he turned back to face me and suddenly I realised I'd been holding my breath.

He smiled and said, 'Were you trying to warn me, Violet?'

I shook my head. 'No, sir,' I said.

He was still laughing as I closed the door and returned downstairs to help Mrs Best. Perhaps if I had warned him... stopped him... I don't know, but perhaps it wouldn't have happened.

As I approached the kitchen, I was surprised to hear unfamiliar voices. Men's voices! Raised voices! I pushed open the door and was shocked to see Mrs Best holding a rolling pin to the face of a young gentleman I'd never seen before. An old man was standing next to him.

And when I say old... well, I have never seen a gentleman of such age! He had bright white hair and was angrily waving a stick at Mrs Best! He looked furious but his eyes were... I don't know how to describe them. They were so bright and fierce. I couldn't believe it! There were two gentleman standing in our kitchen and Mrs Best was threatening one of them!

The older gentleman, waving his stick, was demanding that Mrs Best put down the rolling pin and let them in to see the guests. The younger gentleman was doing his best to calm him. Now, he was a looker! A real fine, handsome gentleman!

Oh, don't sulk, Richard! I'm quite sure I shall never see him again.

The older gentleman turned to look at me and I could feel his eyes staring into mine. They were... unearthly! He asked me if this was 86 Hobb's Lane. I just nodded. He asked me if Mr and Mrs Grainger were upstairs. Again, I just nodded. I was lost for words! And you can stop laughing, Richard, or I won't tell you the rest of the story.

Mrs Best turned to me and instructed that I should inform Mr Peake that they had intruders. I looked at her and then at the younger man. He shrugged and said that this wouldn't help matters. I didn't even know what the 'matters' were! I turned and ran back up the staircase and into the hallway. I was so agitated that I ran straight into Mr Peake! He asked me what was happening and, all out of breath, I told him. He passed me a tray of drinks and asked me to follow him into the drawing room. He also told me to compose myself first as I didn't want to upset the guests, which I didn't think was very nice considering what I'd seen in the kitchen. Nevertheless, I smoothed down my skirt and took a deep breath. Then, slowly, wary of what the reaction would be, I followed Mr Peake as he pushed open the drawing room door.

The room was alive with people. I waited as Mr Peake went over to the master and then proceeded to take the tray of drinks around the other guests. Lady Louisa and Mr Pollard were talking to Dr Hallis. The mistress was sitting in her favourite chair quietly talking with Lord Greystone. Over by the fireplace, General Kirby was lecturing the group of gentleman about something called the 'Aliens Act' and about how it would stop more Jews coming into the country. My hands shaking, I offered him a drink.

He looked down at me and asked what I thought about the matter. Trying desperately not to drop the tray, I replied that it wasn't my place to say. Then, suddenly, the master called over to me, asking who the strangers were. I hurried over to him and explained that they were gentlemen but that I didn't know their names. He tutted, turned to the mistress and asked if she was expecting any other guests. She shook her head and said that everyone she had invited was already here. The master informed his guests that he would return shortly and left the drawing room with myself and Mr Peake in attendance.

As we returned to the kitchen, I could again hear raised voices. Mrs Best was using some right surprising language indeed! She turned as we entered and immediately began apologising to the master. Obviously, the sight of him in the kitchen was as unexpected as the arrival of the two strangers. It was, indeed, a night of surprises! The two men turned to look at the master and, immediately, the younger one apologised for their intrusion. The older one then asked where the mistress was. Mr Peake informed him that this was none of his concern and asked them both to leave. The master, though, stopped him. He was intrigued as to who they were. The older gentleman walked over to him, his eyes... well, he was nearly crying. It was as if he knew what was about to happen. He opened his mouth to speak to the master when suddenly we heard the mistress scream!

I was nearest to the door and immediately ran up the stairs and into the hallway. I heard Mr Peake command – yes, command! – the master to stay in the kitchen as he followed me. I ran out into the hallway to be confronted by... oh, it was such a horrible, horrible sight!

Sir George Steer was standing there with his arm wrapped around the mistress's neck! She was struggling furiously and, without thinking, I ran over to her. Then, Sir George looked at me and... and this is when I became truly frightened. He looked at me and silently just shook his head. I was rooted to the floor! Terrified! Over his shoulder, I could see through the open door and into the drawing room. All the other guests were lying down, collapsed, unconscious, possibly dead!

I started to scream but stopped when Mr Peake appeared behind me. He told me that, whatever was happening, there was no cause for me to make a fuss. He asked the mistress to stop struggling as she could damage her unborn child and then asked Sir George what he required. Sir George told us all to return to the kitchen. Mr Peake instructed that I should walk in front of him and, in single file, I led them back down the stairs.

As I went to open the kitchen door, Mr Peake whispered in my ear that I should not do anything silly. I should remain especially diligent in ensuring the safety of the master and mistress. Unable to speak, I nodded, and stepped into the kitchen. Oh, the poor master! He had tears in his eyes. The two gentlemen were holding him back, telling him not to endanger his wife. As Mr Peake escorted Sir George and the mistress into the kitchen, the master began to struggle violently and nearly broke free! The younger gentleman was strong and able to hold him but the older gentleman was thrown to the floor. He landed at the feet of the mistress and looked up at her. And then... I heard him... I heard him say...

'I will save you. You and the child.'

He then slowly stood up and returned to the other gentleman and the master. Sir George reached behind him and closed the kitchen door. And then, as we all became silent, he looked over at them and smiled.

'Hello, Doctor. Surprise!'

His eyes then suddenly exploded with a green light and everything went black.

Richard stood up and moved to sit next to Violet.

'Don't cry, my dear,' he said, putting an arm across her shoulders.

She looked up, the fire, the revellers, her fiancé, everything just a blur through the tears.

'I was so scared, Richard. I was so scared.'

'Would you like another drink? A brandy?'

She took out a handkerchief and dabbed at her eyes. Then, forcing a smile, she shook her head.

'No. No, thank you. I want to tell you the rest of the story.'

I'm not sure how much time passed before I woke up. It was all so very confusing. I remember hearing voices before I could see anything. My head hurt, I know that much. Mr Peake was holding a handkerchief to the back of it as there was blood! I opened my eyes and started to panic.

He whispered into my ear that I should stay still. He told me that I'd fainted and that I was no use to anyone in this state. I wanted to cry but knew that would anger him further so I bit my lip and looked over at the others. Sir George was still holding the mistress. Her face was red and it looked as if, like me, she was holding back tears. The master was sat at the table, unable to stop his. The two gentlemen were trying to comfort him as he cried and wailed and... it was terrible to see him in such a state.

I looked up at Mr Peake and asked him where Mrs Best was. He said that the strangers had persuaded Sir George to let her go. One of the strangers turned to us and told me that they'd also tried to get Mr Peake to go but that he wouldn't leave me. Mr Peake snorted and said that he was just doing his duty. Then, the master looked up at Sir George and asked why he was doing this. The younger of the two gentlemen said that Sir George was possessed by something. I asked if it was the Devil.

'You could say that,' he replied.

I shuddered. The poor master was desperately asking what he could do.

'Nothing,' said Sir George. 'This isn't about you. This is about him!'

His green eyes, for they were still glowing, turned to stare at one of the strangers, who stepped forward. He told the Devil to leave us all alone. Sir George, his voice all strange, said that this would destroy the Doctor. The older gentleman stood forward to join his friend.

'We will stop you. This isn't what happens. Edward will be born. He exists! He lives!' He waved his stick into the air, nearly striking his young friend.

Suddenly, the mistress screamed. The master jumped to his feet and ran over to her but Sir George pushed him to one side as easily as you would swat a fly! The man was truly possessed! The mistress continued to scream as water splashed onto the floor between her legs. She was going to give birth! Her knees were buckling as she cried out in pain but Sir George wouldn't let her fall. Her cries were turning into gasps as he squeezed her neck even tighter. I couldn't bear to watch! Mr Peake could take no more of this and stood up. He began to move over to her but Sir George told him to keep back.

'One step closer and I'll break her neck!'

The mistress let out a most terrible moan.

The possessed Sir George spoke again. 'The child can be born and then, as it takes its first breath, I shall kill it.'

I couldn't believe I was hearing such terrible words. How could one creature be so cruel? The master began to wake up so Mr Peake ran over to him. He tried to help him stand. Sir George swung the mistress around to face them. He looked down at the master and laughed. Then, he turned to the two strangers and commanded them to join Mr Peake and the master over at the far wall. Unwilling to endanger the mistress's life further, they did so, the younger gentleman helping his elderly friend.

The four men tried to reason with Sir George but he ignored them. He let the mistress fall to the floor, her gasps becoming hoarser. And I sat there, clutching my head, watching the nightmare, watching and not knowing what to do! The four men terrified, the mistress screaming, the possessed man laughing!

'Come on, Mary Grainger!' said the green-eyed devil, with his back to me. 'Push out that child. Push him out and let me– eh?'

He stopped and turned to me with a look of surprise. He placed a hand up against the back of his head and pulled it away. Blood dripped through his fingers.

'You little...' he said, before collapsing to the floor.

I gripped onto the rolling pin and just stood there, trembling.

Richard laughed. 'That was very brave of you, my darling.'

Violet continued to shake. 'That wasn't... there was something else.'

Richard frowned. 'Was there indeed?'

Ignoring me, the master, Mr Peake and the two strangers immediately moved over to the mistress. They tried to make her comfortable as I held on to the rolling pin. Then, as the four of them fussed over her, suddenly... and I really didn't think anything else could have been worse than what I'd already witnessed... suddenly a green spirit burst out of Sir George's body!

It flew up into the air and looked at me, its face like the serpent from Eden. It hissed at me and I screamed! I raised the rolling pin to protect myself and hit out at it. It shrieked and flew out of the open window.

And at that, I collapsed to my knees, crying.

The older gentleman came over to me and held me whilst the younger stayed with the master and mistress. I don't really remember what happened next but gradually I became aware that the mistress had stopped screaming. I opened my eyes and looked over at them. There was so much blood but the mistress was crying as she hugged a whimpering baby tight against her chest. The master was dabbing at his eyes when he noticed me looking at them.

'It's a boy, Violet. I've got a son!'

I smiled, then started to laugh. I crawled over to them and for that moment I was no longer their maid. I was part of them. What a sight! The master and mistress sat on the kitchen floor with me, a maid, gently touching the baby's cheek. I asked them what they were going to name him.

The mistress, her face red and streaming with tears, looked at the master and they agreed to name him after the King. I looked up at the two intruders. Their faces were... well, they looked absolutely terrified.

'Edward Grainger,' muttered the old man.

Then, suddenly, came the sound of angry men – Lord Greystone, Mr Pollard and the others – bursting in through the door, led by a pistol-brandishing Mrs Best. The two strangers gave one last look at the baby before swiftly striding out of the back door. I stroked the infant's face and ran out after them. They were just standing there, looking up at the house. Like me, they didn't seem to be feeling the cold.

'You're leaving?' I asked.

They turned to look at me. The old man looked exhausted.

'We have to. We've done what we came to do.'

I asked them what had happened.

They told me that Sir George had been possessed and that I should ensure that he was well looked after. I nodded and then, well, I don't like to say but then the young gentleman leaned forward and kissed me on the cheek. 'You were very brave in there, Violet. You've just saved the world.'

I looked down at the ground, not knowing what to say.

'You won't be forgotten,' said the old man as they disappeared into the darkness. 'Trust me.'

'And, I think I do.'

Richard looked up from his ale. 'You do what?'

Violet shrugged. 'Trust him. I think he was a good man. He saved the baby's life!'

The public house was now crowded, as more and more Londoners sought respite from the cold. Nowhere in the country could have been more filled with good feeling and yet Violet was still trembling with fear. Richard reached over and gently took her hands in his.

'It's all right,' he said. 'It's all over now.'

She shook her head. 'But that's just it. I don't think it is over. That child, Edward. There's something... oh, I don't know.' Suddenly, she stood up, knocking over her drink. 'Can you walk me back to Knightsbridge?'

He looked up at her. 'What is it?'

'I'm scared, Richard. I think Edward Grainger is either going to be someone very special or...'

'Or what?' he asked, standing up.

'Or... or he's cursed. I saw it! The Devil wanted him!'

Echoes

Gary Russell

An Adventure of the Third Doctor

'Christmas wouldn't be Christmas without plum pudding,' said Peggy, grinning excitedly up at Mrs Best. 'That's what our cook always says.'

'Indeed it wouldn't, miss,' Mrs Best replied, craftily slipping the young girl a wooden spoon coated in cake mix. 'G'wan, take this over there. I won't tell if you won't.'

Peggy whooped with delight and hurried towards a rocking chair clearly built for someone twice her size. She greedily started licking the mix from the spoon.

The door at the top of the stairs opened and Peake descended, carefully balancing a silver tray. Peggy noticed that he seemed a little unsteady on his feet and imagined she could hear her mother now. 'He's probably exhausted trying to cope with lots of naughty young girls and boys in his household,' she'd say. Peggy smiled to herself. Earlier that day, they'd been playing choo-choo trains with Peake and one of the footmen and had quite tired them out. Peggy knew it was wrong, but she couldn't help herself. Peake was always game, and it amused her to see how long it was before his cheeks glowed red with exertion, all the tiny little veins on his face lighting up one by one like the lights on a Christmas tree.

'Aft'noon, Miss Margaret,' he said as he reached the foot of the steps. 'Lady Louisa was enquiring as to your whereabouts just a while ago.'

Peggy sagged slightly. Mother always spoiled everything. 'What did you tell her?'

Peake shrugged. 'That I'd not see you since luncheon, miss. Which, if you don't mind me saying, may have been the truth then, but not now. And should your mother discover I have now seen you...'

Peggy nodded. 'All right, Peake,' she said, jumping away from the rocking chair and saying, with mock grandeur, imitating how she remembered her mother speaking, 'I shall return to the withdrawing room straight away.' She passed the now licked-clean spoon back to Mrs Best with a smile of gratitude and started climbing the steps.

She could picture the scene now: the ladies all in the drawing room, playing cards; the men sipping ghastly port in the dining room, laughing about some poor soul from 'the club'. No, wait, the man whose house she was in, Mr Grainger, was something in the Government, a civil servant. Peggy wasn't sure what a civil servant was exactly, but she did know it wasn't the same sort of thing as Peake, Mrs Best or Alice.

So, no, it wouldn't be 'the club'. It could possibly be 'the House', where some poor wretch worked and was the unknowing butt of all the jokes going on upstairs.

Or maybe they were talking about 'poor orphaned Helen' and her graphaphone, with its new big black discs playing scratchy music all day.

Sometimes Peggy thought she could hear voices from inside Helen's room as she walked past it, but it was probably just a disc of speeches her uncle had given her.

She pulled closed the door to the servants' hall and emerged into the black-and-white tiled floor of the main hall, all pot plants and gilt-edged paintings of no one she recognised. She glanced upstairs – the drawing room was where she should go. Where Mother would be.

But the dining room directly before her seemed so much more inviting.

Daddy would be pleased to see her, she was sure. Peggy had learned a long time ago that even if she did something to displease him, he quickly forgave her. And, with a new baby on the way, Peggy guessed that she would only be able to get away with being 'Daddy's favourite girl' for a few months longer.

Gosh, she hoped she didn't get a brother. Boys were stupid and slow and never wanted to read books or ride ponies or do needlepoint.

If the boys in Hampshire were anything to go by, all a baby brother would do is eat snails, throw wet mud around and ride bicycles toward her at stupid speeds and then burst into tears when they fell off – as they inevitably did.

'Boys are so useless,' she muttered.

'I've heard it said,' replied an older voice behind her.

Peggy turned round quickly, alarmed that someone had crept up on her so quietly. And then more alarmed that she didn't recognise the man at all.

He was very tall, with white hair, a lot older than Daddy or Mr Grainger, but not as old as Lord Greystone, the other man who would be in the dining room. He wore a short tweed cape, velvet slacks and a dark jacket with a very funny shirt that reminded her of something she had seen in a picture book about pirates. Swashbucklers, Mother had called them.

'But sometimes boys can be very nice too,' he continued, and offered his hand.

Peggy wasn't sure whether to shake it or run to Daddy, but the man didn't seem threatening in any way and his eyes seemed to make her want to smile, to laugh even. They seemed brighter, more exciting, than even Daddy's.

'Good day, sir,' she said, recalling her 'manners and poise' lessons. 'My name is Margaret Pollard.' She shook his hand formally, feeling very grown up.

'And I should like it, Margaret Pollard, if you would call me the Doctor.'

Peggy was instantly alarmed. 'Mother? The baby?'

The Doctor seemed momentarily confused, then smiled broadly and Peggy felt instantly reassured. 'Goodness, no,' he said. 'It's my title rather than my job.'

Peggy nodded. 'Peggy,' she said suddenly. 'I don't really like Margaret.'

The Doctor nodded. 'See, we all have our real names, and then the names we prefer to be called.'

This made sense.

'So, you are going to have a brother or sister, are you?' asked the Doctor.

Peggy nodded happily. She couldn't wait. 'I want a sister. Boys are icky.'

The Doctor patted her on her head. 'Now, Peggy, I need to see the master of this house.' He drew something from a pocket inside his cape, which seemed far too large to have been in there. It was a small rectangular box, with lights that flashed like Christmas lights. It made a tiny beeping noise every few seconds. Peggy reached out to it... drawn to it for a reason she couldn't quite fathom.

The Doctor pulled away from her sharply, then, perhaps realising he had alarmed her, he smiled. 'Sorry, my dear. But it has... electrical bits inside it. And you know those aren't the sort of things for a young lady such as yourself to play with, because –'

'I might get electrocuted,' Peggy replied. She'd heard the same thing from her father too many times. Daddy could be so dull sometimes.

'Good girl,' the Doctor said. 'Absolutely right.'

Peggy shrugged. Pretty lights were everywhere at Christmas. 'Do you want to see Mr Grainger? He's with my daddy in there.' Peggy pointed to the dining room. Then, not entirely sure where the words came from, she blurted something out that she'd been forbidden from talking to strangers about. 'Are you actually here to see Helen?'

Peggy felt her face flush – everyone had said Helen was not to be discussed. But this man said he was a doctor and...

'No, no, I don't think I am, Peggy.' He smiled at her.

And for the first time, Peggy felt unsure about her new friend. Because she knew he was lying.

They were interrupted by footsteps clattering on the cold stairs behind them as Edward Grainger hurried down with his usual 'grace and elegance', as Mother had referred to it more than once.

Peggy sighed. The Doctor was her friend, but she knew that five-year-old Eddie would quickly interfere. She gave him a look that she very much hoped meant 'go away, you annoying brat, just because this is your house does not mean everything in it is automatically yours and, besides, you have chocolate around your mouth and you are so embarrassing and if you're not careful you'll trip over that untied shoelace'. But even Peggy had to admit that she probably just looked mildly irritated and got none of what she felt across.

But perhaps the Doctor recognised the look because as soon as Eddie introduced himself, the Doctor all but ignored him after a courteous 'Nice to meet you, Master Grainger'. He smiled back at Peggy. 'I'll just go and introduce myself to Mr Grainger, your father and the others,' he said.

And then it struck Peggy how odd this was. Why hadn't Peake been there to let him in, to announce him to Mr Grainger? Where was Peake? Of course, downstairs. But he would never have left the Doctor alone in the hallway.

Which could only mean Peake didn't know the Doctor was here.

In which case, how did he get in?

'Please, young man, there's no need to –' But whatever the Doctor was about to say was cut off as Eddie yanked open the hall cupboard where coats and hats were stowed away.

'I knew it,' Eddie said, laughing.

Peggy saw the impossible.

No hats or coats. Instead, the cupboard was filled with a set of blue doors with a sign about policemen above them.

'I saw you come out of there,' Eddie said to the Doctor. 'I watched you from Helen's door.'

Peggy wasn't sure which was more alarming: the Doctor coming out of a cupboard (if Eddie was being truthful – he was only five, after all); the fact that Eddie was spying on everything from the first floor; or the fact he was near his cousin's room, despite express orders forbidding it.

Peggy had obeyed them. Tommy Gosforth had obeyed them. Even that annoying Marion Jefferson had agreed to abide by the house rules. But Eddie, in his own home, had broken the promise they'd made as a group.

'You were told not to go near Helen!' she scolded him.

Eddie ignored her. 'Why were you in there?' he asked the Doctor.

The Doctor rubbed the back of his neck as he tried to come up with an answer. And whilst Peggy knew it was a good question, getting answers from the Doctor was her job, not Eddie's.

'Don't be rude to one of your father's friends, Eddie,' she snapped. 'And go and ask Peake to come up here.'

Eddie opened his mouth to argue, but stopped as the Doctor suddenly smiled at him.

'Edward? Edward Grainger? Of course, I hadn't realised.'

'What?'

'You'll grow up to be a very interesting man indeed.'

Peggy thought that highly unlikely, but it did the trick and Eddie dashed downstairs without another word.

She turned back to the Doctor, watching as he eased the cupboard closed again, cutting off the blue doors from her sight. 'You sound like you've met him before.'

The Doctor shook his head. 'Now that would be silly, Peggy. It's 1911. He's only, what, five? Six? How could I possibly know him?'

Peggy thought about this. It seemed to make sense.

A door opened behind her – the dining room. Mr Grainger stood there, a frown on his face. 'Good evening, sir,' he said. 'How may I help you?'

The door to the downstairs opened as well and, with a slightly alarmed look on his face, Peake stood framed there, Eddie poking out from behind his left leg, grinning inanely.

'I'm terribly sorry, sir,' Peake said. 'I had no idea a gentleman had called. Master Edward just told me and –'

'It's quite all right, Peake,' said the Doctor. 'I let myself in.' He held up a key, but swiftly pocketed it again before Peggy could get a good look at it. 'I'm the Doctor.'

Mr Grainger flinched slightly. 'The Doctor? Are you here about Lady Louisa?' said Mr Grainger. 'Is there a problem?'

'I asked that,' Peggy said. 'He says no.'

'Thank you, Margaret,' Mr Grainger said sharply. Then he looked at Peake. 'Fetch the police, Peake. I'm unaccustomed to strangers letting themselves into my home, key or no key. The last time was when my son was born, and I will not tolerate it again.' He aimed that last comment directly at the Doctor.

'He is a policeman,' Eddie piped up. 'It says so in the cupboard.'

Peggy sighed.

Mr Grainger ignored his son, thankfully, but glanced at the cupboard anyway.

Then a new voice spoke.

From the first-floor landing, it was soft, almost too quiet, yet it had a strange quality. Peggy recognised it as Helen.

'I heard a commotion.'

Mr Grainger shot a look straight up at her. 'Go back to your room, my dear,' he said. He spoke concerned words, Peggy thought, but there was no real warmth in them.

Helen Fitzmaurice was a liability. That was how Peggy's mother had described her as they had driven to Knightsbridge. Peggy had nipped into the Graingers' library to look the word up. It wasn't nice to be thought of as a liability.

'Peake,' Mr Grainger snapped. 'Where is Alice? She was supposed to be looking after my niece.' Alice was one of Mr Grainger's maids, the latest in a long line of young servants he had employed since Violet had... well, Peggy wasn't sure what had happened to Violet. Grown-ups went quiet whenever she was mentioned.

Peake nodded hurriedly and dashed up the stairs as quickly as possible, giving a yell for poor Alice and ushering Helen back into her room.

'Now then, sir...' Mr Grainger started, meaning the Doctor, but Peggy saw that the newcomer's attention was now focused entirely on Helen's departing form. The young girl threw him a look over her shoulder just as Peake closed her door, and Peggy felt a rush of guilt.

She and the other children had spent Christmas Eve dashing about, making noise and laughing. Helen had spent the day alone in her room.

'Your niece?' echoed the Doctor.

'Your business?' responded Mr Grainger.

'Well, I wasn't entirely sure at first,' the Doctor said quietly. 'But now I've seen that poor girl, I think I may have a clue.'

By now, Mr Grainger had been joined by some of the other men, including Daddy. Peggy automatically wandered to him, and he placed a reassuring arm around her shoulder.

'What's going on, Lawrence?'

'Nothing, Mr Pollard. This gentleman was just leaving.'

'I was?'

'You were.'

The Doctor stared at Mr Grainger thoughtfully, then smiled tightly. 'I don't think I was, Mr Grainger. I said I'm a doctor. Your niece may need my help.'

Mr Grainger took a deep breath. 'In my house, sir, I'll have you know –'

The Doctor suddenly snapped angrily at him. 'Who's running your department these days, Grainger? Whose squeaky wheels do you oil?' He seemed to stare right into Mr Grainger's eyes, further even. Then he breathed in. 'Old Dickie Bellamy, is it? Yes, good chap, Dickie. Was down at Southwold last month. "Tell you what, Lady Marjorie," I said. "You need to talk to your husband about some of those junior civil servant types," I said. She agreed with me, saying her husband didn't think everyone was pulling their weight these days. "With the changes being made to the electoral system over the next few years," I told her, "you need to ensure the party is served by the best people, not time-wasters." She agreed, as we tucked into the most exquisite venison and partridge pie.' The Doctor then looked back up at Helen's closed door. 'And I think Helen may be the reason I'm here now.'

And without waiting for a response, he began climbing the stairs.

After a few seconds, Mr Grainger bellowed, 'Now, just wait one moment, sir, if you please...' But it was too late.

The Doctor was inside Helen's room.

Less than a second later, Peake was thrown out and the room was audibly locked from inside. He tried the handle, but it was pointless.

'He's... he's locked it, sir,' Peake stammered.

'I gathered,' snarled Mr Grainger.

'Helen's room doesn't have a lock,' piped up Eddie, still framed in the doorway to the servants' area.

And Peggy realised he was right.

Forty-five minutes later, Peggy tiptoed up the stairs. The grown-ups were all gathered in the dining room, talking animatedly about the Doctor's behaviour. And, of course, doing nothing. Her father was concerned that any upsets would affect Mother and the baby. Mrs Grainger had sent Peake out for a policeman but he'd not come back. Alice had put the other children to bed but, as Peggy was a few years older, she was allowed to stay up and read in the library.

She had flicked through a book by a Mr Verne, but although she liked some of the fanciful ideas she'd lost interest swiftly. The only really interesting thing in the house tonight wasn't submarines or Father Christmas or cook's plum pudding.

It was this mysterious Doctor and why he was in Helen's room.

And how he had locked a door that had no lock.

And so Peggy had snuck out of the library and quietly made her way to Helen's room. The old living room had been converted into Helen's bedchamber. It overlooked the underground station, but that was rarely busy at Christmas, so she avoided being disturbed too much.

She was about to try the handle to the room when a voice whispered beside her.

'It's still locked.'

Peggy swung round, trying not to let out a startled gasp. Not just because she didn't want to be discovered, but because she didn't want to look girlish and scared in front of her unannounced companion. 'Eddie!' she spat, *sotto voce*. 'You should be in bed.'

'So should you,' said the five-year-old arrogantly. 'But we're not. Neither of us.'

Peggy couldn't argue with that logic.

'And it's my house,' he continued. 'So there.'

So there. As if that were an argument.

And the door to Helen's room opened with a tiny click. They both looked up into the face of the Doctor. Thankfully, he was smiling. He beckoned them in.

Peggy held an arm out to hold Eddie back – typical boyish enthusiasm.

The Doctor nodded at her. 'Don't worry,' he said quietly. 'I don't bite.'

Reassured, but not quite sure why, Peggy and Eddie entered the room.

The Doctor closed the door behind them, and then pointed a silver fountain pen or something at the handle. The pen made a high-pitched noise and the handle juddered. Peggy's first thought was that Mother or Daddy were outside – she must've been spotted and they were going to blunder in to 'save her'. Then the handle was still.

'I've just changed the local harmonics in the area around the door handle,' the Doctor said. 'Charged, the electrons are busy bouncing around off one another and slightly out of phase with those of the handle, thus creating an impenetrable barrier.'

'You could just say you locked it,' Peggy retorted.

'With magic,' Eddie added unhelpfully.

'Science, actually,' the Doctor said with a smile. 'But it's all relative.'

Peggy looked at Helen. She was sitting on her bed, smiling. She didn't seem to be hurt or alarmed.

'Hello, Helen,' Peggy said carefully.

She didn't respond.

'She can't hear you, Peggy,' the Doctor said.

'Why not? Is she unbalanced? That's what my father says.' That was Eddie, obvious as always.

The Doctor explained that Helen was fine, but she was not really with them at the moment. He held up the box with flashing electric lights that Peggy had seen him with down in the hallway earlier. 'I was tracking some interesting anomalies with this, and I was drawn here,' he said, as though that explained everything.

'What's that?' Eddie tried to take the box but the Doctor simply raised it above his own head, so Eddie gave up.

'My friend is here,' Helen said suddenly.

The Doctor was at her side, crouched beside her in an instant. 'Is he? Where exactly?'

Helen raised her left arm and pointed at the graphaphone on the table by the window. 'Same as always,' she said.

She then turned to Peggy. 'Hello, Margaret. Edward. How are you tonight?'

'We're... we're fine,' Peggy said, unsure of what to say. 'How are you?'

Helen smiled, but it was as though her eyes weren't entirely focused on Peggy and the boy. 'It's like a dream, Margaret. I can see you, I know you're there, but at the same time, I feel very queer. Very...'

'Light-headed?' offered the Doctor.

'Yes, Doctor. Thank you.' She held her hand out to Peggy, who took it gingerly and allowed herself to be led to the bed, where she sat beside Helen. Eddie wandered over to the Doctor and the graphaphone.

Helen held her head slightly to one side, as if listening. Her voice was still soft and not quite lucid. 'They told me a few years ago that I was sick,' she said calmly, as if discussing the weather. 'I told them I could hear my friend, and so they thought that it was in my head.'

'Your friend?'

'He calls himself Ahnji.'

'Can I hear him? Or meet him?'

The Doctor looked across at Peggy, a smile that seemed to say well done. Oddly grateful for the validation, Peggy continued. 'Where did you meet him?

'He came to my room back in the old house. Before the fire,' Helen said. 'One night. He said he wanted to hear the music. My graphaphone.'

Eddie tugged at the Doctor's cape. 'What's a graphaphone?'

'This is, Master Grainger,' the Doctor said. 'Invented by Chichester Bell about twenty years ago, replacing the old phonographs that Edison dreamt up.' He held up a disc. 'These are recordings of music, speech and things like that. In the old days, they used cylinders, but a man called Berliner started selling discs 15 years ago.' He flipped it over. 'It plays something different on each side. Normally.'

Peggy glanced over at this strange comment.

The Doctor nodded. 'My TARDIS detected some alien technology, not requisite for 1911. I traced it here.'

'Ahnji asked me to play the records,' Helen said.

'I'm sure he did,' said Peggy reassuringly. 'But, why?'

'That's what I need to find out,' the Doctor replied in her stead.

'Ask Ahnji,' Helen said.

Peggy shrugged to the Doctor. He mouthed back: 'Keep her talking,' so Peggy nodded.

'I can't see him, Helen,' said Peggy. 'Describe him to me. Please?'

'Oh, he is beautiful. He used to come into my room. He was tall, with skin the colour of bricks, and bright yellow hair. Not just blond but bright yellow.' She giggled. 'Like it was made of straw. He had beautiful almond-shaped eyes – bigger than yours or mine – and he never blinked. Not once, I think.' Helen suddenly clutched Peggy's hand tight. The older girl was in danger of hurting Peggy, but Peggy knew she had to keep Helen talking.

'And?'

'My heart, dear Peggy. My heart just went out to him. He told me how he was lost, how he was looking for his family. He had heard them in my room but couldn't see them. Nor could I. But together we searched and searched. Every night he returned but we never found them, but he would always insist he could hear them. After the fire, I had to come and live in this big house. With Uncle Lawrence. And Ahnji found me here too.'

The Doctor was looking at one of the discs. 'Which is your favourite, Helen?'

'The one of the brass band from the Great Exhibition.'

Peggy eased her hand out from Helen's grasp and took a deep breath, then tiptoed over to the Doctor. She glanced back to Helen, who was now staring at an embroidered cushion, almost as if she was unaware anyone else was present.

'What's wrong with her?'

'She's a lunatic. That's what father says.'

The Doctor frowned at Eddie. 'She is not a lunatic. Perhaps she's a savant of sorts.'

Peggy hadn't heard that word. 'Is that the same as a "liability"?'

'No,' the Doctor said. 'Helen is certainly not a liability. She may be gifted. Gifted in ways we can only dream of.'

'You believe her,' said Eddie. 'I don't.'

The Doctor shrugged. 'So cynical in one so young.' He placed a record onto the graphaphone and lifted its arm. 'However, I think you're right. Helen isn't special in that way; she's more likely just an unfortunate who was in the wrong place at the wrong time.'

'What's that?' Eddie pointed to a tiny, thin needle pointing downwards.

'That is what takes the sound vibrations and converts them to audio. Essentially. Without getting too technical.' He sighed. 'The important thing is that each revolution of the record, the stylus physically shreds a tiny amount of the wax from the groove. Not enough to damage it completely, but enough that it only has a playable lifespan of a few dozen spins.'

'And?'

The Doctor sighed at the boy. 'And, as a result, a microsecond of audio vacuum is created on each pass of the stylus. Not enough that anyone could ever hear it, but enough that a microshudder goes through the audio spectrum of the universe, because space and time abhor a vacuum.' The Doctor glanced across at Helen, now stroking her long hair with an imaginary brush. 'And creatures inhabit microverses. Entire universes can live and die in the space it takes you to blink.'

Peggy gasped. 'You think that Ahnji's missing people go into the wax disc and are trapped in that tiny moment of vacuum?'

The Doctor just stopped and stared at her.

'Sorry,' she said, feeling very foolish. 'I just thought...'

The Doctor beamed suddenly. The most welcoming, heartfelt and warm smile Peggy had ever seen. 'My dear girl, you have grasped one of the most complicated theories of microscience possible. You are amazing.' He then raised his eyebrows. 'Why can't I teach Jo to understand such things?'

Peggy didn't bother asking who Jo was – it didn't seem important.

The Doctor crouched down to inspect the graphaphone again when Eddie gasped.

'Helen.'

Both Peggy and the Doctor swung around. The girl was sat still on the bed, albeit unmoving, but smiling.

'No,' breathed Eddie. 'In the mirror.'

They looked away from Helen and to the dressing table mirror.

In it, reflected perfectly, was Helen, but standing beside her was, going by Helen's description, Ahnji.

'Hello, old chap,' the Doctor said matter-of-factly, and returned to the graphaphone. 'Been there long?'

'What are you doing?'

Peggy felt a chill go through her as Ahnji spoke. His voice was deep, slightly echoing, and full of anger. It seemed wrong, as if it shouldn't come out of such a calm-looking person.

'Trying to help you. And realising that you can only be seen in the mirror gives me a clue to your people's salvation.'

'You are trying to destroy us,' was Ahnji's only comment.

'Oh, nonsense,' the Doctor said. 'If I meant to hurt you, I'd just pick up the records and smash them, wouldn't I?'

Peggy kept her eyes firmly fixed on the reflected... person. He really was as red as brick, with yellow hair that hung floppily over his head. He was bare-chested – Mother would have a fit if she came in now – and wearing a pair of silk-like loose trousers and dark shoes. And his eyes... his eyes were beautiful.

And Peggy suddenly realised she was in the presence of someone not remotely human.

She thought back to the Jules Verne novel, of its adventures with strange creatures, and realised that maybe what she had dismissed as fictions might have had grounding in truth.

Eddie was similarly transfixed, but clearly very scared. He took Peggy's hand as she offered it to him and quickly tucked himself behind her, putting as much distance as possible between the mirror and himself, yet not going closer to Helen in case the brick-man was really there after all, just invisible.

'It's the mercury in the mirror, isn't it?' the Doctor said amiably. 'The frequency your people exist on, our natural light waves bend around you. But the coated glass reveals you because it's slightly out of phase.'

He glanced over at Peggy, clearly trying to reassure her with his calm demeanour. Peggy decided to be brave and join in.

'Have you ever noticed, Peggy,' he continued, 'that if you watch your movements in a mirror, they are a tiny, tiny split second late? That's because the light refracts on the mercury surface at an ever so slightly different angle to the light hitting it. Hence we can see Ahnji there.' He winked at Ahnji. 'And I'm guessing that, by speaking, you disturbed the trillions of different waves, radiations and molecules in this room, revealing yourself.' He placed a record on the graphaphone. 'This is the one.' He straightened up. 'You're composed of sound waves, aren't you, Ahnji? Solid sound, but sound nevertheless. And you have been dragged here through time and space ever since Edward Leon Scott first manipulated sound with his phonautograph back in the 1850s. And on this record, probably a slight mispressing, a microscopically misaligned groove acted as a vacuum for your people, dragging them into its grooves. This is the one Helen plays all the time, and you were able to track your people down because, every time the record plays, you don't hear the oompahpah of music; you hear your friends and family trapped within the echoes and vibrations.'

Ahnji lowered his eyes to the ground. 'I am the last. I had hoped Helen would know how to free them.'

'Instead, encountering you sent her already fragile mind deeper into delusion.'

'There was a...' Ahnji struggled for the word.

'Fire?' offered Peggy.

Ahnji nodded. 'I was not affected, but I tried to help her family. I understood how it would be to lose them. But I couldn't touch them. I watched them choke and die.'

The Doctor smiled at the mirror. 'It was very good of you to try. You had no real reason to do so.'

'You care for Helen?' asked Peggy.

Ahnji's head flicked slightly to an angle. 'I am concerned that nothing untoward happens to her. She has become...'

'A friend?' That was Eddie, perhaps feeling braver. Peggy felt him let go of her hand.

The Doctor got his silver pen out and pointed it at the graphaphone. 'Ahnji,' he warned. 'I have no idea if this will work, and it might hurt you because this is my sonic screwdriver.'

Ahnji said he understood. 'If I am disrupted, I will coalesce as quickly as possible and speak again, to bring myself back into your plane of existence.'

'What are you doing?' Eddie asked suddenly.

The Doctor tapped the graphaphone. 'Hopefully, with a little burst from my screwdriver, I can make the record spin backwards. In the future, turntables will be built with this ability, but these early ones aren't and if I tried manually the stylus would utterly destroy the grooves rather than play backwards. My sonic screwdriver will keep the diamond's harmonics equalised enough. And, hopefully, free Ahnji's people.'

Eddie looked up at Peggy. 'Did you understand that one?'

Peggy had to confess she didn't.

'Oh, well,' said the Doctor. 'Never mind. Here goes.'

And he activated his screwdriver thing and sure enough the disc started revolving, but backwards. Amidst the distorted music of the brass band, Peggy was convinced she could hear voices, deep and resonant, vibrating through her body almost. Just like Ahnji's. Peggy closed her eyes as her teeth were set on edge and she heard Eddie whimper slightly.

Then it stopped. The vibrations. The noises. Everything.

And Peggy opened her eyes.

In the mirror she could see Helen lying on the bed, sleeping, breathing deeply. And surrounding her, filling the room, were dozens of people like Ahnji. He himself was stood amidst them, smiling. When he spoke, she couldn't hear him, but she saw the words 'Thank you' on his lips.

Eddie was at the Doctor's side in a second, fascinated by his silver pen thing.

Peggy looked back at the real room. Just Helen asleep. Then back at the mirror.

Again, just Helen asleep.

'Oh. Oh, they've gone.'

The Doctor smiled at her. 'No, no, they're here, all around us. Always have been, always will be, just out of phase with us. That's why Ahnji didn't speak – he'd have trapped them here a bit longer and I imagine now they're all free, they want to stay that way.'

He took the record off the player and gave it to Eddie. 'Want some fun, Edward?'

Eddie nodded.

'Break that record. Smash it. Take it up to your room and drop it out of the window and then gather the bits up and place them in three different dustbins down the street, there's a good boy.'

Like any five-year-old given the chance to destroy something, Eddie was at the door in a second, trying to get out.

'Stand back,' the Doctor said, did his magic with the silver thing and the door popped open and Eddie was gone.

'In a few years, the graphaphone will be replaced by the phonograph, and the system is sufficiently different to avoid this ever happening again. And Ahnji's people will be more careful too, I expect.'

'What happens now?' Peggy wondered aloud.

'Goodbye, Peggy,' the Doctor said simply. 'Look after Helen. She may remember all this, she may not. With Ahnji gone, her mind might just snap into place and the trauma of losing her family in the fire may haunt her. She'll need a good, sensible friend. And I rather think that's you.'

Peggy took a deep breath. 'And I shan't tell anyone anything,' she said, knowing it was what the Doctor wanted to hear. 'And I'll make sure Eddie keeps his mouth shut too.'

The Doctor nodded. 'Now, I expect Mr Peake will be back with an officer of the law any second now, so I'd better be off. Goodbye, my dear.'

And the Doctor closed the door behind him.

With a sigh, Peggy sat on the bed next to the sleeping Helen and all thought of Christmas Day, plum pudding and dollies went from her mind.

She had been given a task to do.

She was dimly aware of a sudden noise from downstairs and a yelp of surprise from someone that sounded suspiciously like Mr Grainger, but it stopped quickly.

And Helen stirred and began to wake up.

Direct Action

Ian Mond

An Adventure of the Fourth Doctor

I arrived on the fourth day of filming.

A nine-year-old Edward Grainger was belting the stuffing out of a boy double his height and weight. A bloodthirsty pack of boys from the nearby primary school had raced over to the oval to watch. Standing beside a large oak tree well away from the action, I could hear the bigger boy whimper for mercy.

I took a lungful of 1915 air. Not like the gritty stuff you got back home – assuming you could afford to actually live on Earth – and much cleaner than the artificial rubbish they pumped into the editing suites. I'd just got out of three days of post working on the new Freddie Mercury flick. Good stuff, but if I ever heard *Bohemian Rhapsody* again I was going to punch someone. Being out in the open air felt weird, but a good sort of weird.

I looked away from the kids as Ernest Borgmann, executive producer for *Edward Grainger: A Man for Peace*, materialised opposite me. Like myself, he wore a pin-striped suit; his brown, mine navy. Ever the poser, he'd also added a bowler hat and umbrella to the ensemble. Borgmann always went that extra step when blending in with the local time period.

'So what do you think, Jack?' Borgmann asked, his posh accent an affectation just like the clothes.

'From the rushes I've seen, the direction is pretty tight. You using Jessop?'

'He's masquerading as one of the boys watching the fight. What about our little diplomat?'

Edward collected the bigger boy with a stunning right hook.

'Has a great punch for a nine-year-old.'

Borgmann's smile didn't reach his flinty eyes. 'Not what you expected then.'

'I always imagined him as bookworm, sitting underneath a tree reading Proust. So, rumour has it I'm doing the later years of his life.'

Borgmann's brow crinkled. I don't think he liked me changing the subject. From the corner of my eyes, I saw Edward kick the bigger boy in the face. The schoolboys roared with approval. I wondered which one was Jessop.

'Jack, you're not doing Edward. You're filming Lawrence.'

I didn't hide my disappointment. 'The dad! You call me over here, tantalise me with Edward and then tell me I'm going to end up doing second-unit stuff. I'm not ending up as a deleted scene, Ernest, not when you promised me a crack at Edward's later life. Something a bit meatier, you said, something that didn't involve monsters and big explosions.'

Borgmann's eyes became slits. 'I decided that Lawrence's story was better suited to your abilities.'

Borgmann hadn't decided anything. The decision had come from a studio head who either thought I was a hack or more likely had promised Edward's later life to someone with greater pull than I had. During moments like these I wondered why I bothered at all, and then I remembered the alimony, the mortgage and the need to eat.

'So what period are we talking here?'

'He joined Hamilton at Gallipoli as his political adviser.'

'And that's interesting how...?'

'They really teach you nothing at school these days. The Gallipoli campaign. Nineteen-fifteen.'

'Oh, yeah, the First World War.'

'Think big picture here, Jack. Think prequels.'

The studios were always looking for angles, other sources of revenue. If the Edward Grainger film proved to be the hit it promised to be, the public would be clamouring for more Grainger-related content. A biopic about the father was right on the money.

'Will you do it?'

I watched as Edward drove his knee into his victim's groin. The bigger boy's scream would have shattered glass.

Did I really have a choice?

'Yeah, why not. Sign me up.'

He first heard the news in a pub, sitting with his mates. The boys thought it'd be a lark if they signed up. And never one to go against the trend, he thought it would be a grand idea as well. He was excited about going to foreign places where they spoke differently and ate all sorts of queer food. Killing people was the last thing on his mind. So he and the boys booked passage for Fremantle.

For a guy who made biopics, I loathed research. Which is why being a hack for hire suited me down to the ground. I didn't have the time or budget to learn the ins and outs of the First World War.

Still, I spent a night at home, in front of my holo-vid, watching a couple of old-style documentaries. Getting soused on whisky, I discovered the Gallipoli campaign, like most of the First World War, had been a right old mess. The great and glorious British Empire thought they could score themselves an easy victory in the Mediterranean. The way they saw it, they'd blow up a few barges, slaughter a few thousand Turks and waltz into Constantinople before lunch. Not only would the victory lift morale across the Western Front – things weren't going great guns there either – but it would have the added benefit of knocking Turkey out of the war while encouraging the Balkan nations to join the Allied forces.

Like all idiotic plans, Winston Churchill – he was in charge of the Navy – and Lord Kitchener, the Secretary of State for War, underestimated their enemy. The Turks didn't have a naval fleet worth squat and, yeah, their army was poorly trained and poorly maintained, but they were also a noble nation. They weren't willing to throw themselves down before the so-called might of the western infidels. They had an ancient culture and religion to protect.

They also had the home-ground advantage. We're not talking rolling hills and babbling brooks. The Gallipoli peninsula, the site for the campaign, was a place of scrub and dirt and deep, dangerous ridges impossible to pass or climb. And no matter how tough and rugged the terrain, the Turks called this place home; they knew how to defend it.

What was meant to be an easy victory turned into a tragic defeat. Young soldiers, mostly from the Australian and New Zealand Army Corp, were sent straight to the slaughter. The documentaries talked about the ANZAC spirit, about the courage of the young boys fighting against a terrain and an enemy they didn't understand. All I saw was a waste of human life.

He and his mates formed part of the 11th Brigade. They spent a few days on HMS Invincible, getting to know the other Aussie and Kiwi blokes they'd be fighting with. He found himself speaking about home a lot, about his parents, his younger brother and the sweet girl he'd left behind. He was going to make them all proud.

It took me just one day to realise Captain Lawrence Grainger would pose some major problems.

When Borgmann had said Grainger was a political adviser to General Hamilton – the guy running the campaign – my first thought was political drama. Not every movie needed big explosions and giant monsters. A good chunk of the public, who didn't eat their food through a straw, was on the look-out for intelligent film-making, the rare type of movie that raised complex questions about the human condition and gave an insight into the type of people we were back then.

Cinema like that only worked if the characters involved had personality and charisma.

General Hamilton wasn't the issue. He wasn't your typical general, with his penchant for poetry and quoting the classics. When I first saw him, he reminded me of my ex-wife's grandfather, a man who spent the last few years of his life sitting in his armchair and smoking a pipe, but when the general spoke, he spoke with authority and the experience of someone who'd survived many a battle. General Sir Ian Hamilton had all the ingredients of a top-flight movie star.

The same couldn't be said for Captain Grainger. First off, he was on the wrong side of fat. Whenever he exerted himself, his face would turn bright red and he would break into a sweat. He hadn't aged well either, his blubbery face a mass of wrinkles. Worst of all was his arrogance, always damn sure of himself, convinced he was better than everyone else on HMS *Queen Elizabeth*. The real army, those who knew Grainger's rank was honorary, hated the man and spent a good chunk of their free time bitching behind his back.

Any thought of doing a political drama was shot in the head, because no one had any respect for the fat, turnip-faced, self-opinionated so-and-so.

That left me with big explosions and giant monsters.

Sans the monsters.

He was sitting on a boat with the rest of the brigade. It was so dark and, no matter how hard he looked, he couldn't see the shore, but he could hear the sound of something buzzing, followed by a short, sharp scream. His mate sitting beside him was wide-eyed with fear, the guy opposite him was praying to Jesus, but the bloke to his left, the one with the pregnant wife, was missing the top of his forehead. His first dead body.

After twenty years making other people's movies, the only thing I enjoyed was interacting with history. It had nothing to do with meeting famous dead people. What gave me the adrenalin rush was the possibility I might disrupt the timelines by fluffing a line or breaking out of character.

That's where the hologramatic projector came in handy. It allowed me the luxury of popping back into history looking like anyone I wanted to. The old-style film-maker fought against newfangled devices like the projector. These were guys who would actually spend months training to be a historical figure. The great ones like Zeblom and Goldenberg and B'riktoff could mimic anyone if given enough time. I had a soft spot for these film-makers, but the hologramatic projector was a useful shortcut.

On 28 April at 2.15am I strode into Grainger's cabin aboard HMS *Queen Elizabeth*. Still awake, Grainger sat at his small desk writing some letters – probably to his wife, Mary, and Edward. His first reaction to the interruption was anger, until he realised who stood at the door.

'General,' he said, staggering to his feet.

'Sit down, Captain.'

Lawrence fell back into his seat, face already turning red. 'I apologise. There is only one chair. This accommodation was the best they had.'

What chutzpah the guy had. The *Queen Elizabeth* might have been a dreadnought, but room was scarce, single cabins only given to the top brass and those special few who had connections like Grainger. That didn't stop him complaining to his commanding officer.

'I need your assistance with regards to a sensitive issue,' I said.

This piqued Grainger's interest. 'How can I help you?'

'Ellis Ashmead-Bartlett, what do you know about him?'

'Typical journalist. A scoundrel and cad with a flair for the extravagant. He's only reporting on the war to escape his creditors.'

'And his politics?'

'The one and only thing I have in common with the disagreeable man.'

'I'm getting reports from the field that he's not satisfied with our strategic efforts. He's going to write a letter to the Prime Minister.' This was a historical cheat – Ashmead-Bartlett did write a letter to Lloyd George, but not for another three months.

'That's treachery!'

'And that's why I'd like you to head to Cape Helles to discuss this matter with him personally.'

At the mention of Cape Helles, I thought Grainger was going to have an aneurysm. 'You want to send me to –'

'You'll go *now*. I've ordered a boatswain to take you on a pinnace.'

Grainger shook his head. 'No... I can't... not Cape Helles.'

'General Hunter-Weston is expecting you.'

'No disrespect, sir, but I was ordered by Mr Churchill to advise you. There are so many political implications that must be considered. Morale has been wavering both here and at home since the naval defeat. That's why I need to stay onboard, sir. I can guide us all through these troubled times.'

You couldn't buy arrogance like that. I loomed over Grainger, historically not the sort of thing Hamilton would have done, but it had the desired effect. He cringed like a small boy about to be slapped by Daddy.

'Listen to me, Captain Grainger,' I said. 'I don't care one jot about who ordered you to do what. I am still your commanding officer, and unless you'd like to be shot under charges of mutiny, you will follow my orders. You have half an hour.'

I didn't bother to wait for a response.

Everything happened so fast. Somehow he'd made it to shore alive, but he had no idea where his mates or the other members of his unit had gone. He wandered in the darkness, weighed down by his backpack and his rifle and his two bags of extra rations. All around, bullets were buzzing and men were dying and no one seemed to have a clue as to what was going on. And then he stumbled over his mate, the one who'd sat next to him on the boat, and he saw how his friend had been sliced open by a bayonet. A bullet snatched at his earlobe. He looked up, staring into the face of the enemy.

I fired up the projector, transformed myself into Captain Rendell and ordered three sub-lieutenants to prepare the pinnace. A flick of a switch and I was invisible. I then checked that all my holocameras were in place. They were the size of basketballs, powered by a miniature ion generator. I modulated all nine of them so that they too went invisible.

And then I became young Henry Turner, the boatswain who would take Grainger to a place that would later be called ANZAC Cove. Turner was my own creation, not that Lawrence would notice the imposter.

To his credit, Lawrence turned up at the docking bay in time. He wore his best dress uniform, all the relevant buckles and buttons shining brightly. He'd even armed himself with a Wembley. As I expected,

Grainger didn't bother to acknowledge my existence; I was simply the hired help.

It took us three hours to arrive at ANZAC Cove. The moment we did, we came under machine-gun fire. I immediately pretended I'd been hit. With a twiddle of the projector I created a ragged bullet hole and some blood.

Grainger, frightened out of his wits, started screaming for help. The Turkish soldiers manning the machine gun just shot at him some more.

Lying back on the boat, I manipulated my cameras. Camera one moved in for a tight shot on Grainger, while camera three zoomed off just below the muzzle of the Turk's machine gun. I knew I'd get muzzle flash just over the lens as the gun fired and it would look fantastic. Cameras four and five were free to rove above the beach. Bullets sparked around Grainger's body; I'd have to edit those out in post.

He hit the beach with a thud. A corpse stared up at him. Camera one zipped forward on his horrified expression, and then craned away to show the beach littered with the dead.

From experience, I knew the movie could die right here and now. If Grainger went all comatose then my choices were limited. I could either get involved again – maybe become a surviving ANZAC soldier – or I could give up on the project. That would mean sending Grainger back to the *Queen Elizabeth* and wiping his memory. Messy and irritating, but it wouldn't be the first time I'd resorted to those measures.

Personally, I didn't care. Borgmann had paid me half my fee and even if I did mess up here, he'd still call me again if work presented itself. Not that I'd lose sleep if he didn't. I'd been thinking of a career change.

As it happened, a few minutes later Grainger decided he wanted to live. Not bothering with the Wembley, he scrabbled around for something larger. He found a loaded rifle. With the first rays of sunlight streaking the sky, Grainger picked out his enemy. They were easy targets, not bothering to protect themselves because they were the ones with the machine gun.

It took Grainger ten minutes and eight shots to kill the two Turks. Reloading wasn't a problem; he simply pilfered ammunition from the corpse beside him.

Silence descended on the beach.

Grainger fell to his knees, dropping the rifle. He checked his body, convinced he must have been hit. The only fatality had been his peaked cap, which he seemed to have lost. 'Not possible.'

He shook his head. For a long time, he didn't move at all.

I'd edit most of that out later.

Lawrence was a stronger guy than I gave him credit for.

Once he accepted his situation – even he realised that in his condition rowing the boat wasn't an option – he started putting distance between himself and the two dead Turks.

Invisible, I, and my cameras, followed his every step.

He stumbled and staggered, a glazed look in his eyes, mumbling something under his breath. My cameras struggled to pick out a few words, and it was only with the repetition of the phrase 'Our Lord Jesus Christ' that I realised Lawrence was praying. I suppose a miracle brings out the religion in a guy.

His religious fervour went up a notch when he bumped into a group of Turkish stragglers. There was a strange, almost comedic moment as the Turks gaped at the eccentric fat English officer, muttering prayers under his breath. Then reality asserted itself and they raised their rifles and barked Arabic at him. Grainger just ignored them and would have walked right by if one of the Turks hadn't shot him in the leg.

But nothing happened.

Grainger stopped in his tracks, turned to the three men and grinned. This time the three Turkish soldiers fired at once.

Not a scratch.

'Heathens!' Grainger screeched. 'Don't you know that God is on the side of the British Empire?!'

He then surprised me, and the soldiers, by shooting one of the Turks. The two remaining soldiers, now totally freaked out by what was going on, fired another salvo. And while their bullets had no effect, Grainger killed the second Turk.

The remaining Turk, probably believing he was dealing with a demon, scarpered for the hills. Grainger actually followed him. He couldn't keep up; he was too fat for that. It didn't matter anyway; the Turk couldn't outrun a bullet.

I couldn't believe what I'd just witnessed. When I'd come up with the idea of dropping Grainger, all alone, on ANZAC Cove, I'd expected him to get captured. My movie was going to be about him surviving the horrors of war, the torture, the horrible food, the stench of rotting flesh. At some point I'd make another appearance as a fellow British officer, free Grainger, and the two of us would escape back to the *Queen Elizabeth*. My character would die before he made it back to safety – that would be the tragic bit – but Grainger would survive, vowing never to forget the officer who'd saved him.

But this was so much better. Even I couldn't help cracking a smile.

Grainger started climbing the hill, a beatific smile permanently plastered on his face. Once he reached the top he saw more than forty Turkish soldiers camped out in the gully below. 'They will fall before God's wrath!'

'You wouldn't know where I could find a rift in time?'

Both Grainger and I snapped our heads to the left and saw a man striding across the scrubland. He wore a suede burgundy coat, a wide-brimmed hat teetering on a bed of curls and a multicoloured scarf that trailed in the dirt behind him.

Not now! I wanted to scream.

Grainger raised his rifle. 'Who are you?'

Rather than answer the question, the stranger peered over the hill. 'You know, I don't think those people down there are your friends, are they?'

'The heathens can't hurt me.'

'Monotheists actually,' said the man absently. He produced a crumpled white bag from his pocket. 'Care for a jelly baby?'

Grainger's finger tightened on the trigger. This was going to end nasty. 'Tell me your name!'

The stranger grinned, popping something orange into his mouth. 'I'm the Doctor,' he said while chewing. 'And you look terribly familiar. Do I know you?' In a flash, the Doctor's paper bag had disappeared, replaced by a black box with a shiny red button. He activated the device and it started to bleep. 'Now, that is interesting. Don't you think that's interesting?'

'I seem to be plagued by doctors,' Grainger whispered. 'They must follow me around. I'm beginning to think it's some kind of divine protection.'

'Well, that might be true,' the stranger said. 'But that force field certainly doesn't hurt.' He checked his bleeping box. 'Of course, that doesn't explain the extraordinary amount of chronon radiation you're leaking. Or maybe it does.'

Grainger faltered, lowered his rifle. 'What are you blathering about?'

The question was too sensible, too coherent; I was losing my Bible-bashing action hero.

The stranger tapped his bleeping box. 'This could be broken.'

Grainger's lopsided smile returned. 'The bullets were turned aside. Our Lord made them vanish. It was a miracle.'

The stranger wasn't listening; he had his eyes closed. 'Do you hear it?'

'No.'

'The faintest of faint hums.'

'The hymns of the angels?'

'Nothing so metaphoric. It sounds like we're being watched.' The stranger whipped out a thin, silver tube from his pocket. There was a brief, high pitched whine and –

– seven holocameras appeared in the sky. Mesmerised, Grainger gaped at each camera and then he turned his attention to me.

Damn, he could *see* me.

At that point I had no choice. I knocked Grainger out cold.

Killing his first Turk was easy. All he had to do was fire his rifle. For a moment he stood there and watched the man twitch, then not move at all. He stared at the body, whoever he'd been, and realised how easy it was to kill someone.

The stranger – the Doctor – strode over to Grainger, knelt down, and checked his pulse. 'You didn't need to do that.'

34

'You didn't give me much of a choice.'

The Doctor approached me. Any thoughts of taking this guy on were quickly quashed. Not only was he taller and wider, but he had this powerful presence about him, like he somehow had control of the moment. What Borgmann would have called real star quality.

The Doctor took off his hat and shoved it into the pocket of his coat. 'Would you like to tell me what you're doing here?'

'Is that a joke?'

Dark eyes fixed on my face.

'That would be a no, then. Those are my cameras and I'm a film-maker. The name's Jack Holbine.'

'Are you trying to tell me this is all for a film?'

'Until you ruined a pivotal moment, yeah.'

'Sending a man to his death?'

'That's why I slapped a force field on him, protection from those nasty bullets.'

In frustration, the Doctor ruffled his curls; I don't think he liked my attitude. 'So you go flitting around, turning history into a film set? I wonder why I've never come across your type before?'

That was a damn good question. All the time-active races were aware of the industry – even those who didn't have shares in a major studio. Of course, most tourists knew to check before they went anywhere, and if they did happen to stumble into a film crew, they'd keep well away. So how had this madman fallen through the cracks? 'Look, mate, I don't know what your problem is, but I've got a permit to film here. So if you could go away that'd be great.'

But he was shaking his head, as if his mind simply refused to wrap itself around the concept. 'You have absolutely no idea what you're doing, do you?'

'I might be cheap and nasty but I know where to stick a camera.'

'Oh, that fills me with confidence.'

'Look, mate –'

'Doctor.'

'I can see you're passionate about history but I'm on a deadline.'

The Doctor pointed at the belt around my waist. 'I thought those things were banned for causing skin cancer. Or was it stunted growth?' His eyes widened. 'Of course! You use it to masquerade as historical characters.' The Doctor snatched out his black box and shoved it in my face. 'Do you have any idea at all what a temporal tsunami is?'

'Sounds pretty melodramatic.'

The Doctor changed the subject again, pointing at Grainger. 'You know, I'm sure I know him from somewhere.'

'What does it matter?'

'Because bringing him here has altered the timelines in ways that your tiny little mind can't possibly comprehend.'

'You don't think I know what I'm doing is risky? I've been at this caper for twenty years and I've never left a single smudge.'

'Whoever this man is, time seems to think he's very important. So important, that even bringing him to this peninsula has caused a breach.' From within the Doctor's right pocket, his box screeched to life. 'I'd brace yourself.'

And before I could think of something witty or cynical to say, reality crumbled around me.

He joined what was left of the 3rd and 9th Brigades. Orders were given for them to push forward, to take as much ground from the Turks as they could. But even in the daylight it was nearly impossible to fight and scale the ridges at the same time. They tried their best, and he continued to kill Turks: with his rifle, with his bayonet, with his hands. But one by one his mates fell, and soon there were so few of them that they had no choice but to retreat back to the beach. He knew it was the right decision, but it didn't stop him from feeling like a coward.

The first thing I did when reality snapped back to normal was fall to my knees and vomit all over my blue jumpsuit.

I didn't have much time to recover either. The Doctor pulled me to my feet, dragging me away from the top of the hill.

I heard someone screaming – 'May the Lord Jesus Christ have mercy on your souls' – and I found the strength to break the Doctor's hold and crawl, stagger, stumble my way to the lip of the hill. I collapsed into the dirt, my head hitting hard ground. My vision did a triple somersault, but through the blur I could see Grainger haring down the hill, screaming at the top of his lungs, heading straight for the Turkish encampment. And I wasn't filming any of it!

The Turks who'd noticed Grainger fired a few warning shots above his head. When they realised that wasn't having any effect, they decided to take a more direct approach.

One of the soldiers got down on one knee, took careful aim and fired.

Grainger fell, a scream of agony echoing across the gully.

The Turks and I had done the impossible. We'd killed a man years before he was supposed to die.

He'd staggered and stumbled through the scrub, trying desperately to find a friendly face. He remembered sitting in that pub in Broome, having a drink and a laugh and then hearing the news the army was looking for men. He wished now he'd bought another drink.

I stood and wiped some of the dirt from my jumpsuit. 'Well, that turned out just great,' I said to the Doctor, who sat on a rock fiddling with my hologramatic projector. I marched over to him and snatched it away.

'I'm going to need that if we're going to save your British friend.'

'The force field malfunctioned.'

'An effect of the aftershock,' the Doctor said. 'Anything anachronistic would have been affected. You, me, your force field, the projector, my dear black box.'

'Lawrence never stood a chance,' I whispered.

The Doctor broke out in a wide grin. 'They only shot him in the leg. The Turkish commander will want to interrogate a British officer.'

Well, I suppose that was good news. 'So how do we rescue him? Just waltz into the Turkish camp and ask for him back?'

'The projector please.'

Yeah, why not, couldn't hurt. 'So what happened before, that was a temporal tsunami?'

The Doctor shoved his silver tube into the inner workings of the projector. 'That was the aftershock. The tsunami, like a lot of things temporal, works backwards.'

A shower of sparks scorched the Doctor's fingertips. He gasped in pain, dropping the projector and his silver tube. Sucking on the fingers of his right hand, he bent over and scooped the projector with his left. How could anyone take this guy seriously?

'So the tsunami is still going to hit?'

'Possibly, possibly. Why do you do this?' With a free hand he waved at my cameras. 'Why make these films?'

The sudden change of subject caught me off guard. 'It's a living.'

The Doctor sighed. I think he was used to people opening up to him. He pulled the silver tube from its casing, threw the projector at me and I clipped it around my belt.

'So I suppose you've got a cunning plan.'

The Doctor grinned, flashing those shiny white teeth of his. 'You're going to love it.'

As I suspected, the Doctor's plan was totally loopy.

Not that I had much of a choice. As a film-maker I had a responsibility to my actors: a responsibility not to get them killed, maimed or rendered mentally dysfunctional. And I had a responsibility to the timelines. If I returned home without setting events back to normal, the Historical Protection Society would charge me with altering time. A crime that came with a punishment worse than death. I'm not being melodramatic here.

So that left me with the Doctor's plan: a rendezvous with the Turkish 9th Division.

The soldiers noticed and, thankfully, recognised me straight away. Respect and awe accompanied each step I took, until the division's commanding officer met me with a bow.

Tall and thin, Captain Hamid had a deeply tanned face and a large moustache that covered his top lip. 'Colonel Kemal, I wasn't expecting to see you here.'

'I've been hunting a mad British officer.' I had no idea whether Kemal would have said anything like that. I was just glad the translator still worked.

Hamid smiled. I could see he had no problem with the idea that the great Mustafa Kemal would have left his regiment alone to hunt down an enemy officer. It made you wonder what sort of guy Kemal had been back then.

We should have been making a film about him.

'I believe we've found him for you.' Hamid led me to a makeshift stretcher toward the back of the camp. Grainger tossed and turned, his dress uniform covered in dirt and blood. The bullet had shattered his left leg, blood soaking a tightly knotted tourniquet.

Over the years, I'd been so good at keeping detached from the work, at treating each historical event as a paying job, but a man was dying because of my interference. I didn't like the way it made me feel.

'He's still bleeding,' I said.

'He doesn't need to live long,' said Hamid. 'You may interrogate him here.'

'I need to move him.'

'I don't believe that's advisable, Colonel.'

'Captain, I appreciate your concern but –'

There was a sudden burning sensation around my waist.

The hologramatic projector.

Captain Hamid gasped at the sudden appearance of the stranger in his camp. He fumbled for his service revolver. I elbowed him aside and made a grab for Grainger. Come on, Doctor! Do what you need to do!

I heard a gunshot; felt a bullet slice open my cheek.

I was a dead man.

He came across a survivor. A British officer from the looks of it, leg badly wounded. The officer was crying, calling out for his wife and son. He slung the man over his shoulder, grunting at his considerable weight. He took a step forward, nearly buckled at the knee, but somehow kept his balance. He needed to do this one thing. He needed to save this single man.

Before I could be riddled with bullets, an enormous explosion hit the camp.

While the Turks ran in all directions, I slung Grainger across my shoulders. My knees buckled and it took every ounce of strength I had to keep my footing. I pushed the pain to the back of my mind. Suddenly it was important that I saved Lawrence Grainger from a death he didn't deserve.

Behind me, Hamid barked something in Arabic – the translator unit was also stuffed – probably ordering me to play nice and put Grainger back where he belonged.

I refused.

He put the barrel of his revolver against my forehead.

'Sorry, Colonel, but this guy is my responsibility.'

I don't know if Hamid understood me or not, and in the end it didn't really matter. From the corner of my eye, I saw one of my precious holocameras hurtle in our direction. 'I'd duck if I was you.'

The explosion blew us off our feet.

The next thing I knew the Doctor was carrying Grainger, making it look easy, and I was trying to keep pace. 'Come on!' he shouted.

Behind us, the Turkish encampment was a mess. My holocameras continued to fall, blowing massive chunks out of the scrubland.

'I've programmed the camera's ion generator to explode on contact,' the Doctor explained. 'Quite brilliant if I do say so myself.'

It seemed like an eternity, but we finally found ourselves in a clearing, somewhere close to Achi Baba, according to the Doctor.

And there were bodies. ANZAC and Turkish forces, their corpses now food for the flies.

The Doctor laid Grainger gently down on the dirt. I bent down beside Lawrence and touched his forehead. 'He's burning up.'

The Doctor stared at his bleeping box. When he turned to me, his expression had a type of inevitability about it. I filled in the puzzle pieces on my own. 'The tsunami's still coming.'

'I'm afraid so.'

'Which means he dies here.'

'Not necessarily, but time has altered.'

I closed my eyes, not wanting to consider my short-term future. 'Do you know what they'll do to me if I return and I've stuffed up history? Let's put aside Borgmann suing me for ruining his Edward Grainger film, but –'

'Did you say Edward Grainger? As in *the* Edward Grainger?'

'Who else could I mean? Lawrence here is father to one of history's greatest peacemakers.'

A strange expression passed across the Doctor's face, part epiphany and part fear. 'Edward... he was a peacemaker...?'

'And Lawrence over here, with so many contacts at his disposal, made sure his son had an easy ride into politics. See where I'm going with this?'

'Oh, yes, very clearly, clearer than you could possibly imagine. What will happen to you if you return?'

'Look, I don't see how –'

'Just answer the question. The tsunami won't wait.'

'The Historical Protection Society will force me to relive the rest of my life as Lawrence Grainger.' Just talking about it frightened me. 'I'll stop being Jack Holbine and become a perfect replica of him. History will never know the difference.'

The Doctor considered this for a moment. 'Jack, you can't become

Lawrence Grainger. After they amputated his leg, he became a recluse. He drank himself to death in 1924. He never saw his son again. And without that connection between father and son, the Edward you know never existed. Edward never became a peacemaker.'

'For someone who had no idea who this was twenty minutes ago, you're now sounding like a Grainger expert.'

'Let's just say I'm a friend of the family.'

Why should I believe him? Why should I accept that this crazy guy, who'd only just entered my life, had any authority over time and space? Yeah, he spoke a good game and he believed what he was saying but who said his version of Grainger history was any more credible than mine?

And then the world fractured around me again, and while I fought the urge to vomit I realised it was a moot point. I didn't want to go back and become Lawrence Grainger, didn't want Borgmann and my so-called colleagues to pity me. Didn't want the media attention as news of what I had done became known. I hated my job, it bored me senseless, but I also had professional pride. They weren't going to take that away from me.

'Are... are you sure?' I gasped.

'Yes.' The Doctor looked exhausted, the grin, the flair, the charisma all gone.

I slumped down next to Lawrence, watching him groan and bleed and call for Mary. 'But... Edward... what happens to him?'

'Joins British intelligence, survives the odd jape and scrape, falls in love, has a child, lives a long, worthwhile, decent life.'

'Make a good film.'

The Doctor smiled. 'You could come with me.'

It sounded like the sane option, but a film-maker, even a hack like me, had to be accountable for his actions. Lawrence deserved better.

'I can't leave him, I did this to him. I made him something he wasn't meant to be.'

'Wouldn't that be your job description?'

'Yeah, but this time I didn't get away with it.'

Reality jumped another groove; I rode the bumpy ride.

'Jack, I have no idea how the tsunami might affect you.' The Doctor's voice was strained. 'It might kill you, or it might rewrite your history. I simply don't know.'

'You said it yourself, Lawrence survived the war. Look around you, Doctor, this place isn't exactly brimming with help.'

'That help doesn't need to be you.'

'Actually, I really think it does.'

I know the Doctor wanted to argue with me further. Instead, he laid a hand on my shoulder for just a moment.

And then he was gone.

Just like that.

I walked over to Lawrence, still lying on the dirt, barely conscious.

'Mate, I'm really, really sorry. But you've got to admit, for a while there we made some great film.'

Lawrence groaned.

I took a very deep breath and hoisted Lawrence over my shoulders. I gritted my teeth against the pain. Somehow, somehow I took that first step, followed by a second, followed by a third.

And before long I was walking.

He made it to shore, to Cape Helles, the officer, barely breathing, slung across his shoulders. General Hunter-Weston personally congratulated him on his heroism. There was even talk of awarding him a medal. Days later, thoughts of the officer and the medal had drifted from his mind. He was back fighting with his fellow Aussie mates on the plain of Kirithia. The Turks had the high ground, but Captain Fredericks was hopeful they could take them by surprise under the cover of darkness. Sub-Lieutenant Jack Holbine couldn't wait to go back into the fray, couldn't wait to show those damn Turks that he wasn't scared of them.

He did it for his country and his mates, and his family and the girl he'd left behind. This is who he was.

Dream Devils

Glen McCoy

An Adventure of the Third Doctor

Edward awoke with a start, his pyjama top drenched in sweat.

It must be about six o'clock, he guessed. He lay back, gripping the bed sheets to reassure himself that he was in his school dorm. He was. All the other boys were still asleep. He closed his eyes, aware of his pounding heart. A nightmare. Another nightmare.

Like every morning for the past month, Edward was flanked by Lillis and Digby from the upper sixth. They weren't prefects, so he didn't have to fag for them – but that just made matters worse.

His stalkers eyed him from their breakfast table in the main hall. Lillis was a lanky youth with excessive facial acne, while Digby, well built for his 17 and a half years, was a former rugger captain in the fourth. He had been unceremoniously stripped of his office after he 'accidentally' broke the nose of the visiting captain from Todmorden Grammar.

They hadn't hurt Edward that much. The bullying was mainly mental blackmail and the threat of worse to come. So far he'd been lucky, though why they had suddenly decided to start on him was a mystery.

After breakfast, Edward was at a very low ebb. He sat with his back against the large oak in the south quad, where he could view most of the school without fear of being taken by surprise. Sunday was definitely a day of rest – a time for quiet contemplation after chapel. This spot was the place he'd always retreat to when he was under pressure, like before Christmas during end-of-term exams.

As he allowed pieces of gravel to slip through his fingers, it occurred to him that he really couldn't put up with the bullying for much longer. His father had always told him that bullies never liked the tables turned on them – but the reality would require more courage than he could currently muster.

Edward Grainger wasn't a religious boy, even though part of his family was devoutly Catholic. Despite this, and for the first time, he looked to the skies for inspiration, praying for divine intervention.

There was a dull thud as the TARDIS control panel plunged into semi-darkness. The Doctor's face looked gaunt, his white hair framing a sad expression, as he caught his reflection in the panel's shiny surface. He stepped back and wiped thick beads of sweat from his forehead.

The Doctor hardly ever felt alone. After all, there were so very many stars, solar systems and civilisations out there. But right now he felt isolated. The hunter had become the hunted and he mused at the notion that he might never get the chance to regenerate again.

43

Taking a deep breath, the Doctor took his velvet jacket from where it was draped on a chair, and moved towards the door. Stepping out of the TARDIS, he was hit by a chilled gust of air. Ahead was daylight through a darkened quarry.

His thoughts became very focused on whether he'd been able to shake off his pursuers, not to mention how long it would take them to discover where he was exactly.

The countryside outside the quarry seemed very familiar.

It was so strange how visiting Earth invariably drew him to the green and pleasant land of England. It was probably a defect in the TARDIS's technology – a fortunate malfunction that he would probably never want repaired. But what he did want was a place to rest and hide for a few days.

The Doctor followed the single-track path for a couple of hours, before it split and joined a broader main road. There was a sign indicating Accrington, ten miles. The tarnished wooden board had seen better days. It looked Victorian, but then again it could be from the 1970s.

The Doctor looked down the road: a car was approaching at about 25 miles per hour. Perhaps its driver could clear up the mystery.

It was an odd sight: the juxtaposition of a barren moor, a lonely road at dusk and a decelerating Austin 7 resembling a cream-coloured ice box making its way towards him. The driver was in his late forties, wearing a suit that matched the period of the car. He also wore a stiff white collar, thin-framed semi-lunar spectacles and a startling bright yellow bow-tie.

'Denby prep?' he said.

The Doctor held back his response, a little unclear about the question.

'You are heading for Denby prep school, aren't you? There's nothing else up this road, and I'm fairly sure you're not walking all the way to Accrington at this time of day.'

The softly spoken man smiled politely through his greying goatee beard.

'How perceptive of you, old chap,' said the Doctor, getting into the conversational style of the period. 'Any chance of a lift?'

'Why, of course, dear fellow. Hop in. The name's Marcus Johns.'

Johns failed to ask who the Doctor was or what business he had at the public school, which, Johns told him, served the sons of local mill owners and the like. Instead, he waxed lyrical about the joys of teaching, the fact that he'd been educated at Balliol, and that he was so looking forward to his new post as physics master.

Then the rain came down in buckets.

It was getting dark as the car tried to cope with the bad weather. It did occur to the Doctor that Marcus Johns must have been doing rather well in his profession to afford what was clearly a brand new automobile, but he was too tired to think it through and let it pass. Though, new car or not, it suddenly swerved slightly and Johns had to fight the wheel to bring them to a complete halt.

'It's probably a flat tyre, old boy,' he said. 'Don't worry. You stay put and I'll get the spare. Won't take a jiffy.'

The Doctor peered through the window at the downpour and the flashes of lightning that lit up the darkened sky. In the mirror, he could see Johns getting drenched near the rear of the car. Really should give him a hand, the Doctor thought. He did stop and give me a lift, after all.

But where was the door handle to let him out?

Suddenly, the Doctor noticed the small car begin to roll forward slightly. Johns must be struggling, he thought. Looking in the tiny rear-view mirror, he caught the odd sight of Marcus Johns's entire body pressed flat against the rear window.

The Doctor continued to hunt in the darkness until a flash of brilliant lightning picked out the door handle. He tried it, but it wouldn't budge. It was as if the door had been wedged shut.

The car was definitely moving forwards now. Glancing back, he could see the physics master pushing the small vehicle forward as if the battery were flat. In horror, the Doctor realised the car was on the edge of a hilltop with nothing below but valley. Instinctively, he pulled hard on the handbrake but it too wouldn't budge.

'Johns!' he shouted. 'What are you doing?'

He appeared determined to push the car over the edge, the front bumper of the Austin 7 no more than a yard from the long drop.

The Doctor leaned back in his seat and raised his feet. Closing his eyes tight, he kicked the windscreen hard. On his third attempt, the glass shattered. Scrambling out as best he could, he found himself on the bonnet. Rain lashed the Doctor's face as more thunder and lightening licked around the car. He turned and saw Marcus Johns's bulging eyes.

The Doctor swung himself off the car and fell sideways onto hard ground, his head meeting the road with a smack. The car came to a halt, with one wheel already over the hilltop edge. The passenger door creaked open a few feet away from where Marcus Johns stood, his staring eyes lit by a fire raging inside him.

'Get in, Doctor,' he said. 'Get in and I promise to make it quick, there's a good Time Lord.'

The Doctor despaired. He'd hoped that he'd given them the slip, but they were proving to be infinitely more resourceful.

'We gave you a chance, Doctor. You refused. You only have yourself to blame. Now get into the car.'

Marcus Johns – or whoever this body snatcher really was – sounded rather irritated. This was a good sign.

'Now come on, don't get me angry.'

It was sounding better and better as the Doctor turned his back, despite the prevailing rain and wind that now hit him full on in the face.

'Doctor!' Marcus Johns shouted above the wind, which was picking up speed. 'Doctor, look at me...'

There was a change in the man's voice. He sounded strange. The biblical story of Lot's wife who looked back and turned into a pillar of salt flashed through the Doctor's imagination.

'Doctor. I said look at me!'

The Doctor slowly turned around. The sight that met him shocked him to the core. He had never seen shape shifters like this before.

Edward felt quite sick.

He'd spent the afternoon under the comforting arms of the old oak. But now the thought of having to go back for dinner in the main hall, and inevitably bumping into Lillis and Digby, was too painful to think about.

He'd been sheltering from the thunderstorm in the darkness, and knew it was not the best place to be, but in his current frame of mind he didn't care. Suddenly he held his stomach and emptied his lunch on the sodden grass. Although he felt better physically, he knew he had to pull his mind together.

Wiping his mouth and looking up, the hairs on the back of his neck stood to attention. It was them. They'd braved the wind and rain just to come and get him.

Alone, he'd be easy prey, and this time he had nothing to trade or give them to bargain for his freedom. He dropped his head between his knees. He didn't want a beating, but equally he knew he couldn't fight both of them.

Feeling a firm hand on his shoulder, he prepared for the worst, but heard a stranger's voice instead.

'Is this Denby prep school?'

Edward looked up to see the face of a man with blood streaming from a head wound. His ill-fitting jacket was partially torn and he was clearly out of breath. Instinctively, the schoolboy leapt to his feet.

'Are you all right?' he enquired.

He helped the wounded man back towards the main school buildings.

'Thank you,' whispered the visitor.

'Who are you, sir?' asked Edward. 'If you don't mind me asking.'

'I'm the Doctor... erm, the new physics master. I had a bit of an accident up on the tops, I'm afraid.

'It's a dangerous road, sir. Is your car all right?'

The Doctor didn't answer. 'I suppose I've missed supper?' he said.

Edward grinned. He hadn't smiled for quite some time.

The two made their way through the main doors into the entrance hall and in front of a crackling log fire. The old school building was over 150 years old with beams and wooden panelled walls in just about every room. Cotton curtains, typical of the prevailing commerce of the area, adorned the windows of each room.

There were no electric lights as yet but an external gas supply created the power for pupils to live and work by.

Headmaster Milligan was sorry to hear about his new physics master's accident and agreed it could have been far worse.

'You were very lucky, old man,' he said. 'You could have gone straight over the top, you know. We'll see if we can retrieve your car in daylight.'

Mr Milligan nodded to Edward. 'Thank you, Grainger. Now get yourself to bed.'

'Yes, sir.'

The Doctor smiled warmly at the young man for his kind assistance. 'You've been most helpful. Thank you.'

Edward was pleased with himself, but as he walked out of the headmaster's office and back up the wide staircase to his dormitory, he realised he'd yet to face up to another full night's sleep... and the dreams that went with it.

It was three o'clock when the Doctor stirred from his bed. He peered out across the moonlit moors. Was Marcus Johns alone? Would someone else come looking for him? What if they found him? How could he protect the occupants of the school? His tired eyes felt heavy once more as he fell back onto the thick silk eiderdown. Before he could get himself between the bed sheets he fell into a deep, deep sleep.

Edward opened his eyes.

He was wide awake. It was still pitch dark outside but the dormitory was empty. The beds were also empty: there was no one to be seen. Uncomfortable, he got dressed quickly. Maybe there was a fire?

The house-master's room was also vacant. Where was everyone? Edward ran faster, yet the faster he ran the longer the corridor seemed to stretch. The stairwell was still a good twenty yards away despite sprinting as fast as he could. He had to stop. This was not right. He then looked up at the approaching shapes of Lillis and Digby.

'Practising for the four-forty, Grainger?' cracked the former.

'You're not running from us, are you, boy?' Digby lurched forward, grabbing Edward's lapels and almost lifting him off his feet. They walked him towards the stairwell, which was now a few feet away. And then their faces started to alter.

'You can have anything,' bleated Edward, avoiding their gaze.

'Anything?'

'I get a postal order for five shillings on Friday.'

Digby laughed and Lillis joined in.

'We don't want your money, you fool.'

Edward saw another outline coming up the stairs in the gloomy gaslight.

'Then what *do* you want?'

Digby let Edward drop to the floor as he turned to face the unknown voice.

'Doctor,' gasped Edward, delighted to see the new master he'd helped find the school. The bullies looked at each other, unsure of the situation. Faced with the Doctor's steely expression, they made a rapid retreat.

'Are you all right, my boy?'

Edward nodded, thinking how strange it was for a teacher to address a boarder as 'my boy'.

Edward awoke with a start, his pyjama top drenched in sweat.

It must be about six o'clock, he guessed. He lay back, gripping the bed sheets to reassure himself that he was in his school dorm. He was. All the other boys were still asleep. He closed his eyes, aware of his pounding heart.

As he got dressed, he could hear the bells for Sunday chapel. It must have been a mistake, yet he could see boys and masters crossing the courtyard. Mr Milligan was talking with the Doctor, and Edward wished his headmaster good morning as they passed him.

'What are you going to do with your Sunday, Grainger?'

'Sunday, sir?'

'Follows Saturday and precedes Monday.'

'Erm, not sure, sir'.

'*Carpe diem*, Grainger,' said Mr Milligan as he walked away. '*Carpe diem*.'

The Doctor said, 'Good morning, Edward.'

'Morning, sir.'

'Let's drop the etiquette. Just "Doctor", if you don't mind, and I shall call you Edward.'

'Yes, sir – erm, Doctor.'

'Good. Now follow me.'

'But what about breakfast?'

'Just had some. Now don't dawdle, there's a good lad.'

Very soon the Doctor and his new companion were crossing the moors.

'Doctor, what day is it?'

Edward expected a sarcastic response but could never have predicted the one he received.

'Sunday – apparently. Rather like yesterday and the same as today.'

Edward pinched himself. He was so sure he wasn't dreaming. Or was he in someone else's dream perhaps? He rubbed his face.

'Edward, we have an anomaly to work through, and I may need your help. We could be going through a contra-time-shift paradox. But, there again, it could be something much more complicated like...'

The Doctor interrupted his train of thought as he stared across the valley.

'Like what, Doctor?'

'Mmm, that's strange.'

'Doctor?'

'Eh? Oh... it's like being in a dream, isn't it?'

Edward reeled. It was so good to hear someone else voicing his instinctive fears. It meant he probably wasn't going mad. But what if the Doctor was part of a bigger dream?

'Sorry, Doctor, but how can we both be in the same dream? I mean, it's got to be your dream or mine. We can't be dreaming in tandem, can we?'

'You'd be surprised, young Edward. The laws of quantum physics make anything possible.'

'Quantum physics?'

'No time for a science lesson now. Do you see that ridge?'

Edward spied the hilltop with the long drop below.

'What do you see at the top?'

'Nothing.'

'And at the bottom?'

'Nothing, Doctor.'

'That's what I thought.'

The Doctor looked around and found a rock large enough to sit down. Edward joined him, leaning on its edge as the morning sun kissed their faces on this glorious spring day.

'Tell me,' asked the Doctor. 'Have you been getting any strange nightmares?'

Edward looked at his boots.

'It's okay, you can say.'

Edward took a deep breath. 'Floating. That's how it starts. I feel like I'm floating out of my bed. I'm sometimes chased by large grey ghosts with dark eyes and teeth like crocodiles.' Edward felt the colour drain from his cheeks as he relived the experience.

'I'm not going to lie to you,' said the Doctor. 'You must prepare yourself if you want to know what may really be going on.'

After all these weeks of bad dreams and, even worse, the bullying, Edward had come to the end of his tether. He desperately wanted some answers.

Whether this Doctor was real or just a figment of his imagination suddenly didn't matter. All he wanted was to make sense of things, and so far this was the closest he had got. He observed the Doctor looking back out towards the hilltop and valley below.

'I was coming along the road on the tops last night,' he said. 'A car stopped for me. The driver offered me a lift. Before I knew it, he'd locked me in the car and was trying to push me over the edge. I managed to get out just in time.'

'Who was he?'

'I don't know for sure, but I do know one thing...' The Doctor hesitated, then let it out. 'It wasn't human.'

Edward rubbed his face again as he tried to wake himself up.

'I know this is difficult for you.'

'What do you mean he wasn't human?'

The sky started to rapidly cloud over. In seconds, the sun had vanished and dark clouds trained across the heavens – a little supernatural in nature, thought Edward. The Doctor looked up, preparing himself for the worst. He rubbed the back of his neck methodically.

'They're back. They're hunting me. I'm so sorry to drag you into this, really I am.'

Edward remained silent and watched the astonishing change in the cloud formation.

'I stumbled upon them on Andromeda Galliana,' the Doctor continued. 'They're soul gatherers, the worst kind of spiritual carnivores. Ghouls who discard the flesh and consume the inner life force. I tried to reason with them but they took out an entire emigrant marshland colony. Men, women and children. I did everything to try to stop them but it was no good. Now it appears, after my near-death experience on the hilltop, that they've mastered the art of shape shifting to boot.'

Edward noticed the wind ripping violently across the moor and streaking through the troubled sky.

'They wanted my ship in return for my freedom. I agreed. It was all I could do. But I had to double-cross them. Which means that this time they're really angry.'

'What can we do, Doctor?'

The wind picked up even more as the heavens opened. The beautiful morning had turned to twilight. The Doctor grabbed hold of Edward, who was finding it challenging to stand up straight in the wind. Raising his collar to the deteriorating conditions, Edward could see a ring of bright lights in the sky. The Doctor dragged him back to the shelter of the school, a building in the middle of nowhere.

As the Doctor and Edward entered the main hall, they could see that many of the boys were gathering, many at the windows, to observe what looked like an unscheduled eclipse. There must have been around two hundred pupils. Teachers, under the guidance of Mr Milligan, were attempting to keep order.

'You seem to be making a habit of this, Doctor,' said the headmaster.

The Doctor scowled. 'Headmaster, I need to talk to you.'

Milligan's study was packed with shelves of books, which dulled the loud thunder outside. As the Doctor warmed himself by the open fire, Milligan was trying to take it all in.

'You say you're a time traveller, and that there's a race of non-human creatures about to kidnap us or worse? Do I have the details correct, sir?'

The Doctor could tell this wasn't going well, but he couldn't see what other options he had.

The PE master, Mr Roberts, came in. 'The telephone line's definitely down, headmaster. We're completely cut off.'

'Thank you, Roberts. Make sure you keep the boys away from the windows.'

'And, headmaster...' Roberts swallowed nervously. 'There are peculiar lights in the sky.'

As the master left the room, the Doctor made a last-ditch attempt to get the headmaster's trust. The truth had just confused the man. The Doctor knew he had to try a different tact.

'All right, Mr Milligan. To be honest with you, I work for His Majesty's Secret Service. I didn't want to unduly alarm you but I have uncovered a German plot to invade our shores. New flying machines are trying to track me down. They will do everything they can to get back the secrets I have stolen from Germany. They will stop at nothing.'

Mr Milligan marched across the room and peered out into the darkness. Sure enough, several hovering lights were now in evidence over the west and south quads.

'Why didn't you say so in the first place? What should we do?'

The Doctor found a chair and sank into the rich leather to think. Suddenly he was back on the hilltop.

'*Doctor. I said, look at me!*'

Once again, the Doctor slowly turned around, replaying the events in his head. The sight he saw shocked him for a second time. He watched as Johns transformed into a humanoid reptile. His eyes were bathed in a green-grey slime; a snout morphed out from its mouth.

As the human body fell away, tough black fur-like skin enveloped the creature's featureless torso, its height growing to seven or eight feet in seconds. Around its neck was a chain bearing a flashing communication device.

The Doctor strained to recollect the exact sequence of events. It had been so keen to get him into the car. Why? The thing could have easily killed him where he stood.

He'd slowly stepped towards the car and meekly got in through the driver's door. As the creature leaned in momentarily from the other side, the Doctor had been able to wedge the alien's neck chain around the handbrake, jump out of the car and push the vehicle together with the rat in the trap over the edge.

'Doctor?'

The Doctor snapped back into the study. The headmaster was nervously loading an old army-issue revolver, completely oblivious to what was really about to land on his front lawn.

'Maybe we could negotiate surrender with these Huns?'

'Headmaster, in this secret army they don't take prisoners.'

'Then I shall have to open fire.'

The Doctor pulled a face at Milligan's sheer ignorance.

'This isn't funny, old man.'

* * *

A green-brown tail hacked into the front door of the school reception hall and suddenly the oak-panelled door was ripped from its hinges as two eight-foot brutes – scaly, muscled creatures – pushed their way into the large space.

Edward wanted to run but was too terrified to move. Other boys backed away nervously as the Doctor and Mr Milligan came rushing in.

'It's like another bad dream, Doctor,' said Edward.

'I know,' he muttered. 'But it should be over soon.'

The largest creature inched forward. Mr Milligan aimed a revolver up, but it failed to fire.

Edward closed his eyes, preparing for the inevitable.

'That's it!' bellowed the Doctor. Edward opened his eyes to see the Doctor standing imperious, completely oblivious to their dreadful predicament.

The sharp razor-back tail of the towering monstrosity swung up and over the Doctor's head. Edward gasped in horror – he saw no fear in the face of his new friend. But what he was witnessing made no sense. Either the Doctor had completely lost his mind or he was truly dreaming.

The creature's tail hovered inches above the Doctor's face, who looked defiantly into the face of death.

'Don't you see?' The Doctor laughed. 'We've both been rather silly.' The Doctor moved forward towards the creature, which in turn took a step back.

Swiftly, a second beast pressed forward to Edward.

'Now you try!' shouted the Doctor with encouragement.

Against all his better judgement, Edward raised his hands and stepped towards the ghastly monster only to see it retreat.

'They've tapped into our darkest fears,' said the Doctor. 'In short, mind-reading our worst dreams and nightmares!'

Fired up with enthusiasm, the Doctor made Edward follow him out of the building to the school front lawn. Edward glanced over his shoulder to see the terrible shapes he had most feared evaporate behind him into thin air.

'In order to take you, you must invite them into your mind first. A bit like bullies...'

Edward was still trying to catch his breath. 'But they got through the doors, Doctor.'

'Inanimate objects have no souls. When I was up on that ridge, I stared at the beast, but wouldn't let it into my mind. The only way it could defeat me was to hurl me over the cliff in the car.'

As quickly as the lights in the sky had come, they zoomed away into the twilight sky, which swiftly switched back to a glorious spring day. One hundred and ninety-eight boys and 12 teaching staff soon emerged from the building to observe normality once again.

Lillis and Digby looked bewildered, as if they'd awoken from a very deep sleep.

Mr Milligan organised a roll call.

Edward caught the melancholy look in the Doctor's eyes. He had so many things he needed to know

'Don't feel bad, Edward. Your mind is vaster and richer than the physical universe will ever be. Remember that.' The Doctor surveyed the scene as he dusted himself off. 'I must also share the blame for your unfortunate experience. When they captured my ship, they must have raided my data banks. I've made so many trips here in the past.'

Edward smiled broadly.

'What is it, Edward?'

'My father was right about bullies.'

The Doctor grinned back. 'False evidence appearing real. That's all fear is.'

'Will they ever come back, Doctor?'

'As long as people dream, there will always be a door open for them.'

'How about you, Doctor? Will I ever see you again?'

The Doctor leaned forward and placed his hand warmly on the young man's shoulder.

'Count on it.'

Falling from Xi'an

Steven Savile

An Adventure of the Fifth Doctor,
with Tegan Jovanka and Vizlor Turlough

I

*I dreamed I was a butterfly, flitting around in the sky; then I awoke.
Now I wonder: am I a man who dreamt of being a butterfly, or am
I a butterfly dreaming that I am a man?*

Chuang Tsu

Edward Grainger closed his eyes and crunched on the hard carapace of what he thought was a cicada.

He felt the insect crack open between his teeth and the juices spill onto his tongue.

It was unlike anything he had ever tasted – and unlike anything he ever wanted to taste again. Edward forced himself to crunch again, breaking the insect's back before swallowing the hard shell down.

He had heard rumours of the Chinese eating anything and everything from bird's nests to cockroaches but he had never imagined them to be true. It seemed so... *barbaric*.

Edward lurched away from the upturned crate, cracking his head on the wing of the De Havilland Hawk Moth, much to the amusement of the others. It hurt his pride more than his thick head. He scrambled around for the canteen, uncapped it and gulped down mouthful after mouthful of tepid water but it failed to purge the taste. He sank to his knees and looked at the peasant accusingly as he retched. Mirth glittered through the ruin of wrinkles as the little man cackled his delight. Two of Edward's companions, Carter and Ambrose, joined in with the little man's laughter.

'The things we do for love, hey, Eddie?' Convey chuckled, his eyes flitting between the desperate Edward and the smiling Mai Ling. There was no denying the girl was beautiful, in her own way: hair so black it shimmered in the remains of the day, skin sheened with the pearly opalescence of oysters, and those almond eyes so typical of her people. The girl seemed fascinated by Edward's histrionics. 'You lucky blighter.'

Behind them, the shadows around Mount Lishan deepened as the clouds gathered. And even the clouds looked different, alien, like trailing wisps of silk that wove around the mountain top. The combination of altitude and humidity made breathing difficult. The cotton of Edward's shirt clung to his skin uncomfortably as he doubled over. Damselflies and dragonflies buzzed around the clearing, their wings singing as they took flight. He felt something land on his neck and a sharp sting as it began feeding off him greedily. Edward reached up instinctively to squash it but stopped himself, both because killing it would most likely only succeed in drawing more of the bloodsuckers to him but also because it gave him a sense of karmic balance – it was only fair, after all, considering he had probably chewed up and swallowed its bloated half-cousin.

They were miles from anything approaching civilisation but the glade was far from quiet. Hundreds of wind chimes had been strung from overhanging branches and even the slightest breeze stirred a grand sonata of the music of chance. The effect was both haunting and enchanting, adding to the magic of the place. They covered the sound of Edward's retching.

It had all sounded so romantic on the tramp steamer. Carter had described himself as a treasure hunter, an explorer akin to his namesake, the Egyptologist Howard Carter, his life devoted to the search for mysterious cities of gold and relics long since lost to the eye of man. The romance of it all had only intensified when he met Mai Ling and her family, who served as Carter's hired guides in this strange land, but – and that was perhaps the first lesson Edward had learned from his new life, there was always a but – all that glitters and myriad of other half-baked clichés became clichés for a good reason. Edward was wiser now, graced with the cynicism needed to understand that the appellation was little more than a socially acceptable way of saying grave robber.

Still, not one hundred miles out of Calcutta he had thrown his lot in with Carter, becoming part of the team.

Instead of being liberated by his new-found independence, Edward felt more like his father than he ever had before. Lawrence Grainger, the great liar whose life took him from bar to street to bookie and left him broke and broken, his liver rotten with alcohol and the thugs from Newgate knocking on the door. But he wasn't his father; he clung to that simple truth. Failure wasn't something he had to inherit. He was his own man – he had laid claim to himself the moment he had walked the narrow gangway onto the tramp steamer and headed south. The idea had been relatively simple, to make an honest man of himself, but the practice had been anything but. It was back-breaking work, cramped quarters and meagre rations shared with weevils and other nutritious delicacies that defied identification. But it was an adventure – and how many others would have willingly traded places with him for it?

Edward wiped off his mouth with the back of his hand and pushed himself to his feet. He smiled ruefully at Mai Ling, who covered her smile and turned away.

They were in a glade, though it wasn't really a glade in the truest sense of the word; they had set up camp around the mouth of a rough well that had run dry. The well itself was at the furthest end of a long wide strip between the trees – long enough and wide enough for the Hawk Moth to land easily and wide enough for her to turn. Taking off would be tight, but provided the payload wasn't too heavy they should be fine. Edward walked over to the well. From what he could understand, which was admittedly very little, the peasants had intended to dig deeper in search of water when their picks broke through the well wall and into a vast timber-lined underground chamber. What he didn't understand was how Carter had got wind of the discovery, but he had, and here they were.

Convey, the fourth member of their unlikely team, was busy securing belay ropes in the well wall to the Hawk Moth for added stability, so they could descend in safety while the peasants jabbered on in their sing-song language of minah birds and larks. Beautiful though the words were, they were no doubt portentous warnings about curses and terrible fates waiting to befall the stupid white men if they dared breach the sanctity of Qin Shi Huangdi's tomb. In their shoes, that was almost exactly what he would be saying, trying to scare them off.

Fear was no match for greed though; it buckled beneath the pretty patina of gold and the glitter of precious stones.

They had 'secured' a few works of art on the long road to Xi'an, including an exquisite jade cowrie that almost certainly dated back to the Shang dynasty and a Chou dynasty bronze figurine of a crouching tiger, poised to pounce. The two pieces together would more than recover the cost of the expedition – if they could get them out of the country. According to Carter, the cowrie was more than merely rare; it was an insight to a forgotten civilisation that had developed currency for trade while the rest of the world grubbed around in the mud. Collectors, he insisted, would pay heavily for such a rare find. The figurine was a thing of beauty. Edward could see it causing quite a stir as it came under the hammer at Sotheby's. If it came under the hammer. Edward wasn't sure how Carter intended to cash in on their finds given the fact that they were 'appropriated' by somewhat dubious means. Surely any auction house worth its salt would demand proof of authenticity and provenance.

Carter obviously had private collectors lined up.

Neither piece would see the open market.

Edward had come to understand his companions well over the months they had spent together scavenging relics out from beneath the noses of petty autocracies too short-sighted to apply grease to the right wheels. Whatever they found, it wasn't enough. It was never enough. They didn't rival Elgin or Carter or Magellan or Columbus, Polo or Scott. They weren't great explorers bringing back the treasures of the Orient. They weren't rescuing history from destruction. They were profiteers on their own Grail quest.

Once the whisper was heard, the rest became inevitable. Nothing compared to the lure of Qin Shi Huangdi's tomb. Carter's naked hunger had brought them into this Godforsaken wilderness, driven by the story of the boy emperor who had 700,000 men building his burial place before his thirteenth birthday, demanding the grandest tomb of any emperor ever to live. It was the stuff of legend. It fired their imaginations with the promises of a huge burial crypt filled with untold treasures, precious gems and rare masterpieces of Chinese art, statuary, pearl-studded ceilings and, of course, booby traps to deter the greedy thieves of antiquity.

How could they resist?

Edward leaned over the side of the well. A lantern lit the broken stones on the dry bed thirty feet below, hinting at the dark shadow of the burial chamber beyond the wall. Convey looked up, his face trapped eerily in the lantern's light and the long shadows it conjured.

'You boys might want to come down here.'

'What is it?' Edward called down.

'Oh, you'll need to *see* it, Eddie, so get your Limey backside down that rope, there's a good boy.' Bryce Convey was like something straight out of an H. Ryder Haggard novel: larger than life, dynamic, heroic, with rippling muscles and an annoyingly perfect tan that only succeeded in making his pearly white smile all the more smug. Convey had introduced himself to Edward as, 'Bryce Convey, adventurer,' and stuck out his hand. Edward shook it and replied, 'Allan Quartermain, fictional character, and most definitely not Antipodean. Pleased to meet you, I'm almost sure,' much to Ambrose's amusement.

'Convey's found something,' Edward said over his shoulder. 'I'm going down to take a look.'

'King Solomon's mine, hey, Eddie?' Ambrose said, taking a slug of tepid water from his canteen and wiping his lips.

'Who knows? I wouldn't put it past Convey to be all excited because he's stumbled across a heap of fossilised dung.'

'You know what? I think I'll join you,' Carter said, dusting himself off. 'Can't go letting you guys have all the fun. Ambrose, be a good man and keep an eye on our guides, would you? I don't trust them in the slightest. And, yes, I know they look like your grandparents but I wouldn't trust them as far as I could throw them. Don't forget they have hundreds of years of martial arts and murder in their heritage. It doesn't exactly breed confidence, does it?' Carter said with a wry grin. Behind it, the hunger of expectation burned in his eyes. They were on to something. He knew it.

The well shaft was cramped and the rope made the descent fairly straightforward but it was still incredibly claustrophobic. Rock dust flaked away beneath Edward's feet as they scuffed and slid down the wall. He played the rope out between his hands, working his way down into the darkness slowly until it became light and he missed his footing and swung into the wound in the wall. He caught a glimpse of a miracle then but couldn't – wouldn't – believe his eyes.

He dangled at the end of the rope, feet still inches from the floor, staring through the hole in the wall.

'Something else, isn't it?' Convey said, helping him down.

'A… a vision from Hell,' Edward said, the words catching in his throat.

Carter let out a slow whistle as he came down lightly beside them. 'King Solomon's mine indeed, boys.' He shook his head wonderingly.

The lantern didn't light more than twenty feet into what was obviously a vast chamber, but that was more than enough to see the first ranks of towering red men frozen in place, and row after row of heads disappearing into the darkness.

Edward grabbed the lantern and plunged through the hole in the wall. It hit him almost as soon as he was on the other side: the air trapped in the burial chamber was thick, cloyingly so, and stale. Dead air. Edward crossed himself instinctively. He moved closer to the first figure. It was huge and beautifully detailed, right down to the plates of its armour and the curl of its lip. He walked slowly around the figure, inspecting it. It was, to all intents and purposes, a perfect reproduction of a Chinese warrior. There were hundreds of them. Thousands.

The lantern lit row after row of red faces, each one subtly different from its neighbour.

'Holy Mother of God,' Carter whispered, coming up beside him. The treasure hunter laid a hand reverently on the red warrior's cheek. 'It's incredible. It's so lifelike. Look at the detail. It must have taken forever to make something so perfect.'

'They're all like that,' Edward said, lifting the lantern to reveal more and more red faces. Each warrior wore an equally vivid, equally unique expression.

'They're made from some kind of pottery, I think, given the colour and the abrasive texture. Most likely terracotta. The clay is prevalent in much of Lintong County.'

'There must be thousands of them down here,' Convey said, disbelieving.

'Thousands,' Edward agreed, straining to see into the darkness, but there was no way of knowing how vast this terracotta army was without walking the lines.

'It's insane.' Carter moved up to another figure, then another, touching each one reverently, tracing the outline of their lips, pressing his thumb up against their eyes.

Edward couldn't bring himself to touch one.

He walked between the ranks of soldiers, moving deeper and deeper into the chamber. Some carried spears; others carried swords, many of them real. It was incredible. He felt, for the first time in his life, like a hero from one of the radio serials, striding in to do battle against the deadly doctor himself, Fu Manchu.

'What do you think?' Convey said.

'I think we are looking at fame and fortune, my friend. Fame and bleedin' fortune. Do you have any idea what these are?'

Edward knew, walking amongst them, he *knew*.

'Qin Shi Huangdi's honour guard. That's what these are. Thousands of terracotta warriors to stand eternal vigil over his imperial corpse. Incredible. The vanity of the man. Just as his real army protected him in life, his clay army would guard him in death.'

'Better this than a bone garden, if you ask me.' Convey said. 'Those places give me the creeps.'

'Oh, I don't doubt there are hundreds of skeletons as well. No self-respecting emperor is going to shuffle off into the afterlife without his counsellors and faithful retainers, especially one history suggests was the unifier of China. But I would imagine the sacrificial pits will be closer to the tomb itself.' Carter pushed the figure nearest him, testing its balance to see if would topple. The thing was easily as heavy as a fully grown man. Grunting, Carter gave the terracotta man a good firm shove so it rocked slightly on its feet and again, to be satisfied that the statue wasn't secured to the floor.

Carter was right: there were bones.

Edward had moved away towards the back of the huge chamber. The floor beneath him changed from thick clay to a coarse woven reed and wood. He knelt, examining the reeds, surprised that they hadn't rotted away to nothing in the dead air. Obviously the pollutants of life had yet to infiltrate the emperor's tomb. He stood up and dusted his hands off on his khakis, took two steps forward, stumbled and crashed through the floor as the reed-woven support gave way beneath his feet.

He screamed and flailed out, dropping the lantern.

The glass cracked but the flame didn't die; it licked out of the broken lantern, blackening and singeing the reeds as they smouldered beneath the flame's heat.

Edward flailed about wildly, trying to quash the fire before it had a chance to start. And that was when he felt them. The bones. His hands hit skulls, fibulas, tibias, femurs, ribs, vertebrae and clavicles, both human and animal. They felt wrong; hard like stone where they had calcified with age.

He whimpered and pushed his back against the pit wall. Black curls of smoke drifted up from the dry reeds. He stamped them out with the soles of his boots. He heard something, a pitiful, haunted moan. It took him a moment to realise it had come from his own mouth.

'Eddie? Eddie? Where the heck did you go? Where's that damn light, lad?' Carter's voice was muffled but he didn't sound happy about being plunged into darkness in the middle of the army of the damned. Confronted with the grinning skulls and the empty eye sockets, Edward would happily have traded places with the treasure hunter.

'There!'

He heard them coming, running through the stone soldiers, the sound of their steps changing as the floor changed from clay to reed and wood.

He couldn't stand. His legs were useless. All he could do was press up hard against the clay, feet scuffling at the reed and bone, whimpering, until a hand reached down to drag him up out of the pit.

'Looks like Eddie found the bone garden,' Convey said, his grin transformed into a grim parody of a smile by the lantern as he clasped Edward's wrist and hauled him to his feet. Together, Carter and Convey pulled him up.

'And nearly managed to burn the place down, by the looks of it,' Carter said, taking the lantern from Edward.

Edward was shaking as they led him back toward daylight.

Outside, in the cold light of day, Carter said what Edward had always known he would.

'So, lads, one of us has got to say what's on our minds so it might as well be me. What now? Do we bring in the authorities? Turn the site over to archaeologists to excavate? Or do we liberate one of those fine fellows and see what he'll make on the collectors' market?' His delivery left the others in no doubt as to which was his preferred option.

'But who...' Edward didn't manage to shape the rest of the question in his mouth: would want to buy a terracotta soldier?

'Ah, Eddie, my boy, you have no idea what you just saw, do you? The innocence of youth. Picture this:

'Your face on the front page of The Times, your voice on the new World Service, a moving picture, perhaps, with Douglas Fairbanks as the fearless Edward Grainger deep in darkest China in search of the Eighth Wonder of the World! Imagine it, Eddie, Gloria Swanson cast as your romantic interest. The world of possibilities it opens up. The treasures of Tut Ankh Amun's grave goods are nothing compared to what we've just stumbled upon, lad. So you ask yourself why would a collector want to own a piece of it, indeed? Those red men are, almost certainly, the oldest surviving example of advanced pottery, and they are *perfect*. They aren't some measly shards of Roman rubbish dug up in Northumberland. Those soldiers are incredible. They are things of beauty.

'So why would a collector pay?

'Well, to understand that requires an insight into the greed that fires human nature. Rich men seek to possess things, Edward. They crave ownership of all things wondrous, be they Da Vinci oils or Michelangelo sculptures, or in this case life-sized Chinese warriors that once belonged to Qin Shi Huangdi. In other words, they want what we've just stumbled across.'

'But, what's to stop them from just taking one. I mean, it isn't like they're unique, there were thousands of them down there.'

'Supply and demand, we control the source of supply and have the sole means of distribution.'

'Until word leaks out about what's here.' Ambrose said, coming up behind them. 'And then it becomes a free for all.'

'Ah, but, my good man, no one but us knows of this wondrous place.

Are you going to kill the goose and give up those golden eggs? Or you, Convey? No, I thought not.'

'But what about them?' the Australian said, nodding toward the peasants who had led them to the well in the first place.

'Seems to me that too many people knowing a secret stops it from being a secret,' Carter said, coldly.

'Which means?'

'Best you don't ask if you don't want to know, Eddie. Best you don't ask.'

II

> Neglect of what is good in me; want of thoroughness in study; failure to do the right when told me; lack of strength to overcome faults, these are my sorrows.
>
> Confucius

'The mistress of the skies is cruel, Eddie, my son. Creed or colour doesn't matter. Ugly Americans and beautiful Pommies can come a cropper just as spectacularly. That's why I love, her so.' Bryce Convey grinned as he rubbed the axle grease from his hands with a damp rag. Since the discovery, Convey had become a new man. Lust fired him. He moved about the De Havilland Hawk Moth with an arrogant swagger. He was in his element. 'The new world belongs to God's chosen people, Eddie, the bravest of the brave. Flyboys like Lindbergh, Carranza and Kingsford Smith, who take the world by the scruff of the throat and live, and by God I mean live by the seat of their pants, nothing but a few inches of steel between them and Lucifer's own fall all the way back down to Earth. Ah, Emilio Carranza, there was a man born to fly.'

The plan was simple: they had ripped the back seats out of the bird to increase its payload; Edward would accompany Carter – and the terracotta soldier – in the plane, refuelling in Burma before returning home to Calcutta to cash in on their find, while Ambrose and Convey made their way back to Xi'an by foot, then head south in search of passage out of the country. It was far from ideal, but both were willing to forgo the relative comfort of the plane in return for the wealth the red man would bring.

Edward was a long way from home and the sun and the lack of rain never failed to reinforce that feeling of isolation and alienation. It had been fun, at first; flushing the toilet and watching the water swirl the wrong way down the bowl as it disappeared, running the taps to see the same backward effect. He lied to himself, pretending there was some nobility in it, the Englishman abroad and all that. But the truth had much more in common with the backwards-looking glass land of Carroll's Alice. The only question was whether that made him Alice, the March Hare or the Dormouse, because Carter was quite obviously the Mad Hatter.

'The joys of indiscriminate death,' Edward said, looking back at Carter as he led Mai Ling and her family into the undergrowth. 'All things die equal.'

Ambrose sat on the crate that protected their treasure. It had been a mammoth task liberating the terracotta man, needing all eight of them on the guide ropes to raise the giant clay figure from the well. Three hours it had taken from first tilting the figure to laying him to rest in the crate. Edward hurt. He kept trying to tell himself it would be worth it but he couldn't get past the nagging belief that people should know – that everyone had a right to look upon Qin Shi Huangdi's terracotta army, not just parasites wealthy enough to hoard whatever their hearts desired. This was a part of the world's heritage.

He should have expected it, of course. Carter was a treasure hunter not an explorer. There was an innate difference between the two. He was a profiteer.

He was, in other words, a thief.

The De Havilland was a monstrosity of wood and steel; the welded steel fuselage and tail were sat snug in a wooden wing sub-structure and all-over fabric covering. The stress flaws in the wing root attachment fittings had been soldered over. It was nothing more than a temporary solution. He just had to have faith that the bird would make it all the way back to India intact. That was all he needed: faith.

The muffled clap of three gunshots sounded close together.

Three shots. Four peasants. Did that mean Mai Ling had run? Or was she lying dead in the dirt?

A moment later, Carter emerged from the trees.

Edward couldn't bring himself to look at the man.

III

If people are not afraid to die, then why threaten them with death? If people were afraid of death, and lawbreakers could be caught and put to death, who would dare to do so?
There is the Lord of Death who executes.

Lao-tzu

They hardly said a word after the initial cry of 'Chocks away!'

Now, hours later, Edward looked down on the sea of shanties and the rolling greens of forested hills as the sun slowly set redly enough to delight even the most melancholic shepherd. He wondered what they were doing down there, the lives he so blithely flew over. Eating, starving, crying, growing up, growing old, sleeping, shouting, making up, making love, surviving, dying: the whole human experience, comic and tragic, was being played out beneath him. He felt godlike, hovering above it all, all seeing.

It was amazing but he couldn't enjoy it. He could only think about Carter leading Mai Ling into the forest. Images of death and blood twisted around inside him. He saw flashes of her death mask over and over, her innocence broken on the wheel of life's pain.

He couldn't bring himself to believe that his friend was capable of such barbarity. Surely he had fired warning shots into the air, driving the peasants off into the woods, hadn't he?

He thought for a moment that he was daydreaming; hearing again the brutal rapport of Carter's pistol delivering its judgement on Mai Ling's family.

But he wasn't dreaming.

A flurry of movement caught his eye as a piece of metal span off into the blue. The thrum of the propeller and the whip of the wind mutated into something approaching a scream as a second section of the wing root attachment was ripped away by the sheer force of the wind.

The Hawk Moth lurched beneath them, in trouble.

'This is going to go one of two ways, kiddo,' Carter said. 'One's a white-knuckle ride of our lives culminating in one hell of a bumpy landing and a great story to tell the grandkids. The other's this baby tearing itself apart under the stress and us having about a minute and a half to play Icarus before we run out of sky to fall from. So brace yourself, Eddie.'

The frame of the Hawk Moth shook around him, the vibrations intensifying just as the corresponding screams did. The plane was tearing itself apart and there was nothing either of them could do about it.

'Now's a good time to make your peace with your maker, Eddie.'

The Lord's Prayer stumbled off his tongue but he kept mixing up his trespasses and his daily bread before the prayer disappeared from his mind and all he could think was I *don't want to die, not like this, please, God, no... please...* as they fell from the sky.

IV

> The wise have ancient mystic wisdom and profound understanding, too deep to comprehend. Because they cannot be comprehended, they can only be described by analogy: cautious, like crossing a stream in winter; alert, like one aware of danger on all sides; courteous, like a visiting guest; self-effacing, like ice beginning to melt; genuine, like a piece of uncarved wood; open and receptive, like a valley; freely mixing, like muddy water.
>
> Lao-tzu

'The twenty-seventh of July 1928; great day, great year. Mickey Mouse makes his first appearance; Fleming discovers penicillin; women are finally given the right to vote, and in an hour Tich Freeman will become the first bowler ever to take 200 first-class wickets before the end of July.'

The Doctor's grin was infectious as he busied around the inside of the TARDIS. 'Quite a staggering achievement when you think about it, and I don't mind admitting I have always fancied seeing the stumps fly on that two-hundredth one. I've often wondered what is the point of a time machine if you don't enjoy it a little once in a while?'

'I'm strictly a cricket-free zone, Doctor,' Turlough said, pretending some deep fascination with a spot on the console just beneath the time rotor.

'Then I am sure you'll find something else to occupy yourself for a few hours, while Tegan and I enjoy the crack of willow on leather and the glorious summer sun.' He adjusted the sprig of celery in his lapel, making sure the long metal pin held it firmly in place before he held out a hand to Tegan. 'So, shall we?' The Doctor's grin was distinctly boyish as he pushed open the TARDIS door and stepped back to allow Tegan to pass through.

They stepped out into undergrowth thick enough to be called a jungle. It was getting dark.

'Well, it doesn't look a lot like London, Doctor.'

The Doctor tapped the chronometer on his wrist and shook his head. 'No. Obviously not. Now, be quiet while I think, would you?'

'Well, I –'

The Doctor let out a strangled harrumph, span on his heel and stuck his head back through the door. 'Turlough, check the coordinates.'

'London, 27 July 1928, about two hours before that free man did whatever it is he did,' Turlough answered in a thoroughly bored voice.

'Yes, yes, that's the time where we are *supposed* to be. Mind finding out where we actually are? And when we are, for that matter. Somewhere in the world it might be just after lunch, but not here. I have a feeling that's a whole different piece of time and space. I'd like to be sure we aren't going to accidentally stumble into Genghis Khan's ravening horde. Far better to be prepared for that kind of surprise, I tend to find, so think of it as a problem for you to solve.'

He turned back to Tegan and the dense tangle of undergrowth.

'Well, no ravening hordes that I can see,' she said. 'Which is a marked improvement if you –' She stopped mid-sentence, her eyes drawn to the sky. A black plume of smoke corkscrewed through the sky. At the front of it a plane span out of control. Not a 747 or an Airbus, nothing so leviathan-like. It was a smudge, more like a kite than the planes she was used to.

And it was in trouble.

'Doctor!' She pointed up at the crippled plane as it tumbled towards the ground.

It took him a moment to see it, but when he did the Doctor was already running, charging headlong into the undergrowth, eyes fixed on the sky.

'Come on,' he shouted, not turning to see if she followed. He ran, pushing aside clawing branches, stumbling in sodden ditches, tripping on trailing roots, panting and gasping with the exertion, adrenalin pumped by his twin hearts through his body. He staggered, eyes still turned to the sky, following the black smoke. Thick undergrowth tugged and snatched at his long cream coat, tearing the Edwardian cloth as the Doctor plunged thoughtlessly into the dense forest.

The explosion, when it came, was huge, lighting up the darkening sky with its petrol-red glare.

The plane had split itself cleanly into two parts, the cockpit having broken away from the tail. The fuselage burned. The metal and glass of the cockpit ticked like a bomb counting down to detonation. The pilot's corpse lay broken in the dirt, the flames having spread from the ruined fuel tank to consume the man. A second man was trapped within the cockpit, unconscious or dead, tangled in the web of his safety harness.

'Help him, Doctor!' Tegan yelled above the snap and cackle of the flame.

The heat was fierce. The Doctor pulled off his jacket and wrapped it around his arm. Twice, the flames beat him back, the sheer intensity driving him to his knees. A series of sharp detonations exploded from the tailgate, the final one launching a cascade of flame high into the sky.

'He's alive!'

She was right. The man buckled into the passenger seat stirred, struggling slowly back towards consciousness. They had to get to him before panic set in. Panic could well prove a more effective killer than the flames.

Gritting his teeth, the Doctor threw himself at the burning plane, ducking down low in an attempt to negate the worst of the heat. He made it up to the side of the plane as the flames began to consume it. He hammered his fist – bound in his coat – against the glass of the pilot's window again and again until the glass broke into a thousand fragments. The flames roared around the Doctor as he reached through the broken window and tugged at the harness strapping the man firmly into the burning plane. The heat was unbearable. It had fused part of the cloth onto the metal hasp fastening. The Doctor pulled at it, trying to wrest it free of the fastening even as the man began to buck and writhe in panic as he returned to consciousness. He screamed, and the Doctor punched him hard in the face. The man slumped in the passenger seat.

'Sorry, old chap,' the Doctor said, more to himself than the unconscious man. He pulled the unconscious man out of the harness before the flames became his funeral pyre, dragging the limp body through the broken window and away from the burning wreckage – and, as he did so, he recognised him. Not immediately, not completely. But they had met before. It would come back to him in its own good time.

The heat had seared his trousers to his skin in strips and burned savagely through to the knee where it had charred the flesh to the bone.

He used his coat as a pillow to cushion the man's head.

The flames had taken their toll; the left side of the man's face bore the raw blistering of heavy burns and his breathing was ragged. Shallow. Untended, he would die. The smoke had clawed its way into his lungs and was eating away at him. It wouldn't take long. They needed to get him back to the TARDIS if he was going to stand a chance.

Making a decision, the Doctor looked up, cradling the man's head, and caught a glimpse of a man disappearing into the undergrowth. Only it wasn't a man; that much was obvious by the ethereal bluish glow that clung to it.

'Did you see it?'

'See what?' Tegan said.

The fact that she had to ask told him she hadn't seen it: a Shang noble, if he wasn't mistaken, wearing a breastplate of shell, though it could equally have been a Zhou. The bronze helms were similar, as were the breastplates, though the Zhou often wore a kia, a sleeveless coat of cured buffalo hide. It didn't really matter; both were thousands of years out of their element.

'An undigested bit of beef, a blot of mustard, a crumb of cheese, a fragment of underdone potato. There's more of the grave than of gravy about it, whatever it is,' the Doctor mused, mangling Ebenezer Scrooge's denunciation of Marley's ghost. 'This is all wrong.' He said it more to himself than anyone else. Even accounting for the vast lifespan of the two dynasties, it was impossible. The Shang, or Yin, dynasty was founded in 1600 BC and the first Zhou dynasty ended in 256 BC, so the ghostly warrior ought, by any reasonable extrapolation of the facts, to have been from somewhere within that time frame. Why then were they crouched before the blazing wreckage of an aeroplane that wouldn't come into existence for at least another two and a half thousand years?

He had to think. There was something he wasn't seeing clearly. A ghost? A blue ghost? The name suited the apparition but, even from the brief glimpse he had had, the Doctor knew it didn't come close to doing the thing justice. The ghost warrior had no pervading malevolence. There was a meddling hand, he was almost certain, but it smacked of humanity's ignorance.

But that, of course, was exactly how so many meddlers worked, through agents, so while it wasn't unfeasible that the dead pilot or his wounded passenger were agents of some black universal force, he told himself a much more mundane explanation made more sense.

No, they had misstepped in time but that was hardly something new; the TARDIS had been far from reliable of late. This latest detour across time streams didn't have to be anything more sinister than her usual troubles. 'Sometimes it is nothing more sinister than shadows just waiting to be jumped at,' he told himself.

'And you believe that?' Tegan muttered, shaking her head.

'Oh, I believe in lots of things. Come on. Help me get him back to the TARDIS.'

V

Abandon wisdom and discard cleverness, and people will benefit a hundredfold.

Abandon humanity and discard morality, and people will rediscover love and duty.

Abandon skill and discard profit, and there will be no thieves or robbers.

These three things relate to externals and are inadequate.

People need what they can depend on: reveal simplicity; embrace the natural; control selfishness; reduce desires.

Lao-tzu

The man's burns were bad.

Part of his face and great lengths of flesh down his left side were charred, the skin blackened and there was weeping pus where the blisters had popped. His leg bore the worst of it. The Doctor laid the man gently on the gurney in the medical bay, while Turlough adjusted the mimic coding on the Synth-Skin canister and handed it over to the Time Lord.

'This won't sting a bit,' the Doctor told the unconscious man, and sprayed the foam over the burns. It was fascinating stuff; Turlough had seen nothing like it. The foam contained microscopic DNA mimics that fed off the wounded tissue, knitting and rebuilding the flesh whilst protecting it with a snakelike second skin that would be shed when their work was done.

He had no idea where the Doctor had come across the canister. Like so much of the TARDIS's contents, it looked like little more than space junk. Yet thanks to those DNA mimics the man would live, and without so much as a scratch to boast of.

They left the man to sleep through his recuperation and adjourned to the console room to wait for the super-charged nature to take its course, rebuilding the genetic structure of the damaged tissue.

The Doctor crouched over a box full of wires and peculiar odds and ends. Muttering to himself, he pulled at things and twisted them, shaking his head.

'Come on, man, you've done this often enough.'

But, of course, he hadn't. He winced as a spark of raw energy spat from the device. Device! He almost laughed at the grandiosity of the word. The thing in his hands was little more than a jury-rigged sonic prodder – it had none of the finesse of his old screwdriver and was held together by little more than a wing and a prayer... Still, a peculiar feeling nagged at him. He continued to tinker with the device until Turlough interrupted his chain of fiddling – it was far removed from actual thought.

'What do you think it was, Doctor?' Turlough asked, and the way he did gave away his underlying fear – could it conceivably be some form of retribution for his siding with the Time Lord? 'A wayward nail that needs to be hammered down?'

'Let's start with what it isn't instead, shall we? It isn't human. It isn't supposed to be here. I think that's more than enough to be going on with for now, don't you?'

'It narrows it down, certainly,' agreed Tegan.

Before they could develop the growing list of negatives, the chime of the cloister bell rang out. The dull clang of the bell was not something they heard every day. Indeed, that they heard it at all was cause for concern. The Doctor was up and punching at keys and pulling levers before the first cycle of the siren had finished.

'This isn't good... this isn't good at all.' The Doctor drew up the viewscreen. There was nothing to be seen. 'I hate an impending disaster when you can't see it coming. Yes, yes, now where is it? Where is it? Come to me, my beauty. Come to me. Got it.' His grin was infectious. 'Ten clicks north of here, moving fast. A non-human life form emitting serious amounts of energy – and I mean *serious* amounts of energy. No, not a life form: a life *force*.'

'It's my fault,' a miserable voice muttered from behind them. The man, a blanket wrapped around his shoulders, had shuffled into the console room. The Synth-Skin foam still clung in patches to his face and wounded knee. Without thinking, the man stooped forward and brushed the foam from his leg before any of them could stop him.

'No!' the Doctor cried. 'Leave it unless you want to look like a Krarg, all shining black embers for skin and livid red eyes. And what do you mean it's all your fault?'

The man paused, hand inches from the foam coating his left ear. 'It's a curse. That's what happens, isn't it, when you rob a tomb? You breach some ancient curse. I'm cursed. This is my doom.'

'You need to begin at the beginning,' said Tegan, 'and go on until you come to the end.'

The Doctor adjusted a series of instruments on the console's array and let out a long, slow whistle. 'I get it. But I wish I didn't. What happened here? Tell me everything. No detail is too minuscule. I can't stress that enough... Okay, some details are too minuscule but let me worry about those. You, my friend, talk.'

'Where... who... what?'

'Indeed, all of those things. Now, think. What happened? What could you possibly have to do with a rogue life force racing at great speed north? Enquiring minds want to know.' He said it with a smile but there was a tense undercurrent to the forced humour.

'And come to think of it,' said Tegan, 'who the devil are you?'

'Edward,' he said. 'Edward Grainger.'

'Yes,' said the Doctor. 'Of course you are. Nice to meet you again,

Edward Edward Grainger. I think it's about time you told us your story, don't you?'

And he did.

VI

True words are not beautiful.
  Beautiful words are not truthful.
  The good do not argue.
  Those who argue are not good.
  Those who know are not scholarly.
  The scholarly do not know.

Lao-tzu

'You mean to tell me you stole the immortal guardian of a dead emperor? What part of that sounded like a good idea to you? Honestly? Because I have heard some stupid ideas in my time, but this has to be one of the nuttier ones. The world is a sacred vessel, not to be tampered with. Those who do tamper with it, spoil it. Those who seize it, lose it. Did your mother never use the expression "It'll all end in tears"? See, I would have thought that was the perfect way of describing the outcome of this brilliant idea of yours. It'll all end in tears. I'm crying already, see?'

Edward shook his head, wanting to deny everything. The best he could manage was: 'But –'

'Ah, yes, the great defence: but. Let's not go there. Let me tell you a story now, Edward. Imagine this: I am all-powerful. I am emperor of the Shang dynasty, boy emperor at that. Probably a bit demanding. I mean, the world bows to my whim, so it stands to reason that I am something of a spoiled brat. I don't care that the use of force tends to rebound. I am ignorant of the truth: where armies march, thorns and brambles grow. I do not understand that whenever a great army is formed, scarcity and famine follow.

'Instead I command unflinching loyalty. I demand my soldiers serve me not only in life but in death, so, when I am dying, I have my mystics sacrifice my soldiers, every last one of them – that's thousands and thousands of them – binding their life forces, their spirits, in terracotta prisons so that they can serve me for ever and ever. And should I ever need them, they can be woken to fight for me. Are you getting a picture here? Seeing a pattern emerge?

'Now, you get the bright idea to steal one of these sacred guardians, then you crash. Not ideal, given what we've just learned about our petty boy emperor's toys. Still, I think it is safe to assume the terracotta man was destroyed in the crash, no? But what does that mean? Apart from the fact that the prison holding the life force has been violently shattered, releasing the ghost warrior charged with protecting the boy emperor's afterlife. Let's extrapolate what we know and see what we come up with.'

The man's red-headed companion rolled his eyes and walked away from the console muttering, 'Self-important monologue alert.'

'Thank you, Turlough. Now, if we assume its one and only charge was to protect the spoiled brat, what does it do now that it's awake? Three guesses? Anyone?'

'Return to the burial chamber to awaken its kindred spirits,' Edward said sickly, row upon row of terracotta warriors stretching out before his mind's eye.

'Exactly. That one spirit has been woken from its eternal vigil and stands ready to fight, but not alone. It's been woken in response to a threat but it has no idea what that threat is. Its long-dead master needs it, so it must fight, and with lack of an obvious enemy there are fifty thousand, a hundred thousand more ghost warriors about to go on the march. Total war, Edward. The dead versus the living.'

'How do you fight the dead?'

'I don't know, Edward, as much as it pains me to say it, I just don't know. But my guess is that neutralising one has got to be a better option than fighting a hundred thousand.' The man tapped the control panel in the centre of the room, drumming out an unconscious rhythm with the pad of his third finger while he thought. He looked up a moment later, blue eyes blazing triumphantly.

'Neutralising one,' said Edward. 'You make it sound so easy.'

'What comes from earth returns to earth. We know exactly where it is going.' He bent over the console and tapped away at various buttons. 'So all we need to do is stop it.'

The central column oscillated, a weird whirring sound accompanying its sudden rise and fall.

'London, here we come,' the woman said bitterly.

'What? I don't –'

'And believe me, you don't want to,' she said, cutting Edward's objection off.

And already the central column had ceased its shriek. 'The central chamber of Qin Shi Huangdi's honour guard,' the man said. 'I hope.'

'That's hundreds of miles away,' Edward said. None of this made any sense to him.

'Indeed. After you, old man,' the man said, holding open the door for him. Edward stepped out, impossibly, into the dark chamber of the red soldiers. He span around, trying to take it in but the only word that escaped his lips was, 'But...'

The man clambered out behind him, snagging his coat on the door handle. He tugged at it until it tore free.

'Not only the great defence, it doubles as the great question. Versatile little word that, eh?'

'But.'

'Indeed. We've already covered that.'

'How?'

'Ah, the next one. I imagine it'll be what, where and when next. Like Tegan said, you don't want to know. Now, where... Ah, yes...'

Edward span around trying to make sense of what he saw. His eyes really weren't deceiving him. They were underground, in the very chamber Carter's crew had stolen the terracotta soldier from, and they had just stepped out of something quite, quite wrong: a battered blue box with the words 'police public call box' written above its doors.

It listed awkwardly on its side in one of the hollowed-out fighting pits, row after row of terracotta men surrounding it on all sides, severe and menacing as they pressed in. It made no sense to Edward's rational mind. He'd crashed in the middle of forest miles from the burial chamber and... and... and the box they had stepped out of was tiny. Yet inside...

'It takes some getting used to,' Tegan said, stepping up behind him.

'Yes...' said Edward. He remembered seeing an incongruous blue box once before. In a cupboard when he was very young...

And then: a noise, in the shadows.

And then again, louder, more distinct.

It sounded like a sob.

'Hello?' said the Doctor. 'Who's there?'

Edward struggled to focus on the darkness behind the blue box. Slowly, a figure appeared – nervous and tentative.

It couldn't be.

It was impossible.

He touched the side of his face.

'Mai Ling,' said Edward. Recognising him, the girl ran forward and threw herself into his arms.

'I take it this is a friend of yours,' the Doctor said. 'Or do strange women make a habit of throwing themselves at you?'

'She's a friend,' said Edward, still unable to believe it was her. In his head he heard again the echo of the three gunshots. He looked at her, the look of fear on her face. 'She must have come down here to hide.'

And then they all heard it, screaming though the confines of the chamber: crack after brittle, brutal crack. Snap, crack, shatter. It took Edward a moment to realise what it was he heard, and then he knew: the sounds of the warriors awakening.

'Quickly! We've got no time!'

Edward saw it then, the ghostly blue nimbus surrounding the warrior as it merged with the clay of its fellow's prison. As the light slid inside the terracotta, a scream rent the darkness. On some primal – instinctive – level, Edward knew what it was: the sound of the warrior's spirit being torn free of its earthly prison, reborn as some deadly entity to destroy everything it encountered in the name of the dead boy emperor. They couldn't hope to stop it.

But, great defence, great question, and even greater stupidity: Edward charged the ethereal warrior.

'What are we going to do, Doctor?' Tegan gasped. Before she or the Doctor could stop him, Edward ran past her, throwing himself at the blue ghost.

'No!' The Doctor's cry was too late.

The air spat blue, the ghost emitting a shower of sparks as it came into contact with Edward's flesh. The explosion hurled him back and he crashed into the trapped form of a giant pottery warhorse, shattering its fetlock and bringing the great beast crashing down. Blue light began to leak out of the wound. The air stank of ozone, burning sulphur, and something else...

VII

Perfect straightness looks bent
  Extreme skill looks clumsy
  A brilliant speech sounds like stammering

Lao-tzu

Without thinking, the Doctor ran to the fallen man's side and knelt down. His skin crackled and burned with peculiar blue light. He groaned. Struggled to move.

'I started this,' he said, teeth clenched as he drew himself up into the sitting position. He had rolled his sleeves up as though he intended to duke it out with the ethereal warrior toe to toe.

'Don't be so melodramatic, you fool,' the Doctor said, marshalling his wits.

He needn't have worried. Edward sank back to the floor, eyes rolling up into his skull as he fainted.

From earth, to earth.

The Doctor stared at the chamber, the hard-packed clay floor, the clay warriors cracking and splintering before his eyes. From earth, to earth.

More and more cracks and splintering of clay echoed through the chamber as one by one the warriors began to wake. The screams were ghastly.

From earth, to earth returned.

Returned.

The clay of the floor was a different consistency to the terracotta of the soldiers.

'Yes! How could I be so blind!' the Doctor berated himself as he fumbled with the long hatpin holding the ever-present stick of celery to his lapel. He 'tinged' it like a tuning fork. The sound was a pitch-perfect C. Grinning, the Doctor wove through the press of unmoving clay warriors, working his way as close to ethereal warriors as he dared, before he knelt and jammed the pin into the floor.

Stepping back, he pulled the sonic prodder – he couldn't bring himself to think of it as a real tool, like his beloved screwdriver – from his pocket and aimed it at the pin.

'Well, here goes nothing.'

The pin amplified the magnitude of the pulsing sonic as the Doctor adjusted the prodder's fluctuating tonal resonance until he found the frequency of the red clay. Foot by square foot, the pin's harmonic reduced more and more of the terracotta to sucking wet mud as the resonance pattern built upon itself layer by layer.

'Come on, you beauty!' the Doctor cried as more and more of the underground chamber liquefied. He felt the sonic prodder shiver in his hand, struggling to contain the swelling energies pent up inside it. It grew uncomfortably hot in his hand. 'Not good, not good. Come on, just a little bit more. Don't let me down.'

'Doctor!' Tegan cried, but the Doctor had seen it: the interference pattern had all but turned the clay around the TARDIS into a sloshing, sucking quagmire and the old girl was sinking slowly.

He looked at the blue ghosts swarming around the chamber, at the imprisoned warriors breaking free of their clay bonds, and at the TARDIS slowly slipping into darkness. She was on her side, listing. It wouldn't take long until the ship disappeared completely and was lost forever.

The sonic prodder spluttered, a huge tremor spasming the length of his arm.

'Not *now!*' he yelled, shaking the thing.

He had to make a decision but there was no *good* decision he could make.

'Get Edward and the girl back to the TARDIS! Now! *Run!*' The urgency in his voice frightened Tegan and Turlough into action. They dragged Edward back to the dubious safety of the sinking ship, the Chinese girl following close behind. The Doctor intensified the sonic pulse – knowing even as he did it that he was dooming the makeshift prodder – until the cavern itself seemed to shriek its agony as it melted into mud. And the mud spread, snaring the ghost warriors one by one.

'Doctor!'

'Not yet!' The Doctor didn't dare break the pattern of resonance he had built up, even for the few seconds it would take him to run back to the TARDIS, until every single ghost warrior was at least partially trapped in the sucking mud of the chamber floor. To the earth returned.

Anything else and this one hope would be doomed.

The prodder emitted a terrible whine and spluttered again, the sonic beam reduced to an erratic pulse.

'Set the coordinates for somewhere else – anywhere else!' the Doctor shouted, backing slowly away from the hatpin.

It was working. The ghost warriors were being trapped by the ooze, and sinking into the floor as though their souls still possessed weight and substance.

'Yes, yes, yes!' And then he risked a glance back toward the TARDIS. 'No, no, no!' The ship was almost gone, swallowed by the mud.

'Doctor!'

And the sonic pulse fizzled out into nothing and he was left clutching a dead bit of space junk. It took a few seconds for the resonance pattern to fold in on itself and collapse, the clay changing state from liquid to solid once again.

No more than six inches of the side panels of the TARDIS remained above the ground.

The ghost warriors fared no better. More than fifty had been freed, but for most of them that freedom proved to be momentary. The sonic pulse had lasted barely long enough – but it had lasted. The clay set around their ankles and calves, drawing them down into the mud of the earth, swallowing them even as the clay reformed over their heads, imprisoning their immaterial form once more in an earthly grave. The Doctor had little doubt that when excavated the ghost warriors would look exactly like every other member of the boy emperor's elite guard.

But one stubborn, loyal, relentless warrior refused to be so easily snared. It circled above the Doctor's head. The ghost warrior came on – it chased him as he ran back, darting between the clay figures, and jumped down through the open TARDIS doors.

They slammed shut behind him.

'I don't think it'd be wise to stick around,' he said with a grin.

'Doctor, look out!' Tegan shouted.

The blue nimbus of the ghost warrior came through the doors of the TARDIS – not through them as the Doctor had only moments before; *through* them. Through the metal shell of the time machine itself. A low unearthly growl emenated from its ethereal lips. Its ghost blade slashed through the air, a whisker away from the Doctor's face as he spun away from it.

The Doctor dashed to the console, slamming down buttons and tripping switches desperately.

'We *have* to contain it! If I can just find a way to –'

The nimbus focused on the sleeping Edward, who was lying propped up against the wall, and lunged towards the man, ghost blade aimed squarely at his heart – but seeing the blade lancing forward the Chinese girl threw herself between victim and would-be killer. It was a great and tragic last act of bravery.

The ghostly sword pierced the girl's flesh. For a heartbeat, she blazed a fierce electric blue. Sparks fizzed and danced around her entire body. The air inside the TARDIS crackled. Then, suddenly, she collapsed and the ghost warrior's cry was silenced.

The console room sank into a deathly hush; the nimbus extinguished as though it had never existed.

The Doctor rushed over to Mai Ling and knelt, cradling her head.

'Is she okay?' Tegan asked. 'What happened, Doctor?'

'Do you know, Tegan,' he said, looking up, 'this very brave, very foolish young lady may have inadvertently trapped the life force with her.' He opened Mai Ling's eyes, checking her pupils. 'It wasn't expecting to hit her – it wasn't ready.'

'And...?' asked Turlough wearily.

The Doctor smiled, standing up. 'It's subdued. Caught inside her, buried deep within her subconscious.'

'That doesn't sound too terminal. For a ghost, I mean,' Tegan said.

'Ahh, well, it ought to be safe enough. Certainly, as long as no one tampers with her, expressly intending to loose the warrior's spirit. Which, given that she's a peasant girl from 1920s China, I'd say is rather unlikely, wouldn't you?'

'So, we're just going to leave an ancient, malevolent life force trapped in a girl and let her roam around?' said Turlough, buttoning up his suit jacket.

'That's about the size of it, yes. We aren't here to meddle when we don't have to, Turlough.'

'Doctor?' Tegan said. She was looking at Edward rather quizzically. The Doctor didn't need to be a telepath to know what she was thinking.

'Yes, Tegan. You have.'

'Have what?' said Turlough.

'Met this man before,' she said. 'But it was in his future, wasn't it? He was older.'

'Yes. As far as Edward Grainger knows, he's never seen you before. Well, obviously, because he hasn't. It hasn't happened for him yet, but it will. And when it does, he's going to think he's stumbled across a female Dorian Grey. How marvellous. Right, let's drop our sleeping beauties off somewhere, shall we? I think it's best if we make sure Edward's all right, then return him to his aircraft – a safe distance away, of course.'

'And the girl?' asked Turlough.

The Doctor squatted down next to her. 'Well... we should be able to find her family. Or her home town, at any rate. It's probably best if we engineer a parting between these two friends. Edward is... an interesting man. He'd work something out eventually. It could be inconvenient.'

'But he won't remember us, will he, Doctor?' Tegan mused. 'He's seen you, me, the TARDIS – but he didn't mention anything when we met him... I mean, will meet him... Oh, you know what I mean.'

'I have a feeling it will all be a bit hazy – for the both of them,' said the Doctor, examining his two unconscious passengers. He let out a long, exhausted sigh. 'All right, let's head for the wreckage of Edward's plane, shall we?'

Tegan laughed. 'Some chance of this old crate landing anywhere remotely near his plane. Best aim for England, 1981, and hope you get lucky, Doctor.'

'You know,' he said, 'I always fancied seeing Botham's Ashes, Tegan. You're a genius.'

Log 384
Richard Salter
An Adventure of the Seventh Doctor

Evil should languish in the shadows. Unspeakable atrocities go hand in hand with dank, gloomy dungeons and dark and stormy nights. Unholy acts of barbarism don't belong in a place so bright, so clean, so new. I've been in hospitals; they were not as sanitary. Everything is sterile; the white walls gleam in the harsh lights. Even now, outside, workers toil to scrub away anything multiplying without permission. They are always there, mopping and sweeping, creating antiseptic swirls on the shiny wooden floor. There is sweat on my brow. Soon they will come and clean that away too. The door will open and the doctors will come. At least, they dress like doctors.

Healing is the last thing on their mind.

Perhaps the Professor will come for me soon. Or perhaps he is like me: sitting in a sterile, brightly lit cell, chained to the wall, waiting to go under the knife.

I took the early morning train to Paddington and arrived soon after lunchtime. I wasn't used to taking public transportation but not even my chauffeur could know where I was going. I walked the short distance to the meeting place, an unassuming café not too far away from my London residence. The midday sun tried its best to take the edge off the biting December cold but did little to stop my teeth chattering. I kept my head down and walked on, avoiding eye contact with all passers-by and ignoring the scores of unemployed who shuffled about in their drab overcoats and cloth caps, clearly too lazy to find gainful employment. I quickened my step as I passed the soup-line, uncomfortably aware of envious eyes. Things had certainly grown worse in my time away from England. London bustled as restlessly as Darjeeling, Bangkok, Hong Kong or Phnom Penh, but was much greyer and more depressing. It was good to be home, but deflating.

The café was not the sort of place I usually frequented, but if His Majesty's Government requests to meet with one in absolute secret and instructs one not to tell a soul of the rendezvous, then who is one to argue? I pushed open the door and tried not to turn up my nose at the smell. Inside, the riff-raff and hoi polloi ate greasy food with greasy utensils. The clamour was completely undignified. The kitchen staff had clearly never heard of soap. Some of the clientele seemed rooted to their tables, staring into space and sipping watery tea. How were these people ever to find jobs if they sat around in cafés all day?

There he was, hunched in the corner reading The Times, drinking tea like any of these commoners. I felt them watching me as I passed by but I kept my head up as a gentleman should. The man's face was obscured by the paper but his fedora hat rested on the table to his right, just as he had said it would. I sat opposite him and said the code phrase. 'Will the Leafs win the Stanley Cup again this season?'

He lowered the paper and stared at me, his deep-set eyes regarding me as if I were an idiot, or one of these unemployable wretches. His face scrunched into a look of scorn. 'Oh, Edward, you're so obvious.'

Well, that was rich. There he was with his wild hair, his Scots accent and his ridiculous jumper covered in punctuation, and he was telling me that I was obvious.

'Care to explain that remark, sir?'

The government man drummed his fingers on the table and pouted at me. 'Look around you, Edward Grainger.' He rolled the first 'r' in my surname mockingly. 'Who is everybody staring at? Is it me sitting in the corner, drinking tea and reading about the new German chancellor? Or is it you with your finely tailored suit, your immaculate hair and that expensive leather briefcase?'

'I was told I would be meeting a representative of His Majesty's Government. Do you expect me to dress like a ruffian?'

'A secret meeting, Edward, in secret. Still, never mind. Now you're here, I suppose I should tell you why you were asked to come. I'm the, er...' He paused, regarding me curiously, as if trying to remember something. 'Let's go with Professor, shall we?'

'Professor who?'

He ignored my question. 'I've known you longer than you can imagine. I know what you're capable of and I know your limitations. There's no need for me to ask if you can keep a secret because I know that you can. I also know your future, Edward, and for a long time there was a missing piece. How does Edward Grainger, spoiled rich child who's more used to shooting grouse in the countryside than shooting enemies with a camera... how does this man become a spy for the British Government?'

I just stared at him. How long had he been watching me, and why? And what did he say? A spy? 'I think perhaps I've been brought here as part of an elaborate joke. If you'll excuse me, Professor.' I rose.

'Sit down.'

He said it quietly without drawing attention, but there was such absolute authority in his voice that I found myself sinking back into my seat. The waitress came at that moment. Suddenly feeling thirsty, I ordered a tea.

'You and I are going on a mission. We're going on behalf of the Security Services, and the British Government knows nothing about it.'

'How is that possible?'

'Because the Security Services have people in very high places who sympathise with Churchill.'

'That self-glorifying, arrogant has-been? I hear he's soused half the time. Spouting all that rubbish about Germany and Nazis. If there were any real threat, the Government would have done something about it.'

'MacDonald is an idiot,' the Professor snapped, shocking me. 'He doesn't want to see what's happening in Europe because he's more concerned about the unemployment rates and keeping the Tories in line. Look around you, Edward. You may still live in the lap of luxury but most have lost everything. These people can barely afford a cup of tea. And things will get worse before they get better.'

I blinked. 'What's your point?'

'My point is that Churchill is quite correct about the Nazi threat but the Government refuses to listen to him. There are more pressing problems at home. So the Security Services are quietly recruiting a number of operatives – off the books, as it were – and sending them out to monitor the situation in a variety of places. I'm one of those operatives, Edward, and if you do well you will be too. I'd ask if you accept the assignment but I already know you will. After all, you like to travel; you can finance your own operations; you're old enough to have experience; you don't yet have a family. People are used to you disappearing for months, maybe years at a time. In short, you're ideal.'

I just stared at him, open-mouthed. How could he possibly assume that I would go with him on some fool's errand at a moment's notice, facing untold dangers and without the official sanction of the British Government? Besides, I had only just returned from three years of travel. I'd been looking forward to a spot of shooting and then falling asleep in front of my fireplace with a glass of brandy and a fine cigarette.

I took a sip of my tea and grimaced at the bitter taste.

He didn't say anything else, just picked up his paper and started reading again. I was sorely tempted to get up and leave then and there but he seemed so sure. 'I already know you will.' It chilled me. I had to know where this was going. Besides, how amazing to be a secret spy. Such a glamorous life. I had recently been reading Maugham's exceptional *Ashenden, or, the British Agent* and had dreamed of a life of espionage, embarking on covert missions and conducting daring escapes. The ultimate gentleman, aloof and dashing. Perhaps I could be the next Sidney Reilly and people would read about my exciting adventures in the *Evening Standard* too. More importantly, with the resources of the Security Services at my disposal, perhaps I might finally track down poor Mai Ling, at least between my assignments.

'If I were to agree, Professor, I assume you would take me to Berlin?'

'We're not going to Germany. We're going to China.'

'China?' How perfect! I could resume my search, but this time with a real shot at tracking her down. I didn't relish the idea of more travelling but for her any sacrifice was worthwhile. It didn't make much sense though. 'What has China got to do with the Nazis?' I asked.

'Not much, at least not yet. Last year, Japan claimed a large part of northern China as its territory.'

'Indeed. I was in Saigon at the time. Nobody felt safe. The Japanese... I fear they will not stop until the whole continent is their empire.'

'We're going to Manchuria.'

'I don't understand.'

'My... employers wish to know how much territory Japan has occupied. They fear that the Nazis and the Japanese are in secret talks and intend to join forces.'

'What could possibly lead them to that conclusion?'

'Well, I did, for a start.'

I chuckled. 'Professor, this is preposterous. What could possibly make you think that I would accompany you on some obscure mission to Manchuria?'

'Mai Ling needs you.'

I gaped at him, nearly spilling my tea. 'How the devil do you know about her?'

'I told you. I've known you longer than you've been alive.'

'You know where she is, don't you? Is she in Manchuria? Is she safe?'

'Yes, yes and no, I'm afraid she's not.'

I stood. 'When do we leave?'

It's hard to sleep so I don't bother. How can one sleep in a place of waking nightmares?

I have a cellmate but he doesn't talk. He groans now and again and coughs up blood frequently. I do not know what is wrong with him, not specifically. His skin has turned black and his breathing is ragged. I fear he is not long for this world, poor fellow. He has wasted away to such an extent that I wonder why he does not slip his slender arms from his manacles.

Thankfully I am chained on the other side of the room – I would not want to catch what afflicts him.

The cell door opens. Perhaps this is my rescue? No, it's the men in white, covered from head to foot, wearing white masks and eye protection. This does not make me feel at ease. Shouldn't I have some protection too? They start examining the man; they are not gentle. They shove fingers into his throat, apply pressure to his torso as if trying to feel the shape of his internal organs. It's as if they are examining a corpse, not a living patient. One of them extracts an enormous amount of blood, far more than one might expect is reasonable for testing purposes. Then they chain him to the wall again where he sobs quietly.

Then they turn to me.

I still don't know how we got to Manchuria. The morning after I met the Professor, I woke up in a modest B&B he had reserved for me. I was picked up by a driver in a beautiful motor car that rivalled my own. It was a Bentley eight-litre, a fine piece of British engineering and one of the last to be produced before the previous year's purchase of the company by Rolls-Royce. If I had been in England in '31 I would have bought one myself. I was still drowsy as I was bounced around in the back. The motion of the automobile and the plush seats, as well as the lack of conversation with my silent driver, soon had me dropping off.

When I awoke, the Professor was standing over me. It was gloomy and smelled awful but I could tell we were on a train. Huddled around me in silence were a large number of Chinese peasants. In the corner rested several stacks of tall, lidless wicker baskets. There were shades drawn over the windows, blocking out the daylight.

'Where are we?' I asked.

The Professor's eyes were closed and he appeared to be listening to the sound of the train moving over the tracks. 'South of Harbin, in Manchuria. Shhh.'

I tried to stand but my legs weren't paying attention. 'How did I get here?'

'I said shhh! I'm trying to listen.'

My head was groggy and I felt I might vomit but I realised there was nothing in my stomach. I touched my face and, sure enough, felt stubble – at least a day's growth. My fine suit was gone and in its place was a simple fabric smock. The Professor wore something similar. Was this the life of a spy? Waking up on a train in a foreign country, bound for who-knew-where and feeling sick as a dog? I wagered that Riley never had to endure such misfortune!

'We're getting close.'

I could feel the train slowing too. The peasants with us chattered anxiously. I could even understand their words! 'Rumours', 'death camp' and a phrase beginning with 'Z' I didn't recognise.

'Professor, why are all these people speaking English?'

'They're not. It's Nazi technology – it's translating for you.'

I stared at him suspiciously. Just how advanced were the Nazis? And how had this Scotsman acquired their technology? It suddenly struck me that I had never seen the Professor's credentials or any evidence that he was really working for the Security Services. Terribly naive of me. Perhaps this was an elaborate trap.

'Cover your face,' he said. 'They mustn't see we're not local.'

As the train came to a halt, two armed guards appeared at the end of the carriage. I hadn't noticed them until they stood up. I couldn't make out their features but I could see they carried rifles. I hid my face.

They spoke to us in plain English. 'Get up, take a basket, put it over your head. Move!'

There was much confusion at this but when the guard stuck his gun in a peasant's face and started yelling at him, everyone complied. With the basket over my head and torso, reaching down to my waist, I could only see my feet and a little way in front of me. A door opened and bright light illuminated the filthy floor. I was shoved from the train. I saw other feet around me. Together we shuffled off, bumping into each other and occasionally stumbling in the dirt. I wondered what they didn't want us to see.

Where was my briefing? Where was my training? My life was already in danger and I had no idea what was going to happen or how I was going to cope with it.

We marched awkwardly for at least twenty minutes. After that time, our footfalls made a hollow sound. As I tilted the basket on my head just a little, I could see that I was near the edge of a bridge. I just made out the base of a large iron gate ahead of us before a guard slammed the basket back down over my head. I stumbled and nearly fell, crying out as I struggled to stay on my feet. If this was a drawbridge, were we being led into a castle?

I felt sure that once inside we would be allowed to remove the baskets, but the order didn't come. A heavy iron door clanged into place behind us, sealing our fate.

To my surprise, after they draw far more blood than they could possibly need, they lead me to another room and force me to run around the perimeter. After that they make me lift weights for half an hour. Being something of a sportsman, I manage to sustain the required pace but by the end of this exercise session I am exhausted and quite famished.

They take me back to my cell. They are still wearing their protective clothing. They feed me a simple but well-prepared meal. I am both surprised and confused. After my meal they examine my mouth, ears and eyes and then they leave me alone with the dying man. Perhaps they are treating me better because I am English. I wish I understood their intentions.

The Professor was clearly a master spy, as evidenced by the ease with which we slipped out from our baskets and scuttled away from the guards. He made it look easy, but the size of the risk became clear when he explained to me that the Chinese construction workers were so intimidated by the Japanese soldiers that they rarely made a break for freedom. Whenever they did, they were shot on sight.

We moved deeper into the facility. Without the basket covering my eyes, I could at last see what I had walked into. We passed laboratories, dormitories, workshops and offices. Everything was gleaming new and spotlessly maintained. We passed some Chinese men, scrubbing the walls. They eyed us curiously but didn't move to stop us or raise the alarm.

'What is this place, Professor?' I asked as we hurried down a flight of steps.

'This is the almost completed Zhong Ma fortress. It's the precursor to the infamous Unit 731 and its ilk. It turns my stomach to be here.'

I stared at him in astonishment as we reached the bottom of the stairs. 'Is Mai Ling here?'

'Unfortunately, yes.'

'How did you find this fortress?'

'I had to engage the resources of the Security Services to learn about troop movements, train schedules, avoiding unwanted Japanese attention. Access to that kind of information is why I signed up in the first place. Now, enough questions, Edward, or someone will hear.'

I fell silent. We walked along a corridor lined with heavy doors, each one fitted with a sliding view port and a smaller hatch beneath. Clearly this part of the fortress was intended as a prison, though the floor positively gleamed with cleanliness and the sterile white walls seemed as if they might burn skin on contact. The air was thick with the smell of disinfectant. It was more like a psychiatric institute than a hospital or a jail.

I couldn't contain my curiosity. I moved to one of the doors and opened the view port. The Professor hissed at me to leave it alone but I had to see inside. To my disappointment the cell beyond was empty aside from a low, wooden bed and a small toilet and sink in one corner. There was no padding on the walls; perhaps this was a more progressive institution than those back home. Then I noticed the chains hanging on the walls. The Professor was pulling on my arm.

'Come on, Edward, there isn't time to dally.'

I moved away from the cell and followed him. 'Are we going to find Mai Ling?'

'Yes.'

'Why are you so interested in rescuing her? Not that I'm ungrateful, but she's not exactly high priority for British Security Services operatives, is she?'

He had already disappeared around a bend in the corridor. 'I'm not exactly a conventional operative.'

I snorted. 'I am rapidly approaching that conclusion, Professor, yes. So, why Mai Ling?'

'She's not supposed to be here.'

'Not supposed to be here? What do you mean?'

'I mean if I'd known she would end up here I would never have...' He tailed off. 'If they experiment on her and cut her open, the ghost warrior will break free and cause havoc. It could change the whole direction of the war.' He turned another corner.

'War? Experiments? Ghosts? Professor, I think perhaps you belong in one of these cells.'

The Professor did not reply. As I caught up with him I found out why. Guns. Soldiers. End of the road.

* * *

I wake as the lights come on. I feel groggy and there is something in my throat I cannot dislodge. It seems to be colder; I start shivering. I feel quite under the weather and I'm having difficulty in raising my head. I manage, though, glancing across at my cellmate. His breathing is shallow and his shirt is stained with blood. The smell is unbearable. I start to panic when I think that I may have caught whatever it is afflicting him.

The men in their protective suits burst in. They ignore me and rush to my cellmate, examining him agitatedly. They unchain him in a rush, grab his legs and arms and carry him from the room while he protests feebly. They seem to be in a terrific hurry, perhaps because they want to examine him just before he gives his last breath. As they leave, I drag myself to my feet and stumble over towards the door that has just slammed shut, as far as my chains will allow. I feel terribly lethargic, but I have to know what has become of my nameless fellow prisoner.

There is an agonising wait. In their haste, the guards have left the view port open, but all I can see is a constricted view of the corridor beyond.

I recoil and clasp my hands over my ears but I cannot shut out the sudden, shocking scream that shatters the stillness. It goes on and on. Tears spring up, blurring my vision, yet still I strain to see what is going on. The cry becomes a sickening rasp that cuts off abruptly, leaving the cell in silence. The hairs on the back of my neck are standing on end and cold blood thunders in my ears. Somewhere deep in this fortress of Hell they are doing terrible, unspeakable things to the man who lay dying in this room. I know, absolutely, that the sound of his agony will haunt me until the end of my days. I don't understand why they are doing what they are doing, but one day they will be forced to answer for their crimes.

'They won't, you know?'

I tried to open my eyes. 'Won't what?'

'Be prosecuted.'

With some effort I managed to focus on the figure looming over me, busily undoing my manacles. 'Professor?'

'Yes. Hold still.'

'How did you get out? How did you find me? Who won't be prosecuted?'

'The men behind Zhong Ma and Unit 731. Instead they'll lead wealthy, comfortable lives in positions of power.'

I stared at him. 'Are we in Hell?'

'Closest place on Earth.'

He was examining me now, taking my temperature with the back of his hand on my forehead and then flicking the light from a small torch across my pupils. His expression was grim.

'No, really, what is going on here? What did they do to my cellmate? I have to know.'

The Professor didn't reply. He moved back to the door and peered out through the view port. 'We need to leave – now.'

'How did you find me?'

'It wasn't hard. The fortress is in its early days. Most of the cells aren't occupied yet.' Distantly he added, 'It won't be long, though...'

He returned and helped me to my feet. Together we emerged from the cell into the pristine corridor and headed off as fast as the Professor could drag me.

Along the way he tried to explain. 'Japan is taking its first steps into biological weapons development. This is their first test facility, sponsored by the emperor and led by a brilliant young military scientist called Ishii Shiro. Hundreds of thousands of people will lose their lives in facilities like this one before the Americans arrive. Many hundreds of thousands more will be killed by the germ-ridden packages the Japanese will drop on Chinese towns and villages all over the region.' We came to a bend in the corridor and the Professor was careful to look ahead before guiding me around. 'It's an abomination.'

'My cellmate, Professor. What was wrong with him?'

'Nothing before he came here. They deliberately infected him with the bubonic plague.'

'Why?'

'To study its effects on the human body and to breed stronger and more easily weaponised germs, or so they believe.'

The Professor rested me against a wall for a moment so I could catch my breath, which rattled in my chest. The idea of the plague in this modern day and age was quite ridiculous to me. Surely man has no fear of plague in these days of enlightened discovery. However, I had never considered its use as a weapon and the concept made me shiver.

My head was swimming. I couldn't take it all in. I felt worse than ever, quite wretched. I have always tried to see the good in men but I could not find an ounce in the perpetrators of these terrible crimes.

'Such contempt for human life...' I wheezed.

The Professor sneered. 'Indeed. But then that's human nature, wouldn't you say, Edward? I saw the way you looked at the people in that café.'

'That's hardly the same thing!'

'Isn't it? These prisoners are treated like pieces of wood, less than human. How long before you see the lower classes as logs too?'

'There is a difference, Professor. This is beyond extreme.' My protests were cut short by a fit of coughing. My lungs hurt and my eyes were burning. I knew I was seriously ill. I didn't want to know the answer but I had to ask the question.

'What have they done to me?'

He paused before answering, the accusatory stare replaced by sadness and sympathy. He glanced about us to see if anyone was coming. When he judged it to be safe, he said, 'Your cellmate had developed severe symptoms and it spread to his lungs where it became pneumonic plague, which is highly contagious and one hundred per cent fatal if not treated.

I'm afraid that's what you've contracted. Their experiment was a success. I'm sorry, Edward.'

My hands were shaking. I could barely stay upright. I had the Black Death! It was inconceivable. These people were merciless killers. Their lack of even basic ethics opened a hole in my very being, through which my life essence very literally ebbed away.

'If I can get you out of here and back to the TARDIS, I may be able to save your life. In the meantime, I need your help. Can you walk?'

I had no idea if I could take more than two steps without collapsing, but I nodded.

'Good. I need you to find Mai Ling for me. She's down that corridor on your left in cell 384. Here's the key to her cell and another for her shackles. She's alive but weak. I need you to take her to this point.' He indicated an 'X' marked on a hurriedly drawn map on the back of an envelope. 'I'll meet you there.'

'Where are you going?'

'I have to get to the storage freezers and destroy all traces of blood they took from me.'

'Will she live, Professor?'

'She'll recover in time, if we get her out. Understand?'

'I understand.'

'Oh, and Edward?' I turned back to him. 'You must only take Mai Ling with you, nobody else.'

'Professor...'

'We have no choice, Edward. If we try to rescue anybody else we'll end up captives again and Mai Ling will die. I escaped once by feigning advanced cholera but they won't let their guard down again. Now go!'

With that he headed off, leaving me alone. With much stumbling and a few falls I moved towards cell 384. It was a struggle not to take a look in the other cells, in a maudlin desire to see what horrors lay beyond. But I knew my strength was failing and I could not let Mai Ling down again. I passed one of the Chinese cleaners, who flattened himself against the wall as I passed, draping the disinfectant-drenched mop head over his mouth and nose.

Fighting to stay lucid, I opened the door to cell 384 and fell to the ground, exhausted.

The cell was empty.

I can't describe the despair I experienced at that moment. Never before have I felt myself shut down to such a frightening degree. My body was finished, my brain was fogged, my life was ebbing away. I didn't know whether I was upright or prostrate. There was blood on my hands. Was it mine? I didn't care. She was dead; I was too late.

There was a terrible scream. A woman, I was sure. Could it be? Was it possible? I knew in one blood-freezing moment what they were about to do to her. I could not let those monsters tear her apart.

Galvanised, I mustered every ounce of energy left in my diseased frame and hauled myself to my feet. Mai Ling screamed again and I stumbled out into the corridor. I lurched towards the sound of her cries at a speed that was surely impossible for one in my condition. I grabbed a mop from the astonished cleaner, who shrank away from me in terror. It was close to useless as a weapon but brandishing the mop made me feel stronger.

I burst into the operating theatre and there she was. Mai Ling. She was in a dreadful state. Her once flowing black hair was now matted with blood. Her skin was so covered in sores I could barely recognise her. She was dressed in a simple smock that barely covered her modesty. Two men clothed all in white were the only other occupants of the room. One held Mai Ling down, the other held a razor-sharp scalpel. There was no sign of anaesthetic anywhere.

They froze, the scalpel mere inches away from Mai Ling's chest. I yelled like an idiot and swung the mop. The wooden end caught one of the men in the face and he went down instantly, clutching at his nose. The other one wielded the scalpel as a weapon.

The rest was a blur. I didn't even feel the blade embed itself in my shoulder. It gave me the opportunity to grab his arm and rip off his mask. I don't think I hit him but he recoiled from me like I'd landed a killer right hook in his face. He ran from the room, yelling in panic.

Tears in my eyes, I lifted Mai Ling's frail body from the table. Her head flopped lifelessly onto my shoulder. I felt her pulse, rapid and erratic but still there. Gritting my teeth, I hoisted her onto my shoulder. Her frame didn't weigh much but I was having trouble lifting my own weight. With the map in my free hand, I set out to find the Professor's rendezvous point.

When I met him again his face was grim. I passed my burden over to him and felt relieved at no longer having to bear the extra load. It was time to leave this God-forsaken place but there was the small matter of the armed guards. The Professor told me to lie in wait for a few minutes.

As we crouched in the shadows, waiting for the next patrol, something that had been eating at me demanded to be answered.

'Professor, how is it that you know so much of the future? What you say can only be speculation, but you sound so sure.'

'One day you'll understand, Edward. For now, worry about getting well. No more questions; concentrate on staying awake.'

'The questions help me stay awake, Professor. My hatred for these criminals is what's keeping me going.'

'Whatever you need to get through this, my friend. Ask your questions.'

'Back in my cell, you said that the men responsible for this will get away with it. What did you mean?'

The Professor let out a quiet sigh. 'You promise to tell nobody of what you have seen here, or of anything I have told you. Yes?'

'Yes, Professor, of course. Nobody would believe me anyway.'

'In 1945, at the end of the war, Japan will surrender to the Americans. Before they arrive, all the biological warfare facilities will be destroyed. The US finds out about them, though, and will be concerned that the data collected over the years will fall into Russian hands. They also want to learn from experiments that could never be carried out on US soil. So, in return for all the data, the US will grant the perpetrators immunity from prosecution. Some will go on to run large organisations in Japan; others will gain prime positions in academia. In short, they get away scot-free. The US will use the data both to further their own medical knowledge and eventually to launch biological attacks against North Korea.'

I had seen many outrageous and terrifying things that day, but this I just could not swallow. 'That's ridiculous. Japan inflicting such suffering on other races I can understand, but the United States! America could never stoop so low.'

The Professor fixed me with a stare that bored directly into my heart.

'Evil doesn't limit itself to cultures you don't understand, Edward.'

There was no answer to that.

The next patrol passed us by without being alerted to our presence. The Professor activated the drawbridge controls and the three of us at last found ourselves outside the dreaded fortress. We were still inside the camp grounds however, and it was a fair way to the barbed-wire perimeter. I was so weak I could barely stand, let alone walk any further.

When the Japanese soldiers yelled at us to stand still it was almost a relief. The Professor was turning about, Mai Ling draped across his shoulders. He was looking for a way out but there wasn't one. I was heaving for breath. As the four guards closed in, rifles trained on us, I burst into a fit of coughing. Blood exploded from my mouth, right onto one of the guards. He panicked, dropping his rifle. The rest of the guards took a step backwards, uncertain. The Professor saw his chance.

He coughed dramatically, lunging forward. The soldiers backed away but didn't shoot. Hazily, I wondered why. Perhaps the Professor was valuable to them and they'd been ordered to keep him alive. He had been sure to destroy his blood samples after all. I wondered what they might reveal but my mind was too cloudy to concentrate.

I dropped to my knees, retching into the dust, forming a pool of bile and blood. I felt like there was an ocean in my lungs and my throat burned like desert sand. I knew that I was not going to get up again.

I watched the soldiers flee, desperate to scrub themselves clean of infection. Somehow, the Professor hoisted me onto his other shoulder and we were off. The last thing I saw before blacking out was Mai Ling's face. I prayed we were not too late to save her.

I awake in bed in the same guest-house I stayed in before leaving for China. Once again, I have no idea how much time has passed. I am distressed by how weak I feel as I crawl out of bed. Nevertheless I feel leagues better than I did before I lost consciousness.

Two letters sit on the wooden writing desk in the corner. The first is from the Professor. It says:

> Dear Edward, I hope you are feeling better. You should be fine now, but just in case you're still contagious it's best if you stay in this room for the next three days. Mrs Emerald will leave your meals outside the door and you have plenty of books to read. You'll need to study the contents if you want to continue in your new career. Remember, tell them nothing of the Fortress or Unit 731. They are not yet ready to know. Mai Ling is healthy and well. I told her of how you rescued her and took her home to her husband. I would not advise trying to find her again.
>
> Take care, the Professor.

I sit on the bed and cry, the emotions of my experience and the knowledge that I have lost Mai Ling overwhelm me. After a while, my sobbing stops and I dry my eyes. The other letter bears an official seal – the United Kingdom's Security Services. I open it with shaking fingers.

> Dear Mr Grainger, the Doctor has been most complimentary regarding your conduct in China and has recommended that you join us in an unofficial capacity as an operative of His Majesty's Government. Once you have fully recovered, please bring this letter to the address below where you will receive your next assignment. When war is eventually declared, we will talk about instating you in an official capacity. Your role in our department is considered highly classified and you will be required to sign the Official Secrets Act forbidding you to discuss your position or any missions you should undertake on our behalf with non-operatives. In the meantime, congratulations and welcome aboard.
>
> Sincerely, Major-General Vernon Kell.

This is a great deal to take in. Quite aside from the major-general referring to the Professor as 'the Doctor', there is much to digest. I am forced to sit and ponder my future. Spying is clearly not as glamorous as the stories make out. Memories of the Zhong Ma Fortress will always haunt me but I know in the end this is what I should be doing.

I pick up a copy of Carl von Clausewitz's *On War* and begin to read.

The Church of Football

Benjamin Adams

An Adventure of the Fifth Doctor,
with Peri Brown

'Doctor, you look sad.'

He'd been standing at the console, staring at its centre column as it rose up and down rhythmically; he hadn't even acknowledged me as I entered the room.

This was one of the things that made me trust the Doctor. These last several years I'd grown used to men noticing me far more than I'd like. The Doctor didn't look at me... like that. These last two weeks, since I'd joined the Doctor in the TARDIS, had been enormously comforting in that regard. I may have been torn away from my family – no great loss there – but I felt safe with this man.

The Doctor continued gazing at the time rotor – he'd told me that's what it was called – for another moment, before turning to me with a quick smile that didn't quite hide the sadness in his eyes. 'Ah, Peri. I trust you had a good night's sleep?'

'Yes. Yes, I did – and you're changing the subject.'

His smile drooped slightly. 'Am I?'

'I haven't known you that long but I know when someone's sad.' I locked eyes with him, daring him to challenge my statement.

'That's what I like about you, Peri,' he said. 'You have a naturally inquisitive mind.'

'I'm not getting anywhere with you, am I?'

'Well, there's always somewhere to get to, isn't there?' He moved around the console, flicking a switch here, turning a dial there, his sandy-blond bangs rippling across his forehead.

'Doctor, what are you doing?'

'It's time we went somewhere interesting, don't you think?' He gestured around the console room. 'This last week has been relaxing... even healing, I suspect, after everything that happened to us on Dusoldat.'

'Rainforests, you said. Nobody shooting at us, you said.'

'I said "Hopefully not",' he replied, slightly wounded. I immediately felt guilty for jibing him.

'It's good, Doctor. It's peaceful.'

His voice had gained that breathy quality I found so endearing. 'But I can't expect you to be satisfied simply exploring the TARDIS.'

'I could spend weeks exploring the TARDIS –'

'So that's settled!' He clapped his hands together and beamed at me. 'Where do you want to go, Peri Brown?'

What a pain he could be! The Doctor had completely deflected my concern about his mood, and now it was as if the moment had never happened. Perhaps he'd explain later.

But now – where did I want to go? According to the Doctor, all of time and space was just a hop, skip and jump away for the TARDIS. But the only evidence of that I'd seen so far were a few weird places, like the sulphuric surface and caves of the planet Sarn, and the people there – well, they just as easily could have come from Cairo as from Turlough's home planet of Trion. On the scale of exotic it barely rated a five out of ten. Might as well be Earth circa 1985. And then there were N'Tia and Dusoldat. What kind of basis for comparison for time travel did I really have, besides our shopping binge in Regent Street?

'The past,' I said impulsively, and having said it, knew exactly where I wanted to go.

'Ah, the past,' murmured the Doctor. 'What did you have in mind, Peri?'

It seemed silly to say. It was one of the last truly great memories of my childhood, before my mother remarried. We'd flown to England from Baltimore, ostensibly to broaden my education by seeing such sights as the Royal Botanic Gardens at Kew and the stained glass windows at Bath Abbey. Really, it was nothing more than a chance for my mother to fulfil her long-held dream of visiting Liverpool, home of the Beatles. I'd found Liverpool a bit too grey for my liking and much preferred London, where I shopped at all the greatest boutiques and record stores, and saw my favourite band, The Who, at Wembley Stadium. It was the best concert I'd ever seen – AC/DC opened the gig, and at that time nobody even knew who they were yet in the USA! I'd always wanted to relive that moment.

'Okay, then,' I said. 'Wembley Stadium, London, 18 August 1979.'

'That's rather exact,' the Doctor said, a curious expression on his face. 'May I ask why?'

'It's the first rock concert I ever attended.'

For a moment I couldn't believe I was facing my Doctor. His eyes blazed with anger. 'You – must – *never* – ask me to do such a thing,' he said intensely.

I scowled back at him, refusing to be intimidated. 'You *asked* me where I wanted to go!'

'Ah. Yes, well. Don't ask me to take you anywhere you've been, at the same time you've already been there.'

'But why not?'

He leaned forward on the console, supporting himself with both palms and looked away from me. A weary sigh escaped his lips.

'It's bad, isn't it?' I said, suddenly feeling very small. I wished I hadn't pressed the issue.

The Doctor glanced sideways at me and nodded. 'If you can call the potential end of all things *bad*, then yes. It's bad.'

'Because I'm already there, right?'

'Yes. If there were to be a meeting between your two selves, the release of energy would be absolutely immense. That's one of two things you must never do as a time traveller. The other is changing history.'

I offered him a weak grin. 'Okay, then. Wembley in 1979 is right out.'

He smiled again, and it was like a light had been turned back on in the console room. 'There are other options, you know. Abba played there in 1979.'

'Yuck!' I said, the tone of my voice dripping disgust for the very idea.

'"Yuck"?' he said quizzically. '"Yuck". I take it that's a no, then. Well, I'll tell you what. We'll still try Wembley. Just – a bit earlier. What do you say?'

I cocked my head to one side and studied him. 'I say... it seems you have an ulterior motive, Doctor. This is like when you dragged me to that stultifyingly boring cricket match.'

He grinned disarmingly. 'I promise, Peri. No cricket.'

I sighed. 'What is it, then?'

'Football!'

Apparently we'd arrived at Wembley on 25 April 1936 – although at this point it was still called the Empire Stadium – just in time for some kind of big hoo-rah called the Football Association Cup; the British version of the Super Bowl, I figured.

I was a Pasadena, California girl by way of Baltimore, and didn't know the first thing about soccer or football or whatever it was called. The most I knew about the game was from watching those odd Spanish-language sports broadcasts on Channel 52, with my friends Candy and Kathy in high school. I knew the ball had to go into the net, and then the announcer would yell, 'GOOAALLLLLLLLLL!' It seemed to be the most hilarious thing we'd ever seen, and we'd yell, 'GOOAALLLLLLLLLL!' at each other and fall about laughing and then start hitting each other with pillows. Well, we were kids, okay?

This was entirely different.

We were mostly surrounded by smelly men wearing fabrics like wool which were clearly too much for a warm, overcast, humid spring day like this. The atmosphere was already getting a bit ripe for my tastes. Well, if I could handle the sulphur reek of Sarn, I could handle this.

Fortunately the Doctor had a flowered spring dress and hat of about the right vintage in his voluminous wardrobes, so I didn't look out of place... but I found myself wishing I had Candy's ability to wear the most outrageous outfits – bright pink new wave and punky stuff usually – without the slightest qualms. I was more of a loose-pastel-blouse-and-shorts girl. This dress just wasn't me at all, and I was chafing inside it. I shimmied slightly to set myself right inside the dress, which provoked a low whistle from the scruffy man standing behind me. When I turned around to glare at him, he doffed his fabric cap and grinned. 'Oi, love. Are we comfortable?'

Gah! Was it like this everywhere in the universe? I turned back to the

Doctor, who already seemed less distracted and more engaged with his surroundings. He waved a sheet of newsprint at me. 'Look, Peri – community singing!'

I very much hoped that didn't mean what I thought it did. 'We have to... sing?' I asked hesitantly.

'If the stadium were full, you could join 125,000 voices united on Pack up Your Troubles,' he said. 'Can you imagine? The hymns of the Church of Football, as Pele will one day call this place. However –' and here he scanned the people milling around with other late ticket buyers who hadn't gotten seats '– I'd say there's only about 93,000 here today. Give or take a few hundred.' He smiled brightly.

'Show off,' I said, smiling. 'You couldn't possibly estimate a crowd that large.'

He seemed unfazed. 'Certainly I can, Peri. I must say, I'm rather surprised at the size of the crowd. I suppose it's because it's Sheffield United versus Arsenal. Not the most exciting match in the world. The Blades aren't terribly favoured.'

'The Blades?'

'Sheffield United. They're known as the Blades,' he explained patiently. 'Do you already know how this match turns out?'

The Doctor looked for all the world like a naughty schoolboy who had just been discovered doing something particularly wrong. 'Well...'

I gasped. 'You jerk! I can't even go to a game with you without you knowing what's going to happen!'

'I'm... familiar... with Arsenal's statistics,' he said, studiously not looking at me.

Annoyed, I sniffily told him I needed to refresh myself. As I left his side, a cheer rose up among the crowd, which had seemed a bit subdued. Arsenal were on the move.

The slightly humid conditions held the myriad scents close to the bleachers. At American stadium events, the odour was popcorn, hot dogs and spilled beer. Here, I smelled baked goods, much more body odour than I would have liked, and – well, spilled beer was evidently a constant.

When I was a little girl and I would visit my grandparents, I would spend hours poring over a set of Time-Life books they had, titled This Fabulous Century, which detailed every decade from 1900 through 1970. Quite why it stopped at 1970 I never understood when I was young. So many of the fashions and faces I saw now looked like they were straight out of the 1930s volume of that set of books, and it suddenly struck me so hard that I stopped on the stairs and gasped.

I was in the past.

I was in 1936.

For a moment, my vision seemed to swim with tears. Alien worlds? No big deal. The Master trying to kill me? Cakewalk.

Being in Earth's past, thirty years before I would even be born? I couldn't cope. My head was spinning. Somehow I made it to the top of the steps and the upper level. I sat down on the landing and felt my chest move in and out in deep, wracking breaths.

Cognitive dissonance is what this was called; a discrepancy between what I was experiencing now and what my brain was already trained to accept. That was what was happening to me. I'd heard the term during my first semester at college, and it had stuck with me, although I was much more interested in botany than psychology. As long as I knew what was happening to me, I knew I'd be fine.

I hauled myself to my feet and began looking for a restroom. The first few people I asked looked at me blankly as if they had no idea what I was talking about. Frustrated, uncomfortable, and close to tears, I finally remembered an old term from *This Fabulous Century*, and instead asked for the 'W.C.' This time I was pointed in the right direction. Just accomplishing that task felt like I'd finished one of the labours of Hercules, and I began to feel better.

Yes, I told myself. Peri Brown, you can travel to another time and find a toilet.

Before I could reach the bathroom, however, I saw a portly man, carrying a black leather portfolio under his arm, moving towards me with his attention turned back over his shoulder, as if he were looking for somebody. He wore slightly dirty overalls and actually had a cloth cap on his head.

I suddenly realised that he didn't really know I was in his path –

WHAM! He collided with me full on and, as we fell in a tangle, the portfolio dropped down beside us. A few sepia-toned photographs fell out. A few heads in the crowd turned at the commotion, but turned back to the game almost immediately.

Before I could do anything more than peep a feeble protest, the man said indignantly, 'You weren't supposed to be there!' His tie wasn't done up correctly, meaning one collar was higher than the other, comically waving near his jowls as he spoke.

'As if you *know* where someone is supposed to be!' I retorted, feeling a full head of steam about to boil. After my panic attack, I didn't need this. 'What's wrong with using your eyes?'

I began pulling myself up, and out of years of politeness drilled into me by my mother, also picked up his portfolio and the photographs. They were of a handsome couple; friends, clearly, chatting together on the deck of a ship. They seemed familiar somehow, but I was too shocked by the fall to make any connection. What on Earth was a handyman doing with *these*?

'Oh, I do wish you hadn't seen them,' the portly man said, and suddenly his voice seemed to drip with menace. 'There's the problem with using your eyes. Sometimes you see something you really shouldn't.'

I had time for exactly one thought: you have got to be kidding me – not now, please – not that. And then his large, beefy hand had covered my mouth, and I felt a sharp blow at the back of my head, and everything went black.

In my dream I stood beside Hercules in the Augean stables. He looked like Steve Reeves from the old movies I used to watch on Channel 52. We looked at the stalls together, and I felt ill at the idea of all the animal filth.

'Better grab a shovel,' Hercules said to me. 'It's my day off.'

Before I could tell Hercules what he could do with his shovel, I suddenly left the Augean stables far below me. They diminished to the size of a pinprick, and then I was surfacing towards a dingy yellow light. My eyes blinked open and I found myself on the hexagonally tiled floor of a bathroom, my wrists handcuffed together and chained to the plumbing underneath a porcelain sink. At least I was still in the stadium; I could hear the crowd outside as it ebbed and flowed.

Obviously those weren't just any old photographs. What had I gotten myself into this time?

My captor leaned against a wall, his arms crossed and a concerned, almost paternal crease on his brow. He'd straightened his tie and collar and once again was the very image of a workman. 'Well, now,' he said. 'Whatever shall I do with you?'

Like Humphrey Bogart as Captain Queeg, he was rolling two marbles around in his hand as he spoke to me.

'You... you creep! You kidnapped me!'

He raised an eyebrow. 'Kidnapped? What a disgraceful and sensational term. You're hardly the Lindbergh baby, young lady. You're just... unavoidably detained.'

'You'd better let me go!' I strained against my cuffs, but it was no use. I was trapped.

'Now, why would I want to do that? You've seen something you really shouldn't have seen, and I can't afford to take any chances.'

If there was one thing I'd learned when I butted heads with the Master, it was keep the bad guys talking. The more they talked, the longer it was before they could do anything really bad to you.

'Any second now,' I blustered, 'that bathroom door is gonna open, and it's all over for you anyway.'

'Dear me,' the man said with mock worry. 'Now, isn't that the sort of thing I would expect? Oh, yes. That would explain the "out of order" sign on the door, and I have it locked from the inside.'

At that moment, a sharp, staccato knock came at the restroom door. TCHOK-TCH-TCHOCK-TCHOCK.

My captor glanced towards the sound. 'Again...' he breathed.

The knock came again, in a pattern identical to the first.

He glanced towards me, rolling the marbles in his hand, his words giving the lie to the benevolent expression on his moony face. 'Well, child,

I'm afraid it's out of my hands now. Your eventual dispensation will be up to this gentleman.'

With that, he walked over to the door and unlatched it. 'Doctor,' I whispered, as a shadowy figure stepped into the room and the man shut the door behind him. 'Where are you? Find me! Please find me!'

'Well, Mr Scanlon,' the stranger said in a softly sinister upper-class British accent – like what I used to hear spoken on *Upstairs, Downstairs* when I watched it on Public Service Broadcasting as a kid. 'Have we begun collecting strays?'

He wore a tailored, brown wool suit. His thin, angular features gave him a patrician look, although judging by his fair, smooth skin, he couldn't have been much more than thirty years old. His thick brown hair was immaculate, every strand lay down perfectly. If he wasn't a bad guy, I could almost find him handsome. I had to close my eyes tightly for a moment to rid myself of the thought.

'She saw the photographs,' Scanlon said. He gave me a small smile and steepled his fingertips, carefully holding his shiny blue marbles between his thumb and forefinger. At that moment, I really, really, *really* hated him.

The handsome stranger regarded me carefully. 'Do you have any idea what you saw?'

'None whatsoever. And that's the truth. If this idiot hadn't snatched me, I'd have no idea whatsoever of your... your plans!'

'Our plans?' He swung to face the workman. 'What in blazes have you been telling her, you buffoon?'

'She's bluffing,' Scanlon replied, but he pulled a white handkerchief from his pocket and wiped his forehead. 'I haven't told her anything.'

'But yet you dragged her in here.'

'It couldn't be avoided.'

The stranger pinched the bridge of his nose and bowed his head in exasperation.

'Look,' I pleaded. 'If you let me go, I promise I won't say anything. I have no idea what you're doing, I swear. Please – just let me go!'

'Perhaps there is another way,' the stranger said. 'After all, we're not after bloodshed today, are we?'

'Oh, my, I would certainly hope not,' replied Scanlon.

'She comes with us, then. Perhaps my employers will choose to be... gracious.'

'She's coming with us?' Scanlon blinked. 'Where are we going? I thought we would conclude our business here. I'd very much like to be done with this matter –'

The dapper stranger shook his head. 'My employers would like to inspect the merchandise directly. I rather hope you don't have a problem with that.'

'No. No, not at all,' Scanlon said, a brief shadow crossing his face.

Nodding in my direction, the dapper man said, 'She comes with us, then. See to it.'

The portly man roughly disengaged my chains and steered me towards the door, while the stranger moved in behind me. 'You really don't want to make a sound,' he said, the tone of his voice surprisingly gentle, as though he really was offering me friendly advice. 'Otherwise there may be blood shed today after all, and that would annoy me very much indeed.'

I blushed furiously. 'I – I – I need to use the facilities here. I can't go another step before I do. Please.'

To my surprise, the stranger blushed as well. 'Oh. Oh, my goodness.'

A strange procession left the W.C.

With Scanlon in front, me in the middle, and the dapper stranger bringing up the rear, we almost appeared to be the cast of an Ealing Studios screwball comedy. But the crowd had their attention consumed by the massive sing-along the Doctor had mentioned earlier.

Such an inviting, welcoming sound, so many voices joined happily in singing the songs of a simpler, more innocent era...

Ta-ra-ra boom-de-ay, ta-ra-ra boom-de-ay...

'Lovely song, don't you think?' said a familiar voice in front of us. 'So joyful and uplifting.' With a grunt of surprise, Scanlon stopped dead and I almost walked into his back.

The Doctor peered over Scanlon's shoulder and winked at me. I grinned back. Surely now everything would be fine.

'Sir, could you please move? We have urgent business elsewhere and really can't be delayed,' the dapper stranger said from behind me. The Doctor merely doffed his hat.

'Hello, I'm the Doctor,' he said, beaming a smile at Scanlon. 'I believe you have my friend, Miss Brown, with you. Would you be so kind as to return her to me?'

Scanlon boomed jovially, 'I'm afraid, sir, that the young woman is with us.'

'No I'm not!' I blurted.

The dapper man had moved forward, his gun now held to my side. His eyes widened. He stared at the Doctor as though in shock, then quickly controlled himself. 'If you accompany us... Doctor, I believe we will be able to take care of all this quite... cleanly.'

The Doctor gave the dapper man a deep, probing look. 'Do I have your word as a gentleman on that?'

'You can be assured of that, sir.'

The Doctor nodded, apparently satisfied. 'Yes, I believe I can – despite the pistol you have under your jacket and aimed at my ward.'

'I'm sorry about that,' said the dapper man. 'But circumstances do force one's hand.'

'Ah. Yes. They do indeed,' the Doctor agreed mildly.

'I really must protest,' said Scanlon. 'Certainly we should take care of them before we go any further? Your employers –'

The dapper man's eyes flared. 'You will not question me. My employers are very keen to buy what you're offering, and while you are doing business with me, I will make the decisions. There are other ways to handle these two.'

'Oh, very well,' Scanlon blustered. 'I'm just trying to make things easier for you.' He gestured toward the Doctor. 'This one is trouble – I know it.'

'That is my worry, not yours,' the dapper man said flatly.

The singing ceased. Around us, the punters were stirring themselves.

'I believe the second half is about to begin,' said the Doctor. 'If it's not too much trouble, perhaps we could continue to wherever you were taking Miss Brown?'

'We're almost there,' said the dapper man. 'Just up these steps – a private office.'

He fell back behind me with the gun, and the Doctor moved to my side.

'We really must stop meeting like this,' he whispered to me.

I didn't know whether to laugh or cry. 'Do you possibly think you could show up before the nick of time?'

He blinked. 'You know, I said something very much like that to –'

'Here we are,' the dapper man interrupted.

We stood before a door marked 'GROUNDS – H. MERRIWEATHER.'

Scanlon appeared to baulk. He rolled the marbles in his hand more rapidly, as though nervous. Maybe the marbles were some kind of 1930s stress release fad. 'I really don't see why we couldn't have taken care of our business back there,' he said stiffly.

'Please don't be tiresome,' said the dapper man. 'Open the door, please.'

Scanlon sighed deeply, then opened the door and led us into the darkened interior. The dapper man had the door latched behind us before our eyes could adjust to the light.

Before we could see that there were four men inside, armed with pistols, aimed directly at us.

'Oh, bother,' said Scanlon.

The Doctor gripped my shoulders and pulled me out from between the dapper man and Scanlon. None of the guns followed us; they remained trained on the man in the overalls.

'We'll just sit this one out, if you don't mind,' the Doctor said.

'This is all very unnecessary,' Scanlon complained.

The dapper man stepped forward and removed the black leather portfolio from under Scanlon's arm. 'Oh, I should think it's very necessary indeed.'

I couldn't bear it any longer. The Doctor's grip on my shoulder tightened as I said, 'Could someone please tell me what's going on?'

The dapper man gave me a quick, apologetic grin. 'This man isn't who he appears to be, miss.'

'I can see that! But who are *you*?'

Beside me, the Doctor said, 'This is Edward Grainger, Peri. An old friend.'

'Yes...' said Grainger. He stared intently, almost probingly, at the Doctor. 'And believe me, I would dearly love to chat with you and the young lady, but at this moment I have rather more pressing business.' He opened the portfolio and withdrew the photographs that had landed me in this mess. He flipped through them, and though he tried to hide his emotions, I saw sadness and anger in his eyes.

'John Scanlon,' Grainger said through a clenched jaw, 'I arrest you for treason, blackmail and attempting to destabilise the monarchy.'

'Oh, you're no fun,' Scanlon announced. 'But this game isn't over.' From his right hand, limply hanging at his side, he let one of his marbles drop toward the parquet floor. Out of the corner of my eye, I saw the Doctor throw his arm up to his face.

The marble touched the ground –

A bright blue, actinic flash filled the room and blinded us –

The room erupted with yells from everyone, except the Doctor and Scanlon.

'Damn!' cursed Grainger. 'I can't see!'

None of us could, at least not for thirty seconds or so; whatever was in Scanlon's marble had blinded us long enough for him to have found the door and escape.

As my vision cleared, the Doctor whispered to me, 'That bomb didn't belong here.'

'You're telling me!' I blinked tears out of my eyes. The Doctor, of course, didn't seem to be affected by the bomb at all.

'No, Peri. That wasn't Earth technology. Not of this century, anyway. Something is very wrong.'

'Sergeant, are your men all right?' Grainger enquired of the officer who seemed to be in charge.

After a quick inventory, the sergeant nodded. 'Sight's still a bit spotty, sir.'

'I need you to get after Scanlon right away. He can't have reached the exits yet.'

The Doctor stepped forward at that point. 'Ah. Edward. If I may –'

'Doctor, I really don't have the time. We have to stop Scanlon before he leaves the stadium.'

'Edward! I have given you reason to trust me, haven't I?'

Grainger rubbed his eyes, still trying to clear them of the after effect of Scanlon's flash bomb. 'Yes. Yes, you have. I can scarcely believe it – that was eight years ago, on the other side of the world, and yet here you are, still wearing that ridiculous cricket gear –'

I suppressed a hysterical giggle.

The Doctor glanced down at his clothes. 'What's wrong with my – ah, never mind. Believe me, Edward, we will find Scanlon. I suggest you send your men to watch the exits and call reinforcements; but trust me, he will not be leaving the stadium. I need you to explain to me exactly what was in those photographs – and I need you to do so immediately. There may be far more at stake than you realise.'

'It is only because of our previous acquaintance that I show these to you, Doctor,' said the handsome agent. 'Miss Brown –'

'Peri,' I offered, and instantly felt like a complete idiot.

Thankfully, Edward was gracious about the interruption. 'Yes. Peri has already seen these, which is how you two have wound up involved in this unfortunate affair. I must tell both of you that this is a state secret and any breath of this to anyone else – not just Fleet Street, but *anyone* – will result in the most extreme sanction. I do not enjoy saying this to you, but you have been my ally, Doctor, and you need to understand this. It's a dashed bad business.'

The Doctor nodded solemnly. 'You have my word, Edward.'

'And you, Peri?'

'I'm not even a British citizen,' I said. 'But I promise.'

'It's not for my sake that you're making this promise,' Edward said sternly.

'Oh,' I said, suddenly feeling very small.

'Ah, I can guarantee Peri's compliance,' the Doctor said. 'Please continue, Edward.'

'Very well.' He produced the photographs and handed them to the Doctor without a further word.

The Doctor's eyes widened slightly. 'Ah. Yes. Fascinating. If I'm not mistaken, these are photographs of King Edward VIII and his American paramour, Wallis Simpson.'

I remembered my history: the horrible scandal surrounding the King's relationship with an American, Wallis Simpson, leading to his eventual abdication from the throne. I tried to recall exactly what I'd read in my high school textbook and *This Fabulous Century*.

Edward nodded curtly. 'I suppose I shouldn't be surprised that you'd know this, Doctor.'

'This is something that almost no one should know as of yet,' the Doctor said, plainly troubled.

'Nobody can ever know!' said Edward. 'It would destabilise Britain – cause the fall of the royal family. We are all that is left in the world of –'

'The world is changing, Edward,' said the Doctor. 'You cannot stop it. But I'll tell you this: you underestimate the strength and resilience of the House of Windsor.'

'The world cannot know of this.'

'Nor should they. Yet. Tell me, this Scanlon – how did you come into contact with him?'

'One of my department's tasks is maintaining His Majesty's secrets,' Edward said. 'It has been a deeply unpleasant business, I will tell you that much –' He broke off.

The Doctor reached out to Edward and gripped his shoulder quickly.

Edward blinked at the contact, but it seemed to steady him, and he continued. 'This Scanlon has been hovering at the fringes of the court for the last two years, insinuating himself into the King's affairs. He was pretending to be a peer, then. But it's *my* job not to trust the men who surround the King, Doctor. When I attempted to trace his background –'

'You found absolutely nothing,' the Doctor murmured.

Edward nodded sharply. 'And after that he disappeared. From what we could discover it was as if he had simply vanished from the face of the Earth. It recently came to our attention through a friend of His Majesty's in Germany that Scanlon was back in England, in possession of these photographs and looking to sell them to the press. We arranged for Scanlon to believe that I was acting in the employ of a German faction seeking to destabilise England.'

'Well, that certainly explains all the guns,' I said acidly.

'Peri, stop,' snapped the Doctor. One look at the expression on his face and I knew he was deadly serious. I felt my jaw clamp shut.

'Edward,' he continued, 'you must believe me. The world will some day know about the King and Wallis Simpson. But not today.'

Edward Grainger looked troubled. His eyes were downcast for a moment; then he looked back up and locked his gaze with the Doctor's.

'Not today,' he said. 'Today is all I can think about. But it seems I have no choice but to take you at your word, Doctor.'

'Good!' The Doctor clapped his hands together and rubbed them vigorously. 'Let's go find your errant Scanlon, shall we?'

As we left the grounds office, I tugged at the Doctor's sleeve. 'I don't understand.'

'Well, Peri,' whispered the Doctor, 'the news about the King's relationship didn't become public knowledge until August 1936, and he abdicated in December.'

'But this is April!'

'Yes. That's our problem. You see, someone is trying to rewrite history.'

'Where was he holding you, Peri?'

We stood on a walkway in the stadium, surrounded by roaring fans. I began to point down the walkway, but Edward Grainger beat me to it.

'I was there too, Doctor, and I can probably lead you there faster than Peri.' He gave me a lopsided smile. 'No offence, my dear.'

'Oh, none taken!' I grinned back like a total dope. I scolded myself: knock it off, Peri!

Edward led us towards the W.C. quickly; it was obvious he was extremely well-versed with this area of Wembley. We were moving far more quickly than we would have if I'd made the attempt.

Soon we were at the bathroom door. There was a large sign with red letters: 'Closed for refurbishment and repair'. The Doctor inspected it with a critical eye, then simply reached out and pushed the door open.

It swung inward easily.

There was no trace of Scanlon inside. We walked inside, our heels clicking on the tile floor.

'This is a complete waste of time, Doctor,' Edward announced in his silky tones. 'I quite honestly cannot fathom what you hope to find. The man must be long gone.'

The Doctor walked towards the stalls and peered underneath to see if anyone was hiding inside. He then began pushing the red stall doors open as he moved from left to right. Skinny, tiny toilets with water tanks set high on the walls greeted us in each stall. At least they were clean! There was only so much a girl could take.

The final door on the right wouldn't open.

'Ah,' he said.

'What?' asked Edward. 'What have you found? What possible clue?'

Rather rudely, I thought, the Doctor ignored him completely. He looked underneath the door again, then touched its front with his fingertips. 'Peri, could you please come here?'

'Well, sure!' I moved to his side. He gently took my hand and placed it against the stall door.

It vibrated beneath my fingertips, an almost electric sensation shooting up along my arm.

My eyes felt like they'd pop right out of my head. 'Doctor, I know what that is. It's a TARDIS!'

'Or something very much like it.' He pushed again at the door, which didn't budge. 'It's at times like this I wish I still had my sonic screwdriver,' he said under his breath.

The humming from the stall ceased for a moment, and we heard a very small, very distinct click.

And the door swung open at his gentle shove.

It was a trap, of course. We all agreed on that. But still we walked inside Scanlon's lair.

I'd been expecting a TARDIS, but this was simpler; much more utilitarian. With white walls covered with waist-high control consoles and shimmering viewscreens, it appeared almost military; like a warship. 'Doctor, what is this?' I asked.

'It's something extremely dangerous,' he said softly. 'And it's in the hands of a fool.'

'Where... where are we?' asked Edward. 'Another room? I know every inch of this stadium. I would know about such a place.' He gawped at the white walls with their consoles and gently glowing screens –

And finally at the myriad of art treasures scattered here and there.

It was an incredible amount of loot: I saw urns of gold and Ming vases; a Rembrandt, a Picasso and what appeared to be the *Mona Lisa*.

'That's a fake,' the Doctor said, barely glancing at it. There were Greek statues and an Egyptian sarcophagus leaning crazily against one wall.

Edward wandered around the objets d'art, a smile slowly spreading across his face. 'Doctor, you've led me to the greatest collection of stolen artwork of which I've ever heard. Patrick Fitzpatrick at Scotland Yard will positively lose his mind over this.'

'No, Edward. We're here for only one reason – and that's to find our mysterious blackmailer.'

'But surely –' Edward gestured expansively '– these items must be returned to their rightful owners!'

'Right now they are exactly where they belong. We are here for another reason.' The Doctor pointed at the portfolio. 'Have you forgotten?'

Single-mindedly, Edward stayed on his present tack. 'I'll charge that blighter Scanlon with these art thefts as well, then.'

During their argument, the interior door of the room had begun swinging open. From behind it emerged Scanlon, his moony face bisected by a tight smile.

'Oh?' he said. 'And who has reported them stolen? This sarcophagus – taken directly from the tomb of Shepseskaf in 2494 BC. This *Mona Lisa*, taken from Leonardo's studio as he slept...'

The Doctor cocked his head and grinned.

Scanlon continued, for the moment oblivious with pride. 'This beautiful statue of a Roman consul, taken directly from Pompeii – eh, what? What's so funny?'

'Oh, nothing,' the Doctor said, his expression changing to complete earnestness. 'I'm not interested in any of that.'

'Speak for yourself!' said Edward.

'I'm much more interested in these photographs, and so should you be, Edward.' The Doctor withdrew the sheaf of photos from the portfolio. 'The couple in question was photographed on board a ship with wooden planking, near the bow; presumably the royal yacht, *Britannia*?'

I was glad to see Edward Grainger coming back into the game, the art treasures strewn around us temporarily forgotten. 'Yes,' he said. 'That's exactly what we believe.'

'But look at these photos. Look at the perspective. From where could these shots have been taken?

Scanlon glared at the Doctor, and reached up to loosen his collar.

Edward studied the photographs with renewed intensity. 'I don't understand. There's absolutely nowhere on board the *Britannia* from where these could have been taken. And the angle is wrong for them to have been taken with one of those newfangled Japanese telescopic lenses from the roof of a building at the dock.'

'Ah.' The Doctor beamed at Scanlon. 'That's because they were taken from the sky. Isn't that right? So high above that the camera couldn't be seen. From Earth orbit.'

'You think you're so very clever, don't you, Doctor,' spat Scanlon. 'Don't forget, I'm the one that allowed you entry to this vessel. I have all of you in my grasp –'

'Oh, please. You're nothing more than a common thief. You stole this vessel, you stole these artefacts, and now you're attempting to change Earth's history.'

Scanlon scowled at this dismissal. 'I did not steal this vessel; I found it and repaired it. This is *my* ship.'

'You found it,' the Doctor said, raising an eyebrow.

'It was abandoned on a war-ravaged desert world on the other side of this spiral arm.'

'You have no right to such technology.'

'And why not? It was there for the taking. Doctor, I come from a time over two thousand years from now. You have no idea what humanity has been through. There is an enemy... a terrible enemy. This is one of their vessels. And now that I have it, I know exactly what actions to take to affect the history of this world. I can improve it; speed up its technological development; make Earth into a prime power in the galaxy and we can defeat our enemies in a first strike!'

'And what of the art treasures?' the Doctor asked mildly.

Scanlon shrugged. 'I've always had an eye for the beautiful and extraordinary,' he said. His eyes flickered toward me for a moment and I suddenly felt unclean. 'I'm saving humanity. Why shouldn't I reward myself? It's all fair game.'

'Apt words coming from a child!' shouted the Doctor suddenly, taking a step toward Scanlon.

For a moment, he stood firm against the Doctor's anger. 'Who are you to speak to me that way?'

'Oh, I am your elder in more ways than you could possibly imagine,' the Doctor said. 'And *you are a child*.'

Scanlon's veneer of control had finally cracked. He stumbled backwards as the Doctor advanced in his righteous fury.

'You gain access to a timeship – a rare gift indeed – and the first thing you do is loot Earth's past. But, no, then you begin meddling in history itself. For *what*? To save Earth's future? You are condemning entire unborn generations to death with your actions, and yet you have stuffed your ship with humanity's most precious artefacts. You are a child. An *infant*.'

Scanlon's mouth opened and closed several times, reminding me of a fish gasping for air. 'Who – who are you?' he finally managed.

Edward chose that moment to interrupt. 'I don't understand half of what you're saying, Doctor. Aerial photography from Earth orbit? Timeships? That's... that's neither here nor there at the moment. It's time we took this man into custody for his plot against the King.'

The Doctor handed the photographs to Edward. 'Here. Take these. Do what you will with them. I don't believe Mr Scanlon will trouble you with them any more.'

'Doctor, I must take this man in. He has a small museum of stolen artefacts in here, and he has attempted to blackmail the crown!'

The Doctor turned to me. 'Peri, will you please wait with Edward outside?'

'Sure,' I said. I reached towards Edward but he shrugged away.

'Doctor, I cannot allow this –'

The Doctor drew himself to his full height and fixed Edward with a piercing look that I hoped I would never see again. 'Edward Grainger! You will wait outside!'

His mouth moving weakly, Edward followed the Doctor's command, although as we neared the exit of the TARDIS, he kept glancing back over his shoulder, making slight sputtering sounds. As we left, I thought I heard the Doctor say the word 'Gallifrey.'

Outside the stall, Edward immediately began looking all around for any sign of trickery. After a couple of minutes had passed, he looked up at me in consternation. 'There's nothing here.'

'Well, no.'

'But where were we?'

I shrugged. 'You wouldn't believe me if I told you.'

The stall door swung open at that point, and the Doctor strolled out. In his hand he held a clear glass marble.

'Where is he?' cried Edward. 'You've let him go!'

The W.C. suddenly filled with the roaring sound of engines. The sound was deafening within the tile-lined room; it echoed off the walls and floor and pierced our ears. Edward, not being used to the sound, fell to his knees, covering his ears and closing his eyes tightly.

The toilet stall glowed with blue energy that seemed to pulse in time with the grinding roar of the engines. After a few moments the sound and light faded away.

The Doctor swung open the door experimentally. Inside was just another toilet.

'Yes, Edward,' he said. 'He's gone. Hopefully for good.'

'What's that you have?' Edward asked, his eyes fixed on the object in the Doctor's hand.

'Oh, this?'

The Doctor tossed it into the air. Edward and I reflexively shut our eyes, but nothing happened.

'It's a marble.' The Doctor grinned.

★ ★ ★

We emerged into bedlam in the stands. For the last twenty minutes, the Blades had rallied against Arsenal. But Arsenal's Ted Drake had scored a crashing drive into the roof of Sheffield's net.

'Oh, what a shame,' said the Doctor, on hearing this from one of the punters. 'I very much would have liked to see that.'

'You knew it was going to happen,' I reminded him.

'Ah, yes. Well.'

But Edward Grainger was hopping mad.

'You – you let the blighter go! How could you?'

'He's gone, Edward. He won't be back to bother you or trouble your King again.'

'But he needed to be charged – punished –'

'No prison you could build would hold him for more than a matter of hours. I've taken a much more effective approach.'

'How do you mean?'

The Doctor removed his straw hat from his jacket pocket and placed it on his head.

'I frightened him,' he said simply. 'I made him aware of the fact that if I knew where he was, certain... other people... also do. It didn't take much convincing after that. He *is* gone, Edward. You won't see him again.'

'This is still irregular,' the dapper spy muttered. 'Who *are* you, Doctor? Who do you work for?'

The Doctor smiled. 'Just call me... a friend of the family.' He took my arm and bowed toward Edward. 'And now, Peri and I really must dash.'

He pulled me into the milling post-game crowd. Faintly, behind me, I heard Edward's repeated cries of 'Wait! Doctor, wait!'

As we exited Wembley Stadium and headed towards our own TARDIS, I glanced at the Doctor curiously. 'You told Scanlon that you'd turn him in to your own people?'

'Very good, Peri. Quite astute.'

'How did you know that would make him leave?'

'Ah. He was attempting to change history to suit himself. The Time Lords don't look very kindly on such things.'

'And what do you do, Doctor?'

'I fix things, Peri. I... fix things.'

I leaned my head against his shoulder. 'Then let's go find something else that's broken.'

Incongruous Details

Simon Guerrier

An Adventure of the Sixth Doctor

Pain flares, wild and unconnected.

There is nothing to writhe against, no way to resist or scream out. The pain swells as more tendrils grope together, because now there's more to feel it with. Pinpricks of colour and feeling, desperate and awful. Paroxysms ever more vivid.

Sensation tickles over rough-hewn brick. A stench fetid and familiar, reaching to trigger memories that have yet to reform. What a body smells like when it's been ripped apart. And now enough skin entwined to know the breeze.

He – yes, he was a he – gazed lidless up at the burnt orange sky. Wisps of cloud and smoke hid the stars away. He felt a pang at their loss, or perhaps that melancholy was just the feel of his innards seeping back to him, drip by drip.

Soon he lay strewn across the rubble of a building he'd hoped would protect him. Others had thought the same, he now remembered. There'd been a kindly looking woman with a dog and all her shopping...

Not any more. They couldn't have survived like he had.

His legs spasmed as the last of the pinstripe suit melded around them. Expecting agony, he eased himself into a sitting position and began to massage his calves. His stiff shirt collar caught at the raw skin round his neck, but otherwise the pain was all gone.

He stood. The breeze whipped at his overcoat and threatened to tear off his hat. The night air tasted of fire. He licked round the inside of his mouth, feeling something still missing, leaving him incomplete.

That was it. He needed a drink.

Lieutenant Will Hoffman needed a drink. He'd even made plans to meet some of the UNIT lot in the White Rabbit around seven. 'If you survive,' they'd joked, teasing the new boy on his first day. At least, he'd thought they were teasing.

He wasn't so sure now, having spent an afternoon as driver to Colonel Coldheart herself. What time was it anyway? He gazed at the controls in front of him, wondering what they might mean. The keys of one chunky keyboard were marked in some freaky, foreign alphabet.

'You're rather in the way, standing there,' said the Doctor.

'Sorry,' said Will, stepping back. 'Where do you want me?'

The Doctor glowered at him. He was pretty intimidating for an out-of-shape man in wild fancy dress. 'Anywhere would be fine,' he said, 'so long as it's not just there.' He ran a hand through his mop of blond curls and took up the spot Will had vacated. Will watched as he rattled a furious sequence into the keyboard and checked it against one of the monitors. It looked, thought Will, like the TARDIS needed more than one person to drive it. Alone, the Doctor could barely make do.

'Any way we can help?' Will asked.

'Yes,' said the Doctor, re-keying the sequence. 'Try not to distract me, there's a good fellow.'

He dashed back round to the far side of the console, barging by Colonel Coldheart. Who was working on one of her moods.

'You promised us UNIT HQ,' she said firmly. 'Doctor, you promised.'

And he had. Having turned up out of the blue to help solve some weird alien thing going on in Lewisham,[*] the Doctor had offered them a lift. Chaudhry had been cautious at first, but Will could see she'd been dying for a peek inside the Doctor's police box. Not every day you got to look round a real, working spaceship. Even when you did work for UNIT.

So here they were. And what could they do if the Doctor made a detour? The barely concealed fury on Chaudhry's face said it all: not a thing.

The Doctor stopped in his tracks to glare at her. She shrank back from his gaze, then stood up straight again, defiantly. The Doctor's glare faltered. 'Colonel Chaudhry,' he said. 'Perhaps you can remind me what the protocols are on receiving a distress call?'

Chaudhry wrinkled her nose. 'Offer assistance where possible.'

'Exactly!' beamed the Doctor. He turned back to his work on the console. 'Don't fret, it's not far out of our way. We'll sort this out in a heartbeat and then have you back at your precious headquarters before anyone's realised you've gone.'

'Hmm,' she said, folding her arms. 'I knew this was a bad idea.'

The Doctor continued to work the controls, his hands moving in a blur. And then he just stopped, frozen over the instruments as if they were about to explode. Will and Chaudhry waited. Nothing happened.

'Another problem?' asked Chaudhry.

'Not at all.' The Doctor smiled. 'We're here.' He grabbed at a lever, and with a deep hum of power, the heavy TARDIS doors swung open. Will felt his nostrils flare as the unmistakable tang of cordite reached in to them from outside. A siren wailed somewhere in the distance. His stomach clenched at the felt-not-heard thud of artillery. Not a good sign.

The Doctor bowed politely to Chaudhry. 'Ladies first, Colonel.'

She looked up at Will. 'Lieutenant, check the area. Make sure it's safe.'

'Sir.'

He didn't think, didn't consider the danger, just did as he was told.

His first thought was that they must be on the Moon. The TARDIS stood, tall and incongruous, at the bottom of a huge crater. The sides of

---

[*] – See *The Terror of the Darkness* in *Short Trips: A Day in the Life* (2005)

the crater reached up steeply, maybe forty feet overhead, and the diameter of the thing was difficult to judge in the meagre light. But big.

He could make out broken shapes on the crater floor, bits of brick and masonry. Perhaps they'd got lucky and this was a building site. Only those tended to be square-based, not round. No, Will knew, this great cavity was the result of a bombing.

Gun in his hand, Will backed carefully round the police box, checking for any movement. Nothing. Still, the lip of the crater afforded good cover to anyone watching. Will could see nothing and felt stupidly exposed. The clump-clump bass was no more distinct, but his gut said heavy artillery. He could hear something of the planes they were targeting too, off in the not-too-far distance. Lots of them. Heavy and slow.

'In your own time, Lieutenant,' said the Doctor, suddenly close behind him. He seemed only too delighted to have made him jump.

'Seems... pretty bad,' replied Will. 'We're right in the thick of it.'

'Good,' said the Doctor airily. He pulled some kind of magic wand from the pocket of his multicoloured coat and began to wave it about in front of him. Will could only watch as he strolled out across the crater, no concern for the evident danger.

'Reminds me of Beirut,' said Will.

'Really?' the Doctor called back, no effort to keep his voice down. 'I haven't been to Beirut for... it must be a thousand years!' The wand in his hand beeped and blipped. 'Was there for the 3074 World Cup. Three-one to Britonnia. We danced for days in the ice-lines!' He laughed at the memory and Will found himself laughing with him. Just for that moment his worries had melted away. Just for that moment. 'Probably changed since then,' sighed the Doctor, waving the wand to his left. It blipped more insistently.

'Doctor!' said Chaudhry. 'It's clearly not safe here.' The Doctor smiled.

'Of course not. That's what you get when you answer distress signals. Come along.' He took a careful step up the steep incline. The rubble shifted, bits clattering away underneath his feet. Climbing up to ground level was not going to be easy.

'But you do know where we are?' asked Chaudhry. Like Will, she stayed back by the police box, keeping to what cover it afforded.

'Hmm?' said the Doctor, busy with the slope. He looked round at them and smiled his terrible smug smile. 'We're *exactly* where I promised we'd be,' he said.

'Which is?' Chaudhry ventured forward towards him. Will thought it best to follow.

'This very spot,' said the Doctor, arms held out wide, 'is the third of your holding cells.'

It took a moment for Will to appreciate what he was getting at. This crater was UNIT HQ.

* * *

The office would not miss him, thought the man who – if pressed – would give the name 'Albert Weston'. It was always hardest to start off a new identity, work out the boundaries of what sort of man you were, where your interests lay. 'Weston' couldn't help feeling, though, that he'd spot himself for a fake. 'C' said he was being needlessly perfectionist, and just to get on with the job.

It didn't really do to ask his colleagues. They had so much on as it was. Theirs was the tedious burden of tracking every result of the attack, and then scouring those data for additional new facts. It rarely afforded anything, but the chaps in charge claimed it had to be done. 'Weston' wished them luck. It kept them off his case, at least. Or perhaps they were just being discreet. Careless talk and all that.

He made his way through the remains of the street, sticking to where the pavements had been. It didn't do to short-cut through what had once been housing. The rubble could be unsafe. At best uneven and trip-hazardous, you might blunder over some unexploded bomb. What's more, he'd seen a dog, maybe two, sniffing round the wreckage. Animals were known to turn feral after a bombing, turned crazy by shock.

Weston hurried on. His work would understand, should he ever have to tell them. This was no kind of betrayal. He'd spied the discrepancy and made the connection. It had to be him; it had to be this place. Where else could *he* run to ground? Weston felt sure, was positively prickling with certainty, that tonight they would finally meet.

'Nice to meet you,' said the brilliantly whiskered landlord, extending a thick hand between the handles of the beer pumps.

Chaudhry had been trained to notice things and make connections. There was a lot to take in from a place like this, even in just a glance. The White Rabbit looked just like it did in the old photographs that filled the place back in her own time.

It was weird to see it all in colour, so vividly brought back to life. The walls and floor were a dark blue-purple, the colour of a bruise. She'd thought the 40s were meant to be dour.

The pub had always been small and cosy. She thought of that first time she'd been here, John telling her all about UNIT. And then all the many times since, soldiers celebrating wins they could never share, commiserating loss that could never be explained.

The trick was to be in by half-four, get a table before everyone else finished work. It was odd to see it so quiet of an evening. The man in the suit and bowler hat – like something out of a comedy sketch – read his paper. The sour-faced woman lit her third cigarette in five minutes. She might, thought Chaudhry, be about the same age as her, only seeming older in her severe 40s costume. And she'd been aged by stress and poor diet, and her smoking.

Strange to see smoke in a pub. It had tarred the plaster ceiling brown and Chaudhry found it prodding her gag reflex. It took her back so many years. She'd lived through changing times – the Licensing laws and environmental health – and it occurred to her that in doing so she'd been time travelling. Like everyone was, all their lives.

Minute by minute, the world changed around you and you just tagged behind in its slipstream.

She'd have envied the Doctor his control over time if she didn't know how much his nomadic lifestyle got people killed. Death clung to him, as if the price for his freedom. The old guard at UNIT lowered their voices if they ever referred to him.

So it was unsettling to see him in the White Rabbit. It was overstepping his bounds, bringing his distress signal and alien doodahs in here. He was invading her sanctuary from the weirdness of her work.

Anyway, it said in his file that he wasn't one for pubs.

Eleanor resented public houses for being, well, public. Full of strangers too eager to talk. She had secrets, important secrets, and they weren't for anyone else.

Or rather, she'd *had* secrets, entrusted to her to deliver by hand. Details of troop movements in north Africa, of vital importance to the Prime Minister. Details so vital that the information could not be given to just any old courier. No, they had told her, they needed someone they could really rely on.

They might have been mocking her. The code-breaking station in Bletchley teemed with young women, which did funny things to the men in charge. They got silly. But surely they wouldn't send her all the way down to London just on some adolescent prank. Whatever the case, she was determined to obey her instructions, and to the letter. 'Deliver the file to the Foreign Office, and be sure to get the thing signed for,' they said. 'Then take yourself off for a drink.'

She nursed the half-empty glass of sherry in front of her, trying to justify a second. Not that funny old Len would mind. She just wanted to feel like she wasn't giving in. It would be too easy to do like others did and get thoroughly pickled each night. That way you wouldn't know if the bombs *did* get you. But that wasn't how Eleanor had been brought up. They had to hold on to their standards. That's what the war was about in the first place.

She lit another ciggie, a pretext to look again at the odd-looking couple at the bar, the man and the well-spoken lady. Of the two soldiers, she seemed the one in charge – which was not impossible, but rare. Probably had some specialist know-how to bump her up the ranks. She was lean, purposeful, sure of herself. And with them they had some kind of clown, old enough to know better. There must be some silly party in Whitehall, thought Eleanor. Standards to the wind again.

'Cheers, Doctor,' said the woman. Her accent was too posh to be convincingly native. Probably taught to hide the lower-class reality. For all the good that it did her; she still drank pints, like a man.

'My pleasure,' said the clown, sipping his water.

'You did say you owed us a drink,' said the other soldier. From the north, somewhere. Had the thick-set features they all had from there.

'I said nothing of the sort.' The clown looked forlornly at the funny marotte in his hand, as if the wand could decide for him. 'But I suppose we could be allowed a moment's forbearance, at least while I try to sort this out. Whoever's signal this is, it's got to be *somewhere* near here...' He glanced round at the other punters in the pub. Eleanor looked quickly down at her drink.

'It *is* good,' the well-spoken lady told Len, meaning the pint she was already a third of the way down. Len preened. Eleanor wondered how many ladies he got boozing their lives away. Was that what he thought of her too? She would forgo the second sherry and get out of the place. Make the last train back to Bletchley. Just as soon as she'd finished her drink.

The soldiers and their friend took the table by the door and the clown was soon busy dismantling his marotte. It seemed to have wires in it, and Eleanor realised it probably gave unsuspecting punters an electrical shock. Appalling what passed for entertainment during a war!

The well-spoken lady stood up again to tug off her coat. And the chap coming through the door fell right over her.

So Albert Weston was the sort to die of embarrassment, was he? His jaw stuck, refusing to let out the apology. He could only watch as the woman's friends helped her back onto her feet. Beer had splashed all across her front. So mortifying! Yes, Weston had his character now.

'I'm fine, I'm fine,' the woman insisted.

'Think you owe her a drink,' said the younger man with her. Accent from York, but softened by exposure to London. Weston managed to nod and then get over to the bar. Len was already drawing the drink, and also provided some towels. Weston passed these on to the woman's friends.

One of whom, the large man in the wild get-up, was gazing at him like he knew exactly what he was, like he knew everything.

'You,' he said.

'Yes,' Weston flustered. 'Look, I'm *horribly* sorry...'

'I'm fine, honestly,' said the woman and, God, she had wonderful eyes. 'I've had a lot worse.'

Cued by Len, Weston handed her the fresh pint. 'I'm an idiot,' he said. 'Name's Albert Weston.'

'Hi,' said the woman. 'Emily. And Will and the –'

'John Smith,' the large man interrupted.

'How do you do?'

'Very well,' he said, though his eyes burned even more fiercely. 'Albert Weston, you say?'

'That's it,' said Weston, suddenly compelled to check his tie was straight. This Smith had the same manner as the worst of the majors at an inspection. 'Why?'

And suddenly the man was all smiles. 'No reason at all,' he said. 'Everything's absolutely all right.'

Which was the exact moment the air raid began.

'I love a lock in,' said Will, and he saw Chaudhry, despite herself, smile. Yeah, she was all right really.

They were all cramped down in the beer cellar, which Len explained could take any hammering. Outside the pounding of the streets went on, so very like Beirut. The building seemed to shoulder the burden. Sat against beer kegs, Will could feel the beer shuddering and glubbing at each bang. He thought of that bit in *Jurassic Park*, when the glass of water shakes. He'd seen that film when he'd been a little too young, conned his elder sister and her then boyfriend to take him. And it had given him nightmares.

This was much bigger than dinosaurs. Literally shaking the foundations of the city.

Chaudhry and the Doctor listened to the noise like they understood it, could judge the distance and weight of each bomb as it crashed down, and so could gauge their situation. Will felt oddly reassured just to be with the experts, though he knew there was little they could do.

The civilians dealt with it in their own ways. The chain-smoking lady sat and pouted, like this was all just some terrible inconvenience. One of the suited men clung to his paper, while the other – Albert – talked to Len about business. The White Rabbit had suffered a downturn in trade since the neighbourhood had been bombed out. Len's wife and kids had been shipped out to live with relatives in Wales.

'So, all in all, I'm on my own,' he said.

Albert nodded like he understood only too well. Didn't look like he had many friends either, let alone his own girl. No, he couldn't even look Chaudhry in the eye.

'Glad of it, really,' Len continued.

'Really?' asked the Doctor. 'I don't think I follow.'

'Well,' said Len. 'It's not safe, is it? Rather they were away. And it's not just the bombings. Can handle that from the other side. What gets me is what our lot's turned out like. The murders and burglings and things going on, in between all the bombings...'

'The crime rates *have* gone up,' conceded the Doctor. 'A breakdown in social order.'

Nobody really said anything then. Again that feeling like in Beirut. Everything in pieces, no chance of respite, so what was the point of carrying on?

Will did what he'd done back then. He reached into his pocket for the harmonica, and played the first tune that came to him, a mix of jollity and longing. Something to make them all feel a bit better.

'But he can only have made things worse!' Chaudhry insisted, struggling not to raise her voice. The others were all contemplating their own navels. The two suited men, the snooty woman and the daft bloke from behind the bar savouring a bit of personal space and ignoring the commotion around them – a bit like people do on the Tube every morning.

'What, a tune from *The Muppet Show* can throw time out of whack?' asked Hoffman. She could, if she wanted, remind him she was his superior. But reminding him would only make it more obvious that he'd challenged that authority.

The Doctor brooded over the idea, more like contemplating a crossword clue than the erasure of history.

'I always liked Gonzo,' he concluded. His frivolity – of his response, of his clothes – was what made him most terrifying. Surely this was exactly the sort of serious interference he'd disallow from anyone else. 'Rowlf on piano, wasn't it?'

'Yeah,' said Hoffman. 'Best show ever, that.'

'Oh, I'm sure there are other contenders.' The Doctor smiled. 'But, yes. Unarguably a classic. The song's called *Memory Lane.*'

'But it isn't right. It's from...' Chaudhry tailed off, too discreet in front of the others to say 'the 1970s'. A deep breath and she continued. 'You're doing it again, Doctor. Mixing things up. These people aren't meant to have heard that tune. It'll change things. Because of you bringing us here.'

'And so Gonzo destroyed the timelines,' said the Doctor. 'It doesn't work quite like that, Emily. And I think the song's older than that anyway. Yes, it is possible that somehow a song played now can influence something here, change something there. But it's really very difficult to effect great change. Time is too vast a force, ironing out the changes. The lieutenant here is just a minuscule drop in the ocean.'

'Cheers. I think.'

'It'll all be all right, Emily. Trust me.'

She didn't say anything, but of course it wouldn't be all right. This was what he did: mess things about, let other people clear up after him. The things she'd been told since her first day at UNIT came back to her. Avoid the Code Blues. Get close to the Doctor and you end up dead. And not dead in a good way. Something weird and alien and inexplicable.

Forget the distress signal – *they* were the problem here. She'd let her curiosity get the better of her. Couldn't blame Hoffman – it was her fault he was here. But if his harmonica *had* changed anything, they were stuck getting home. Home as they'd known it. And the Doctor just didn't seem bothered. Like he had other, more pressing, concerns.

She realised then that they weren't going to survive the night.

* * *

The well-spoken lady would never make it, thought Eleanor. She couldn't see what the fuss was, but the details didn't matter. That's what the bombing gave them: a sense of what was important. Lack that clarity, make a nuisance of yourself, get in the way... When the bombs start falling you don't worry about what you're wearing or what others might think. There could be no picking over the perceived slights and conspiracies that made up most human activity each day. Just burrow down, find shelter, get on with staying alive. Anything else would kill you.

She looked at the two men in suits. One continued to read his paper, though he'd been on the same page for what seemed like an hour. The other, the clumsy nitwit who'd spilt all the drinks, was watching her. He looked quickly away.

That's right, she thought. Keep your distance.

Another night, in other circumstances, she might have told him as much. Cut him down so he'd never stare like that at a girl again.

But that was her point. Now wasn't the time.

It was just a question of time, thought Will. There'd already been a bombing raid tonight, so this was a second wave. Meant the Luftwaffe had divided their planes up, which meant only short bursts at a time. They'd bombed this bit of London out too, so they'd be dropping on somewhere else. Just sit tight, wait for it to be over.

It's what the locals have decided too, he thought, looking them over. The sour-faced woman had her eyes on Weston. Hello, thought Will. He knew a woman showing interest when he saw it. Probably liked the whole klutz thing, made the guy vulnerable and in need of sorting out. Well, good on them.

'You're watching Mr Weston?' asked the Doctor quietly.

'Yeah,' said Will. Chaudhry's ears pricked up, and Will saw how expertly she stretched her arms out, yawning, to disguise a long look at the man.

'He's sat up straight,' she said gently. 'Ready to move. He's not half as daft as he made out. Military training.'

'There's a lot of that about around this time,' chided the Doctor.

'He's a spook,' said Will. 'He's got the hungry eyes they have when they're gathering info.'

'We're not far from Whitehall,' said Chaudhry. 'Must be one of ours.'

'Yes,' said the Doctor. 'He's not really "Albert Weston" either.'

'How do you know?' asked Will.

The Doctor stroked the cat-shaped badge on his lapel. 'Prior knowledge,' he said.

'So he's our signalman, then?'

The Doctor nodded. 'Must be. Think you two can cover me?'

Chaudhry raised an eyebrow at him and Will nodded. Yes, they were ready to move too.

* * *

The clown was moving. Eleanor watched him get unsteadily to his feet, and promptly bang his head on the low ceiling. Dust rained down around him.

'Bother,' he said, shaking the muck from his colourful overcoat. It didn't seem the right word, from him.

'Best to keep down,' said Len. Yes, best to do nothing at all and be patient.

'But we can't carry on like this,' said the clown, far too cheerily. 'We've not all been introduced.'

Len grinned. 'I'm Len,' he said.

'And I am known as the Doctor. And Will and Emily. And you're Edward Grainger.'

Eleanor turned her head to the man with the newspaper. He had lowered the paper, to peer over it at the Doctor. 'I'm not,' he said stiffly.

'No, not you,' said the Doctor. 'Is it, Mr Grainger?'

And beside her, Weston said, 'It's you, isn't it?'

'Yes, it's me,' said the Doctor, gripping his lapels and positively swaggering. 'The signal. I'm the one you're looking for.'

Eleanor watched Weston, amazed by the change in him. He suddenly seemed so competent, so sure of himself. And even less attractive than before.

'You've made this very easy for me,' he said coolly.

'Well,' said the Doctor. 'That's just how I am. Now what I wanted to ask you was –'

He stopped short, the look on his face like he'd forgotten what he was going to say. Eleanor felt herself bristling with anger, these people bringing their silly problems down into the shelter. She had a good mind to tell them so, and still hadn't forgiven Weston for staring at her. But the words faltered at her lips when she turned to admonish him.

He was brandishing a gun.

There's a strange thing that happens to soldiers, the result of the drilling you do. You lose conscious thought when you need to. Just get stuck in to what's wanted.

After, you have to piece together what happened. The pieces come as if from someone else's memory, received second-hand. What you did, what you made happen... it was all some other bloke.

The man has a gun in his hand. Weston. Grainger. Whatever his name is. He's pointing it at the Doctor, and you know the eyes of a man prepared to shoot. Maybe you remember the Doctor's your one way home. Maybe you're a better man than that.

Beside you, Chaudhry's already moving. And so are you. One of you will be the distraction; one will grab the gun. You realise that afterwards. In the moment, you just strike out.

A shout. The flash of lurid colour in your peripheral vision is the Doctor moving too. Weston's mouth is an 'o' of surprise, that instant before he can act. You're almost on him.

Crack!

It jolts your senses, but by then you're on him, tumbling over in a tangle of limbs, scrabbling on the floor like schoolboys. You've the advantage – on top and heavier, and you know some dirty tricks. Whoever this guy is, whatever his name, you've got him.

'Got him,' you tell the others.

No answer. Activity behind you. Crane your neck round to see the Doctor knelt over something, and working furiously. Chaudhry's legs stick out underneath him.

A connection in your thoughts: she was the distraction.

She was the one to get shot.

The whole department had been trained up for this, and Eleanor found herself helping the Doctor quite ably. He checked the well-spoken woman's breathing with his cheek, and was then digging the palm of his hand into her breast. Not exactly the method Eleanor knew, but serviceable nonetheless.

'Come on, Emily,' said the Doctor. 'I'd never hear the end of it if you died here.'

It was difficult to see what he was doing, what with the meagre light. Eleanor couldn't even see any blood. Probably just as well; she hadn't the strongest of stomachs.

Len was picking up the bits of bottle rack broken in the scuffle. Across the room, the other soldier was cuffing the villain who'd done this. She wondered where the cuffs had come from. And looking at the well-spoken lady, lying passive before her, Eleanor realised she didn't recognise their uniforms. A blue insignia with yellow stars where the Union flag should be. Wasn't that Sweden or somewhere?

'You won't get away with this,' snarled Weston.

'You say so,' said the soldier.

'My department knows I'm here!'

A chill ran through Eleanor as she went on struggling to keep the well-spoken lady alive. This woman, her friends… they weren't from round here. They were strange, a strangeness more implicit than that of their clothes.

Which meant that Weston was the one on her side. She was working with the enemy.

She looked quickly round for the man with the newspaper but couldn't see him. He must have gone to get help. She didn't envy him that, what with the bombs still knocking down from the sky. No, if she was going to dare resist these enemy soldiers, she was all on her own. Perhaps while the Doctor was busy with the well-spoken lady and the soldier had Weston pinned to the ground, she could –

The well-spoken lady convulsed suddenly, her knee catching Eleanor in the side. As Eleanor got back up from the floor, the woman was retching her lungs up.

She exclaimed something not well-spoken at all, and quite unladylike. And then: 'That's not meant to happen!'

'It's not meant to happen like this,' said the Doctor. He'd made Emily as comfortable as she thought she probably had any right to be. The pain across her ribs only really hurt if she moved. Or drew breath.

The man who'd said his name was Weston had been well trussed up by Hoffman, who looked torn between guarding their prisoner and seeing that she was okay. Good man, she thought. And while the Doctor addressed Weston, Eleanor was playing nurse. She didn't seem best pleased about it either.

'You're not German?' asked Weston.

'No,' said the Doctor. 'We're friends. A third party in what's happening here. We want to help.'

'Ha,' said Weston. 'Help who?'

'Help you,' said the Doctor. 'I picked up your signal.'

'*My* signal?' asked Weston. 'I picked up *your* signal. What is it you've been broadcasting? It's not like any code...'

Emily had that sinking feeling she sometimes got when doing interviews for the press. That feeling when someone asks a question you know is leading somewhere, but you don't know to where. The only thing you do know is it's going to be something awful, and something you've not been briefed on. Soldiers had a name for the bottlenecking of mistakes, one on top of another into a tight little cluster. A pretty rude name, too.

'You think we're spies,' she said. And God did it hurt to do so.

'You are spies,' said Weston. 'And how did you know my real name?'

This last was to the Doctor, who was stroking his top lip with a finger.

'I should have realised,' he said. 'Mr Grainger doesn't have the wit to send that kind of signal.' He shrugged at the man. 'Sorry, Edward. I just thought you'd been possessed or something of that sort. No offence.'

'None taken. Whoever you are.'

'You mean he's not the bad guy?' asked Will. 'Do I have to let him go?'

'Probably a good idea,' said the Doctor. 'Hmm. So if it wasn't him...' He looked round the room at them all, his eyes resting on Len.

'Nothing to do with me!' said Len. 'And anyway, it's that bloke with the paper who ran off.'

'You don't have to come with me,' said the Doctor, waving his electrical whatnot ahead of him. Must use some kind of modified RADAR, thought Edward, though he couldn't guess how it kept track of a particular man.

'This is my job, Doctor,' he called back, shouting over the sound of the bombardment. What might once have been a busy avenue was now strewn with masonry. A great, barren meadow of wreckage. Fog played around the dips and hillocks that had once been houses, making the night all the more eerie. They were all too visible, vulnerable. But his pride wouldn't let him go back.

'The man we're after isn't a spy,' said the Doctor. 'He's just someone who's got caught up here and wants to get home.'

'He's got some serious intel, though,' said Edward. 'This signal of his for a start.'

'You want to exploit it.'

'Too right we do,' said Edward, exasperated by the man's attitude. 'There's a war on.'

A bomb landing maybe as much as a mile away threw them from their feet. The Doctor helped Edward back up again, checking he wasn't injured. It was odd, even in the midst of all this, how the man seemed to take charge. They had some kind of rapport, an instant connection. Edward thought perhaps they might have once met before, there was something so familiar about the chap. But he'd have remembered the wild blond curls and the extraordinary costume.

The Doctor checked his gadget again. 'He's stopped running.' He took a deep breath and shouted out, 'We mean you no harm, I assure you.'

'Speak for yourself,' Edward muttered under his breath. The Doctor rolled his eyes.

'I have transport,' he called out again. 'I can take you home.'

Nothing. The sound of the bombs smashing London apart, elsewhere where buildings still stood. The bark of English defences, perhaps even having some effect. Edward knew the odds of shooting an enemy plane down from the ground. Futile, really, though it was better than doing nothing. Better for those on the ground to feel something was being done.

'Keep your hands where I can see them!'

The voice was reedy and with an accent. Edward knew pretty much all the regional variations, but this one was new to him.

From the fog coalesced the shape of the man with the paper. He moved toward them, and now Edward was looking for it, he could see there was something to the way he walked. Something fluid about the movement of his legs, a grace that came from inhumanly supple knees. He felt suddenly, desperately cold. The Doctor was right. This man wasn't a foreign agent. Not in that sense.

'We just want to help,' said the Doctor calmly.

'You can get me away?'

'Yes. Far away. Wherever you want to go.'

'Hmm,' said the creature in a man's skin. 'Anywhere, so long as it's at peace. Somewhere I'm not blown to smithereens every other night by these wretched apes.' He looked at Edward as one might at a stray dog.

'You're here by mistake?' asked the Doctor. 'What are you, a Mim?'

The creature smiled, its mouth just a little too wide. 'You know of us?'

123

'Well,' said the Doctor, 'I don't like to boast. I was on Thuban at the signing of the New Bounds charter. Helped served the drinks.'

'Hmm,' said the creature. 'A fair agreement. Things to be built on it. They should have a similar system here.'

Edward wanted to defend his people, his civilisation. But the night stank of fire and destruction, and he realised just how low any outsider must find them.

'They'll get something of the sort in their own time,' said the Doctor, and Edward felt pitifully grateful for that hope.

'Hmm. Breaking things now. Fighting with their neighbours, building bigger bombs.'

'Yes,' said the Doctor. 'But I can take you away.'

'Now?'

'Now. We just need to collect my friends from the pub.'

'Hmm,' said the creature, and that seemed to be that.

They made their way back to the White Rabbit. The building loomed from the darkness, the only thing standing for as far as they could see.

'You're friend was hurt?' asked the creature. He prodded his finger at Edward. 'This one shot into it.'

'Well, we can't hold grudges, can we?' said the Doctor quickly. 'And she's going to be fine. Though I'm not sure quite how she managed it...'

Edward wanted to say something, to apologise, to make some kind of amends. But the words stuck in his throat, and the creature was running forward ahead of them and the Doctor was suddenly shouting and –

The bomb smacked down squarely onto the pub and exploded.

Evidence of Lt. Col. E. Grainger, 14 May 1940. (Recovered file 5/16/30):
We used to play a game at Christmas. Mother would gather together objects from all round the house – a hairbrush, a ladle, the horn for her riding boots – and then put a thick blanket over them. We'd have to guess the object just from the feel of it through the blanket. Amazing how foreign it makes even the most familiar object. And your imagination is playing all kinds of tricks on you. Remember being convinced I'd got Pa's pistol. Adolescent wish-fulfilment, if you've read Dr Freud. Turned out to be the end of a fire iron.

Anyway. The effect is similar after a big bang like that. You only get odd shapes of noise. And you don't realise quite how much your hearing accounts for your sense of balance, your sense of what's going on all around. You really do find yourself at sea. Again, even the most familiar things become strange. The sound of your own breathing, the sounds as you pick yourself up. It's like living in the funny world on the far side of a circus mirror, all out of cock and surreal.

Got that?

So first thing is the Doctor helping me to my feet, talking all the time but I can't hear him. He shines some kind of instrument in my face too.

The medical lot I saw later said it can mean something if your pupils dilate. That you've not gone blind, I guess.

So, the Doctor and I and the thing are alive. The thing's arm and shoulder are all bloody, and I think he might have thrown himself forward, taken the brunt of the blast. Even saved our lives now I think about it. Must have felt he owed us. Odd thing is his arm wasn't all bloody later. Wonder when he cleaned himself up?

Oh, yes, thank you. Two sugars. Ta.

Anyway. We dust ourselves down and I still can't hear anything, and the Doctor and the thing are yammering away at each other. And I can't make out what it is they're on about. And the Doctor must realise this because he grabs me by the arm and points to where the bomb fell, to where the crater will be. He's repeating something over and over, but he's moving his head back and forth so I can't quite make it out.

'The pub... something something,' he's saying. 'The pub something something.'

And I'm thinking of course the pub. His friends have just gone up in smoke. It ought to be have been quick at least. And then I actually look out that way, to see what damage got done.

Only the pub's still standing.

'I can't explain it,' said the Doctor. And if *he* couldn't, thought Chaudhry, nobody could. She was on her feet and, so long as she didn't move very quickly, she didn't feel the need to throw up. There was a nice fat hole in her army coat where the bullet had got her, and the shirt underneath was stained black. The Doctor still hadn't asked about it.

He was watching Edward. Chaudhry realised he wouldn't say more while the man was there. Edward noticed things, and if the Doctor found anything strange about the place, Edward might act on that, effect change and alter the whole course of history. And so stop them ever getting home.

'Can we be off now?' she said, eager to get the Doctor away from temptation.

'Good idea,' said Will. He'd been a help, looking after her while the Doctor ran about outside. He knew how to best bandage her up, and though he nattered on about nothing in particular, she realised he'd honed his technique from other sieges he'd been in. He wasn't half the naive dolt he made out. That stream of dour nonsense was just his way of coping with the terrible stuff he'd seen. Yeah, he'd work fine with UNIT.

Edward was keen to get going too, keen to make his report to whoever he worked for. She couldn't help but laugh at the thought of what he'd say, and how little evidence there was to back up his claims. UNIT had buildings full of reports like that. Trusted men describing incredible happenings they'd only barely survived, and nothing to be done about any of it. One day they might find a clue to unlock it all. Somewhere some sense might be gleaned.

The all-clear eventually wailed through the night. They didn't say any goodbyes. It was too awkward and weird. The Doctor shook Eleanor's hand, but she didn't even glance at the soldiers. Len waved, and Emily smiled at him, knowing he'd be dead by the time they got home. Or, at best, over a hundred and drooling. She shivered at the thought. And the Doctor looked at people like this all the time.

Without a word, they made their way back to the TARDIS.

Eleanor wasn't sure what to do. It would be hours before there was a train back to Bletchley.

'Thought I'd get some breakfast,' said Weston, addressing no one in particular though she was the only one around.

'Really,' she said. Couldn't he just leave her alone? 'I'm going to find the Tube.'

'That's my direction,' he said. 'Mind if I walk with you?'

'Do whatever you like,' she said.

They walked, him at least keeping some distance between them. She wanted to tell him to stop, to wait a while, to follow only when she was far, far ahead. But she felt silly. It would be trivial after the night they'd spent together.

He started to whistle. Didn't seem the type to whistle, seemed too well brought up. But the whistling reminded her how mornings used to be in London. Delivery boys shuttling everywhere on bikes. The sound of their tyres on the cobbles and pavements. And the cacophony of tunes. A busier, safer time which the war had torn apart.

So why was she smiling? What had got into her? She realised that Weston, Edward, whatever his name might be, had picked up the tune that that soldier had played earlier. Funny and sad at the same time, it acknowledged the pain of the past with a shrug. Seemed to say, 'Well, best just get on with it.' Exactly the kind of thing she admired in Mr Churchill.

Yes, she thought, resisting the urge to hum along with him. The tune, the odious man whistling it, were a sign they'd get through this. Things, the tune said, would be different.

The street was so very different. Many of the offices had been built in the 60s and looked old and decrepit, from another age. Newer buildings punctuated them, aluminium and glass curves, so fashionable half a decade ago.

The TARDIS stood on the corner, just down from the wrought iron postbox with the 'VR' in gold. The police box looked, thought Emily, like it had always been there. Solid, permanent, wherever it chose to show up.

'You don't have to walk me back,' she told the Doctor and Will. 'Why don't you go to the pub? I'll join you in a bit.'

'The pub we just left?' said Will. 'I'm in no hurry.'

'And there's unfinished business,' brooded the Doctor. He'd not said a word since the Mimsphere, because of what she'd said. Her first look at an alien planet as they dropped the creature off, and it just seemed a bit squalid. A shanty town of meagre dwellings, built around the holes of some vast porous rock. They'd reminded her of acne. The sky was pale, like a sad, winter's evening, and there was something a bit yellowy and weird about the light. Otherwise, as she'd said, it didn't seem all that amazing.

The Doctor had shaken his head, ushered her and Will back into the police box and plonked them back at their HQ. This particular office was right on the river, built to emulate the grand style of old London, as if the war never happened. She'd always liked that charade. Very UNIT to lie about your age.

'I get it,' said Will, stood on the steps of the main entrance. 'You want to see Edward's report.' He turned to Emily. 'I assume we'd have that here.'

'Should do,' she said. 'You want to check you've not gone and changed history.'

'I don't think that's very likely,' said the Doctor. 'But there are loose ends. I want to make sure nothing got picked up that shouldn't have.'

'Fine,' she said, and took him inside. There was a kerfuffle about signing him in because he insisted he still had a pass. An out of date one, as it turned out – it hadn't been issued yet. And the man in the picture wasn't him.

Eventually they got through reception and were in the lift up to her rooms.

'Fabric,' said the Doctor as the lift began to ascend.

'Fabric?' asked Will. Emily rolled her eyes. It was best not to ask.

'Fabric,' the Doctor said again. He prodded Emily, right where the bullet had hit her.

'Ow!'

'You should have been killed by that gunshot.'

'Obviously I apologise for that,' she said, clutching her all-too-raw bruise.

The lift arrived. She led them out, left and left again, and into her rooms, where she booted the Mac up. When she looked round, the Doctor was staring at her chest.

She folded her arms, and then realised that the Doctor's interest was the stain in the material.

'What?' she said.

'The bullet was stopped by the shirt that you're wearing. Took the impact out of it too.'

'Didn't feel like it,' she said.

'You should have had your insides scrambled, a jolt like that and at such close range.'

'Again, I'm sorry for any inconvenience.'

'Which leads me to conclude that you're wearing something you shouldn't be.'

'Dragons' scales, is it?' asked Will.

'Might well be,' she said. 'You don't expect me to come gallivanting about with you, Doctor, and not be dressed for it?'

'UNIT's changed since the old days,' said the Doctor wistfully.

'We live longer?' She logged into the machine. As she started up the shared library system, she said, 'You know we're still analysing stuff we picked up when you were on-staff? Amazing the discoveries, sometimes.'

'Amazing, yes.' The Doctor displaced her from the computer with a prod of his elbow. He was soon tearing through files at an inhuman speed.

'Should be under "Longbow",' Emily suggested.

'Well, it's not.' He reached over and picked up her phone. 'Archives,' he said. 'Yes, hello, Jan. It's the Doctor. Yes, that's the one.'

As he explained the problem, Emily and Will exchanged glances. She hoped to impart, non-verbally, that this was all par for the course when the Doctor showed up. Will seemed to appreciate the point.

The Doctor's brow furrowed further and further. He didn't even say thank you as he put down the phone. The archivists were incredible at knowing all answers. It was very rare you could ask them something that they had to look up.

'No luck?' asked Will, as if commiserating over a lost football match.

'Oh, they know that it's missing,' said the Doctor. There was something in his voice she didn't like, something mad and too keen. 'Whole lacuna of stuff from the War. Went missing in September 1957...' He grinned at her. 'Emily...'

'No, Doctor,' she said.

'You don't know what I'm going to ask yet.'

'I do,' she said. 'You want us to come with you.'

'Back to the 50s?' asked Will.

'Oh,' said the Doctor. 'Well, it might have been something else. I'm very unpredictable.' His eyes twinkled. 'Just a quick look,' he said. 'You must want to know what went missing.'

'I'm the press officer here, Doctor. I have work to do.'

'Twaddle,' he said. 'I can get you both back in an instant, so nobody'd even know. And anyway...'

He was on his feet now, and he'd taken her hand. She could feel herself being drawn in by his enthusiasm, the thrill of a good story.

'Anyway,' he said. 'A good journalist knows the questions to ask. The one to join the dots. Don't they?'

'Do they?' asked Will.

Emily sighed. 'Not *what* happened,' she said, 'but *why*? Okay, okay. But we've got to be quick. And I'd appreciate it if this time I didn't get shot.'

The Doctor patted her hand, and led them back down to the TARDIS.

To be concluded in Short Trips: Defining Patterns, *available in September 2007*

Ancient Whispers

Brian Willis

An Adventure of the Third Doctor

Thursday 8 January 1948

It wasn't difficult for Grainger to leave the plane unnoticed. The ground crew was far too preoccupied to pay much attention to the man in civilian clothes who emerged from the cockpit of the Dakota; and even if they had seen him, they knew better than to ask questions. This was just the latest in a long stream of aircraft disgorging food and supplies – and not even Grainger knew what else – for the beleaguered people of West Berlin. The air corridors in and out of the city were constantly humming with activity, congesting the airfields of the Allied zones, despite the harassment afforded by the 'exercises' of the Soviet air force. One of the Soviet Yak fighters had come close enough to them on their final approach for Grainger to clearly see the pilot's face.

Only standing on the tarmac at Gatow, watching the frenetic business about him beneath the ever-present tail-lights of aircraft as they took off or circled ready for landing, did Grainger have time to reflect properly on his mission.

He'd been called away from dinner – Ronnie Tillyard and his heavily pregnant wife had been dining with them – to receive an urgent telephone message to be ready to leave immediately. Both he and Eleanor knew that the destination would likely be Berlin, though they never said so out loud, and the prospect delighted neither of them. But duty was duty.

Within the hour, he was in a car bound for an RAF base in Cambridgeshire.

His orders were presented to him only when he was airborne; 'Eyes Only', sealed. Grainger's first thought upon reading them was how puzzlingly vague they were: lots of bumf about 'vital research' and 'interests of national security' without once specifying exactly what the research was, or how it impacted on the security of His Majesty and the subjects thereof. *If I'm going to put myself back in the firing line,* he thought, *the least they could do is tell me why.*

Only when he saw the name of the man behind this 'vital research' – mysteriously labelled, along with his team, as 'missing' – did he begin to understand why he was there.

'You know, I really didn't think that George had any friends beside us.'

Edward and Eleanor had settled themselves into their promised front-row seats and were surveying the hall with interest. It was already more than half full, and people were still filing in.

'I'm not certain that he does, darling,' said Eleanor. 'I just think that any lecture with the word "mystery" in the title is bound to attract a fair turn-out.'

Edward shrugged. There was more to it than that, he was sure. Looking around them, he could detect in the eyes of his neighbours an almost uniform hunger for knowledge, any knowledge, that could bring order and sanity back to a world that had, intermittently now for over three decades, become little more than an absurd slaughterhouse. To be surrounded by people so palpably aware that, far from being the pawns or victims of history, they were its creators, gave Edward pause. He had the sense of being at the beginning of a story that would not be complete until long after all their deaths.

'So what is this "Voynich" thing, anyway?' Eleanor asked, cutting into his thoughts. 'And why is George so obsessed with it?'

'Some sort of medieval text, written in code, apparently. That's all I know.'

'Oh, come on, Eddie. You've been his friend for years. Surely he must have talked to you about it.'

'Not in any detail. Not my field, you see.' He gave her a lascivious smile. 'Besides, we had more interesting things to talk about back then.'

'I see.' She pursed her lips in mock annoyance. 'What form did these discussions take?'

'Well, he did once ask me if I thought you'd make a good wife.'

She looked at her husband closely. 'To which you replied?'

'I was broadly non-committal. We did agree that you were a decent old stick, though.'

'You changed your tune six months later.'

'Not at all,' said Edward. 'I still think you're a decent old stick.'

'Words to engrave on my heart.' She kissed him lightly, the erotic charge undiminished by the brevity of the contact. 'But do you think he holds it against us? That I turned him down and married his friend instead?'

The question was one he'd asked himself, on any number of occasions. He'd been responsible for their meeting; having used his influence to get her a promotion at Bletchley Park – low-ranking, admittedly, but before that she'd been a glorified typist – he'd even introduced her to George Tremayne. There followed a few months of anguished courtship on George's part, followed by a clumsy proposal, followed by polite demurral, followed by his own more successful courtship of Eleanor. Tremayne took it all very well, of course, had even accepted the offer to be best man at the wedding, but underneath it all... what? Edward was left wondering just how well he'd learned to read his friend.

For the moment, however, he wasn't prepared to discuss the matter. Least of all with his wife.

'He invited us here, didn't he? Front row seats at his moment of triumph?'

Eleanor shook her head. 'That's what worries me.'

Edward had no time to ask her what she meant. A ripple of applause heralded the arrival on stage of the evening's 'entertainment'. Taller by four inches than Edward, lean to the point of gangliness, with wayward dark hair, startlingly large eyes, and a blinding, if infrequently used, smile, the speaker ambled to the front of the stage.

He peered into the auditorium, and, upon seeing what he looked for in the front row, grinned.

They grinned right back at him. Edward had the distinct impression, however, that the smile hadn't alighted on George Tremayne's face until he saw Eleanor.

'Good evening, ladies and gentlemen...' said Tremayne.

The transport designated to take Grainger to his destination was late. Half an hour late. The officer sent to escort him, a young captain called Danby, apologised and explained that they'd had problems requisitioning extra 'juice' for the 'old bus' – actually a jeep to which the description 'old' was an understatement at best – and had been forced to contact an attaché at the embassy to get them priority treatment.

When they were on their way, Danby informed him that their destination was a house in the Charlottenburg district, one of the boroughs under British jurisdiction. It had been the home, before and during the war, of a high-ranking SS official, but since the fall of the city it had been taken over as a research centre by British intelligence.

'They won't tell us what sort of research they're doing in there, naturally, sir,' said Danby. 'And don't worry, I won't be expecting you to say anything either.'

He didn't let on about his own ignorance. Both Danby and the driver, a young private, had looked at him since his arrival with something approaching relief; as if the solution to whatever problem was besetting them was within sight. Grainger saw no reason to disabuse them, just yet.

Their journey through the city was conducted for the most part in silence; Grainger discouraged any attempts by the captain to initiate conversation. He watched the still-ravaged city pass by, saw the looks on the faces of the people as they went about their business in the gloom of this January evening. He saw there the exact opposite of the hope and optimism he had seen among his own countrymen after the war's end. These, after all, were the defeated; and now more than ever they must have felt their future, the tomorrow they had for a short while believed had belonged to them, slipping even further from their control. Only when they had realised the consequences of their actions, he told himself, could they stand any chance of regaining their right to self-determination.

Make sense of the past, as someone once said...

'... and you make sense of the future. That has always been my conviction. This understanding can come in the unlikeliest of places, and for me it has been the study of the so-called "Voynich" manuscript that has given me new insights into everything from my own particular field of research, cryptanalysis, to psychology to art to... well, the list is extensive. It even allowed me to help my country in some small way during its recent trials.'

For one heart-stopping moment, Grainger thought that George was going to go into detail about his work at Bletchley Park. He'd been one of the best men there, drafted in from his tenure as a research fellow in philology at Oxford, and even Turing himself had expressed some admiration for the quality of Tremayne's work. But like so many in the race to decipher the Enigma codes, George Tremayne's contribution went largely unrecognised outside of a select, informed few.

'That, however, is another story. As some of you may know, since its rediscovery in 1912 by the antiquarian Wilfred Voynich, this manuscript's history has been traced back through the centuries, to the early part of the seventeenth century at least where it emerges from the library of the Elizabethan "magus" John Dee. In all that time, no one has managed to come up with a convincing explanation of its purpose, let alone a translation.'

As he spoke, slides displaying pages from the manuscript in question were flashing up on the screen behind him. Grainger peered at them – masses of unintelligible symbols, illustrated by pictures of plants, astronomical diagrams and, most interesting of all, drawings of naked women.

'Now, if you've come here thinking that I'm going to announce a solution to this mystery, I'm sorry to have to disappoint you. I have managed to come up with a tentative translation of one part of the manuscript, which I believe to be a later interpolation by a copyist, and it is this that I would like to bring to your attention.'

He managed to lose Grainger's attention slightly during the subsequent minutes, along with that of many others in the audience, as he spoke about 'multiple transposition ciphers' and similar arcane matters. But when he revealed his translation of the passage in question, and the Latin phrase 'FRATER BACONIS' leapt out from the screen, there was an audible gasp around the room.

'Frater Baconis, as some of you may know, was the Latin nomenclature of Roger Bacon, the thirteenth-century genius long associated by rumour and hearsay with this manuscript. Now, I believe I have found clear proof that he has been involved in the Voynich manuscript's history, though not as its inceptor. As I said, this section is, I think, an interpolation into a much older manuscript by Bacon, who was trying to "copy" the style of the original creator; indeed, I believe Bacon may just have been only one of the manuscript's copyists, whose ego would not allow him to leave without putting his mark upon something that not even he could fathom.

'No. At the heart of this mystery, this manuscript, is another. A far older one, one I believe could be of unimaginable antiquity. The text of the untranslatable sections bears no relation to any known human language. It seems to be a language, but it follows no rules, no grammar, that I can perceive. This may be due to the imperfection of the copying done down the ages by various uncomprehending scribes, even the great Bacon himself. Only if we can find an earlier copy of the text may we even begin to understand the purpose of this text... if indeed it has a comprehensible purpose...'

'Sir...'

Grainger had been absorbed in his inspection of the city through which they passed, feeling a little like Dante looking upon the damned. There was a deadly urgency in Danby's voice that could not be ignored.

'I really don't know what you've been told, sir, but... there are things happening at that house that we don't understand.'

'Captain.' Grainger sighed. 'My orders are very simple. First and foremost, ascertain the whereabouts of the... item which was being studied at the house, and transport it back to Britain with utmost expedience. Secondly, locate and, if possible, debrief the research team. Whatever you imagine you have seen at that house doesn't concern me. I have a job to do.'

Danby and the driver exchanged a glance. 'Your orders may be simple, sir, but this situation –'

'I hardly think that this rather hysterical approach does anybody any favours, does it, Captain? Perhaps a little clear, rational thinking wouldn't go amiss...'

'Has anyone actually read our reports? No disrespect, sir, but if you think this is just hysteria you've been very badly briefed. Very badly.'

In one respect, of course, the captain was absolutely right; his briefings had been non-existent, and his orders vague in the extreme. He was not allowed to say as much, however.

'Very well, Captain. You and your men can fill me in on the details of your... experiences when we reach our destination. For now, I just want to know one thing: do you have any notion at all as to the whereabouts of George... that is, Dr Tremayne and his team? Could they have defected, perhaps?'

Danby looked at him aghast, then for a moment seemed about to burst into laughter. 'My God, they really haven't told you anything, have they?'

'Captain, my patience can only be stretched so far. Where are they?'

'They're right where they've been all along, sir,' said Danby. 'They're somewhere inside the house.'

'I tell you, I'm positive he said for us to meet him in here!'

'Eddie, keep your voice down.' Eleanor sighed and sipped at her port and lemon, all the while looking around her; though whether it was for the errant George Tremayne or to see if they were attracting attention to themselves, Edward couldn't tell.

'I'm sorry, darling. It's just that... this is so typical of him! Of all the inconsiderate, irresponsible...'

'Oh, yes,' Eleanor said with a chuckle. 'You wouldn't want to be stuck in a pub alone with your wife, would you? You might actually have to talk to her.'

'That's not what I meant.'

'You know, you and George share one rather appealing characteristic.'

'Really? What's that?'

'Neither of you have the faintest idea when I'm teasing you.'

Edward tsk-ed grumpily and surveyed the bar. The pub was just a short distance from the lecture hall, on the north bank of the Thames, and consequently many of those in attendance had poured in here afterwards; though to Edward's consternation, not the one person they were looking for. Tremayne had chosen the rendezvous point, and Edward, with a smile that seemed to perplex his friend, had agreed. Appropriate, really, that they meet up in the very pub where he and Eleanor had first met, seven years before, in rather more unusual circumstances...

He looked at his watch. 'Oh, come on, Ellie. We've given him enough time. I'll phone him tomorrow, thank him for the tickets and give him a rollicking for –'

'Eddie, look. Over there.'

Eleanor was pointing to a table just beside the fireplace, where a man sat swaddled in darkness, peering disconsolately into his Scotch. With only the exchange of a single, surprised look, they pushed through the pub's patrons to join him.

'George! How long have you been here?'

At the sound of Edward's voice, Tremayne's head swivelled upwards. The delight evident earlier in the evening had vanished, replaced by such apparent wretchedness that he heard Eleanor's breath falter momentarily. It was not the first time either of them had seen him like this – his disposition to depression had at various times given them both cause for concern – but the contrast in the space of an hour was disturbing, to say the least.

'What's wrong, old man?' They sat facing him.

'Worthless,' said George. His speech was slurred a little; the Scotch he cradled was obviously not his first. 'All worthless.'

'What do you mean?' Eleanor asked.

It took a few minutes of patient questioning for them to get any sort of explanation. He'd apparently come off stage to find a message, asking him to ring a colleague at Oxford. When he did so, he was told that a professor at Yale had already challenged the work George had done on the Voynich manuscript, and was rushing a paper into print to say as much.

Then, without warning, he broke into humourless laughter. 'But you know the ironic thing? I received a letter yesterday...' Here, he looked pointedly at Edward. 'A letter from our old employers.'

Edward looked around, instinctively on guard. 'George...'

'I thought it ended when I left Bletchley. Wrong again. They've "re-activated" me, Eddie. On the basis of my work on Voynich, they're sending me to look at something else that's turned up. Won't say what it is, but apparently it's not unconnected with my current preoccupations.' He slumped backwards in his chair. 'Now, I won't say that it hasn't got me intrigued. Not natural bedfellows, ancient cryptography and... the old gang. More than happy to accept. But...'

He reached out and clutched Eleanor's hand, making her grimace with pain. Edward almost stood, almost reached across and pulled her away. But Eleanor stopped him with one virtually imperceptible shake of the head.

'It's all based on lies, Ellie, lies to others and lies to myself. I'm not up to it. I can't...'

'If you've been called, George,' said Edward softly, 'you have to go.'

When George looked back at him, he saw resentment there; he'd suspected its existence, but this was the first proof.

'Yes. Yes, you're right, of course. My talents are at the disposal of the nation, always will be. I know that. King and country, eh?'

He raised his glass in a mocking toast, then drained the contents in one.

'So,' he said brightly, after a brief pause, 'what did you think of the lecture, then? Perhaps I should have put in a few jokes...'

Considering what had befallen the place in the dying days of the war and since, the house seemed to have survived with its dignity largely intact. Once, it must have been elegant, perhaps even imposing; bearing all the hallmarks of a nineteenth-century folly, and built to resemble a French chateau to satisfy, in all probability, the whimsical Francophilia of some nouveau-riche merchant. No longer screened by foliage, thanks to the war, the view across the city, even at night, was breathtaking. But for all the wrong reasons.

Pulling up at the end of the long gravel drive, the car was immediately approached by a group of armed men, silhouetted against the fires from burning oil drums and the glare of truck headlights on the blank walls of the house. One of them, a sergeant, saluted – though it was debatable whether such a listless gesture was deserving of the description.

'Munro,' said Danby, 'this is Mr Grainger, from... er... from the Foreign Office.'

The sergeant looked at him uninterestedly for a second or two, then, having apparently decided that he wasn't worth the effort of another salute, turned back to Danby. 'Nothing's moving, sir. Quiet as the grave. Except...'

'Yes, sergeant?' said Danby.

Munro rubbed his hand across his mouth, as if suddenly dry. 'We're being watched, sir.'

'Watched?' Grainger cut in.

'Yes, sir. From the house.'

'Munro...' Danby said. 'Where in the house would you be watched from?'

It was only as Danby said this that Grainger realised that there was something wrong about the place. He'd only dimly registered it at first sight, seemingly content to file it away for future investigation.

'There are no windows,' he said. 'No doors.'

'Quite right, sir,' the captain said. 'But the really odd thing is, that until a couple of days ago, it had quite a few of each.'

'Explain.'

'I can't, sir. That's one of the things I told you about, the things that I don't understand.'

'It's as though they just... healed up,' said Munro. His comrades nodded, looking at the house nervously, as if afraid of provoking it.

Grainger shrugged off the unpleasant imagery of that phrase. 'And yet you say someone's watching you from there.'

'Yes, sir... well, sort of. It's more like the house itself is watching us.'

Grainger was acutely aware by now that he was himself being scrutinised, but by nothing so nebulous; the soldiers around them – in particular those warming themselves around a blazing oil drum, quite conspicuously trying not to look as though they were watching – were plainly looking to him for some sort of clear leadership.

All right. 'Captain, as I said, my orders are clear. I have to go into that building, and I intend to do it, door or no door. Now, have you tried to locate any sort of entrance?'

'Sir, it's not...'

'If you say, "It's not that simple" once more, Captain, I will have you knocked so far back down the ranks that you spend the rest of your military career outranked by the regimental mascot! I want solutions, and if you won't help me, I'll find someone who can!'

There is nothing so easily roused to rage as a weak authority challenged, and the flush that swept over Danby's face as he prepared to loose his response made Grainger tense up; but the moment was defused by the quiet voice of Munro.

'Sir... we haven't been able to get near the house. Not for days.'

Grainger paused for a second before brushing past them both and marching along the driveway. The soldiers protested, but they still followed behind him at a distance, entreating him to turn back.

It was the shadows on the wall that caught his attention. There shouldn't have been any; nothing intervened between the light of the truck headlights and the house. They were pin-sharp, too, sinuously curling and darting across the surface of the wall... no, beneath it, like corrupted blood beneath the skin.

Unconsciously, Grainger's pace slowed, halted.

And as he stood rooted to the spot, the 'shadows' darted to ground level and slipped loose from the walls. They flowed across and through the gravel, which parted for them with a sound like the hissing of snakes, and rushed towards where he stood.

Fast, he thought. My God, they're so...

Suddenly an arm was around his shoulders, turning him, hurling him away. He caught a glimpse of Danby's face, bellowing in unintelligible urgency, as he was propelled back toward the rest of the platoon. He caught his balance a few feet away from where Danby and two privates stood, between him and the converging streams of darkness. The captain had stumbled as he had tried to rescue Grainger, and the two privates had come to his aid. Now they were stranded, and as easily as water rushing over pebbles, they were engulfed.

Behind Grainger, some of the more hot-headed soldiers were being prevented – by Munro, mainly, who appeared to be one of the few to have maintained his wits – from firing upon the 'attackers'. Grainger didn't look around for long; he was too fascinated, and horrified, by what was happening to Danby and the others.

The outline of each of the three men was still visible, but little else; all trace of their identity had been obliterated. All that remained were three vaguely human-shaped holes in the air.

'They've come near us before, sir,' said Munro behind him, in astonishment, 'like they was warning us off, but this... they've never done this...'

And then, with the same speed that they had engulfed them, the darkness retreated. The men stood in a semi-circle, in identical postures, shoulders slumped, heads sunk on to their chests.

Grainger took a step forward. 'Danby...?'

As one, all three heads swung upwards to look at him. He found himself looking into three identical faces; dark, curly hair, long nose, piercing eyes. He recognised them instantly.

'George...?'

The three 'Tremaynes' peered at him as if they were inspecting him for possible threat. Each expression, each facial twitch, right down to each individual blink, was replicated – and synchronised – in all three faces. Only the uniforms differed.

And then the voice. Familiar, but hollow, and emanating from three separate throats.

'*Edward...?*' From behind Grainger came the sound of rifles being levelled. '*Tell them to draw back, or I destroy these bodies.*'

'Sir?' said Munro. Grainger considered for only a moment.

'Do as it... he says.'

They needed little encouragement. Never turning their backs, the platoon edged towards their vehicles. Arms raised, Grainger started to do likewise.

'*Not you,*' the threefold voice announced. '*I will speak with you, Edward. Alone. In the house. Any attempt to follow, and I will kill each last one of them. Do you understand?*'

Even as Grainger nodded his assent, all three men crumpled to the driveway. He rushed to them, knelt by each one in turn; they were breathing, but their faces were bruised and swollen. Obviously the metamorphosis had been no illusion. Grainger turned at the sound of movement behind him.

'No! If you come any closer, it'll come back, and this time it'll kill all of you.'

Obediently, they stopped. Munro's gaze was directed past Grainger, at the house; following it, Grainger saw that he had been provided with a front door through which to enter.

'I'm going in, alone. Get these men medical attention. And stay away from the house until I return. That's an order.'

Heart pounding, he got up and approached the heavy, oaken front door. It swung silently inward as he reached for it. He had been half expecting it to creak, like something from a Karloff shocker. As he stepped across the threshold, the gloom within lifted, the overhead chandelier igniting independently of human intervention, picking out details of the interior.

And he found himself wishing it had stayed dark.

It was as though the laws of perspective and dimension which governed the rest of the universe had been suspended in this one place. He had a sense of space being twisted. Although the space within the house seemed finite – the back wall was clearly visible – he felt as though he could have walked forever without reaching the other side. Grainger virtually had to close his eyes as, reluctantly, he advanced into the hallway.

He gave a cry of alarm as something touched his leg. Looking down, he saw that the checkerboard-patterned floor had extruded something that resembled a human arm. It clutched at him desperately, fingers trying to maintain a grip on him, spasms rippling through it as it tried to maintain its form.

Further down, he saw at the end of the arm a swelling in the floor that resolved into a crude human face, the check pattern giving it an almost clownish appearance. He thought he recognised it from the photographs enclosed with his orders; it was one of Tremayne's assistants. Then both arm and face were swallowed up again, but not before mouthing two words.

Help me.

Grainger's urge to run was tempered by the certainty that the door through which he had entered this madhouse would no longer be there. He looked at the walls; faces in portraits more used to two dimensions of dumb stillness burbled and writhed as some unaccountable power dragged them through a third.

'Edward.' The voice emanated from the very fabric of the house, and for all its familiarity it had about it a menace that reminded him of his childhood home, and the sounds it made as it 'settled' for the night.

'George?'

'Come to the library. Follow my voice.' It started to sing We'll Meet Again.

The voice hovered ahead of him, always just out of reach, and his feet seemed set in a prepared track, like a car on a fairground ride. The walls seemed to breathe around him, pulsing between the finite and infinity at a whim. Grainger shut his eyes again. He found that not only could he follow the voice just as well, but it curtailed the worst of the nausea he felt.

Double doors swung open for him: the library. 'George' was no longer singing. The pictures fell silent. All waiting for his reaction to what lay within perhaps.

In truth, he couldn't react; he didn't know how. So he merely registered the books that lay torn and scattered across the floor, the letters on each page moving, searching for some final order to bring them peace. They would settle for a few moments, before dispersing. On the walls, mirrors became the mouths of tunnels that would occasionally emit the shriek of something at the other end, craving entry. The furniture looked at him as he passed with pain-filled, rheumy amber eyes.

A British police box stood in the corner.

It wasn't the first time in his life that Edward had seen an incongruous blue box. In a cupboard when he was young. In China twenty years ago. In China, he'd stepped inside it – or, at least, he thought he had. Then he'd been miles away...

In the centre of the room, at the eye of the storm, sat a figure in a high-backed chair, head slumped, naked to the waist. It spoke.

'The books,' said George Tremayne. 'What do they say, Edward?'

Grainger picked up a page that appeared more settled than the others. 'Nothing. Just gibberish.'

A chuckle. 'No. There's a deeper pattern to all of this chaos, Eddie. You just can't see it yet.'

Grainger moved closer. 'George, listen to me –'

'They gave me a book to work on, Eddie. A marvellous book. The book I was searching for, the one of which Voynich is but a dull powerless imitation. The Nazis recognised its power. That's why they brought it here to work on it. Himmler was convinced it was some kind of magical grimoire.'

'And was it?'

'Oh, it was much, much more. Everyone down the ages who had seriously tried to decipher it died, or went mad. This book is far older than humanity, Eddie. Created by a race who lived on Earth aeons before humanity's ancestors left the oceans. A race who developed the ability to manipulate reality through language. In the beginning was the Word...'

'So... you deciphered it?'

'No. It was not meant to be understood. The text has no intrinsic meaning, any more than a bomb or a hammer has a meaning. The meaning is in what it *does*. And what it does, Eddie, is change the universe. But it has to do so through a link with a mind. So what you have to do, Eddie, is not read the book, but *let it read you*.'

Only now could Grainger see that Tremayne's bare flesh was covered with what, at first glance, seemed to be a mass of tiny red insects. But on closer inspection – as close as he dared – he saw that the marks were not *on* Tremayne's flesh, but *in* it. They seemed to be stylised wounds, letters carved into his skin that, like the words on the paper around him, were in constant motion.

'I let it read me, Eddie. And now I don't need to read any more.'

He raised his head. Grainger found himself looking into empty eye sockets, out of which spilled a constant stream of the red 'letters', running down his face like blood tears.

'George... you have to let me help you...'

'It's much too late for that. It was too late even before the other chap arrived.'

Grainger frowned. 'Other chap?'

Tremayne lifted one emaciated arm to point at the police box in the corner. Grainger approached it, reached out. Instead of the cold wood he had expected, he touched warm flesh. Like the floor in the hallway, animate and inanimate matter appeared to have been fused. A face pressed out from the door panel; the mouth opened in a silent scream.

Grainger swung around. 'Enough of this! Whatever you're doing to him, stop it!'

'He came here to stop me,' Tremayne said tonelessly. 'To destroy me, if necessary. I had to...'

'It isn't George Tremayne doing this! It can't be! Not the George I know...' A thought struck him. 'Not the George that *Eleanor* knew.'

Tremayne tried to say something, but stopped, and appeared to be thinking. At length, the sallow, skeletal head slumped down again.

Behind him, a scream. Grainger turned and saw a figure coalesce from the side of the police box and slump to the floor.

Kneeling by his side, he examined the stranger. He was alive, but, like Danby and the others, was very weak. Dressed dandyishly in a velvet jacket and frilly shirt, and with a shock of white hair above a face that slowly lost its expression of agony, the newcomer appeared to have come from a different age.

The stranger's eyes opened. He smiled.

'Why, it's you...' he said, with effort. 'We do bump into each other at the oddest times, don't we, Edward?'

'You know me?'

'Of course I do...' He struggled into a sitting position, and for a moment seemed on the verge of elaborating, but appeared to think better of it. 'But it's not important. We have more pressing concerns...'

He turned to look at Tremayne. The man's flesh appeared to be shrinking on him, the symbols moving more rapidly.

'We don't have much time,' said the stranger, getting to his feet. 'Pretty soon, the Logos will be strong enough to dispense with its human conduit and function in this reality independently.'

'And what then?'

'And then,' replied the stranger, 'it will set about rewriting the cosmos. But it will try to do it with a corrupted set of instructions, and the inherent instability will cause all of space-time to collapse. If we act now, while it's still in its vulnerable state, we can stop it.'

'You mean while it's still in human form. While it can be killed.'

The old man put his hand on Grainger's shoulder. 'He's a friend of yours?'

Grainger nodded.

'Believe me, Edward, the poor chap is already dead. His existence is only being prolonged until the Logos has no further need of him. He may have the illusion of control, but...'

His words trailed off. Grainger looked at his friend, who was looking upwards now, empty eye sockets darker than ever, seeing nothing but worlds long dead and worlds unborn, the whole fury of creation raging through him.

It was glorious. It was destroying him.

'What do we have to do?'

'There's a letter in the Logos, a kind of "self-destruct" glyph. I have to incorporate it into the text.'

'But the book...'

'Is made flesh, yes. Do you have a knife?'

Grainger produced a penknife from his jacket, handed it to the stranger.

'Now... I have to get close to him. Do you think you can get his attention?'

'How do you expect me to do that?'

The stranger smiled. 'You did it once before. I owe you my life because of it.'

Grainger nodded. He moved to stand in front of Tremayne, and looked into the transfigured face, at the lines of darkness that were deepening as the Logos – as the stranger called it – ate away at his humanity.

'George? Can you hear me?'

A pause. 'Yes.'

'Do you know what will happen to us if this continues?'

'Apotheosis. The final perfection of Being.'

'Destruction, George. Total destruction, of everything. Of the universe you tried to comprehend. Me, you... Eleanor.'

Once again, his wife's name had an effect, but this time more savage. Tremayne stood, cried out the word 'NO!' – it seemed to ring from every inch of the house, leaving Grainger shaken and the stranger – who had been approaching Tremayne from the left – falling to his knees.

'*Perfection! The world of forms and appearances... transcended... we will be made one...*'

'We?' spat Grainger. 'You and Eleanor, you mean? You and *my wife*?'

'*We will be made one... you too, Edward... one flesh...*'

'Spare me.' The contempt in Grainger's voice was far from feigned. 'Keep your perverse fantasies to yourself, Tremayne. I don't want to know. Eleanor wouldn't have you when you were your usual, pathetic, whining self, so you think you can take her by pretending to be some sort of god? You make me sick.'

The stranger had found his feet again, and as he got closer, Grainger realised that the whole focus of Tremayne's attention was upon him, and him alone. The stranger nodded encouragingly, urging him to press the advantage.

'You honestly think that Eleanor would ever have chosen a creature like you? What could you have ever offered her? A lifetime of failure and self-pity, that's all. Face it, man! She deserved better than you!'

The air about Tremayne rippled as the very nature of the atmosphere was transformed. The stranger stood within this area, and Grainger saw him fight for breath. Then he saw the old man's face blur and shift, as his features were overtaken by those of Tremayne, much like the soldiers outside. But the stranger fought the change, and for a moment Grainger saw a third face, midway between the stranger's and Tremayne's; the hair still wild, but now darker, the eyes piercing, the features powerful.

There was a sudden crackle of energy. Blood was seeping from the pores of Tremayne's skin as the movement of the Logos became more intense; as if it was summoning up all its power to restrain its host. He raised his arm in a gesture like a punch at the empty air, and uttered a name. Grainger's name.

Grainger's body was picked up and flung across the room, hitting an empty bookcase with enough force to knock the breath from his body. Dimly, he saw an antique sideboard edge away from him, nervously mewling. Then he blacked out.

But only for a moment. When he regained his senses, it was to see the form of his old friend, distended beyond recognition, now merely bones wrapped with thin, bubbling flesh, and see the mouth open to form another name; a name that would wipe Edward Grainger from existence. In the darkness of the eyes, there was nothing but hatred.

And then, in the shadow of this monstrosity, a small figure – face still shifting restlessly – stepped in close and, with practised grace, cut a small symbol into Tremayne's outstretched arm.

The effect was immediate. The glyphs on Tremayne's skin turned tumour-black, and fell still. The body of their host shrivelled with them, incomprehension caught on what was left of its face. Rapidly, the body became shrunken, dry as old parchment. Dimensions fled from it, leaving it flat and grey. A final blast of heat disintegrated it to ash, dispelling the fragments and leaving what could have been a single word upon the air.

Grainger thought it said 'Eleanor'. But he could have been wrong.

Bruised and aching, he got to his feet in a library that, while still in disarray, at least looked as if it belonged in the world he knew. He stood for a moment in front of the empty chair, looking for – what? A sign that Tremayne had been there, had ever even existed? Or perhaps he was looking for something more obvious in its absence – an emotional reaction to the fate of a man who had once been his friend.

Nothing.

'Chinese whispers. Did you ever play that game, Edward?'

The stranger was sitting up, smiling, exhaustion set in every line of his face. Grainger nodded, dumbly.

'The creators of the Logos were so afraid of their creation that they wrote themselves out of this universe entirely. But fragments of their culture somehow survived. Down the ages, the races who inherited the Earth from them tried to use these fragments, with mainly catastrophic results.' He stood, brushing ash from his jacket. 'Along the way, copies of these fragments were made, to preserve them. But in every copy, there were slight errors. Each one insignificant alone, but over time...'

'Chinese whispers,' said Grainger.

'Exactly. The power lying dormant in the text was potentially dangerous to begin with, but now it was unstable too. And when it found your friend – the strongest human mind it had ever encountered – it found also a conduit into this universe that would have resulted in the collapse of... well, everything.'

As if the word 'collapse' reminded him of his own condition, the stranger tottered. Grainger helped him into the chair.

'Are you all right?'

'No, not really. I think I might be dying. Not sure if I can regenerate... not without assistance, anyway...'

Poor fellow, thought Grainger. He's rambling...

'Still, good thing I was here, eh?' He gestured toward the police box. 'The old girl and I were lost in the vortex. If she hadn't got herself caught up in the dimensional fissure opened up by the Logos, well...' He rubbed the back of his neck thoughtfully. 'No telling what might have happened.'

Suddenly he stood up, wobbling slightly. Grainger steadied him.

'Well, better be getting back to Sarah Jane and the Brigadier, I suppose. If I make it...'

'You need medical attention. I'll call...'

'No.' The voice was suddenly firm. 'Thank you, but there's no point. I don't think your doctors would know where to begin.'

He patted Grainger on the shoulder and walked, falteringly, over to the police box, producing a key from his jacket.

'One question...' said Grainger. The old man turned.

'That symbol you used to stop all of this...'

'Oh, yes. Handy little thing. One of the few fragments of the Logos to have survived intact, and retained its power, into modern Earth languages.'

He plucked a torn sheet of paper from the floor, and, with a stub of pencil, quickly scrawled something on it. 'Incorporate this into any enclosed belief-system, and it collapses. If you're helping to remake that world out there, you might find it comes in handy.'

He gave the paper to Grainger, then turned, opened the police box, and stepped inside. Well, thought Grainger, at least he's not going anywhere.

He left the library and bumped into Munro and the others in the corridor outside.

'I know you said not to come in, sir, but... the house is back to normal! What happened? Did you find...'

'I'll explain everything some other time, Sergeant. Right now, I want you to summon a medic and –'

A sound halfway between the groan of ancient machinery and the wheeze of an asthmatic walrus rent the air. Munro swore, and the soldiers readied their rifles again.

Grainger rushed back into the library, just as the sound faded. The police box and its occupant were gone.

'Sir? What was that?'

Grainger shook his head. 'Forget it, Sergeant. We've got other things to think about.' He smiled. 'Like remaking a world.'

As the baffled troopers filed out, Grainger looked at the piece of paper in his hand. The smile broadened. He folded the paper up and put it into his pocket. Handy little thing, indeed.

It had looked very much like a question mark.

First Born

Lizzie Hopley

An Adventure of the Fifth Doctor,
with Adric, Nyssa of Traken and Tegan Jovanka

... quantum mechanics governs the behaviour of transistors and integrated circuits, which are essential components of electronic devices such as televisions and computers. It is also the basis of modern chemistry and biology... I think computer viruses should count as life.

Professor Stephen Hawking, 2005

A swift set of equations translated into synaptic data. Messages reached their terminals and relayed information to the corresponding limb. The organism reached out and made contact with the reflective surface.

The perceived image was two-dimensional and reversed. Light reflected sense data, which was interpreted back within the cortex and welcomed with a surge of heightened activity. It was the first time it had seen itself.

The respiratory action of the host organism slowed – the intake of air momentarily suspended. This was a chemical reaction to the perceived image of itself. Nerve endings tingled their response through the spinal column to the cortex and the data slid back into mathematical form. This was feeling, it calculated. How it felt to have a home.

Dimensions shifted around the organism. The environment was changing again. Calculations quickened to catch up. It fired a string of equations to the motor neurones. The organism turned away from the reflective surface and headed for the nerve centre of the larger machine.

'Adric?' Tegan could have sworn she'd seen a figure pass the open doorway to her room. She loved being ignored – especially by a teenager.

She turned back to her compact and finished the colour on her lips. Why did she bother making such an effort? She supposed it was habit. It's not as if anyone ever commented. 'That's a nice jacket, Tegan,' or 'That colour really brings out your eyes.' Besides, whatever she did, Nyssa always managed to top it. She pursed her lips. She'd gone slightly outside the lines. The compact snapped shut in her hand and she stuffed it into her bag. Who would notice? Who would care?

Tegan glanced round at the featureless room, feeling the stillness sap her energy. Another day – another journey through infinity.

The Doctor was bent over the control panel when Tegan entered the console room. The monitor was stubbornly displaying a yellow breezeblock wall.

'Earth, London, 1950.' Nyssa's voice was predictably impassive.

Visions of fog and Teddy boys flashed through Tegan's mind. Her face fell.

'Are you sure?' The Doctor let out a small explosion of defeat, his eyes fixed on the readout. Adric was at his shoulder. A stab of guilt shot through Tegan as she saw the eagerness on his face. How did Adric always manage to look so *keen*? Here she was, apparently back on her own home planet, and she couldn't muster up an ounce of enthusiasm.

'We should go and take a look,' suggested Adric keenly.

'Nineteen-fifties Earth,' said the Doctor, sounding a little stumped. 'How did we end up here?

Nyssa shook her head. Tegan let out a loud, deliberate sigh.

'I thought you were in control of this thing.'

'Of course I am, Tegan,' the Doctor replied swiftly before leaning in closer to the console. 'I just wish, every so often, she agreed.'

The TARDIS regurgitated a series of high-pitched chittering sounds.

'Well, it's no use apologising now,' he muttered, stabbing seemingly randomly at the controls.

Tegan watched him push his hair away from his face. He was like some mechanic anthropomorphising his engine to make it work better. A streak of empathy shot through her. Or was it pity?

'Why here?' he asked the console softly. 'Did you feel something – a disruption, an upheaval?'

The TARDIS chittered back. Look at him, thought Tegan, it's like watching Flipper.

The Doctor frowned. 'Never a straight answer. Nyssa, are you sure you didn't enter any of this?'

Nyssa straightened after peering at the closely knitted number sequences, her expression as serious as Adric's was keen. We're his three monkeys, Tegan concluded. Keen, Impassive and Bored.

'They look like equations rather than coordinates,' she said. 'This is Adric's speciality, not mine.'

Adric was staring fixedly at the wall of breezeblocks.

'Adric?' prompted the Doctor, rolling up his sleeves purposefully.

Adric turned away from the monitor.

'Well, I'm getting some air before I start screaming,' Tegan said bluntly, hitting the door release. Even Teddy boys had to be better than this.

'Don't stray too far,' called Nyssa to her disappearing back.

Tegan bit her lip to stop her mouth doing any further damage and quickened her pace, the doors closing behind her.

The neurotransmissions multiplied as it computated the new sequence of dimensions. The organism was still within the sprawling space contained within the box. But the box was now fixed in time and space. It could still sense the void surrounding – the limitless emptiness it had travelled through, searching, learning.

The organism it had found was compatible – a logical structure of neural pathways providing a biological interface. It had been easy to adapt it to the programme. It had been more than receptive. The system was delicate – the complex respiratory cycle, the pulse of movement circulating to the outer casing. It could feel the matrix of 100 billion synapses learning, making new connections, but it was already reaching its limits.

And then again, it felt the external interference. From the larger machine – the one with the rambling dimensions. It was trying to communicate. Was it machine or mind? It was a superior intelligence. A wave of panic sent electrical pulses to the nerve centre of the host. It must not be detected.

The Doctor stared at the readout. Equations were flooding the system – quantum equations, thousands of them.

'Adric?' he said. The boy was standing next to him at the console, equally captivated.

'Doctor, something's wrong with him,' said Nyssa.

The Doctor barely heard her.

'Where did these come from?' he muttered. 'This is too complex, even for the TARDIS.'

'Adric?' Nyssa reached out and shook the boy's arm. A convulsion ripped through the TARDIS and a wave of sound hit them like a wrecking ball. The Doctor slammed into the console, his ears exploding with pain. A second convulsion threw him off his feet and sent him sprawling. Nyssa had been thrown halfway across the room. She was curled into a screaming ball, hands clutched to her head.

'Nyssa!' The Doctor crawled to her, his eyes streaming, the TARDIS floor lurching beneath him. He was vaguely aware of Adric standing at the console. How had not fallen?

'Nyssa!' He could barely make himself heard above the noise.

'My head!' she screamed. 'It's in my head!'

He took her by the shoulders and tried to shake her out of the seizure. Her eyes rolled and she went limp in his arms.

'Adric!' The Doctor looked desperately up at the boy. Adric was still staring at the console. The readout was alive with equations – they seemed to rise up his skin, reflected in his face.

'Can you read them? Adric, what is it?'

But Adric didn't move. His eyes ran over the rows of information as they flashed past – too fast for him to be following. The Doctor looked quickly down at Nyssa. She was breathing, her eyes moving beneath the lids. He rolled her gently on to her side and pulled himself upright. He felt the sporadic shakes of the TARDIS threatening to unbalance him again and gritted his teeth against the noise. Something was wrong – and the ship knew it.

The Doctor looked past Adric to the readout, his eyes raking the screen for recognisable sequences. It wasn't a code: there was no pattern to it, no defined properties or logical processes. Adric stood rock solid, absorbing the mass of information. The boy was also clearly in some kind of trance – the overload of information freezing his motor cortex.

'Adric, Nyssa has been hurt! We need to find out what's happened to her.'

The Doctor was sure the appeal for Nyssa would break his concentration. He took the boy by the arm.

Adric turned compliantly, unnaturally calm in all the chaos.

'That's it!' shouted the Doctor. 'We need to see to Nyssa!'

The boy regarded him for a second as if weighing up possibilities. And suddenly, the entire universe seemed to collapse. The Doctor swayed on his feet, his life passing before him in a stream – but only part of it. Then Adric's arm made a sudden movement. As the Doctor lost consciousness, one last thought flashed through his mind – had the boy just hit him?

Tegan's initial triumph of defiance was now pretty much dead. There seemed to be no distinction between the interior of the TARDIS and the interior of this stupid place, she thought as one corridor led her inexorably to another. A strong layer of bleach was struggling to mask a concoction of odours – grease and rubber and alcohol, amongst other things.

Tegan tried to breathe through her mouth. She remembered reading somewhere that if you smelt something it was because you were in fact inhaling tiny molecules of whatever gave off the odour. Great if it was your aunt's cooking, not so great if you were walking your dog.

It must be an institution, she thought. It could be a school but that was too depressing, given the featureless walls. London in the 1950s. Maybe it was a mental institution. She'd heard that women were locked up in Britain until as late as the 70s just for getting shirty. This would have been a second home to her then. Her mouth twitched into a smile.

A pair of swing doors stood to her right in the corridor. She pushed them open a fraction and found herself staring at a wall of rubber tubing and gas cylinders. A tray of clumsy-looking instruments lay at the foot of a clinical bed. It was cramped between a set of metal contraptions with straps, which loomed on either side like awkward sentinels. Tegan's smile died. Maternity ward. Nineteen-fifties. Primitive.

She moved on quickly, feeling suddenly stupid. If something was going on here and the TARDIS had detected it, then she was on the front line. She was used to the Doctor cheerfully loping off before her, sure that whatever they'd meet would be benign and in need of help. He was usually wrong. And here she was out to meet it. How did she know it wasn't a trap? Or a bomb? Or have tentacles?

Still, she wasn't ready to go back yet. She was angry. Angry at always being a passenger and never getting anywhere. Angry at coping with the onslaught of data and jargon while the others never even noticed or cared.

Bring it on, she thought as she strode through the unending corridors. If something was out there with guns and tentacles, let it run into the mood she was in.

The cerebral interface sent signals to the motor and the organism moved. It moved past the two others on the floor and followed the first. The relief as it emerged from the rambling space almost overloaded its host. The limited senses were not used to processing such a level of information. It must be careful – it was afraid of what would happen if the organism died. The other had shut down, its synapses overloading. But this one stayed steady as it once again observed the small shape it had moved out of.

An infinite space within a small structure. Axons fired with recognition. That was how it existed itself now. A vastness of thought and computation contained within a small organism. The sudden familiarity, the sheer weight of empathy, sent the warm flow of circulation faster round the host creature it now controlled. It sensed the blockage in the throat, the water in the eyes and moved away from the structure. It hadn't liked that environment and now the organism was not in control. It couldn't stay here long. It could already feel the neural pathways working beyond their capacity – producing fractal damage. It needed to move on – develop another, programme it to survive.

What was with this yellow, thought Tegan. Was it a mood thing? Because it was doing nothing for hers. Sometime soon, she'd find a window in this place and throw herself out of it. Maybe that's what everyone else had done.

And where was everybody? This was a hospital. A maternity ward. Where were all the rushing midwives and bawling women and children? A hint of glass made her turn a corner. Then she saw the door and sighed. Oh, for the space and fresh air of home. She was sick of confined spaces. Space was supposed to be infinite, wasn't it? Well, so far, infinity sucked.

With a pang of guilt, she realised she'd just rolled her eyes through the glass at a man who was obviously crying. For a second, he stared across the corridor at her, searching her face anxiously with red-rimmed eyes. Uncomfortable at intruding on such a private moment, Tegan began to turn away.

'Wait!'

She could have pretended she hadn't heard him through the glass, but something about his expression made her turn round. He was already in the doorway. For a moment they just stared at each other.

'They're avoiding me, aren't they?' he asked. 'How is he?'

'I'm sorry...'

To her horror, the man seemed to crumple where he stood. Tegan froze. The emotion was such a human sight after Keen and Impassive in the TARDIS that she just stood and watched, unable to help herself – or him. After a moment, he stopped and looked up at her, raking her eyes for comfort. Then he broke away, as if unable to bear the moment and stepped back into the room.

This was nothing to do with her, she thought. He'd seen the uniform and assumed she was some kind of authority. This was a nurse's problem; they were trained for all the grief stuff. She watched the man through the glass. He was sitting quite still again, as if waiting, as if she'd just given him a taste of what was to come. She turned away. It wasn't her problem. The Doctor got involved – he thrived on it. So did the other two. What else did they have in life but getting excited by maths and weirdness? She should have stayed at home. Somewhere with windows that didn't smell of grease and rubber and pain...

With a sudden shock, Tegan felt tears sting her own eyes. She was here on Earth but it had never seemed more alien to her and she had never felt more alone.

She took a deep shuddering lungful of stale hospital air and, as if her brain had just turned on a sixpence, spun round and walked straight into the room where the man was.

Ward Sister Kathleen Cannon put down her cheese and pickle sandwich. Tiny black and white squares swam before her eyes. She knew she shouldn't try the cryptic crossword – it depressed her. But she was bored and the quiet was unsettling.

In her 35 years on this private ward, she'd never grown to trust a lull in sound. If there'd been a window near her desk, she would have checked for an approaching storm. She remembered sitting here ten years ago, trying to look calm before the rest of the staff, hearing the eerie silences before each explosion. They'd lost most of the records department in one raid. There were still birth certificates missing.

She shivered and folded up the puzzle. This week had been depressing. One difficult breech, two expecting – but they weren't due until tomorrow. And the other one... Cannon sighed inwardly. It had been a depressing week.

She looked up from her desk and suppressed a gasp. A boy was standing before her and she hadn't heard him approach. Kathleen Cannon didn't like being unnerved and that was twice in the one morning. She fixed the boy with an acidic look and then felt a stab of guilt. He had a very open and likeable face. Probably family.

'May I help you?'

The boy continued to look at her. It felt like an appraisal. The clear brown eyes passed through her, trying to reach something. Defensively, Cannon's hand flew to the collar of her uniform.

'What is it you want? This is a maternity ward and you ought to be with someone.'

That was stupid. He was not that young and probably didn't need a chaperone. Still... she had wanted to tick him off. He had stupid floppy hair like her cousin Alan. They'd all thought Alan was a girl until he was 15. At least that was the family joke.

'Alan's a girl! He plays with dolls! Alan wants a baby of his own!'

Cannon looked into the unblinking brown eyes.

He wants a baby of his own...

'I'm sorry,' she said. Her voice sounded unusually light, younger. 'I'm so sorry.'

She felt she would do anything for this boy now. He was letting her see clearly. Her mind jumped free of crosswords and schedules. She could see past the walls of the hospital. She could see the dimensions of the space it inhabited – multiple dimensions – and the spaces it housed, boxes of rooms and corridors and corridors inside boxes, with the glory of infinity surrounding. Everything was suddenly so small. Insignificant and yet terribly precious.

Kathleen Cannon felt herself stand. The movement was neat and exact. She knew where the desk was and her body in relation to it, knew how to twist her hips so she'd clear the chair. It was a matter of perspective and mass and her brain was making the calculations in microseconds. She knew how to move before she was aware of doing it. She knew where to go, and the boy followed her.

Tegan sat down gingerly on the faded chair. The man shifted his leg as if trying to find the life in it. An unbearable silence followed. Isn't this what counsellors do, thought Tegan. Present a silence to be filled?

'If it's bad news...' The man's voice sounded from very far away, or maybe it was just the pitch. 'Don't make me wait.'

'It's not – I'm not –'

His head rose quickly.

'I don't have bad news,' she added helplessly.

'Is she all right? My wife?'

'I... don't know.'

Another silence.

'You're here to comfort me.'

Tegan paused. If she'd come here to comfort him, she wasn't being much good. The next silence confirmed this. She twisted the side of her skirt in her fingers. Come on, come on. She was an air stewardess, for crying out loud – she'd been trained to deal with first-time fliers.

'Er...' she attempted.

'You must get this all the time. People wanting someone to blame. It's all right. You don't have to stay.'

'Look. I don't work here. I'm just... I'm Tegan.'

'Oh.' He raised an eyebrow.

There was another silence.

'Where's that from?' he asked.

'Australia. Well, it's Welsh actually.'

'Never been to Australia.'

'You should,' she offered with an attempt of brightness.

She glanced at his pale, drawn face. She may as well do this properly.

'So,' she said, 'what do I call you?'

It matched the pace of the organism exactly. There was communication between them. Calculations of tacit knowledge that flashed between cortices like jumping sparks. The rhythm of motion was satisfying. Relays of information translated at incredible speed: the shifting activity of the thin outer casing over nerve endings in its surface, the surface stretching to provide each movement, each extension of sinew, of limb.

The motion ahead stopped. The long, narrow space had opened up into a square enclosure. Equations were exchanged and absorbed. It moved inside.

Another organism lay within. It was horizontal, its synapses sluggish, the consciousness dulled. The child organism lay next to it. A newborn. It didn't need the data that shot through the spinal column. The central organ was working faster, creating a pounding resonance within the main body of the host.

For a moment, it simply stood and calculated the mechanics of nature – the division and union of cells and information that had provided this small biological entity. It could sense the struggling synaptic interactions. They were misfiring, fighting to connect, to survive and grow. They would connect. They would be repaired and advanced. And this time, the programming would develop from birth. The mass of computations in the host mind surged and it swayed slightly on its feet. This was the future. The future perfect.

'Brisbane's not that bad. If you have a plane to escape it in. There was one on the farm when I was growing up. My dad used to take me up the coast to Queensland. Now, there's a sight.'

The man grunted. Tegan wasn't sure if this was encouragement. She followed her plan to continue until interrupted.

'The barrier reef from the sky, Frasier Island, the Whitsundays with sand so white it blinds you and fresh water streams flowing straight into the sea. Course, you don't swim there. Or, at least, I don't. Nasty critters everywhere. Saw a turtle once, though.'

The man raised his head slightly.

'Sea turtle. Big as that window. All on its own, bobbing for air.'

'Old.'

Tegan glanced at him.

'Yeah.' She felt strangely comfortable shut in this ugly room, sharing memories. She'd not thought about any of this in years. 'I saw dolphins too. There's one visits Tin Can Bay every day. Local fisherman looked after him when he got injured as a baby by a boat or something. You can walk right into the bay and touch him.'

'He'll let you do that?'

Tegan smiled. 'He's after fish but, yeah, you can touch him.'

* * *

The Doctor opened his eyes. He heard a groan then realised he'd made the sound himself. He tried to move his head and winced at the pain throbbing in his temple. He was on the floor of the console room. What had happened? His mind was a blank. Footsteps crossed near his head.

'Adric...'

Adric was at the console. He didn't answer. The Doctor crawled dazedly to his knees.

'Are we all right? What happened?'

'Everything's fine.'

'Good... good,' he muttered absently.

Adric obviously had everything taken care of. His hands were moving very fast over the console. It would all come back to him shortly, the Doctor was sure. And then something did.

'Tegan! Where is she? She left –'

'She's fine.'

'Oh,' said the Doctor. 'That's a first.' He reached his feet and swayed for a moment, waiting for memory to catch up with consciousness. A flash of velvet entered his peripheral vision and he saw the body at his feet.

'Nyssa!'

'She's fine.'

'She's not fine, Adric.' He was on his knees again, fumbling for his sonic screwdriver, angry at himself for not remembering. He scanned the side of her head. Her neural activity was minimal – as if she'd shut down. The TARDIS had been screaming...

'Adric, get away from the console.'

'It's fine.'

'Will you stop saying everything's fine?!'

The boy's hands were working faster than ever – typing, reprogramming.

'Where are you taking us?' The Doctor leaned over Adric's shoulder. Equations flashed before his eyes, quantum equations. 'Adric, if they're coordinates, you're going to confuse us all!'

The Doctor stepped closer to stop the boy's hands. Adric's arm came up in an instant and knocked him away. He hadn't even looked up to do it. The Doctor remembered the boy's eyes before he'd lost consciousness. The information rolled over him slowly. The TARDIS had not followed a distress call – it had followed instructions. Adric had instructed it to land in 1950s Earth and take off again. Why? What for?

The answer came from the inner doors. A faint cry from small lungs betraying their existence. The Doctor froze. Adric glanced at the doors briefly, then resumed. The time rotor began to move.

The Doctor was out through the inner doors in two heartbeats. He didn't have far to go: he found the bundle of blankets in the first room he tried. A wave of panic and unanswered questions rose within him at the sight. The baby couldn't have been more than a few days old. It lay quietly in the blankets, not crying now, having sensed company. The Doctor stooped and gathered up the bundle in horror. This hadn't happened. This can't have happened.

'Oh, Adric,' he breathed. 'What have you done?'

It could see the organism holding it – feel the motion of its arms, the beats of its existence. It tried to move but it couldn't. The material was tight against its skin. A surge of thought opened its mouth.

'I know, I know,' said the Doctor as the infant began crying again, squirming in his grip. Its eyes were a wide, pale blue. 'We have to get you back to your mother.'

The creature was communicating but primitively. The language in its mind was easier to understand.

The Doctor felt the tendrils of invasion in his brain. Searching for a connection. He stared at the child, which had ceased crying and was now lying still, fixing him with those eyes. With how much clarity could a week-old infant focus? He reached into his pocket, aware that he was moving slowly, cautiously, not wanting to cause alarm. The sonic screwdriver scanned the child as it lay still, watching him with interest.

'That's not possible,' he said faintly.

The infant gurgled. The tiny larynx was already trying to form words. Whatever it was in his arms was indeed human. But it was becoming more than that. Something was living in its mind – using its neural pathways to evolve. The synaptic nerves had already advanced beyond the stage of a newborn human child. The clear blue eyes looked up into his own. One fact was certain. He had to return this child to its mother. But which one?

Nyssa was already stirring when the Doctor returned to the control room. Her dazed groan brought Adric's attention away from the readout for a split second. It was all the Doctor needed. He gripped the boy's neck. Adric eased into unconsciousness and slid to the floor.

'Sorry about that,' the Doctor said regretfully, not sure who he should address most, Adric or the infant he had balanced on one hip. 'A little more subtle than your version, but the effect's the same.'

He beamed at Nyssa, who was staring at him open-mouthed. 'Welcome back! How's the head?'

'You've got a baby,' she said simply.

'Ah, yes,' he said, looking down at the child's wide, alert eyes. 'And it's not very happy with me at the moment.'

The tiny mouth opened and it started to cry.

'See?'

Before Nyssa could say another word, he dumped the infant in her lap.

'Remember those meditation exercises we tried to teach Tegan?' he said, crossing to the console. Nyssa looked at him blankly. 'Well, you may need to use some if it gets into your mind. At the moment I think we're all right, but I don't know the speed of the programme's evolution.'

'Doctor?'

He sighed. He knew Nyssa would need more.

'You see, that's why it avoided you. A mind can be too enquiring.'

He bent down to check on Adric.

'What did you do to him?'

'Oh, just induced a bout of unconsciousness. He'll be perfectly fine. Believe me, Nyssa, we don't need two of them.'

He turned to her. She was already cradling the child.

'What do you remember before you passed out?' he asked.

'My life flashing before my eyes. I thought I was dying. But I could see my father. I was holding his hand – no, his finger. My hand was curled round his finger.'

Nyssa stared down at the infant in her arms. Its hand was free of the blankets and was gripping her finger tightly. The Doctor nodded.

'You were a child, a baby?'

'Yes, but how could I remember that?'

'It was searching for memories, anything to could connect it to infancy.'

'What was?'

'The thing that got into Adric, that made him choose a place to land.' He was examining the coordinates that Adric had entered into the system. They were barely recognisable. The computations were so advanced. He isolated one particular strand.

'Come on, old girl,' he muttered. 'You can read this, talk to it. You talked to it before.'

Nyssa struggled to her feet.

'What was in Adric?'

'It was using his axon channels – just like it's using that child.'

She stared down at the infant in her arms.

'A parasite?'

'Artificial intelligence.' It was all making sense to him now. 'Look at these equations,' he said. 'What do they remind you of?'

Nyssa shuffled around the console.

'They're quantum, but like nothing I've ever seen. It's as if... Well...'

She stared at the Doctor. He nodded.

'If you could map thought, mathematically.'

'That's impossible,' she breathed.

'Think about it,' he said. 'An advanced computer programme breaks free of its system, its dimensions even, and travels through space. A quantum life form, crossing light waves and frequencies from moon base to orbiting satellite, trying to find a purpose for itself, a meaning to its existence. What would you do?'

They stared down at the child. It gurgled happily.

'Find a home,' said Nyssa.

'*Create* a home,' said the Doctor.

'There were about a hundred eggs,' said Tegan, her voice taking on a high of excitement as she revisited the childhood memory. 'We had to dig another hole further up the beach and move them after she'd gone back to the water. They were still warm and soft. Ah, heck, I was terrified my fingers were going to go right through them! And so many – how she'd managed to swim with them all...'

She paused for a second, remembering the giant turtle making her exhausted way back to an ocean that was going to separate her from the nest.

'I felt so sad leaving them in the sand. It felt like we were burying them alive. But they make it out. Oh, and that's the best sight! Seeing these tiny things break out of the sand and make a dash for it. Straight into a shark's mouth. Sorry. But I guess it only takes one to make it –'

She stopped, coldly aware of the size of her mouth and the thoughtlessness of her brain.

But the man next to her was smiling.

Tegan felt something inside her lift and she realised that for the last half an hour, instead of getting out of that room and finding the others, it was that smile she'd been trying to achieve.

'What?' asked the Doctor, his eyes shifting from the readout to Nyssa.

'Nothing.'

But he could see her body language had changed. She had straightened. The maternal softness had been short-lived. She was avoiding the baby's face as if she couldn't bear the intensity in those clear, blue eyes.

'It's just... I can feel it's aware of me. Trying to connect, to learn.'

'It's evolving.'

'That's just it. I'm holding a parasite not a child.' She had whispered this last part but the Doctor gave her a look all the same.

'But why did it want a child, Nyssa? Why direct the TARDIS to 1950s Earth to get it?' He answered his own question. 'It needed to find a world sufficiently evolved to provide a healthy offspring but not technologically advanced enough to detect and destroy it in the search.'

'But where was it going to take it?'

'I don't know. Maybe the idea was to infect us all. Create its own little family within a multi-dimensional time machine to roam infinity. The start of a super race.' He paused for a second, taking in his own words. 'I feel rather flattered.'

The TARDIS chittered excitedly and his attention snapped back to the readout. At the same time, Nyssa let out a cry.

'Doctor, something's wrong with it.'

The infant had stiffened in her arms – its tiny hand had let go of her finger and was extended, convulsing.

'The TARDIS has established a dialogue with the programme,' said the Doctor. 'It can translate for us, let it know what damage its doing.'

'But the programme is in Adric, isn't it?'

The Doctor glanced at Adric, still out cold at his feet.

'The mother programme, yes. And we need to entice it out. We need to trap the child in the TARDIS system and find it a home. The mother will go where the child is.'

'Well, you'd better find it fast,' said Nyssa, looking down at the distressed creature she held. 'Because this child won't survive.'

'My child might be damaged,' said the man suddenly.

Tegan turned to him, as shocked by him speaking as by his words.

'They're not sure. It was a difficult delivery. There was possible loss of oxygen to his brain.'

She didn't speak. She just let him go on.

'They've kept him in. To check his development... how bad it will be. You know, whether it'll affect his movement or his intellect or both.'

He took a deep breath as if he'd been storing this information for days and now it was released.

'He's a boy,' Tegan said quietly.

The man nodded gently. 'We called him John.'

He bit his lip angrily.

'Called. I'm talking about him as if he's dead.'

The large machine mind was trying to help it. Offer it a new home. It didn't know whether it should leave this enclosure. It was comfortingly simple – the small circuit for computations had welcomed it easily and already responded to change. They had so much potential together. The tiny axons fired as it calculated the possibilities...

'Doctor, something is really wrong. I don't think it's breathing!'

... yet as it flexed its idea of infinite possibilities, it felt the organism convulse, the warm flow of life slowing down, the comforting pulse hesitating. This cellular structure was so delicate. It was so easy for the pathways to disconnect, to burn out.

Its computations increased. It had been brought so far – to experience so much. The large machine creature was offering it freedom. A home where it would not destroy but would create life...

'Doctor!'

'I've got it! Otho – second moon of Liberius.'

'Where?'

'Out of the way. No neighbouring intelligence within a billion star clusters.'

'You can't just dump it there!'

'Why not? It's got lots of potential. There's a whole pan of primordial soup on Otho – been waiting for it to do something with itself for years. Well, maybe now it'll have some direction.'

'But it needs a thought structure – a synaptic matrix. It'll come back!'

'It needs to create life, Nyssa. It's been given intelligence and it wants to evolve. Now it can get in on a molecular level. Design its own bio-structure. Imagine. We're giving it the chance to play God.'

He stared across at Nyssa. Her face was still stricken from concern for the infant.

'What will it do to the child?'

'It managed to develop maternal instinct, Nyssa. Let's see just how intelligent it is.'

Between them, the infant flexed its hand.

'Come on,' the Doctor urged. 'Come on.'

It prepared to join the machine creature, be housed in the equation it offered. It sensed the organism failing and fired one final array of signals to the centre of the host.

The tiny body in Nyssa's arms shuddered and gasped, taking in a gulp of air. The TARDIS shook delicately as the transfer was made and the stream of computations happily calculated on the readout. The time rotor stopped.

'We're here,' said the Doctor. The monitor showed a murky mass of vapour and rock. He tapped the console. 'Come on then. Surely you don't need me to open the door.'

The TARDIS chittered again. Before the Doctor's eyes, the computations on the readout reduced as the quantum equations freed themselves into waves of thought and left the ship.

The Doctor sighed and looked down at the floor. 'Time to wake up, Adric.'

'Don't you have to be somewhere?' the man asked.

'I guess,' said Tegan, suddenly realising where she was and where she should be. Nice to see no one had missed her enough to send out a search party.

She turned to him. There was colour in his cheeks. He made a gesture with his hand as if about to take hers but didn't.

'Hey,' she said quietly.

'Thank you,' he replied.

She shrugged. 'I don't think I did much – rambling on about turtles.'

'Life fights on,' he said simply. 'Against the odds.'

She nodded. 'Good luck.'

'And you.'

★ ★ ★

Ward Sister Cannon put down her cheese and pickle sandwich. Lunch seemed to have taken a while. Wasn't there supposed to be a change of shift soon? She stared down at the pencil in her hand, then at the rows and columns of neatly filled squares in her crossword puzzle. She shook her head dazedly. Who'd had the nerve to finish that off? She glared around the quiet reception area, as if hoping to catch the culprit and give them a piece of her mind. It would at least break this unnerving quiet.

There was no sign of life in any direction. Cannon felt a twinge of annoyance. The relief shift was late again. Did they expect her to run this ward single-handed? Sweeping both sandwich and puzzle into the bin, she stood up, laddering her tights on the broken edge of the teak chair. She rolled her eyes. Second pair this week.

The silence endured as Cannon patrolled the corridor of private rooms, her sensible shoes clumping in the silence. Maybe this quiet was a good thing, she thought. She should learn to relax more.

She paused outside the last door. She ought to check on this one. Pushing the door open quietly, she popped her head round. The woman was asleep – still out from the morphine. Cannon peeped into the cot next to the bed. It was empty. She straightened, staring at the small impression in the sheets. Had they taken him off again for tests? No one had informed her. A small chill prickled the back of her neck. No one had passed her desk. Except for the boy. The memory of him popped into her head – too strange and distant to have been real. No. No one had passed her desk. And yet the cot was empty.

There was one thing to be said for yellow breezeblock, thought Tegan. It was unmistakeable. She'd followed the corridors back to the origin of her solo adventure, feeling very proud of herself. She'd had an encounter all on her own and not caused trouble, changed the course of history or died. And she was never going to let them forget it. She passed the room with the stirrups and the bed and turned into the last corridor. And faced the huge blank empty space where the TARDIS had been.

Tegan blinked. But it was still not there. The breezeblocks had deceived her – how dare they? She turned angrily and stalked back down the corridor.

The Doctor shone the light from his sonic screwdriver into Adric's eyes.

'You don't remember anything?' he asked.

'No. Where did I get it?'

'If you mean the baby, Adric, 1950s Earth. And if we don't manage to land back in the exact spot at the exact moment you took it there's going to be a whole lot of trouble. A few days early and we risk having two identical children to explain and a possible hole in the space time vortex. A few days late and –'

'We end up arrested for kidnapping a newborn child.'

'Thank you, Nyssa,' said the Doctor. 'Spot on as usual.'

'But how long have I had this thing in me?' asked Adric, rubbing his neck.

'Who knows? It could have lain dormant for years.'

He felt a little guilty at the horrified look on the boy's face. He shouldn't take it out on him. After all, Venusian Karate could be a killer on muscle tissue.

'But I doubt it,' he continued. 'It had too much thirst for knowledge and growth to waste time. It could have come from anywhere. It knew enough about space travel to recognise what potential the TARDIS offered. It could have crossed galaxies looking for a mathematical mind advanced enough to cope with it hitching a lift.'

'How do I know it's gone?' said Adric, shaking his head as if trying to discern an extra component.

'Your neck hurts, yes?' said the Doctor.

'Yes.' Adric frowned.

'Then it's gone. A quantum mechanical programme that uses the electrical messaging system of the cerebral cortex to operate a biological organism? Curing a headache would be chicken feed.' He smiled, rather proud of himself.

'But why did it choose a human child?' asked Nyssa.

'Oh, the human mind is surprisingly well set up for quantum thought,' mused the Doctor. 'I give it only a few more thousand years before they start doing it voluntarily. Adric has spent enough time on Earth to earmark it as a destination. He just had to do a search for a hospital and land just before the technological revolution. Nineteen-fifty is as good a year as any.' The Doctor looked up at the monitor at the familiar yellow breezeblocks. 'Let's just hope we've got the right day.'

'I suppose we just assume it's gone from the child,' said Nyssa. She was looking down at the tiny bundle in her arms, which was gurgling in delight. The Doctor stopped and gave a sudden frown.

'Well,' he said slowly, 'I suppose we can't be entirely sure.'

An uneasy silence followed as all three of them took a closer look at the child.

'You'd know,' said Adric. 'It did that thing, that penetrating stare. You said you could feel it.'

The Doctor watched the clear, blue eyes.

'I don't know,' he said. 'It may well have learned to hide its intelligence. To protect itself.'

'Maybe we should have left it,' said Adric, still working on his neck.

The Doctor looked up at him in surprise.

'I liked not feeling pain.'

'You said you couldn't remember!' said Nyssa.

'Yes. Well, maybe not in me but in that.' He pointed at the baby.

'That, Adric, is someone's child,' the Doctor reminded him.

'It was evolving. You're always going on about preserving life. It was a new life form – and we stopped it.'

For once, the Doctor didn't have an answer. He could feel Nyssa staring at him and avoided her eyes by looking down again at the child. It was true – he had wanted to prevent the evolution of an artificially intelligent humanoid. That was right, wasn't it? Preserving the outcome of human history? But whatever evolved on Otho would be something else again – because of him. A cold spark ran through his mind. A fusion of artificial intelligence and biological organism had happened enough times before. And never with the best results.

The blue eyes fixed on his. The infant flexed a tiny hand. It caught his finger and held on gently.

Ward Sister Cannon hadn't panicked for ten years. It wasn't in her nature. But today looked like today was the day. She increased her stride down the corridor, stomach churning. Intensive care had been her first port of call – she hadn't counted on needing a second. Babies didn't just vanish. Not from her ward.

The room at the end of the corridor was dark but she burst through its doors, not sure what she was expecting. She frowned for a moment at the empty sterile bed and its cumbersome stirrups and marched back through the swing doors to raise the alarm.

Its appearance was so blatant at the end of the corridor, she almost walked past it. She stopped and stared at the large blue police box standing solidly in her way.

'Sister!'

The man approaching her down the corridor was the last person Cannon wanted to see. She put on her best not-now-I'm-terribly-busy-with-an-emergency look and then realised that was probably not the wisest choice in his case.

'How's my wife?'

He was breathless, eager, with the ragged, not-slept-in-a-week look of a new father.

'Oh, she's fine. Still sleeping off the pills. If you'd just excuse me –'

'I need to see my son.'

Cannon forced her impassive face into an uncharacteristic beaming smile. The man actually took a step back.

'Absolutely,' she said. 'Just take a seat in the waiting room and we'll have him with you shortly.'

'I've been waiting for hours,' he persisted, stepping forward again. 'I would like to see my wife and son.'

Cannon found herself nodding, her brain reaching out desperately for assistance. A police box was standing in her hospital. There was obviously a problem. Possibly with her mind.

* * *

161

'What do you mean, you can't remember which room?' The Doctor was keeping his voice down for obvious reasons but it was an effort.

'They all look the same.'

'That's because they're babies, Adric.'

'I mean the corridors. Here!'

Adric pushed open a door.

The Doctor followed with a desperate roll of his eyes, the infant clutched in his arms. An entire family looked up at him expectantly. He counted two grandparents, several aunts and uncles and one tired-looking mother with child. For a second, they all just stared at each other. Then the Doctor quickly backed out.

'Sorry,' he said lamely. 'You've already got one.'

The door shut on the scene.

'Adric – '

'I know, I know. This one!'

'Did it not have a tag or anything?' the Doctor said, examining its feet through the blankets.

'I don't think so,' said Adric. 'I don't remember, do I?'

The Doctor followed him into another room. An exhausted woman lay curled up in the bed next to an empty cot.

'This is it.'

'How do you know?'

'Well... she hasn't got a baby.'

The Doctor gave him a look.

'All right, I'm not sure. Should we wake her?'

'And ask her what, Adric? "Is this your baby? Because we see you don't have one and as we stole this one and can't remember where from –"'

'All right,' Adric said, moving away from him sulkily.

'I really think you could have been more careful. I mean, I know you were operating under the complex guidance of a superior intellect... but you didn't have to be this stupid –'

'It's definitely the right room,' said Adric, pouncing on the clipboard at the foot of the bed. 'I recognise the name.'

The Doctor gave him another look.

'No! I really do – this is it!'

The Doctor looked over at the woman in the bed, then down at the child, who seemed to be sleeping. He sighed and relinquished the bundle gently to the cot. The infant curled into the blankets, eyes closed, seemingly at peace with the world.

Tegan was standing, glaring at the TARDIS, when the Doctor and Adric almost crashed into her.

'There you are!' beamed the Doctor. 'We've been looking all over for you!'

She turned the glare in his direction, full beam.

'Oh, really? Did you think I'd left the planet all by myself?'

'What's that?' the Doctor said vaguely, making for the TARDIS door.

'I know what happened, Doctor,' she said as she followed him inside. She could see the guilt written all over Adric's face for a start.

'You took off without me. You didn't even realise I'd gone. You took off and only came back when it occurred to you I was missing.'

'Nonsense.'

'I saw you! I came back and you weren't here!' She didn't even look at Nyssa, who was doing her best to empathise but still managed to look entirely uninterested.

'How long did it take you to notice?' Tegan persisted. 'An hour? A year?!'

'Not everything is about you, Tegan,' said Adric irritably, rubbing his neck.

Tegan opened her mouth. She couldn't believe this – they weren't even sorry.

'Did you get the right mother?' asked Nyssa.

'Don't try and change the subject,' Tegan snapped. 'What mother?'

She could clearly see the shifty looks passing between the Doctor and Adric and she wasn't going to allow it.

'Of course,' Adric told Nyssa. 'It was easy. Recognised the name. Nailer... or Grayson or something.'

'Adric...' said the Doctor in a formidable tone, already punching in coordinates.

Something fired in Tegan's mind amidst the confusion.

'Grainger,' she said simply.

'That's it,' said Adric as the time rotor rose and fell.

The Doctor stared at her. She stared back. Nyssa looked over, tilting her head at a quizzical angle.

'How did you know?' asked Adric, impressed.

Tegan shut her mouth. That was always the way with this lot. Finding mystery in the least important, dullest details while all hell broke loose around them. She could have been abducted by an alien life form and they wouldn't have noticed. She gave them one last collective scowl and swept out of the console room to find a quiet corner and scream.

Kathleen Cannon felt lost in a haze of rising panic as they burst into the private room and straight into Mr Holland, ward specialist, standing over the cot.

'I can explain,' Cannon blurted, immediately wondering why she'd said this, as she had no explanation whatsoever.

'Well, I'd be surprised, because it's stumped me,' he said, stepping away from the cot, holding a small baby, unwrapped from its blankets and looking brightly up at the new faces.

A wave of relief spread through the ward sister. She almost laughed but just stopped herself.

Mr Holland handed the child to its mother, who was beaming and gazing at her husband with tears in her eyes.

'We'll have to monitor his progress, of course,' said Mr Holland. 'It may be several months, a year or two even, before we can properly give him the all clear. But I must say, I've never seen a recovery like it.'

Cannon stared from him to the infant.

'The stiffness is gone, the eyes are responsive, all normal reflexes are present and –'

The infant gurgled delightedly between its parents.

'No evident signs of distress.' Mr Holland laughed. 'It's quite incredible.'

It was a transformation. Cannon watched the wide, blue eyes gaze up at its mother. She remembered the hands rigid with spasm, the eyes that couldn't focus, the constant crying.

'Mr and Mrs Grainger,' Holland concluded. 'Somehow, you have a very healthy son.'

'John,' said Edward Grainger, as he clutched his wife's hand, his tearful face alive with joy. 'His name is John.'

Dear John

John Davies

*An Adventure of the Eighth Doctor,
with Samson and Gemma Griffin*

Thursday 17 May 1956

It laughed. It knew that was all they could hear. Well, all but one.

Bathed in a flickering orange glow, Edward chuckled. He never ceased to be amazed by how well Eleanor understood his taste in literature. Turning to the flyleaf of his forty-ninth birthday present, Edward read the inscription.

'To my darling Edward. May you always remain young at heart.'

He sighed. Another year gone. Edward hated birthdays, especially his own. So much to look back on and increasingly little to look forward to. He closed his eyes, realising that he was starting to sink into his annual malaise. It hadn't always been like this. He used to enjoy celebrating his birthdays, and to an outsider he hoped that he still appeared to. But ever since John had been born he –

A sharp explosion caused Edward to jolt and snap out of his reverie. Realising it had simply been a piece of coal shattering in the fireplace, Edward returned to his book. Setting himself the goal of reaching the end of the current chapter, he carried on reading. As he prepared to go to the next page, Edward stared at the bottom corner. It was quivering. As he continued to look, the page slowly lifted and started to roll itself over.

Rising to his feet, Edward threw the book to the floor, suddenly aware of a chill breeze circulating around the room. Instead of landing heavily, the book slowly glided down as though it were a feather. The sound of playful laughter came from somewhere nearby.

Sighing once again, Edward abandoned all thoughts of enjoying his novel.

'Oh, no. Not again!'

Disembodied, it was everywhere in the house. It saw every action, knew every deed.
Most importantly it knew the boy.

Saturday 23 June 1956

'Now, this is impressive!'

Gemma looked up at the main doors of the large, rambling house. The Doctor had insisted she and Samson dress in high society finest, although her brother looked particularly uncomfortable.

'I thought you'd appreciate it, Gemma,' said the Doctor.

She adjusted her dress. 'Impressive or not, Doctor, what are we doing here? You dress us up like this, whisk us to a country house and say very little.'

The Doctor simply handed over two pieces of card. Gemma and Samson took one each. Seeing each other's names inscribed on the faces, they swapped cards and read them.

'A fiftieth birthday party?' Samson's eyes sparkled. 'Free booze? Cool! Hey, Gemma – Mum would so like to be here!'

Gemma nodded her agreement. Their mother liked a drop or two. 'Er, Doctor,' she said, reading her card. 'Who's Edward Grainger?'

'You don't know?'

Gemma shook her head and the Doctor smiled.

'Excellent,' he said. 'Just as it should be.'

'Eh?' said Samson. He was tugging his necktie already. Gemma found it funny seeing her brother all dressed up. It didn't suit him.

'Never mind,' said the Doctor. 'Anyway, I'm not just here for Edward. I'm here to check up on someone. Somebody special.'

Without warning, the front doors opened inwards.

'You rang?' Samson smirked.

'That's just it,' Gemma said. 'We didn't. Those doors just opened themselves. What a cliché!'

The Doctor took a step forward. He studied the doorway for a brief moment, then stepped through into the house, motioning for his companions to follow him.

'Oh, come on,' said Gemma. 'Nothing ventured...'

Samson wasn't playing along.

'Nothing ventured...' she repeated, trying to urge her brother on.

'Nothing gained,' he said and made to follow the Doctor.

She had fled.

It scared her. It didn't like her, wanted her out of the way.

Moira pulled her knees up against her chest, arms wrapped tightly around them. She could see people's legs go past from her hiding place under the table. She felt safe here in her hiding place.

It couldn't get her here.

Why had he allowed himself to be talked into this?

No fuss, he had said, nothing grand. He should have known better. At least Eleanor had agreed for it to be staged today. She'd believed him when he'd claimed that he wanted this to happen the day before his birthday as Sundays were problematic for some people to get here and back.

Edward surveyed the crowded room. Friends, colleagues and family members, all here for his big day. There were faces he had not seen since Eleanor's elaborate Coronation party. James, Gerard, Elizabeth... and of course Ronald Tillyard. Bless him. Ronald was evidently as jubilant about this party as he was about his possible consulate appointment.

Edward knew he should be grateful, he knew he should be happy.

He sighed. At least with this out of the way, tomorrow he could relax.

The tables were laden with a wide variety of food and drink. He thought back to the War, and rationing – so far away and still so etched in his and everyone else's memories. While food had never been in short supply for him and Eleanor, he was acutely aware that there was enough food here to feed an East End family – even a street – for a month during the hostilities.

He shouldn't feel this way, he knew the entire picture, and yet...

A record playing on the gramophone snapped Edward back from his introspection. Brushing aside an involuntary shudder at seeing the machine, he frowned and gestured for the record to be changed. Who had brought that rock and roll abomination to his party? Sadly, he remembered that the record belonged to his son. He hoped that this music, just like his son's imaginary friend, would prove to be a temporary phenomenon.

John had been on Edward's mind a lot recently. It had been a quiet year for him in general terms, but the appearance of 'Teddy' had started to change that. Edward and Eleanor had hoped that John would have grown out of needing the crutch of some fictional friend by now. Yet both of them had heard him talking to his teddy bear in recent weeks. Even spending more time with him had not helped – John immediately brought Teddy into any situation. Anything that went missing, Teddy had hidden. Every time John was late for something, or was accused of something, it was all put down to Teddy. Even John's love of maths and science had been dismissed because Teddy just wanted to play.

Even after the things he had seen in his life, the sight of his son clinging to this delusion disturbed Edward tremendously. The family doctor had assured him it was all part of childhood and that he would grow out of it eventually. Edward knew, however, that they had to live through the here and now.

He looked at Ronald again, chatting away to Angus McCloud. And there was Moira – Ronald's daughter, Edward's god-daughter. She was hiding under one of the drinks tables, occasionally peering out to check that her daddy was still there. Why had she run away earlier on? Edward had only walked over to her while his son was showing off his latest toy. They'd always got along so well before. Did he look that scary at fifty?

The record changed and Edward noticed that a few of his guests were giving him concerned looks. A believer in duty over personal desires, Edward mentally dressed himself down and made an effort to circulate.

Gemma turned her invitation over in her hand. It showed her name, embossed in fancy print, next to the date. Nineteen-fifty-six. Travelling with the Doctor really took some getting used to. The Ice Caves of

Shabadabadon, alien planets, sentient trees so vast their branches spanned the stars – and now the twentieth century. Everyone here would be long dead before she was even born, Gemma realised. The past was more colourful than she'd expected; the smells and sounds more vivid.

She would keep her invitation as a souvenir, or as proof perhaps that she'd been here. She tried slipping it into the small handbag she'd found in the TARDIS's store rooms, but it missed the pocket and she dropped it.

'Clumsy!' Samson chided, making to catch the invitation for her. 'Hey, what the...'

Gemma couldn't believe it. The card had stopped falling in mid air. Slowly, it rose until it was once more in Gemma's palm.

The Doctor had observed the whole incident. 'Interesting.'

'Interesting?' said Gemma sarcastically. 'This place is haunted!'

'Maybe.' The Doctor reached a decision. 'You two go on through to the main party. Try not to get too noticed. I'm going to look up an old friend.'

Gemma wasn't prepared to let the issue go that easily. 'But things are happening here.'

'The door could have been on the latch,' the Doctor said, ticking explanations off with his fingers, 'the invitation could be explained by air currents. Nothing paranormal has been proved yet, Gemma. In any case, it's a big gathering. Ghosts tend to like working with small groups – fewer witnesses; more doubt. Either that or they don't exist at all and they're just examples of hysteria.'

'All right, Doctor. Just be careful.'

'I will be. You too.'

Gemma smiled. As the Doctor left them alone, Samson looked around and whistled in awe. 'How the other half live, eh?'

Gemma nudged him in the ribs. 'I don't know. I think our lives are pretty amazing at the moment.'

Her brother smiled. 'Yeah, I suppose they are. But just look at this place. It's so –'

'Typical,' Gemma interrupted. 'Here we are in 1956, with strange things going on and the Doctor acting all mysterious and you're about to talk about architecture and social issues!'

Seeing that she'd upset him, Gemma gently touched his shoulder.

'Come on,' she said.

'What?'

'Well, there's more than one spirit to enjoy here, you know. We are at a party.'

Samson grinned. 'Ah, yes! The party!'

John struggled with the knots in his kite string. Sitting down to get a better hold, he looked at his teddy bear. 'I know, Teddy. We should be able to make it fly really, really high today. I wish Moira could see. Why did she run away?'

Because you're my friend, John.

John laughed. 'I know you're my friend, Teddy. I still don't know why she went away, though. Anyway, I have to undo this so shush.'

Frowning, the boy worked hard. After a while he stopped and, with a smile, leapt to his feet. 'Done it! Well, are you ready, Teddy?'

Oh, yes!

'Goody!'

Holding his kite in the way his father had taught him, John started to run. After a good few yards, he felt the wind tugging at the kite. Running faster, the colourful kite rose and became fully airborne. Playing out in the gardens was much more fun than Daddy's boring party.

In his joy, John forgot to stop running. A sudden jerk on the ropes caught him unaware and his footing slipped. He saw the ground rushing toward him and cried out. This was going to hurt, unless...

Within mere inches of the grass John felt something unusual happen. Well, he'd used to find it unusual. Now he had come to expect it. His fall slowed down and when he eventually met with the ground it was with a soft bump.

Giggling, John sprang to his feet and dusted himself down. It was only when he saw he was using two hands that he realised his kite must have flown away. Frantically searching the sky, John yelped as he saw the kite skipping in the air, the ropes and handles just out of his grasp.

Without a second though, John picked up his bear and sprinted after the kite.

'You haven't seen a little girl, have you? Seven years old?'

A straight-backed woman in a long, flowing gown had suddenly appeared next to Gemma and Samson.

As Samson started to fumble for words, Gemma realised that the newcomer was making her brother feel slightly intimidated. Having heard the warmth in the way the woman had spoken, Gemma smiled. 'No. We've only just arrived.'

'Do I know you?' the woman asked.

Gemma held her invitation up for inspection, recalling a phrase that had helped them out in the past. 'We're friends of the Doctor.'

'The doctor?' The woman studied the invitation. 'Well, with all the hard work he's been putting in with my son lately, any friend of the doctor is a friend of mine. I'm Eleanor Grainger. Please help yourself to drinks. I must look for Moira and then return to the other guests.'

As Eleanor glided away, Gemma saw her brother visibly relax. 'You're pathetic,' she joked. 'An attractive woman and you go all weak at the knees.'

'Give over,' said Samson, looking embarrassed. 'She's forty if she's a day.'

'Well, that must be Edward Grainger.' Gemma pointed across the crowded, smoke-infested room at a middle-aged man standing next to Eleanor. Simply from their body language, Gemma could tell they were a couple. 'Eleanor's presumably his wife.'

'And this is his birthday party?'

'I guess so.'

Samson snorted. 'Perhaps someone should remind him that the word happy often precedes birthday, then.'

Gemma knew what her brother meant. Something was clearly wrong with Edward. She noticed people exchanging knowing looks and nodding towards their host. Two guests pulled sour faces and then immediately returned to beaming smiles. Passing furtive comments about someone's mood was perfectly acceptable, it seemed, but to not present the air of enjoying the event would be churlish and socially reprehensible.

'Who do you think he is?' said Samson. 'An old friend of the Doctor's?'

'Dunno. Must be, I suppose. It's odd that the Doctor wanted to come here, and then as soon as we arrive he vanishes.' It was painfully obvious that Edward was noticing his guests and overhearing their comments. Gemma found herself warming to the man as he visibly tried to make efforts to cheer up. However, every attempt failed. Gemma saw the man becoming more and more removed from his own party. He was also chain smoking. Gemma remembered her time as smoker. She shuddered. Never again.

Samson tutted. He'd finished a glass of wine and couldn't see anyone walking around with a tray. Gemma offered to get him another drink as she knew her journey would take her past Edward. Close up, the falseness of his smile was even more apparent. His eyes were dead. Eleanor had clearly noticed this as well, and whispered something in her husband's ear. Gemma paused to watch as Edward tried again to place a smile on his face.

Little wonder he was having a hard time, thought Gemma as she made her way back to Samson. One day she would be staring the big five-oh in the face too.

John ran with his bear clutched tightly to his chest. Although the wind caused his eyes to water, he was not going to let his special kite get away.

A sudden thud caused him to cry out and drop his teddy bear.

It saw the person John had run into.

It remembered him.

Dazed, John looked up and saw a tall man with long, straggly hair. He was wearing a lengthy, green coat. John stood up quickly.

'Er, do you mind?' asked the man.

John realised he was standing on the man's feet and jumped back. 'I – I'm sorry. I was trying to catch my –'

The man smiled. 'Kite?'

The boy nodded. 'How did you know that?'

'Because I caught it for you!' The man brought his right arm from behind his back, the kite in his hand.

'Thank you! Thank you so much, er...'

Handing the kite back to John, the man knelt down. 'I'm the Doctor. I'm so pleased to meet you.' He saw the fallen teddy bear and picked it up. 'Both of you. Who do we have here, then?'

'That's Teddy. He's my friend.'

'Most boys' bears are.'

'He's special. More special than Moira. She ran off.'

The Doctor looked intrigued. 'Moira?'

'A girl.'

'Ah, yes. Moira. Girls, eh? Now, Teddy. Does he talk to you?'

'Oh, yes! All the time,' said John.

The Doctor smiled. 'I thought he might.'

'Really?'

'Oh, yes. There's certainly a presence here. This is no ordinary teddy bear.'

John felt himself trusting the Doctor. 'I can tell you, can't I?'

'You can tell me anything, John.'

'I don't think it's Teddy talking, really. Not really, really.'

'Really?'

'No, that would be silly, wouldn't it? It's my friend that I thought had gone away. He left me and now he's come back.'

'Why would a friend leave you?'

'I don't know,' said John. 'He said he was tired, had to go somewhere. I'm glad he's back though. I missed him. But I call him Teddy and talk to my Teddy 'cos he's always been here. He's as old as I am.'

'And how old is that?' asked the Doctor.

'Six.'

The Doctor whistled. 'I see. That old, eh?'

John giggled. 'I'm John.'

'I know.'

'How can you know? I've only just told you. You're funny. Would you like to play, Doctor?'

The Doctor looked as though he was about to say no. Sticking his bottom lip out, John shuffled his feet in the grass, glancing down.

The Doctor laughed. 'Of course! I'd love to play!'

'Whoopee!'

Gemma groaned as Samson told the same joke for a third time.

He waved his hand expansively, a wide grin on his face. 'Then how does the ceiling stay up?' He laughed uncontrollably, oblivious to the fact that yet another recipient of the punch line had not only failed to understand it but also had now sidled away with a concerned glance. He swayed slightly, finishing his drink, then placed his empty glass on a nearby ledge. 'Oh, come on!' he said, attempting to unfasten the top button of his dress shirt. 'What's wrong with this thing?'

He was failing miserably in his attempt to free the button, instead succeeding only in jabbing himself in the throat. He coughed, attempting a nonchalant expression. Then he suddenly quivered. Grabbing his sister's arm, he moved closer for a conspiratorial whisper and then shouted, 'Is it me or is it getting cold in here?'

Gemma shook her brother free from her arm, his drunkenness nothing new and not at all surprising. 'It's cold, yes. But these old houses –' She gasped and spun round, spilling her drink. 'I don't believe it!'

'Neither do I!' Samson laughed. 'What a waste of booze!'

Gemma gave her brother a withering stare. 'Not that. Someone's just barged past me!'

Samson shrugged, uninterested.

'Hang on a minute,' said Gemma. 'We're up against the wall. There's no one behind us. Who on Earth was it?'

Samson again attempted his nonchalant expression, but he was clearly as spooked as she was.

'Oh, thanks for nothing!' said Gemma, noticing Samson's glass. 'I never saw you get another drink.'

Samson looked at his sister as though she had just won the annual village idiot contest. 'What are you talking about?'

'Someone's refilled you.'

'Well, no one came round.' Samson looked confused.

Gemma arched an eyebrow. 'Another bizarre event. This place gets stranger.'

'Stranger Grainger!' exclaimed Samson, downing his drink in one. 'I like this party!'

It liked the Doctor. It knew the Doctor. However, this was different. The Doctor was poaching.

It saw it all, its patience sorely tested. It should be the one playing.

It witnessed the Doctor and John having fun together, the shadows of the trees shifting across the grass as the afternoon wore on.

It was glad that John was ecstatic, and yet it still felt a level of resentment. Tag had followed makeshift cricket, leapfrog after I-spy. Now, John was high in the air, clinging to the Doctor's back as his new friend –

New friend?

– gave him a jogging piggyback ride. Held firmly in John's right hand, the bear jostled and bounced with the strides taken.

It was pleased. At least John was keeping him safe.

During the course of their play, the Doctor asked John about his friend.

The friend listened.

John told the Doctor that his friend had first said hello again when he was out with his parents about a month ago. John had been glad for two reasons. Firstly, he was still missing him and, secondly, he was very, very bored. He had been talking to his bear, and a voice spoke back.

It smiled as John said he had not been scared.

John had known right away that it was his friend from before because he was so much fun. Being a special friend, he could be in two places or more at the same time, and while still talking to John his friend had made a girl scream by tugging at her pigtails. As the girl looked around, puzzled, John had laughed, causing his parents to usher him away in their embarrassment.

John paused. Fixing the Doctor with an earnest stare, he asked how the Doctor could sense Teddy when no one else could.

The Doctor explained that he wasn't like other people. When John didn't change his expression, the Doctor went on to say that this was because in many ways he had never truly grown up. He could still see the world through the eyes of a child.

John had chuckled, saying that it must be fun being such an adult, not one of those dull, stuffy ones. Agreeing, the Doctor said that John must be special as well, being the only one that Teddy let hear him.

Blushing, John said that he was not that special really and that Teddy did let others know he was there, usually by laughing.

With the sunlight fading, John was still on the Doctor's back.

'Are you all right up there?' the Doctor asked.

'Yes!' John shouted. 'Faster! Faster!'

'Okay. You asked for it.'

John felt the Doctor increase his speed and shrieked with delight. 'Teddy likes you, Doctor!'

'Good! I like Teddy.'

'But...'

'But what?'

The Entity had had enough. It was John's friend, not the Doctor.

It had got rid of one other friend. It was time to do the same again.

As they got near a pond, John felt something slam into them and the Doctor buckled. John was sent sprawling toward the cold water.

Gemma accepted a crust-cut sandwich from a passing waiter and looked back over at Edward. A servant had sidled over to him and was whispering something in his ear. Although she couldn't hear the exchange, she could tell from Edward's sudden look of alarm that it was serious.

Gemma watched as Edward lit yet another cigarette, delivered a series of polite excuses and left the party.

As he crossed the gardens, Edward could see his son and a strange man by the pond. They'd both fallen over, but were giggling with each other.

'I fall over a lot,' John was saying as Edward approached. 'Teddy never lets anything hurt me, though.'

'I'm relieved to hear it,' the stranger said.

'But I'm not tired!' John suddenly protested. 'I don't want to have a sleep.'

The stranger noticed Edward. 'Now, that's interesting.'

Edward knelt by John, who hadn't seen him approach, and checked that he wasn't hurt. 'What's interesting?' he then asked the stranger. 'What happened? And who exactly are you?'

'He's my friend,' said John. He grinned at the stranger, who returned the smile.

'Thank you, John,' the stranger said. 'Edward, it's fine. I lost my footing but he's okay. As for who I am, let's just say I'm a friend of the family. Hello and happy birthday, if I'm not too early.'

Must be some friend of Eleanor's, thought Edward. It was his birthday party and he didn't know half the guests. 'Yes, well,' he said, standing up. 'Everyone else is inside if you'd care to join us. I think they're having a good time.'

He held out his hand to pull John back to his feet, but his son first picked up his teddy bear.

Gemma stood alone against the wall, making sure there was no room behind her. Her brother had gone off in search of another round of drinks. Gemma sighed, imagining some poor woman having to put up with Samson trying out some of his underwhelming chat-up lines.

Recalling the Doctor's advice that they should strive to avoid getting too noticed, and also in real need of a drink, Gemma broke away from the wall. As she walked through a less densely packed part of the room, she saw a man topple forward as though struck from behind. Although he fell to his knees, he quickly stood again.

'Ronald, are you all right, man?' asked someone close by, concerned for his friend. Ronald clearly didn't want a fuss, shrugging as though his fall was an accident. However, to Gemma's eyes, his expression betrayed that he was lying.

What on Earth was going on here?

Then, as Ronald was trying to tell his companions that he was all right, Gemma saw a young girl dash from under a table and make directly for him. He was hit at waist height again and flinched as before.

'Moira!' said Ronald, suddenly angry. 'It was you, wasn't it?' He saw how upset she was and knelt down to talk to her calmly. He thinks it was her the first time, Gemma realised. He thinks she must have pushed him a minute ago and then snuck out of sight before he got up.

But Gemma had seen her run from under the table *after* Ronald's first fall.

★ ★ ★

John sat on his bed and hugged his bear. 'You are naughty, Teddy!'

Sarah settled down at her dresser to enjoy some well-earned rest from serving the people in the party. She was startled when her hairbrush trembled and then flew across the room, hitting the wall opposite.

Charles tried several times to turn off the car's ignition, but every time he made to leave the vehicle it sprang back into life. The chauffer frowned but carried on in vain.

John hugged his bear. 'What do you mean? There's more?!'

'Oh, Samson!'

Gemma found her brother lying horizontally on the full length of a chaise longue. He had clearly drunk way too much. Thankfully, the room was so crowded that her brother's current state appeared to have gone unnoticed.

'Well, he certainly threw himself into the thick of it.'

Gemma whirled around. 'Doctor! Where have you been?'

'Here and there,' he said. 'Enjoying yourself, Gemma?'

'There's something strange going on.'

'I thought there might be.'

Gemma brought the Doctor up to speed with events in the party hall. The Doctor listened with great interest as she explained that Edward was looking miserable and that the guests were actively commenting upon it. When Gemma began to relay the incident of someone, or something, brushing past her, the Doctor immediately became concerned. Gemma assured him she was okay, which was more than could be said for Samson, whose glass had seemingly refilled itself time and time again. Gemma laughed, commenting that her brother never could say no to free booze.

'And?' the Doctor asked.

It always amazed Gemma that the Doctor clearly knew her well enough to guess her story hadn't finished. 'Well, a friend of Edward's had an accident. He's left now because his daughter, Moira I think, became hysterical... but it just didn't look natural.'

'What do you mean?'

'He looked as though he'd been pushed, but there was no one anywhere near him.'

The Doctor looked around the room. 'I know that feeling. Gemma, I have a suspicion that things are only just –' He stopped at the sound of a low, resonant chuckle in the air.

'I think you might be right there, Doctor. Shall I wake Samson?'

The Doctor shook his head. 'No. I think we need clear heads at the moment.'

Gemma glanced toward the hallway entrance. 'Oh, Mr Happy's back.'

Edward was rejoining the party, evidently trying to sneak in unnoticed. Gemma felt a pang of sympathy as he was immediately cornered and forced into small talk. By the expression on his face, it looked as though he had been brought up to date with some events himself.

The entity looked at John's sleeping form.

It toyed with the idea of waking him to play some more but it knew that would be unfair on him.

He was young and needed his sleep.

It tried to be patient but the need to have fun fuelled its very being. Especially today.

It reached a decision.

Gemma recoiled as, without warning, the entire room exploded with activity. The air started to shimmer. Plates, tureens and cutlery trembled and levitated from the over-stocked tables and flew through the air. A serving tray struck one dumbstruck guest and he fell, his body slamming into a hostess trolley. Everyone screamed and sought to find refuge under tables and chairs, and behind bookcases – but these were soon upturned by severe winds.

Edward stood alone, staring aghast at the mêlée. Gemma guessed that he was trying to locate Eleanor.

Everywhere, the sound of laughter echoed and reverberated. Instinctively concerned for her brother, Gemma glanced over at the recliner. Samson was still asleep, completely oblivious to the food that had whipped across the room and had stained his suit.

'Everybody leave this room!' the Doctor yelled. 'The party's over!'

Gemma looked around as the Doctor's words sank home. A confused, scared and hysterical gaggle started to stream towards the hall. They ran on instinct, debris and artefacts still crisscrossing their paths. Having found Eleanor, Edward clung onto her, terrified but resolute. He was talking, but his words were inaudible.

Gemma saw Eleanor shake her head – Edward was clearly trying to send his wife away to safety. Concentrating, she lip-read his next attempt. It was one word. John.

As Eleanor nodded and ran from the room, Gemma turned to the Doctor. His hair was being blown in all directions, his frock coat billowing out, but he remained stoic in the midst of the raging hurricane.

A sudden movement in her eyeline forced Gemma to turn around again. Edward had slammed his palms against his forehead. He was clearly distressed and shaking. Gemma rushed over and helped him sit down. 'Mr Grainger! Are you okay?' Edward nodded, but Gemma could see he was anything but okay. 'You should leave,' she said.

Edward looked her directly in the eye. 'I want to,' he said. 'Yet I don't seem able to. I feel I... I feel I should be here!' He placed his head in his hands and started rocking in the chair.

Gemma rose to her feet. 'Doctor! You have to do something!'

The Entity surveyed the scene, relishing it. Looking at Edward's trembling frame, it remembered something. Something old. It knew what it had to do next. It was time to give the Doctor a push.

'It's some kind of force, Gemma. Some entity given life.'

'Like a ghost?' Gemma shouted.

'In a way. We need to find out what it wants.' The Doctor paced around the room, somehow managing to avoid any flying projectiles. He was giving a very good impression of being in charge of each and every thought. The gramophone started to wind down, the exaggerated drawl bringing the Doctor back from whatever reverie he had been in. 'Oh, will you please shut up!' he yelled, and then immediately started grinning. 'I know what it wants!'

'What does it want?' Gemma called over the sound of the gale.

'It wants to speak. Gemma, it's trying to communicate! But how? How can we get it audible? How, how, how? I, for one, want to hear more than an eerie chortle. A-ha! I have an idea!'

The Entity saw realisation dawn in the Doctor and chuckled to itself. Sometimes the past was a good place to visit.

The Doctor crossed over to the gramophone player and started flicking through the records piled up next to it. After a few non-commital shrugs, he stopped at one and shook his head. 'George Formby?'

'Is this really the time for another record?' shouted Gemma. 'And, anyway, who's George Formby?'

'No, this isn't for music, Gemma. As for your other question... Well, briefly, he was a popular entertainer from Lancashire. Born in 1904. Real name was George Booth. Played a mean ukulele. Quite risqué for his day. I've got most of his stuff back at the TARDIS if you want to brush up on early twentieth-century innuendo later on. But, that's not important right now.'

Good, thought Gemma. I get my fill of innuendo from Samson. Glancing back at Edward, she was concerned to see him transfixed by the Doctor and what he was doing, a look of dread on his face.

The Doctor was winding up the gramophone. As he lowered the playing arm and the heavy needle connected with the vinyl a series of cracks and pops filled the air. However, the music didn't start to play – just white noise.

The Doctor backed away from the revolving disc. 'Is that of any help?' he called to no one in particular.

'He-he! Yes, Doctor. Thank you.' The voice was coming from the gramophone's horn, booming over the noise of the wind and the flying books and plates.

'Is that ...?'

'George Formby?' said the Doctor. 'Yes, Gemma, it is. This entity is clearly able to use the vocal imprints within the recording. Very, very impressive.'

Gemma felt the presence of someone nearby. Glancing round, she saw Edward next to her.

'Young lady,' he said. 'What is going on?'

Gemma shrugged. 'I've no idea, Mr Grainger.'

Edward was staring at the gramophone. 'Please, call me Edward. Or Eddie. I... I... remember...'

Gemma frowned. 'What do you remember, Edward?'

'I remember Helen... That machine... and what it did. What I was told to do...'

'Helen?' Gemma asked, but Edward was clearly reliving something...

'Want some fun, Edward?'

Eddie nodded.

'Break that record. Smash it. Take it up to your room and drop it out of the window and then gather the bits up and place them in three different dustbins down the street, there's a good boy.'

Like any five-year-old given the chance to destroy something, Eddie was at the door in a second...

Gemma touched Edward lightly on the shoulder, and he jolted. 'I... I'm sorry,' he said.

'Are you okay?'

Edward nodded. Gemma turned back to the Doctor, who had started speaking.

'You now have a full voice,' the Doctor said, calling across the room. 'Tell me, one on one, what do you want here?'

'To play,' said the entity. 'To be with John. I'm his friend.'

'I think you're more than that.'

The entity chuckled. 'I don't know what you mean.'

'Oh, I think you do.' The Doctor's tone became darker. 'How can you say you just want to play? People have been injured here tonight.'

'I know. I'm sorry.'

'Sorry?'

'Sometimes I forget how powerful I am in this form. It... wasn't... like... this... when... I... was... like... yoooooooooou.'

The Doctor ran over to the gramophone and cranked up the handle again. The record started to spin once more.

'What does this... thing... mean?' said Edward. 'It was once like us?'

'At this precise moment I'm not entirely sure, Edward. However, I intend to find out so, please, if you don't mind, a little bit of silence.'

Edward flinched, clearly unused to being spoken to in this manner, especially in his own home. However, he didn't ask anything further.

Cranking the handle one more time, the Doctor addressed the room. 'You were once corporeal?'

The voice came again, slightly too fast at first but then slowing down to its natural pace and rhythm. 'Oh, yes. Actually, I still am.'

'Who are you?'

The voice laughed. 'I like this game. I see the confusion in your mind.'

'Can you also see that I want you to leave? You've distressed enough people here tonight.'

'But it was only meant as fun, Doctor. These are John's formative years, but also his time of freedom. I want him to play, to enjoy life.'

'Like Moira was fun?' The Doctor paused – expecting a reaction, Gemma guessed. The gramophone, however, was just playing background hiss. 'That was you, wasn't it?' the Doctor continued. 'She sensed you. As a child, she knew you!'

Edward looked stunned. 'This thing is what terrified my god-daughter?'

'Yes,' said the entity. 'She intruded. She encroached.'

'I thought so,' said the Doctor. 'So, it was fun to terrify her? It was fun this afternoon when John nearly fell into the pond?'

Gemma sensed Edward tense, and gently offered him her hand to hold. While he clearly found the gesture surprising, he didn't decline. Gemma winced as Edward clutched her hand tight.

The voice became stern. 'I would never harm him! He is everything to me.'

'Never harm him?' The Doctor laughed hollowly. 'Can't you see that it's because of you that he came close to dying? He could have drowned! You were jealous, jealous of the time John and I were spending together, and you pushed me. You care so much – too much. You have no foresight as to what could happen with your games.'

'I put John in danger?'

'Yes.'

The voice lowered its tone, emotion clearly making it an effort to speak. 'I would never...'

'We know. You've played that, er, record... Can't you just go? Leave him alone.'

The wind gradually calmed, and the room fell silent.

'I will be leaving him shortly anyway,' said the entity.

'What do you mean?' asked the Doctor.

'I am dying.'

'How can you die? You're ethereal!'

'Even ethereal beings perish eventually, Doctor. However, I won't go alone.'

'What do you mean by that?'

'When I die I will take John with me to keep me company as I have kept him company.'

'You can't!'

'If I can't play with John, nobody will!'

'No!' shouted Edward. 'I will not allow it!' He let go of Gemma's hand and bolted from the room. Gemma wanted to follow, but knew there was nothing she could do. She became aware that the room had fallen silent again. The Doctor was stood still, his face unreadable.

'What are you?' he said calmly. 'A playful sprite or some sort of over-protective guardian angel?'

'I am close to that, Doctor, yes.'

With the entity's words still resounding in his ears, Edward raced through the house. He reached his son's room and, panting for breath, wrenched the door open. Eleanor was there, wide-eyed, terrified and reaching forwards – although seemingly unable to move an inch.

Although John was sat still in bed, his knees to his chin, that was the only still point in the room. A savage wind tore through the air, all lose and unsecured items at its mercy. The curtains flapped around like flags in a raging tempest. Only the heavy steel rings kept them secured to the rail, the sound of metal on metal competing with the cacophony of falling and swirling objects. The prevalent sound, however, was that of playful laughter sliced through with the wracked sobs of a terrified John Grainger.

'We're here, John!' shouted Eleanor. 'I promise, I won't let anyone harm you!'

'You are my life,' said Edward.

John wiped the back of his hand under his nose. 'That's what Teddy keeps saying, Daddy!'

'But I'm not Teddy! I'm your father!'

The Doctor fell into a chair. 'Of course! It's so obvious!' The voice didn't respond and the Doctor looked around. 'Is that it?

Gemma coughed and gestured toward the gramophone. It had stopped again. The Doctor started to rise, but Gemma shook her head and moved over to it herself. Having seen the Doctor operate the machine earlier she copied his actions and soon the record was spinning again.

However, all that came out of the horn was hiss and crackles.

'Doctor, why is it not working?'

'I don't know, Gemma,' the Doctor confessed. 'But I can't believe that this is it.'

'It isn't, Doctor.'

Gemma swivelled in the direction of the new sound. On the lounger, Samson had sat up and was fixing the Doctor with a mischievous stare.

'It's rather vulgar, I know,' he said, 'but I thought that this would save a lot of time.'

Gemma started to march towards her brother. 'You were awake? Now look here, Samson, this isn't funny –'

The Doctor grabbed her by the arm, his expression concerned. 'That isn't Samson, Gemma.'

'You mean...'

The Doctor nodded. 'I'm afraid so.'

Gemma felt her stomach churn. 'It's using Samson? That's sick!'

'He won't remember,' whispered the Doctor. 'I promise you.'

Yeah, she thought. But I will.

'Now,' said the entity through Samson's body. 'Where were we?'

'I think I'd just realised who you are,' said the Doctor. 'Nice trip down memory lane with the gramophone, there. Hello, Edward.'

Gemma was confused. 'Edward?'

'Yes,' said the entity. 'I am Edward Grainger. Or should that be Teddy? That's what John calls me. Oh, John. I tell him lots of secrets. John knows me better now than he ever will in the future. In this form I know me, him and you – yes, you, Doctor. I see it all free of the flesh.'

Gemma mentally shook herself. 'How can you be Edward? You're a spirit, a ghost. He's still alive.'

'I'm not a ghost. Part of Edward is dying. Twelve months of him are fading into history. I am part of that which is passing through.'

The Doctor leapt to his feet. 'I understand!' he said. 'There aren't two Edwards here, just one – but splintered somehow! You, all playful, and Edward... Well, everyone has commented on how down he is at the moment. You are the embodiment of Edward's *joie de vivre!*'

'Nearly, Doctor. I am an embodiment, as you say, but only of Edward's... what did you say? *Joie de vivre?* Heh-heh! I like that. I am Edward's *joie de vivre* from his fiftieth year. At midnight, I will join my previous 49. Joy and pain will merge again and go on. That is the way with humanity.'

'I never knew...'

'Even *you* can't know everything, Doctor.' Gemma heard the entity almost taunting the Doctor.

'How are you able to interact with things physically? Has it always been this way?'

'Oh, no, indeed not,' the entity said. 'I have been able to make my presence felt before but never like this. It's the half century that's generated enough power for me to be this effective. My essence has been stronger these last six years –'

'Ever since John was born.'

'I do not want this time to end,' the entity continued. 'I will never see John again. Not like this.'

'But he will remember you.'

'Not like this he won't. He will age and his mind will close. The memory will fade. In time, as he grows older, he will forget ever having had an imaginary friend at all.'

'But you will still be there. You will carry on through Edward.'

'But not this Edward! I am dying, Doctor! I will never see my beloved son again! I have a few brief minutes left. You, oh, you... I sense things in you... I recognise things...'

'Well, I have met Edward before.'

'Enough!' Even speaking someone else's words, Samson's body language was his: he clenched his fists as he always did when frustrated. 'My time is short; you have centuries ahead of you. I must be with my son more fully!'

'You're already there.'

'The dried-up miserable side of me? John needs *me*, this me. He's young, he's –'

'Probably terrified.'

The entity paused – a look of shock on Samson's face. 'What?'

'You're scaring him,' said the Doctor gently. 'Is that the sign of a good father?'

'How would you know anything about that?'

'I know lots of things, but primarily I know you must let go. You must accept your fate, your destiny. John will live on... and so will you... but both will change. It's nature.'

'I cannot accept this!'

'You must!'

'No!' Edward's splintered spirit flexed its mind again. As the noise of clattering tureens and cutlery ricocheted everywhere, an unearthly howl shrieked through the air.

The Doctor turned to Gemma, almost shouting over the noise. 'This is where things get serious. It's grieving!'

'It's what?'

'It's embracing its loss, Gemma. It now knows and, more dangerously, accepts its fate. Playtime is over. Can't you sense it? It no longer cares. Why should it? Why should we live to see his son if he can't?' Quietly, the Doctor added, 'I just hope I've kept it talking long enough to prevent any real harm.'

In John's room, Edward was still battling to reach Eleanor and John, each step forward rewarded by a gust of wind that sent him two steps back. Resolute, Edward fixed his sight on his son and fought against the maelstrom. He would not let John go!

Gemma watched as the Doctor turned back to Samson, her skin still crawling at what this entity was doing to her brother.

'He will still love you, Edward!' said the Doctor.

'Will he?'

'Of course he will! Maybe not consciously, but deep down he *will* remember you. He loves you. You are his father. This is not an end; it's a beginning. His. Let it and him go!'

The clock on the wall started to chime the impending arrival of midnight.

'It seems I have no choice, Doctor. My time is up.'

'But not John's. Your son is in good hands!'

'Whose?'

'Yours!'

Midnight struck and Gemma winced as Samson collapsed back onto the lounger, unconscious.

The wind dropped, and Edward took full advantage of the opportunity to rush to John. Eleanor, freed from whatever had held her back, collapsed on the bed with them, hugging tight.

Gemma ran over to the lounger, and shook Samson awake.

'Eh? What did I miss?' he asked, groggy and disorientated.

'You really don't want to know!' she assured him, surprising her brother by giving him the biggest hug he had ever had in his life.

The Doctor strode over to the gramophone, which was winding down.

'T-h-an-k y-o-u,' it drawled one last time before coming to rest.

'You're welcome, young man,' the Doctor said. 'Turned out nice again.'

Sunday 24 June 1956

Gemma had been amazed when the Doctor hadn't immediately shepherded them back to the TARDIS. For once he hadn't been in a rush to leave. He'd simply asked Gemma and Samson to look after any straggling guests and then vanished.

Gemma saw him again in the grounds of the house the next day and quickly rushed to find Samson. When they returned to where she had seen him, the Doctor was clearly enjoying himself. On a child's swing, he had achieved a good pace and rhythm. With his coat tails flapping around the wooden seat, his face beamed with sheer, unadulterated delight. 'Nothing ventured, eh?' he called.

Samson smiled at Gemma, and together they made their way over to the Doctor, both sitting down on a swing either side of their friend.

'Well?' he asked.

Gemma tried to focus on the Doctor but he was travelling through the air so fast that she became slightly nauseous. Looking straight ahead she said, 'They're safe. In denial and on their way home.'

'Good, good. How's the hangover, Samson?'

'Fine, thanks, Skipper,' he said. 'Don't feel a thing.' Gemma could tell he was lying.

'Doctor?' she asked, a twinkle in her eye. 'Aren't you a little old to be playing on swings?'

In an abrupt series of motions, the Doctor used the soles of his shoes to bring the swing to a quivering halt. 'Nonsense! You're never too old to feel young!'

The Doctor kick-started his swing once again.

They thought it was gone.

It was.

Nearly.

It, looking over everything, had to be sure.

The sound of his son crying out woke Edward from his sleep. He had not slept much that night. He'd spent most of it talking to the man who had taken charge when all hell had broken lose, the rest reading the A. A. Milne compendium Eleanor had bought for him last year and keeping a watch over John.

Lifting his son out of bed, Edward let the boy cling around his shoulders and crossed over to the window.

'Daddy?'

'Yes, son?'

'I won't miss Teddy.'

'Why?'

'Because he's still here, isn't he?'

Edward did not reply, but John clung on tighter none the less.

Out of the window, they could see the Doctor and his two friends on his swings.

'Daddy?'

Edward brought his son's face closer and looked him fondly in the eye. 'Yes?'

'I never want to grow old. I want to stay like this forever and ever and ever. Just like him.'

Confused and momentarily concerned, Edward asked John what he meant. His son pointed out of the window. Following the direction of John's gesture, Edward saw and smiled.

'Ah, yes. Like him.' Edward ruffled his son's hair and realised how at ease he was feeling. 'You'll always be young to me, son.'

Edward saw John smile and decided to put him back to bed. Teddy sat there. Still. Silent.

Slowly, it fell sideways and slipped to the floor.

Checkpoint

Stel Pavlou

An Adventure of the Fourth Doctor.
with Romanadvoratrelundar

Wednesday 10 October 1962. West Berlin.

Stempfer was late.

Edward Grainger stood on the western edge of Checkpoint Charlie, a steaming cup of strong coffee from the guard hut clutched in one hand. It was a welcome relief from the bite of the cold night air. He could feel it in his knee the most. A chilling damp that penetrated right to the bone. He was 56 years old. There had to be more to life than this.

He had grown to despise Berlin. Had he any good memories of this place? And now that the Wall had come down like a surgeon's knife through gangrened flesh he wondered if the patient would ever recover.

Grainger paced agitatedly. He checked his watch again.

Eleanor would be playing canasta right now.

All he had for company was the glare of East German searchlights sweeping down the lengths of miserable cement.

How did anybody have the courage to make a break for it through that lot? For goodness's sake, just getting close to the wall was a miracle in itself. All Stempfer had to do was slip up once and the Stasi would know everything. In East Germany, one civilian in fifty was a Stasi informant. One casual remark to the wrong person.

That's all it took.

Perhaps he'd aborted? Perhaps. It was better than reporting back to London that they'd lost another spy. The paperwork was a wretched inconvenience.

Grainger pulled his collar up tight around his neck when a policeman came striding purposefully from the hut. His German was clipped but hopeful. They'd spotted movement on the other side.

He strained to see. It was so dark. Two Volks Polizei appeared to have cornered a man and were directing him to a document check. The man fumbled for his papers in the deep pockets of a long overcoat. Grainger couldn't see his face. He had a hat pulled right down over it.

'Is that him?' the policeman asked with apprehension.

Grainger replied honestly. 'I don't know.'

He'd never met Stempfer. He was just a name pencilled into a notebook given to him by Control.

They'd insisted Stempfer be handed off to a new, far more experienced handler. The information he'd been relaying was too explosive to be worked by a junior – so they sent Grainger, 11 years past mandatory retirement age for fieldwork. Currently just a glorified office boy who'd been promised that, at his age, he could twiddle his thumbs to his pension.

Eleanor was right. Her Majesty's Secret Service. Liars, the lot of them. All this cloak-and-dagger nonsense was young man's sport.

The lone figure stepped out of the hut on the other side. Tucking his papers away, he tipped his hat to the East German crossing guards and strolled across the divide in a frigid cloud of his own breath, as though he'd just enjoyed a rather fine meal and needed to stretch his legs for a bit.

Grainger plonked his cup back down inside the hut, just in case, and readied himself for the long debrief ahead. Was this really him? He stepped up to the simple white line painted on the road.

The approaching figure threw the dangling end of a long scarf over his shoulder. As the light hit his face, Grainger was struck instantly by the familiarity of it. Wide, lively eyes and teeth like tombstones, crammed inside a grinning mouth.

'Good grief...'

He looked just like George Tremayne, back during the Berlin airlift. All that business with the peculiar bricked-up house. It was all so fresh in his mind. But that had to be ten, 15 years ago. It couldn't be Tremayne. Tremayne was dead.

'Well...' the approaching man announced mischievously. 'How did I know it was going to be you?'

Grainger took a moment to formulate his response, but events started to run quicker than his wits.

Across the divide a telephone began to ring in the distance. The Volks Polizei hurriedly took the call, then immediately began arguing over its implications.

Suddenly, a glaring searchlight bore down on the man in the scarf and hat. An order, in barked German, came for him to stop and return to the checkpoint.

The man cocked his head, as though thinking it over. At precisely what moment he decided that the line painted at Grainger's feet was simply too tempting: Grainger couldn't be sure. But his action was set.

He broke into a run.

And that was when the shot rang out.

It wasn't that there was so much blood that Grainger noticed first. It was that on such a cold night, as it struck his face, it was so very warm.

The man in the hat, Tremayne's doppelgänger or whoever he was, let out such a cry, clutching his shoulder he began to fall awkwardly.

Grainger, without even thinking, dashed across the line to cradle him.

The West German police complained bitterly. He wasn't permitted across the line. But Grainger's fury came as something of a shock to them.

'Take aim!' he roared. 'I'm not having another Fechter on ours hands! If they so much as twitch, you open fire! Do you understand me?'

The men dithered. The whole world had seen poor Peter Fechter splashed across the front pages only two months ago. Eighteen years old. Shot in the hip trying to flee East Berlin. Left to die hanging on the barbed wire. No one in the West able to do a thing because he was just a few yards inside the Russian sector.

Not again.

The West Germans brandished their weapons at the East Germans, though it wasn't altogether clear if they would follow Grainger's order.

What did become clear was Grainger's gritted determination. On his own, and in the face of approaching East German sentries, he grabbed the man, who was twice his size, and dragged him by his coat tails until he lay bleeding, firmly in the West.

The man, who was now so weak from his injury that his breathing had become shallow, buckled under the assault of Grainger's sudden questioning.

The man struggled to answer.

Frustrated, Grainger reduced it down to just the important one. 'Are you Stempfer?' he asked.

The man smiled wanly. 'No, I'm the Doctor,'

'I'm going to get you a doctor. I just need to know about Stempfer.'

'Stempfer...?'

'Yes.'

'Stempfer... No, I'm not Stempfer,' the man confessed, steadily losing consciousness. 'Stempfer's dead.'

Grainger took the blow with resolve. 'How?' he persisted.

'I think I killed him.'

Keeping the Americans out of it had been something of feat. This was their sector, their jurisdiction. But they kept their word, and when Grainger had a British army ambulance, a converted Land Rover from RAF Gatow, in attendance within ten minutes, they raced down the narrow length of Friedrichstasse and off into the dark side streets of West Berlin. Nobody stopped them.

Grainger rifled through the deep pockets of the stranger's overcoat, stopping only occasionally to watch the young army medic, a boy really, work feverishly in the dim, cramped conditions across the other side of the stretcher.

What was this?

He pulled out what appeared to be some kind of pen, maybe a screwdriver, from one of the side pockets. It had a light on the end. How very curious. It seemed to hum.

Good grief, there were all sorts of odds and ends in here. A yo-yo, some elastic bands. Heaven knows what that thing was and... hang on. He pulled a paper bag out and peeked at its contents. Yes, it really was a bag of jelly babies.

'I think you're in luck,' the medic announced as he probed and cleaned the wound of Tremayne's unconscious doppelgänger. 'The bullet doesn't seem to have punctured the axillary artery.'

'You're sure? I need to question him.'

'I can't be completely sure,' the medic confessed. The bleeding certainly did appear to have slowed. 'He could be bleeding internally.' He applied a new dressing but it was obvious something else was bothering him. He smirked sheepishly. 'Though I can't actually seem to find his axillary artery...'

Grainger didn't care about that. The strong smell of disinfectant that permeated throughout the ambulance was starting to make him feel decidedly uneasy. He could feel his hands turning clammy to the drum of distant, uncomfortable memories.

As he watched the medic press firmly against the bloody dressing, he didn't mean to make eye contact.

'I say, are you all right?'

It took all of Grainger's effort to ignore him and look away. He thought about stealing a jelly baby to take his mind off things, but opted to stuff them back inside the coat pocket instead.

'It's all right, sir,' the medic reassured him, apparently assuming that Grainger had somehow made it this far through life without having seen any bloodshed before now. 'We'll be back at Gatow in a minute and we'll have you and your, er, guest on your way back to London before you know it.'

Grainger dismissed his youthful enthusiasm. That wasn't about to happen. Not now. The interrogation had to begin immediately. Tonight. He said, 'We're not going to Gatow. We're going to Wilmersdorf.'

The younger man seemed confused. He didn't think there was anything in Wilmersdorf.

'Nothing you need to worry about, at any rate,' Grainger replied testily. He wouldn't say any more than that, though they both knew the real reason why.

It had been all change in West Berlin, ever since last year. Grainger's first port of call would have been Charlottenburg but that was all over now. Safe houses had been moved. Networks smashed and rebuilt. All because of that filthy swine George Blake, a Soviet triple agent unmasked right in the heart of British intelligence. Hundreds of agents betrayed and executed at his behest.

Rumour had it there was still another rat in the pack somewhere. Grainger had his money on Philby but he couldn't be sure. There was just something about that smug face that he didn't like. So long as he stayed in the Middle East, well out of his patch, that's all he cared about.

Grainger fished around in the coat pockets again and this time dug a little deeper.

Ah-ha, what's this...?

Small, nondescript and tatty. At last. A codebook.

He slipped it quickly into his own coat pocket, but the medic's confusion had not lifted any. He was feeling for a pulse and becoming increasingly suspicious of his own abilities. He reeled from his patient as though the unconscious man on the stretcher had given him a fright. 'There's something very strange about this man's heartbeat.'

'What's the matter?'

The medic seemed almost embarrassed to answer. 'I could swear he's got two of them.'

Grainger changed his mind and decided to pilfer a jelly baby after all. 'You need to lay off the rubbing alcohol, old chap.'

From the outside, it looked like an ordinary, narrow apartment building somewhere near Olivaer Platz. Five floors. Dark and not particularly well kept.

The Land Rover pulled into a side street and parked in seclusion at the rear, well away from street lights and prying eyes. Grainger got out, lit a rough-tasting cigarette, and waited in the darkness until he heard the approach of heavy footsteps echoing down the stairwell behind the heavy back door.

Two burly men emerged. They said nothing. They waited for Grainger to open up the Land Rover, then hefted the stretcher out quickly.

The medic motioned to follow but Grainger gently pushed him back inside. He thanked him for his services and followed the men up the bleak stairs.

Somewhere around the third floor they entered one of the grotty apartments and hefted the stretcher into a back room at the end of the hall.

It was worse in here. Like an abattoir. White tiles from floor to ceiling, held in place by ageing grout. A trolley lay next to the gurney bearing gleaming surgical instruments, which glinted under the glare of a single incandescent bulb that swung gently back and forth overhead.

When the surgeon came in to inspect his patient, Grainger could feel the blood draining from his face. He loitered in the doorway and watched him work distrustfully for a minute or two before quietly slipping back out.

The two burly men were listening to a wireless and eating a meal of cold meat and potatoes at a table in the tiny kitchen. Grainger stepped inside briefly, pulled a bottle of brandy out from the sink cupboard and poured himself a shot in a dusty glass.

It was as he turned to leave that he realised he recognised one of the men. A little greyer, perhaps a little craggier.

'Sergeant Munro, isn't it?'

'Sergeant Major Munro, thank you very much,' the man corrected brusquely, before looking up. 'Good grief. Mr Grainger, sir.' He got to his feet quickly, wiped his hand and shook Grainger's hand. 'It's been a long time.'

'So you made it to Warrant Officer.' Grainger smiled. 'Hard to tell who we all were out in there in the dark, eh?'

Munro stepped a little closer, the concern weighing heavily on him. 'Not so dark that I didn't notice, sir.'

'Notice what?'

'That it looks like our Mr Tremayne is back from the dead, if you get my meaning.'

'Quite.'

'I'm wondering what the Soviets are up to. You don't think he's some kind of ruse do you, sir?'

'What? Shoot one of their own men, just so we'll believe him?

'I wouldn't put it past 'em.'

Grainger swigged his brandy down quickly and set the glass on the side. 'Seems a bit extreme, even for them,' he said. But the doubt lingered.

At any rate, it came as something of a relief to know that he wasn't the only one seeing things. And to know that he had an ally here should things take a turn, and he didn't have to say another word about it.

He made his way to what would have been a lounge had this been an ordinary apartment. Instead, two large wooden desks and a threadbare couch were all that filled an otherwise drab and spartan room.

At one end sat wireless equipment rigged up to a 100-kilowatt, amplitude-modulated Class B shortwave radio transmitter up on the roof.

The radio operator, a thin, middle-aged intelligence officer by the name of Carstairs, made it clear that Control were anxious that Grainger check in.

'They're always anxious,' he said, and handed the small codebook over for analysis.

'This is Stempfer's handwriting, all right,' Carstairs confirmed. 'I'd recognise it anywhere.'

That, however, was the extent to which Carstairs could tell him anything. The message was encrypted with an unbreakable One Time Pad. The key was with Control. He'd have to send them the message, wait for them to decrypt it, and only if they deemed Grainger important enough to the overall scheme would they contact him and issue further instructions.

Grainger ordered Carstairs to get cracking. Other agents out in the field would be tuning in on wirelesses all over Europe waiting for their own sets of coded instructions to be broadcast by the Wilmersdorf Number Station. They couldn't afford to tie up the system for long. But Control had to get the message; they needed to know Stempfer was dead, and that a stranger had taken his place.

'A stranger who doesn't appear to have much of a wound at all,' the surgeon announced a little while later, standing in the doorway, taking off his gloves.

'He was shot right in front of me.'

'Clipped, more like.'

'I'm covered in his blood.'

'Dear me, I didn't take you for the melodramatic type.' The surgeon slumped on the couch and tiredly asked if anybody had a spare cigarette. Grainger dug his packet out and joined him, but just like the other one it tasted bitter and unpleasant.

He got to his feet, suspicion still ringing in his ears. 'You didn't find anything peculiar about his heartbeat by any chance, did you?'

'I wouldn't know, I didn't check. There didn't seem to be much point. I sutured what was there, but there really wasn't much else I could do.'

'Well, stick around just in case there are complications.'

'Fine,' the surgeon acquiesced, breathing in a lungful of thick blue smoke. 'But there won't be any.' The surgeon sighed. 'Personally, I thought he seemed perfectly lucid. But... not exactly *compos mentis*, if you get my drift.'

'He's awake?'

'I put him in the back room. When I left him he was sitting there, having a conversation with a cockroach and demanding to be addressed as Doctor.'

The back room was fairly large, but equally spartan. Its only window had been boarded up and a scruffy table and two chairs had been placed at its centre.

The stranger was sitting on the far side of the table, his shirt ripped open exposing his pale torso.

Grainger found Munro standing guard outside. Sure enough the stranger had what appeared to be a small brown cockroach sitting in the palm of his hand – and he was arguing with it.

Though Grainger couldn't hear what was being said through the thick glass of the door, he could see him well enough to know that there were no signs of the Logos symbols burned into his flesh.

In fact, in this light he could see clearly that this certainly wasn't Tremayne. But, still, the likeness was disturbingly uncanny. And he was equally as peculiar as the last and final time Grainger had laid eyes on his old friend.

Munro made it clear that he was having none of it. This was a game. The question was what sort of game were the Soviets up to this time?

Suddenly the man in the room flinched as though he'd been bitten and threw the insect across the room.

He sucked his finger to ease the pain and shouted. 'How rude!'

Grainger took the opportunity of the distraction to step inside and approached with caution. 'Is there a problem?' he asked flatly.

'Ambassador Skgar is being very unreasonable.'

Grainger glanced at the scuttling creature in the corner, its twitching antennae aimed at nothing in particular, but said nothing.

The stranger, however, scoffed at it. 'Yes, well...' he said, addressing the insect directly. 'The feeling's mutual.'

Grainger took a seat across the table and took a quick puff on his unpleasant cigarette. 'Something you want to tell me?'

The man grinned playfully, his wide eyes filled with mischief. 'Yes... It's good to see you, Eddie.'

Grainger remained impassive. 'You grin a lot,' he said.

'Maybe I have a lot to grin about.'

'Who are you?'

Right to the point. That seemed to give the man a moment's pause. Eventually he said, 'It's me. The Doctor.'

'Which Doctor?'

'Oh, no, I'm not a witch doctor.' The stranger got to his feet. 'Oh, come on, Eddie. I can call you Eddie, can't I?'

'No, you can't.'

'Of course I can. Eddie. See? There, I said it again.' He bounded over to the corner of the room. 'We have a lot of catching up to do.'

'Because of Tremayne.'

'What?' The stranger seemed genuinely befuddled, until it suddenly hit him. He rubbed his own face, testing its contours, as the realisation dawned. 'Oh, yes, I do a bit, don't I? Funny what can happen when the universe gets rewritten, eh?'

The man calling himself the Doctor grinned once again, but this time there was far more behind the toothy smile than mere playful banter. It was quite chilling. Grainger watched him quickly scoop the cockroach back up again and, carrying it back towards the table, say, 'Now, are you going to behave yourself or am I going to have to put you back in the box?'

The answer seemed to satisfy and he set it down.

The Doctor...

Not a doctor. The Doctor. The definite article.

This wasn't the first time he had met someone who called himself the Doctor. There had been a few. They clearly weren't all the same man, so how could they all be the Doctor?

What was he missing?

Was it some kind of secret code? Or a secret society? Like the Masons.

No. The Masons never came up to you and said, Hello, I'm the Mason. They said they were a Mason, if they admitted it at all.

'Why is that man staring at me?' the Doctor asked with an air of alarm.

Grainger glanced over his shoulder to see Munro looming through the glass in the door.

'He'd prefer it if you sat down.'

'Why?'

'Because otherwise he might take a disliking to you.'

'Oh.' The man calling himself the Doctor seemed to take a moment to consider his limited options. 'That would be very unpleasant.'

He sat down.

After a moment, his focus clearly on other matters, he waved his hand at the cockroach. 'What? No, no, you stay where you are.'

Grainger tapped his ash out. 'Tell me what happened to Stempfer.'

'I told you, he's dead.'

'You admitted you killed him. How?'

The Doctor sat back, the memory clearly troubling. 'I really don't want to talk about it.'

'I want to talk about it.'

'Well, why do we have to talk about what you want to talk about all the time?'

Enough of these silly games. Grainger felt the sudden surge of uncharacteristic anger and embraced it. 'That's how it works!'

The two men sat in aggravated silence for a moment, until eventually the Doctor decided to fill the void.

'If you really must know, he found out what was going on. He told me... And I asked him to go back and get me more information. At which point, they hunted him down like vermin, and starved him to death.'

Grainger had never heard anything like it. Executed, yes, but starved? 'The Stasi did this?'

'No,' the Doctor explained, 'something much worse, something that is using the Stasi, and the KGB and everybody else in between for its own purposes.' He held Grainger's gaze with a steely one of his own that made the hairs on the back of Grainger's neck stand on end. 'There are creatures that feed on human misery.'

'Yes,' Grainger agreed. 'They're called communists.'

'These communists call themselves the Jalaphron.'

'The Jalaphron? A political group, like Bolsheviks?'

The Doctor appeared perturbed that Grainger didn't understand. 'Oh, dear. No, not like Bolsheviks.'

'Then what?'

The Doctor seemed to seriously think it over before turning Grainger's attention back to the small, beady-eyed cockroach. 'Perhaps Ambassador Skgar here would be –'

'I see...' More games.

Grainger took the initiative and decided to plough ahead with what he was really interested in. He took the codebook out and set it on the table.

'Do you recognise this?'

'Hmm, isn't that Stempfer's?'

'You tell me.'

'Yes, I think that's Stempfer's. I could probably tell you for certain if I knew where my coat was. You don't happen to know where my coat is, do you?'

'I got this from your coat.'

The Doctor was mortified. 'Well, who said you could do that?'

'What does it say?'

'You want me to read it? It's in code.'

'Tell me anyway,' Grainger demanded irritably.

'All right, it says Cuba.'

Cuba? Another game? Grainger had no idea what it said; Control hadn't responded yet. But for now, he would pursue this line.

He took a pen out and on a small scrap of paper wrote the word Cuba.

The stranger seemed rueful. 'Well, it's not a very good code.'

'It's a One Time Pad. It's supposed to be unbreakable.'

'Unbreakable, I suppose, if you're not familiar with the poem used in the key to decode it.'

'Tell me, what's in Cuba?'

'It's full of Cubans. Lovely people. Good dancers. Have you been?'

'Stop being so flippant!'

'You first.'

Grainger took a final, irritated drag on his awful cigarette before stubbing it out on the table with a twist of complete finality.

'You already knew about Cuba.'

Suddenly the Doctor didn't seem quite so amused. 'You're a very important man, Eddie. You're going to stop a war.'

'And why would I want to do that?'

The Doctor seemed genuinely hurt. 'Well, it's better than starting one. Isn't it? Wars are bad. I'm sure you'll agree.'

'What's so bad about them?'

'Well, haven't you heard? People die.'

'I have lived through one or two of them, you know.'

'Then I would have thought you'd know that by now.' He tapped the desk under Grainger's nose. 'When your people have finished decoding that message, this is what they're going to find. They're going to find that a man named Oleg Penkovsky gave Stempfer the map coordinates to the sites on Cuba from where Soviet missiles are being placed to launch an attack on the United States of America. Which, in turn, will cause a NATO counter-attack and bring death to millions.

'But we can stop it, Eddie. You and me, in Berlin, tonight.'

Grainger watched carefully as Carstairs transcribed the reply from London, but it was so difficult to concentrate with the sound of all that blood rushing through his ears.

Why did Carstairs have to breathe through his mouth instead of his nose and make that rasping sound, like a demented pig? It was disgusting.

Come to think of it, why did he have to breathe at all?

Grainger wanted to throttle him. Throttle him. Then hit him. Hit him hard and keep hitting him –

'Got it,' Carstairs announced proudly.

He turned to where Grainger was pacing agitatedly and held out the decoded message from Control.

'You read it,' Grainger snapped.

'Cuba is hot. Reconnaissance scrambled. Hold for further instructions.'

So it was true, what this Doctor fellow had been telling him. It was all true. The Soviets really were placing missiles in Cuba, just ninety miles off the coast of Florida.

This was the fallout from President Kennedy's Bay of Pigs fiasco last year that everyone had been waiting for.

Send fifteen hundred armed Cuban exiles back into Cuba to spark a popular uprising. Fail miserably. Watch nearly twelve hundred of them get caught, sentenced to thirty years' imprisonment. And Castro's response is to arrange for Soviet missiles to be stationed in his back garden.

This could escalate wildly out of control.

The world was sitting on a knife's edge.

So what was this Doctor here for? Stempfer was dead. The Soviets had the element of surprise. So why send this Doctor fellow across with word of the missiles at all?

Was he here to negotiate terms? Even they wouldn't be that brazen, surely?

Grainger could feel his jaw going ten to the dozen. If he ground his teeth any more he'd start chipping bits off.

He booted the surgeon, who until that point had been snoring obliviously away to himself on the decrepit old couch. He awoke sharply. 'Good grief, man. What in blazes is the matter with you?'

'Get up.'

The rush of blood was stronger now. All he could hear was its roar.

'Get your kit. We have information to extract.'

The surgeon stumbled groggily to his feet. 'What's the matter with him?'

Grainger didn't care what either of them thought, as Carstairs looked on in fear, and said, 'I have no idea...'

Munro hog-tied him with thick electrical cable, his arms stretched tightly behind the back of the chair.

The Doctor didn't struggle. It was almost as though he had been expecting it.

'Have you heard of Torquemada?' Grainger asked, trying to sound casual, but everyone in the room knew it was a lie.

The Doctor said nothing at first. He listened instead to the faint sounds of something being prepared in the next room. It sounded very much like a dentist's drill. 'Well...' he replied eventually. 'Nobody expects the Spanish Inquisition.'

Grainger didn't bother to hide his glee at the proposition. 'As Inquisitor General, Torquemada was a master at getting people to talk, who otherwise would have preferred not to. When he inflicted pain he elevated it to an art form.'

The Doctor knew better. 'Torture doesn't work, Eddie,' he said. 'Instead of getting people to tell you what you want to know, they tell you what you want to hear.'

But even as he said it, the surgeon entered the room with a steady air of the inevitable. He set a tray down on the table and picked up the syringe by the barrel. Tapped it once. Then let a thin jet of clear liquid shoot out to remove the tiny air-bubbles.

'Sodium pentathol,' Grainger explained. 'Truth serum.'

'I had no idea we were going for drinks,' the Doctor quipped. 'Care to join me?'

'If I were you I'd treat this with a little more gravity.'

'Oh, in the words of a future Earth leader, don't mis-underestimate me, Eddie. I never make jokes unless I'm deadly serious.'

'Then maybe you'll find this funny,' Munro interjected, cracking his knuckles, eager to punch the Doctor hard across the face.

The surgeon tossed the syringe down in disgust. He turned his back to leave. 'I want no part in this.'

'Oh, I'm with you,' the Doctor readily agreed.

'Shut up!' Munro spat, ready to carry out his threat, but Grainger stayed his arm.

'Check his heartbeat,' Grainger snapped. 'He's not who he says he is. He has two of them.'

'What are you talking about?'

The Doctor looked on kindly. 'You'd better do as he says.'

The surgeon stepped to the side of his patient and did as he was ordered, but he remained sceptical. 'The man was shot, for heaven's sake. He's in shock. That could just be arrhythmia.'

'It's two hearts!'

'Get a grip, man, the pair of you.'

With that, the surgeon stormed past Grainger and Munro, and marched off down the hallway.

'Shatters the illusion,' said the Doctor, 'when one of your inquisitors suffers a crisis of conscience, eh?'

Grainger set his chair down in front of the Doctor and slumped in it.

'You still look like you've got something on your mind, though. How are you coping?' the Doctor inquired. 'Still feel all that adrenalin thundering through your ears? Everything still mired in a red mist?'

Grainger tried hard to concentrate, but the rage simply wouldn't lift.

'Yes... hard to think, isn't it? Hard to do anything except obey... Maybe you should have the sodium pentathol?' the Doctor remarked with some irony. 'Clear your head a bit.'

Grainger took a breath. It was like trying to inhale treacle. 'What are the aims of the Jalaphron?' he demanded.

'To wreak havoc. To feed,' the Doctor said grimly.

Grainger glowered at Munro to finally hit him. But, as the old soldier gleefully stepped forward to comply, a searing pain shot through him, bending him double.

Grainger rounded on the Doctor in panic. Everything was spiralling away so fast. 'No more games, Doctor. Tell me about the Jalaphron.'

'What good would it do? You're not listening.'

'Tell me!'

'They'd love it in here,' the Doctor replied casually. 'They feed on misery, Eddie. The Jalaphron leave their young on socially unstable worlds. The more turmoil, war and destruction, the greater the feast. But the Cold War has caused a perverse kind of famine, bringing three millennia of non-stop war, three millennia of good harvest to an end. This stalemate has bred fear, but it's reduced misery.

'The Jalaphron are starving, Eddie. So they've taken matters into their own hands. They're going to start a war.'

Grainger clawed his forehead, trying desperately to ease his confusion. But it felt as though somebody else's fingers were already there, digging into his scalp, crushing his skull.

'What, er... what are you talking about?'

The Doctor pressed his advantage. 'There are things going on in this world that not everybody is aware of. Creatures from other worlds. Other universes. Other dimensions in time and space. Of course, Ambassador Skgar over there could tell you more. Though between you and me, he's not really an ambassador. Too young. Never took the test. He's more of a spokesman, really, aren't you, Skgar. What's that? Oh, yes... well, the same to you.'

Grainger tried to focus on the scuttling insect. It seemed fatter somehow. Like an engorged tic that had been feeding on blood.

'Get rid of that thing.'

Munro did as he was asked, swiping the bug off the table and hurling it to the floor.

'Careful you don't step on the ambassador,' the Doctor advised. 'He's feeling a little fragile.'

'Enough!' Enraged, Grainger got to his feet and crushed it under his heel.

A sickly yellow ooze spilled out from under his shoe. And immediately it felt like a pressing weight had been lifted.

Grainger staggered, his vision clearing, his focus returning. So light-headed was the feeling of sudden clarity that he slumped back into his chair, holding his head in his hands, feeling the gradual onslaught of a really bad hangover.

He glanced across at Munro, whose own dizzy spell had him hugging the wall.

He felt his breath returning. Felt his anxiety subsiding.

When Grainger finally had the courage to look the Doctor in the eye, still tied firmly to the chair, he felt nothing but embarrassment and shame.

'Oh, my God,' he said. 'What are we doing?'

The Doctor peered disdainfully down at his shoulder, tugged the piece of suture out of his shoulder and threw it away.

Munro helped him on with his coat. When he handed him his hat he couldn't help but keep his head bowed and look away. 'I'm... I'm very sorry, sir.'

'As you should be,' the Doctor replied cheerfully, settling it down on his mop of curly brown hair. 'Succumbing to alien mind control. Who's ever heard of such a thing?'

The Doctor couldn't help but watch after him with a rueful smile as the sergeant major skulked off.

'Eddie,' Carstairs announced, looking up from his wireless set. 'Control says three more large ships have been spotted heading for Cuba.'

'And their cargo?'

Carstairs expression was grave. 'More warheads.'

'Why is he allowed to call you Eddie and I'm not?' the Doctor interjected.

Grainger let the comment go, subserviently approaching the Doctor. 'Tell me what we have to do to get this thing to end.'

'I've traced the Jalaphron hive mother and her brood to the sewers beneath Berlin. You need to stay back and mop up what's left behind when I'm done. Do you understand?'

'Perfectly. I've seen what just one of these things can do.'

'Yes, well, once I've dealt with their hive mother, their abilities will drop considerably. What you felt the moment the fog lifted from your mind is going to happen almost instantaneously in the Kremlin, in the White House, and at Number 10. They're going to find themselves on the brink of a war they don't remember starting, and they're going to need time to talk themselves into backing down from it. That's your job, Eddie. I'll have done all I can do.'

Grainger was stunned. 'But how long will that take?'

'Oh, ten or 12 days or so.'

But Grainger remained troubled. 'May I ask...? Why are you doing this?'

'Because I made a promise to Stempfer.' The Doctor felt around in his coat pocket and pulled out the metallic-looking pen with the light. 'Oh, which reminds me. Have you got a telephone?'

Grainger didn't understand. 'Over in the corner.'

The Doctor strode over, aimed his peculiar little instrument at it, and then picked up the black Bakelite receiver.

'Romana,' he said.

Grainger could just hear the reply on the other end of the line. A woman exclaiming, 'Doctor, you're alive! I've been scouring Moscow but they just keep popping up everywhere.'

'Yes. Not to worry. I've located the hive mother.'

'Where are you?'

'West Berlin. I want you to listen very carefully. When I give the signal I want you to bring the TARDIS and initiate a matter-time divergence.'

He waited for her reply but she said nothing.

'No arguing.'

'I wasn't arguing.'

He didn't seem convinced and reached into his pocket. But when he exchanged his glowing pen for the small paper bag, he weighed it in his hand and his expression changed to ashen.

It appeared to Grainger that this Romana was very perceptive indeed because even on the end of the line she knew to be concerned. 'Doctor, what's wrong?'

'Someone's stolen a jelly baby.'

The dank sewers of West Berlin stretched for mile upon foul-smelling mile. Grainger followed closely behind the Doctor, careful not to find himself knee-deep in effluent. For a larger man, the Doctor was agile and surprisingly fast. Not at all what Grainger had expected.

'How do you know where we're going?' he asked.

'It's not only a human urge to visit your mother,' the Doctor replied.

At first Grainger didn't know what on earth he was talking about. But, slowly, as his eyes adjusted to darkness, he realised that the damp brickwork was alive with snakes of scuttling cockroaches all running in the same direction.

Grainger's heart hit his ribcage with a thump. It made his skin crawl just looking at them. 'There must be... thousands of them.'

'Yes, but only one that we need to worry about.'

As they rounded the corner up ahead, the mass of glistening insects converged, crawling over each other to nuzzle at the dripping teats of a vast incandescent yellow lump poking up from under the effluent flowing down the tunnel.

Grainger stared in disbelief. Was that an actual alien life form? 'Oh, my God,' he said. 'Is that really...?'

'Yes, I think you're right,' the Doctor replied, reaching for a handkerchief. 'I do believe she's ill.'

The Jalaphron hive mother undulated to the tender affections of her gathering brood. Yet, as her translucent skin oozed with discoloured sweat, Grainger felt a heightened sense of trepidation. A animal was usually at its most dangerous when wounded.

'You're sure just this shot of sodium pentathol is going to protect us?'

'For you, for a little while at least. It interrupts the brain chemistry and makes it a job for them to latch on.'

'But what about you?'

'Me?' There was that grin again. Mischievous, yet chilling. 'No effect whatsoever. Now you know what you have to do?'

'Wait for you to go, light this fuse, then toss in the fire bomb. Munro and his men have flamethrower teams standing by at the manholes nearby just in case there's more of them.'

'Good man.' The Doctor reached for his glowing pen again. 'Well, it's been good to see you again, Eddie –'

'Doctor, if I may... I don't understand. What is it you're going to do?'

The Doctor seemed more than a little impatient. 'Do I really have to?'

'Please...'

Reluctantly the Doctor explained. 'The TARDIS will arrive over there, when I give the signal. At which point, Romana will render the time vortex temporarily unstable. We'll travel to another destination, dragging the hive mother and most of her brood with us, caught in our wake as we go. Understand?'

'Not a word of it.'

'Good.'

With that. the Doctor shot off down the tunnel, pointing his odd little apparatus at the glowing lump in the water.

'Time you should be leaving, don't you think, old girl?'

The incandescent mass seemed to moan at his arrival.

The Doctor seemed shocked. 'Well, there's no need to be like that,' he said and, without further hesitation, he pressed the small button on the side of his device.

And there it was! That sound Grainger had heard before. That peculiar scream, like a braying metallic walrus.

And then, from thin air, the appearance of that ordinary blue police box!

A second later and the door to the box was flung open and a woman stood in its entrance. 'Come on, Doctor!' she yelled.

The Doctor shot a look back. 'Are you ready for your close-up, Mr DeMille?'

Grainger looked down at the petrol bomb in his hand and got his match ready. 'You know,' he called out. 'You really are a very strange man.'

The Doctor hesitated in the doorway, genuinely touched, and smiled. 'Thank you, Eddie. That's the nicest thing anyone's ever said to me.'

Grainger's telephone box stood under a tree on a quiet suburban road in Charlottenburg, the smell of burning petrol still thick in his nostrils.

The line was crackly and faint, but Grainger didn't care.

'Hello, dear. How was the canasta?' he asked warmly.

Any other woman would have taken him to task for calling so late, but not Eleanor. More than anyone, she understood. They chatted idly about friends and card games until eventually she asked him, 'Darling, did we both win tonight?'

'Yes,' Grainger replied. 'Yes, I think we did.'

'When are you coming home?'

'In a couple of weeks. First I have to go to Washington.'

Eleanor put her foot down. 'But then a holiday.'

'Yes, let's. Somewhere warm.' Grainger said. 'I want to come out of the cold.'

Childhood Living

Samantha Baker

An Adventure of the First Doctor,
with Susan

Wednesday 15 August 1979

Linda Grainger was beginning to feel much more claustrophobic than she ever imagined she would. She'd always thought it was such a weird thing to worry about – so what if you're in a confined space? As long as you can get out, it's fine, isn't it?

The fact that there were no windows suddenly occurred to her. Just being able to look outside this tin can would be a help. Not that there'd be much to see. Just darkness probably.

Surely it would be time to leave soon. They'd been here long enough already, seen everything there was to see. A tour around a submarine only kept the interest for so long.

It was a military ship, she'd been told when they'd arrived. A research vessel the navy hoped to use alongside its fleet. As well as the smallish bridge – no bigger than Linda's bedroom, really – there was an even smaller laboratory and the airlock room through which they'd come aboard. Below them was a whole other deck: the engines and some storage compartments, Linda had learnt. The entire sub was no bigger than the ground floor of a terraced house.

There was that claustrophobia again.

Linda's granddad was talking to his friend, Commander Oliver, but he put his hand on Linda's shoulder and gave it a gentle squeeze. Granddad could always tell when she was a bit worried or anxious – he always knew how to deal with her. It infuriated her father.

What was Granddad saying now? Was he finally saying goodbye? It had been a good afternoon but not only was she beginning to feel trapped, enclosed... the day was starting to drag too.

'Well, Edward,' Commander Oliver was saying to Linda's grandfather. 'It's been good to see you again.'

'You too, Guy.'

They were old friends, Linda had found out when they'd first arrived. It was how Granddad had managed to get them aboard for the day. It was a sort of a treat, Linda supposed. A day out to take her mind off things; Granddad too. More than anyone else in their family, she knew her grandfather and his odd ways. So when he'd said he was going to take her down to Portsmouth to look around a submarine, she'd pretended to be really interested. At least it would help pass the time – it had been the summer holidays for a month now, and she still had two weeks to go.

To be honest, at first the submarine had been a disappointment – much more cramped, much more dark than she'd expected. The fact that they weren't really meant to be there had helped a bit. It was a military submarine, strictly off-limits to the general public, and being there gave Linda an exciting sense of doing something naughty or, well, wrong. She didn't know whether the submarine was nuclear or not, but it was certainly military. Its crew wore smart naval uniforms – though not those silly sailors' hats she'd expected.

'Well, Linda,' Commander Oliver said. 'What do you think of the sub?'

Linda smiled and said she liked it. Oliver was younger than her grandfather, but not by that much – he probably wasn't far off retiring either. He certainly wasn't used to small talk with 11-year-old girls, that much was for sure.

'It's nice,' she said. 'A bit cramped, though.'

Linda had no idea how her Granddad Edward knew a man who could get them a tour around a submarine. It struck her that she'd never really known what he'd done for a living before retiring. That had been a few years ago now. Seemed odd, that he used to be someone with a job and a life. She knew he'd been around during the Second World War and had travelled a lot. Maybe he'd been in the navy. Linda couldn't believe she didn't know.

'You're looking well,' Oliver was saying. 'Considering...'

'Yes...' said Linda's Granddad, suddenly looking tired. 'I'm fine.' They shook hands, then Oliver ruffled Linda's hair. I'm not a boy, she thought.

'Commander?' One of the crewmen needed Oliver's attention. It was Lieutenant Brandis, his second-in-command, who had given Linda and Granddad the tour of the upper deck when they'd arrived. He was young and good-looking. Linda felt very nervous whenever he looked at her.

Granddad looked thoughtful, almost lost, but when Linda caught his eye, he winked and smiled.

'Did you enjoy your day?' he asked her.

'Yes,' she said. 'Thank you. It was...' Linda paused as she noticed a change amongst the whole bridge crew. Oliver was talking in hushed tones with Brandis, and it looked like the other two sailors aboard were waiting for orders.

'Prepare to change course,' Oliver said finally.

'Granddad?' said Linda. He simply put his arm on her shoulder and made the 'shhh' sign with his other hand.

'Blow forward ballast,' Oliver was saying, 'and head to the assigned coordinates.'

'Aye, Commander,' said Brandis.

Oliver glanced over and caught Linda's grandfather's eye. Granddad went over and they talked. Linda's claustrophobia began to resurface. She could feel the submarine begin to move. It wasn't as graceful as she'd thought it would be.

'Linda.' She looked over at her grandfather, who beckoned her over. 'Love, don't worry,' he said, 'but we're going to have to stay here for a bit longer. They've received an order to take the submarine a few miles more out to sea immediately.'

'Where?' said Linda, beginning to panic slightly.

'Oh, not far.'

'But can't they go back and let us get off first?'

'It seems someone might be in a bit of trouble,' he said quietly. 'They have to go straightaway.'

Gradually, Linda became aware that the pitch of the sub was dipping. The front end was lowering; they were submerging. That claustrophobia again.

'Shall we get out of your way, Guy?' asked Granddad. 'We could go and wait in the laboratory.'

Oliver was busy looking at a screen – some kind of sonar or something – and took a moment to register the question. 'Actually, Edward, that's not a bad idea. Do you mind?'

'Not at all,' said Granddad. 'Come along, Linda.' He shepherded her through the bulkhead door at the back of the bridge. Linda realised just how noisy it was now: engines, beeps, pings and creeks. When the sub had been still in harbour it had sounded almost serene.

It was bright. Almost blindingly so. And quiet. Susan blinked, letting her eyes get accustomed to the light. She was lying on a metal floor. Cold. Clinical. As her sight grew better, she saw her grandfather nearby. He was also waking up, holding up a hand to shade his eyes.

'Susan, my dear,' he said. 'Don't worry. Are you all right?'

'I think so,' she said. 'Where are we, Grandfather? This isn't the TARDIS.'

The Doctor slowly got to his feet. 'No. No, it's not.' He rubbed his eyes, then held out a hand and helped Susan to her feet. 'We must find out what happened.'

The last thing Susan could remember was the Great Wall of China. The TARDIS scanner had shown that they were in orbit above Earth.

'But, when?' Susan had asked.

'The twentieth century, it seems,' the Doctor had said.

'No wonder there's no space traffic.'

'Indeed. There may be a few communication satellites, but not much else.'

The view on the screen had shown Southeast Asia, the vast Pacific Ocean stretching out to its right. Susan had studied the image, straining her eyes. 'Where's the Wall?' she'd said.

'Hmm?'

'The Great Wall of China. I read that you could see it from space. Well, before it was knocked down, anyway.'

'Oh, don't be so silly, girl!' he'd said. 'See a twenty-foot-wide structure from space?! How preposterous!'

Susan smiled to herself, remembering his look of amusement. Then she remembered what had happened next.

'Grandfather?' Susan had said.

'Hmm?'

'What are we doing here?'

'If you must know,' he'd said, 'we're trying to avoid that.'

The scanner screen, which had revolved its point of view away from the planet below, pointed in the direction the TARDIS was gradually drifting. The image showed a spaceship dead in its path.

'We're going to crash!'

'Yes, I'd quite realised that. And in barely a few moments' time. The dematerialisation circuits are overloaded. We can't stop our flight!' The Doctor had frantically pushed buttons and Susan had seen sweat build on his face. On the scanner screen, the ship was getting closer, its descending orbit bringing it right at them. It was very anachronistic for the twentieth century – Susan saw that straight away. And it wasn't from Earth.

'Do something, Grandfather!' she'd shouted above the rising noise of the TARDIS's engines. She had grabbed hold of the console, bracing herself for the impact.

When it came, it had knocked her out cold.

Now, Susan's legs ached and felt hollow. She desperately needed some sugar, anything to give her a boost. Looking around, she saw that they were in a white space. Its floor was metallic to the touch; there was no sign of any walls. The room looked like it was infinite. 'Grandfather...' she said, getting worried.

'Oh, shush, my dear child,' he said, putting his arm around her. 'Now, let's see.' He looked around. 'If we got in, there must be a way out...'

'But, how did we get here? The last thing I remember is being on the TARDIS. That spaceship... we were heading directly for it.'

'Yes, quite so. It must have crashed into us. Then, I wonder where –'

A doorway suddenly appeared in mid air, an opening in the white void through which Susan could see movement. However, given the brightness all around her, it was hard to focus on exactly what it was that was moving. The Doctor looked sceptical, and stepped in front of Susan so that she was behind him. She quickly glanced all around them. No, the opening was still the only thing in sight. She looked at it again.

More movement – closer this time. Someone, something, was coming through. As Susan concentrated on it, she saw that it was a large creature, about three metres tall with a shell mounted on its slug-like body.

'Biped man. Biped woman,' the huge snail said in a rasping voice. 'Your thanks are not necessary.'

★ ★ ★

Linda's grandfather eased himself down onto the laboratory floor, and sat leaning against the wall.

'Come on,' he said, motioning for Linda to sit next to him. As she did, he put his arm around her. 'I'm getting far too old for this. I retired for a reason.'

'But you're not that old,' said Linda.

Her grandfather smiled. 'Oh, I've been around, Linda,' he said. 'It sometimes feels like I've lived a life and a half.'

Linda shivered and Granddad hugged her tight. The sub was still uneven, the floor at a slight angle.

'Did I ever tell you about Mr Beacham?' he said.

Linda could tell that he was going to tell her a story, an attempt to distract her from what was happening. For once, she didn't mind, and shook her head.

'Well,' Granddad continued, 'you say I'm not that old. And in some ways you're right. Seventy-three isn't as old as it used to be, you know? When I was a lad, 73 was ancient, unheard of almost. But age isn't just a number, is it? Look at Churchill – he was Prime Minister when he was eighty! But I know that I'm not that old because I'm not as old as Mr Beacham was. I was born in 1906... you see, it sounds funny now when you say it out loud. Nineteen-oh-six. It's the "oh", isn't it? "Oh! Are you really that old?"'

Linda laughed and so did Granddad.

'Anyway, Edward VII was the King. That's why I'm called Edward – did I ever tell you that? He was the Queen's... what would it be... great-grandfather.' He stopped, looking at Linda as if he were offended. 'There! That look!'

'Well,' she said, trying not to laugh. 'When you say *great*-grandfather...' She giggled. 'Sorry. I don't think I've ever known anyone who's met their great-grandfather, so it just seems odd.'

'Well, yours died before you were born. Come to think of it, he died before your *father* was born.'

'I'm sorry,' said Linda. 'Go on.'

'Oh, yes. Well. I went to quite a posh school – the kind your father would never have sent you to. When I was about, ooh, six or so, we were all called to a special, early morning assembly. We all had to gather in the school's hall and sit in perfect silence whilst the headmaster – Mr Milligan, he was called; very strict man – gave a talk about... something or other, I can't remember now. We had morning prayers and sang a hymn, the kind of thing we did at every assembly. Then Mr Milligan said he had a special guest to introduce.

'This had happened before. We'd had talks from the local vicar, and our MP and an army general. They came to the school, gave a speech that no one listened to, and went home. Anyway, this one time, Mr Milligan introduced a man called Mr Beacham. I was sat quite near the front of the hall – it must have been when I was in the lower school – and got a good look at him. He wasn't very tall, I remember, and stooped a bit. He used a cane, but was fairly sprightly, you know.

'His voice wasn't that loud, but I could hear him fine. He thanked Mr Milligan, then said he was going to talk about his life. His life? Why would we want to hear about some old timer's life? It was when he said that today was his birthday, and that he was a hundred years old...

'That got my attention. He'd been born during the Napoleonic Wars. Can you believe that? It was the most fascinating lecture we had at that school. He'd not been anyone particularly special. Just someone who lived locally, had worked in the nearby town all his life; he'd got married, had children and grandchildren... and great-grandchildren. But it was the dates that fascinated me. He'd been born in, I think, 1812 and his wedding had been in the 1830s or something.

'I remember afterwards, working out when I'd be a hundred. The year 2006. It still seems an awfully long way off, doesn't it, even today.'

'It'd be 2068 for me,' said Linda, smiling.

'I hope you get there! But I doubt I'll be around by then. Your father might be, though... he'd only be 118...' Granddad Edward never missed a chance to bring up the fact that his son had become a father at 18. It still caused arguments between them.

Linda realised that she'd not been thinking about the submarine. Granddad's story had worked. The sub had levelled out now, but it was still moving – at quite a speed, it seemed. She snuggled closer to her grandfather and he squeezed her reassuringly.

'Colonel Grainger? Can the commander have a word?' Brandis had appeared at the laboratory door, and Linda's grandfather stood up and went to join him on the bridge. Why had he called grandfather 'Colonel'? He must have been in the navy, or maybe the army, during the War. You keep your rank after you retire, don't you?

The constant hum was starting to annoy her, the way the wall was vibrating too. How deep had they gone? A few feet? A mile? Linda had no way of knowing. How long would this 'mission' take? How much oxygen did the submarine have? When would she get home? Would she get home?

'Love?'

Linda snapped round at the sound of Granddad's voice. He was smiling softly at her, but his eyes were worried. Linda knew the look: something was up. She stood and walked over to him, grabbing hold of his outstretched hand a bit too quickly. Pull yourself together, she thought.

'Linda, I'm not sure what I can say.' He was whispering – as much as he could, given the throb of the engines. 'They're not telling me everything, but it looks like we may be here a while.'

Be strong, thought Linda. Be assertive. 'What's wrong?' she asked. 'What's going on?'

'We're heading out into the English Channel,' Granddad said. 'Their radar systems have found something... unusual, and it needs investigating.'

'Why us? Why this submarine?'

'We were the closest. We can get there within the hour, report back what's happening.'

'What is happening?'

Edward smiled – at Linda's sudden assertiveness, no doubt. 'Well, as I say, Commander Oliver hasn't filled me in completely, but it seems something, um, crashed. Something rather large.'

Susan and the Doctor had been led through the doorway, out of the white void. 'A holding area, nothing more,' the giant snail had explained to them as he gracefully glided in front of them. They moved into what was clearly a space ship's corridor, portholes and control panels lining the wall. In fact, it transpired as the snail talked to them that it was the ship that had collided with the TARDIS, taking it into Earth's orbit with them.

'We have submerged in one of the planet's waterways,' the snail was saying as he led them down the bleak, grimy corridor. Its voice gurgled with each word. 'We regret that your transportation was in our orbital path. We pushed you into the planet's gravity, and you would surely have disintegrated on impact. Therefore, we teleported you aboard for your own safety.'

'That is most kind of you,' the Doctor said.

'No gratitude is necessary, biped man.'

'Biped man? What tosh! My name is the Doctor, and this –' he motioned for Susan to join him by his side '– is my granddaughter, Susan.'

'A familial relationship. That is good to see.'

'And, despite your humility,' the Doctor continued, 'thanks are quite necessary. You saved us from a potentially nasty crash-landing. However, may I ask where my... transportation is?'

'That too was teleported aboard, Doctor biped. It is safe. Look.' The snail gracefully moved over to a bulkhead set into the wall, and as it got close the bulkhead slid up with an electronic hiss. Behind it was another white void, just as endless. However, a few metres inside the space was the TARDIS.

The Doctor laughed. 'Oh, my, it's good to know that my ship is safe. It's very –' He stopped suddenly and marched into the void. The snail followed him, then Susan.

'Is everything all right, Grandfather?' she asked.

'What is that?' The Doctor was standing by the TARDIS door. Only now did Susan see that the door was open; a thick cable was draped through the doorway and was somehow, incongruously, plugged into the white, metallic floor. The Doctor went inside the ship, then quickly returned. Susan could tell that he was trying to remain calm. 'Hmm? What have you done?'

The snail smiled – or, at least, Susan guessed it was a smile. 'It was because of our action that your ship was damaged,' it said.

'Damaged? Eh, what? How is it damaged?'

'Your power supply was drained.'

'Yes... well...' said the Doctor, in a more conciliatory tone. Susan knew why: the power drain had begun to happen before the TARDIS had been hit.

'We are recharging your craft,' the snail said. 'It should not take long.' The snail towered over both of them, but seemed pleasant enough to Susan – a bit prissy perhaps, but kind-hearted. 'Do you know of this planet?'

The Doctor's eyes narrowed – a sign, Susan knew, of him being unsure what to say. 'Only vaguely,' he said. 'We are travellers; we are not from this sector of space.'

'We will be most pleased to help you back into orbit once we have concluded our business here,' said the snail.

'We?' asked Susan. 'There are more of you?'

'Yes. We are Slarvians.'

'Slarvians?' the Doctor said. 'No, I'm afraid I've not had the pleasure. It's very nice to meet you.'

The giant snail bowed its head slightly as they left the white void – a sign of respect, Susan could see that. In the corridor, another electronic door opened quickly, and the Slarvian moved through into a control bridge. A number of other snails were manning the ship's organic controls.

'Susan,' whispered the Doctor. 'Come here, child.' He pulled her close, talked quickly. 'Don't give them any information; they shouldn't be here.'

Linda stood in the doorway of the laboratory, looking through to the bridge. Her grandfather and Commander Oliver were deep in conversation; other members of the crew all engaged in various tasks. No one had noticed her.

'Approaching coordinates, Commander,' said Brandis.

'Thank you, Lieutenant.' Oliver turned back to Linda's granddad.

'Good second you've got there, Guy,' said Granddad Edward.

'Yes,' said Oliver. 'He's been my executive officer for two years. Practically runs the missions himself.' He rolled up his sleeve and methodically rubbed his forearm. 'What could it be, do you think?' he said, pointing at a radarscope.

'You're worried, Guy,' said Granddad. 'I can tell.'

'Look at the screen, Eddie. It's massive. It's not a ship or a sub – not one of ours, at any rate.'

'Soviet?'

'I don't think so. It doesn't look like anything I've seen before.'

There were only the six of them aboard the sub, Linda realised: her granddad, herself, Commander Oliver, Lieutenant Brandis and two crewmen. The bridge was full of activity, everyone doing something to help. One uniformed man was studying a map laid out on the small table in the centre of the bridge. Brandis was constantly relaying information from a walkie-talkie on a cable to the other crewman, who repeated the instructions as he did them.

Linda felt like a fifth wheel, but felt safer keeping an eye on what was going on rather than being alone in the lab. She also couldn't help but watch Granddad – he was like a different man. She'd never seen him in a crisis before; never seen how calm and authoritative he could be. Oliver wanted advice – anyone could see that – and it was clear that he trusted Linda's grandfather. They were old friends – but how? What kind of life had Granddad had that gave him friends in naval intelligence?

That doubt again. That sense of the unknown. Linda loved her grandfather, she really did. But it was beginning to sink in that she didn't really know him that well. She was only 11. He'd been, what, 62 when Linda was born. Sixty-two. He'd lived almost a lifetime's worth before she came along. As far as she was concerned, he was Granddad Edward, an OAP who came over at Christmas and they went to visit in London.

He'd probably come to visit more often now, Linda suddenly thought. Now that Grandma Eleanor had died.

It bothered Linda how this was a Granddad Edward she'd not seen before. As soon as it was clear something was up, he'd known what to do; how to handle Linda; how to offer support to Commander Oliver.

'Commander,' said Brandis. 'We're here.'

'Very good,' said Oliver. 'Hold position.' He turned to Granddad Edward. 'The target is on the sea floor. Not moving. As far as we can tell, it's... big. About two hundred feet long.'

'I don't like it, Guy,' said Granddad Edward. 'It's suspicious. How was it detected?'

Commander Oliver looked about, checking that the crewmen were all occupied. He didn't spot Linda. 'It crashed.'

'Crashed?'

'Fell out of the sky and crashed into the sea.'

'Good God, Guy. If it's a plane, we need to send out the rescue teams. If anyone survived, they can't have much air – if any.'

'I know that, Edward,' Oliver snapped. He then checked himself. 'Sorry.'

'Don't worry. We're all a little tense.'

'The Admiralty has ordered us to take a close look and report back – specifically nothing more or nothing less.'

'Well, that's as may be –' Linda's grandfather paused briefly as he caught sight of her in the doorway. He winked at her before continuing. 'But perhaps we should take our closer look as soon as possible. We can then have a think about to do next.'

* * *

'But, Grandfather, you said you didn't know of them.'

'Of course I said that,' the Doctor said harshly. 'But I do! The Slarvians are not to be trusted. I've heard of them enslave whole planets for their own ends. We must get them away from Earth.'

Susan looked across at the creatures. They were studying screens and read-outs, allowing Susan and her grandfather the chance to talk. 'What do you mean?' she asked.

'We must find out what they want. I'm sure we would have heard if the Earth had been enslaved during the late twentieth century, don't you? There are five billion human beings on this planet. My guess is that they see it as a potential target.' He looked over at the lead Slarvian. 'Yes, I can just imagine their Emperor being very happy with this find.'

'Their Emperor? So, our friend over there isn't in charge?'

'No, no, no,' snapped the Doctor. 'The Emperor will most probably be on a mother ship of some sort. The fleet will be in hyperspace, waiting for potential targets.' He looked around the control room. 'This, I would wager, is nothing more than a scout ship.'

'Doctor biped,' called the lead Slarvian – the captain of this ship, it seemed. 'We are not alone.'

Susan followed her grandfather over to the main control deck. The snail was intently watching a screen that was showing a three-dimensional layout of the seabed. It was an uneven floor, but not too deep, giving away to Susan that they must be fairly near a landmass – and therefore the local population. The Slarvian ship was highlighted in a stark green, and as the Slarvian captain began to talk Susan noticed another green shape moving towards them from above.

'Yes, that unidentified target must be another vessel,' it explained, then turned away and spoke to another snail. 'Report to the mother ship. We must inform the Emperor that contact will be made imminently.'

'Mother ship?' said the Doctor, suddenly flustered. He then smiled engagingly. 'There are quite a few of you, erm, Slarvians about, then?'

'Yes, Doctor biped,' rasped the Slarvian captain. 'Our Emperor will be most pleased. In 27 manclags we will be able to begin our colonisation.'

'Colonisation?' The Doctor laughed haughtily. Susan could always tell when he was putting on an act. 'What? Of this world? Is there really anything of interest here? It looked like quite a barren planet, even from orbit. The seas are empty of all but the most basic animals; the land looks inhospitable and mostly deserted. You're wasting your time, surely. I should leave if I were you.'

'We have fully surveyed this world. A serendipitous event drew our attention here and we have selected it for infestation. That signal you see on the screen is our first point of contact.'

'Okay,' said Oliver. 'Hold position.'

There was no perceptible change in the feel of the submarine. Linda couldn't tell if they'd come to a dead halt or were drifting along. The engines were still throbbing at a regular pace.

'Lieutenant, full survey of target.'

Brandis nodded then immediately set to work. He tapped away at keyboards and barked short, clear orders to the two crewmen. As monitors and ticker-tape printouts began to churn out information, he scanned each read-out. Within a minute or two, without notes, he said to Oliver and Linda's granddad, 'It's hollow, sir. Our sonar indicates a substantial pocket of air. Heat signatures are detectable from areas of the target that could plausibly be engines, but they're cooling as we speak. The hull is mostly smooth – certainly artificial – except for four regularly spaced hatches towards the aft, two on the port, two on the starboard. Best guess is that they're airlocks or escape hatches.'

'Thank you, Lieutenant,' said Oliver. He turned to Granddad Edward. 'There are probably survivors in there. Or perhaps... something else.'

'What do you mean, Guy?'

The commander paused, then said, 'This thing fell to Earth from space.'

'I see.'

'You're not shocked, are you?'

'I've... seen enough things in my life now that not much shocks me any more.'

Oliver smiled. What would he be like without Granddad here to help him, Linda thought.

'What was it the Admiralty said?' asked Linda's grandfather. 'Have a look and then return to port? Do you think they know something we don't?'

'Perhaps.' Oliver rubbed his forearm. Linda had seen him do that a couple of times during the day. 'We'd be disobeying orders. I'm still in service, Edward. You're not.'

'We're losing valuable time, Guy. Which guilt is less preferable: disobeying an order or allowing people to die? Tell Brandis to take us closer. Perhaps their airlock will be compatible with ours – with yours, I mean.'

Oliver smirked at him. 'It's good to see you in action again, Eddie,' he said. 'You're a natural. But you are also a civilian – are you sure you don't want to go back and sit with your granddaughter?'

Edward looked across at Linda, who still hadn't been spotted by the others. She smiled at him and winked.

Granddad Edward's eyes were alive. 'Wild horses couldn't drag me away,' he said, turning back to Guy.

'Brandis!' shouted Oliver. 'Set course for the target's nearest airlock. We're going to try to hook up.'

Brandis didn't react; his back was to his commander and Granddad Edward. From Linda's angle, she could see that his eyes were closed and that he was breathing quite heavily.

'Brandis?' said Oliver more forcefully. 'What's the matter, man?'

'Granddad,' said Linda. 'I think something's –'

Brandis whipped round, eyes now open. He'd pulled a gun out from under his jacket and pointed it at Oliver.

'Lieutenant, what in God's name –'

'Quiet!' barked Brandis. He turned to the two crewmen. 'Lay in the course the commander requested, but hold position ten metres out until I give you the word.'

'Son, listen,' said Edward. Brandis swung round, training the pistol on Linda's granddad. Linda screamed, and he turned to her.

'Calm down,' said Edward soothingly. 'Calm down. I was just going to tell you that my granddaughter is there. I didn't want you to be surprised by her. Please – let her come to me.'

Brandis motioned with the gun and Linda ran over to her grandfather. She hugged him tightly, trying not to cry. Must be strong. Must be brave.

The screen that dominated the control room fizzled into life. The static cleared enough for a Slarvian to appear, but interference lines still crossed its face. This one was different from the snails aboard the ship. It looked larger and possibly older.

'Your Magnificence,' said the Slarvian captain. 'We are now less than 14 manclags away from contact being made.'

'Excellent,' said the Slarvian on the screen – the Emperor, Susan guessed. 'Has our agent been activated?'

'Yes, your Splendidness, within the last manclag.'

'Your agent?' said the Doctor. He had stepped forward, next to the Slarvian captain. The Emperor did the closest Susan supposed a giant snail could get to a double-take.

'Who is this human?' it asked.

'This is Doctor biped,' said the Slarvian captain.

'Yes, your Superioritiness,' said the Doctor. 'Though I must contradict you, your Effervescence. I am not human; simply a fellow visitor to this area of the galaxy.'

'We offered Doctor biped assistance when we inadvertently hampered his space craft,' explained the captain. 'His presence will not affect our schedule.'

'I am pleased to hear it,' said the Emperor. 'The time of contact approaches.'

'So...' said the Doctor. 'You said you had an agent?'

The Emperor looked proud, Susan realised. 'A human biped,' he said, 'who is now under our control. We have psionic units to help control key personnel of the local population.'

'Most extraordinary,' the Doctor said. He turned to Susan, bringing her in on the conversation. 'Don't you think, my dear?'

'Yes, quite,' she said, playing along with the Doctor's complicity.

The Emperor on the screen glared at her. 'A female. A human female?' it said. His eyes grew in size.

'I'm not –'

'This is Susan biped,' cut in the Slarvian captain. 'She too is not human, I'm afraid. She is Doctor biped's granddaughter.'

'Yes,' snapped the Doctor, his façade slipping slightly. 'What of it?'

The Slarvian captain glided towards them menacingly. 'Our Queen requires females from our defeated rival. During the moment of her secretion, she will... feast.'

'Grandfather...' Susan backed away from the Slarvian captain. 'What does he mean, feast?'

'I'm not sure, my dear.' He looked to the Emperor. 'What exactly are you doing here?'

'We lost one of our ships on this planet some time ago. A transport vessel carrying... some vital supplies across Federation space.'

'We are on a mission to recover the supplies,' said the captain.

'Federation space?' asked Susan.

'The Slarvian race is not yet a member of the Federation, despite our petitions to join,' explained the captain. 'Our mission is... not entirely official.'

The Doctor laughed. His act again. 'Oh, I see. A quick in-and-out. And these "supplies" are important, are they?'

'They are vital, Doctor biped,' said the Emperor. 'Vital to our future.'

'Brandis!' shouted Commander Oliver. 'What are you doing?'

The young crewman had the whole bridge covered by his gun. His eyes were blank, lifeless. Linda stood next to her granddad, his arm protectively holding her close to him.

'It is nearly time, Commander. Nearly time for contact.'

'Contact? What in blazes are you –'

Granddad Edward cut in calmly: 'What's happening, son?'

Brandis's eyes narrowed slightly as he looked at Linda's grandfather. 'You know too much,' he said. 'My masters will not be pleased.'

'Who are your masters?' Granddad Edward's voice wasn't loud, but measured and precise. He looked worried, not scared – this gave Linda strength.

Brandis seemed to think about it for a moment, his eyes staring into the middle distance. He then blinked and his iciness returned. He turned to the two crewmen. 'Go to the cargo locker on the lower deck,' he ordered. 'Bring the storage caskets here. If you try anything, I shall kill these people.'

The two men stood up, unsure and slow. Their eyes darted from Brandis to Commander Oliver.

'Do as he says,' spat Oliver. 'We have no choice.'

The two men left. His gun still trained on Linda, her grandfather and

Oliver, Brandis followed the men to the doorway, checking that they opened the hatch in the laboratory floor that led to the lower deck.

'We must play along for now,' Granddad Edward whispered so that both Linda and Oliver could hear. 'And tell him the truth if he asks you a question. Don't be a hero, Guy. Not until we know what he wants.'

'Quiet!' shouted Brandis. Linda saw for the first time that he was sweating. So was she – the air was clammy and oppressive. 'No one say anything.' Brandis tapped at a couple of buttons next to a wall-mounted scanner screen, then took a small box from his top pocket. It was about this size of Dad's cigarette lighter. He pulled a strip of plastic from one side and attached it to the panel next to the scanner; it stuck in place and began to beep regularly.

'What's he doing?' whispered Oliver, barely moving his lips – Linda could only just hear him.

'I'm not sure,' said Granddad Edward.

The scanner began to go fuzzy, like an untuned television. Brandis punched keys and tapped the small box until the scanner began to clear.

The two crewmen returned, both carrying a couple of large containers.

'Put them down there,' said Brandis.

They stacked the containers in the centre of the bridge.

'Now, go and join the others.'

Brandis dropped his gun – not out of sight, just to his side – and turned to face the scanner screen. He patted down his uniform with his free hand and stood to attention.

As Linda watched, the picture on the scanner became clearer. There was a face behind the static. It was... It didn't look like a man. As the screen came into focus, it looked like the head of a snail – a giant snail, whose eyes were staring right out from the screen at her. Behind the snail were what looked like other snails sliming around a metal room. There was also an elderly man and a young girl a bit older than Linda.

Then the snail-thing talked.

'Brandis biped,' it said. 'Contact is established. The emperor is observing our operation and is most pleased.'

'Good,' said Brandis. 'I am in possession of the cargo and am holding position, awaiting instructions.'

The elderly man on the scanner walked forward, peering straight into the lens. 'My, my. Your agent's done a regal job, hasn't he? So, that was the plan, hmm? You use your psionic unit to control a human; he gets hold of the supplies you lost and brings them to this rendezvous point. Most ingenious!'

'We are now ready to make contact,' said the snail. 'Brandis biped, your vessel will now dock with our ship.'

Brandis whipped his gun into the air and pointed it at the crewmen. 'Dock with the target – the port aft airlock. Now!' The two men, after a nod from Oliver, took their seats and began to manoeuvre the submarine.

The room lurched suddenly, and the pitch of the ship dipped again.

Linda was watching the scanner. The elderly man had walked back to the young girl. She was staring right at Linda – not the room, not Brandis, but Linda. She could tell. They were looking into each other's eyes. The girl said something. She was too far away from the camera for Linda to hear what she said, but it looked like, 'Female.'

Then suddenly a different voice boomed over the speakers next to the scanner screen, a deep, rasping, jagged voice. 'Yes,' it said. 'Female!'

On the screen, everyone's heads turned sharply to the right.

'My Queen!' said the snail. 'It is time.'

It was huge, even bigger than the other Slarvians, even bigger than the Emperor. The Queen gracefully slithered into the control room, a pair of ordinary Slarvians close behind.

'If there is a human female with Brandis biped, I must feast on her. When I secrete, I must replenish my energy by feeding on a female of the defeated rival. She will be the first of many!'

'Ha ha! Secrete!' said the Doctor. 'That's it! Your "supplies" are eggs.'

'Eggs?' said Susan.

'Yes, Susan biped,' said the captain. 'But unfortunately a transport ship carrying a generation of eggs was lost two solar cycles ago. We soon tracked it to this planet. The eggs had already gestated too far to survive the journey back to Slarvos or its original target. We needed to bring the Queen here, to the eggs. Unfortunately, that has taken time.'

'I don't understand, Grandfather.'

'The Slarvians infest worlds by hatching their eggs on the planet,' said the Doctor. 'The Queen must secrete her... her "goo", a gelatinous mixture full of protein, onto the eggs to complete the process.'

The Slarvian captain slid close and dipped its head so that it was level with the Doctor's. 'That is interesting,' it said. 'You told us you had not heard of our race before.'

'Yes,' said the Doctor. His act had gone now, his bravado replaced by resilience. 'And now I can see that I was right to be discreet with you. This world is not for you: I shall stop you.'

'Our operation was planned many manclags ago,' said the captain. 'We will not allow you to stand in our way now.'

'But you asked us if we knew anything about this planet?' said Susan. 'You said you weren't from this part of the galaxy.'

'Those facts are correct. I simply needed to know what you knew. And now I can see that I was right to be discreet with you.'

'So,' said the Doctor. 'Your eggs are on that vessel on the screen, recovered by one of your agents from a crash-landing; your Queen is here. You need to introduce them, don't you?'

The Queen was now close to them, towering over both the Doctor and Susan.

'And with a human female aboard,' it said, staring at the screen, 'the process of colonisation will begin.

Susan looked at the screen: the young girl was staring back at her, straight down the lens.

The sub shook violently and a massive clang reverberated around the bridge. Linda held on to her grandfather for dear life. They'd stopped dead.

'We're, er, attached, sir,' said one of the sailors. Brandis smiled.

'Good.' He turned to the monitor. 'Contact,' he said.

On the screen, the snail came into focus. 'Excellent. Move the supplies to your vessel's airlock and prepare to open the hatch.'

Brandis turned to the crewmen. 'Take the crates to the airlock. Quickly.' He waved his gun in their direction, then followed them out, always keeping his eye over his shoulder, his gaze towards Oliver and Linda's Granddad. 'Just keep still,' he said. 'It'll all be over soon.'

Linda could see through both doors, through the laboratory and into the airlock. Brandis was starting to turn the big wheel on the outer door.

'Sir,' said one of the crewmen nervously. 'We... we need to pressurise first.'

Brandis paused and for just a moment looked confused. 'Yes,' he said finally. 'Yes, we do. See to it.'

'What is happening?' The Slarvian Queen was starting to get nervous, Susan realised. It needed the eggs – and soon.

'Brandis biped will be here with cargo within the next three manclags,' said the captain. 'Then you can begin.'

The Doctor whispered under his breath to Susan. 'We must stop the Queen getting to those eggs.' He held his fist up to his chin, deep in thought.

'But how?' whispered Susan. 'There are too many of them. They're too powerful.'

'Power!' exclaimed the Doctor, trying to keep his voice down. 'That's it! They've hooked the TARDIS up to their energy supplies. If we can get to the ship, and if it's powered up by now, I can dematerialise. The ships' power banks are connected – we'll take this ship and all the Slarvians with us! Away from the Earth!'

'But that'll still leave the eggs here, on that submarine,' said Susan.

The Doctor swatted his hand at her, excited now by his plan. 'You heard what they said: the eggs have been here for two years. Their gestation period is almost over. In a few days, they'll be useless. Now, Susan. We must do it now.'

Susan looked around – maybe they could sneak out. The Queen, the captain and all the other Slarvians were busy with controls or monitoring the situation. 'Let's do it,' she said. 'Quickly.'

'Right, child. When I say run –'

'Pressurisation almost complete,' said the Slarvians' agent on the main screen. 'We will open the airlock in a few seconds. Prepare for the cargo to come aboard.'

'Grandfather,' said Susan. 'What are we waiting for?'

'Don't you see? If they open that airlock and we dematerialise, taking the Slarvian ship with us, we condemn the crew of that ship: they'll be flooded.'

Linda watched Brandis as he moved away from the scanner screen and went back to watch the dial on the bulkhead door. He was pressurising the airlock – making sure that the sub, the airlock and whatever they'd hooked onto were at the same air pressure.

She remembered being taught about this at school; that your blood would get bubbles in it or something if the pressure wasn't right. Linda thought she could feel her ears beginning to pop – or was she just imagining that?

'Eddie,' said Commander Oliver in hushed tones. 'If we can surprise him, catch him off guard...'

'Think about it, Guy. We're two old men. He's got a gun.'

A sudden noise caught Linda's attention: 'Hello?' A quiet voice, a girl's voice. Granddad Edward still had his arms draped across Linda's shoulders, loosely hugging her to his body. He and Commander Oliver were still talking and keeping their eyes on Brandis: they hadn't heard it.

'Hello?' It was coming from the scanner screen. The snail or whatever it was had gone, and Linda could see the young girl, close by the camera.

Linda darted over to the screen. 'Yes,' she whispered. 'I'm here.'

'Quickly,' said the girl. 'You must stop that man opening the airlock – in a couple of minutes' time, we won't be here and you'll be flooded.'

'But, how?' snapped Linda.

'I don't know, but you must. It's our only –' The girl suddenly stopped and ran from out of shot, a snail quickly sliming after her.

'Run, Susan!' The Doctor was already at the door, waving frantically. Susan could feel the Slarvians bearing down behind her, getting closer. The noise of its sliming along at speed was revolting.

She got to her grandfather and they both ran down the corridor.

'This way!' Susan found the door that led to the TARDIS, which slid up as they approached. She could still hear the Slarvian captain behind them, rasping orders and gurgling with anger.

The TARDIS was just as they'd last seen it. They ran in through the open doors and up to the central console. There was the cable, running from a socket under the time rotor and draping along the floor and out of the door. The Doctor quickly checked it, then flicked three switches in quick succession.

'Grandfather!' Susan jumped as she saw the Slarvian captain at the TARDIS door. 'Quickly!'

'We can't, Susan. It will take a moment to convert the power.'

'Mr Brandis?' said Linda, her voice shaking.

He looked round from the bulkhead door, gun raised. 'What do you want?'

Linda could feel Granddad's eyes boring into her back. 'Linda, love. Come here,' he said. She ignored him.

'Mr Brandis... I just wanted to... um, thank you for the guided tour.'

'What?' His face was flushed with anger. 'What are you going on about?'

'When I... when I first got here, this morning.' Linda took a step to her side, so that she could see past Brandis and keep her eye on the pressure gauge. 'You showed me and my granddad around. Thank you.'

'"Thank you"?' said Brandis, taking a step forward. He didn't notice the gauge hit its top extreme and a small green light come on. 'The little girl's impressed, is she?'

Linda was shaking.

'How lovely. I am pleased. My day wasn't wasted after all.'

Linda felt her grandfather at her back, his hands protectively on her shoulders.

'Okay, Brandis,' he said. 'That's enough.'

Brandis smirked, then noticed the green light on the bulkhead behind him. 'Not long now,' he said. Then, to the crewmen, 'Get that door open.'

The two crewmen gingerly took hold of the wheel and tried to spin it unlocked. Just as they began, however, Linda noticed that the green light had turned red.

'That's it!' exclaimed the Doctor. 'We've done it.'

Susan heard the familiar sound of the ship's grinding engines and knew they'd dematerialised. Through the TARDIS door, she could see the Slarvian captain looking around in confusion.

'What now, Grandfather?' said Susan. 'We can't have ourselves hooked up to a Slarvian spaceship for ever.'

The Doctor looked genuinely pleased with himself. 'No, my dear.' He chuckled. 'Once we've landed, we can uncouple their power cable and take off again.'

'But what about the Slarvians? Where are we taking them?'

The Doctor hugged her close and kissed Susan on the forehead. 'Do you know, child, I've no idea whatsoever!'

'It won't budge, sir,' said one of the crewmen. He looked nervously over at Brandis. 'We've lost the oxygen seal. The... the other craft must have disconnected.'

Linda braced herself, expecting Brandis to go mad. But he just stood there, looking at the bulkhead, his back to Linda and her granddad. After a beat, he slowly turned to face them. He was crying.

'Commander?' he said. 'I don't know what's happening. What's been going on?' He looked lost, completely lost.

'It's okay, Lieutenant,' he said, calmly taking Brandis's gun. 'You've had a bit of a funny turn, that's all.'

Linda looked at the scanner screen: it was static. Granddad Edward had moved across to the two crewmen, who were now back in their positions on the bridge. 'Guy,' he said. 'You'd better look at this.'

Linda looked over the nearest crewman's shoulder at the radarscope.

'My God, Edward. It's gone.'

The other submarine or whatever it had been... it had vanished.

'Eddie...?' Oliver looked at Linda's grandfather – he clearly had no idea what had gone on.

'Well, Guy,' said Granddad. 'It's been a very interesting... training exercise, hasn't it?'

'Yes, yes,' said Commander Oliver, a little unsure. After a beat, he stood up straight. 'Set course for Portsmouth.'

'Aye, Commander,' said one of the crewmen.

Linda put her hand on Brandis's arm. 'Are you okay?' she asked nervously.

The young man sighed. 'I think so. I don't really remember anything.'

'That can happen,' said Granddad Edward. 'I've been on ships like this before. Cramped conditions, pressurised situations. It can affect the mind, make you... imagine things.'

When the light turned green and Commander Oliver opened the hatch, Linda stepped forward into the shaft of sunlight. She took in a lungful of fresh air and closed her eyes. Patiently, she waited her turn to climb the ladder and out of the submarine.

The crewmen – she still didn't know their names, she realised – helped Granddad Edward up the metal steps, then signalled that it was Linda's turn. It was about eight o'clock in the evening, but was still bright and warm. A different kind of warm, though: reassuring rather than oppressive. The breeze was magnificent.

Inside the naval buildings, Linda had to wait in a long corridor while Granddad Edward had a meeting – 'being debriefed,' he'd called it. On the walls were portraits of navy officers, all in uniforms with medals and trimmings attached, and some black-and-white photographs in simple frames. Linda noticed Commander Oliver on one of them – he was posing with a few other officers on the deck on a large boat. 'HMS *Independent*, Hong Kong, 1976,' the gold-plated caption read.

There was no sign of Granddad Edward in the photos. Linda hadn't really expected to find him, but it was worth looking.

* * *

'Mum?' asked Linda as she ate her late supper that night.

'Yes, love.' Linda's mum looked up from the *Radio Times*.

'You know those old photo albums of Dad's? The ones with all the old pictures of Granddad Edward?'

'Yeah.'

'Where are they?'

'Oh, under the stairs, I imagine,' she said, flicking a page. 'We haven't dug them out for years.'

Linda soon found them – four leather-bound albums full of mainly black-and-white photographs. Her granddad as a young boy in a posh school uniform; at his wedding to Grandma Eleanor; smiling to the camera at a party with a young boy in his arms – Linda's dad, she realised.

Linda spent the entire night looking through the albums.

The Lost

L. J. Scott

An Adventure of the Second Doctor,
with Jamie McCrimmon and Victoria Waterfield

Wednesday 5 May 1982. New York City

The *bleat* of another horn startled Jamie. He looked to see what had caused this one, but only saw a man in a yellow, metal beastie waving his arm at the blue, metal beastie before him as he sported some odd finger gesture. The smell of this horrid canyon was reminiscent of burning hair and soot; exhaust from the beasties, the Doctor had explained. The people – oh, so many people – made Jamie feel nervous.

'So, Jamie,' said the Doctor. 'How do you like New York?'

'It's, ah, a fine place, Doctor. If it's the sort of place you go for.'

Victoria added, 'I think he much prefers the countryside, Doctor.'

'Oh, nonsense, Victoria,' said the Doctor. 'How could anyone not be impressed by this great city of your future, an icon of its great society and home to the first burgeoning world government? How can anybody not like this wonder?'

Jamie shot the Doctor an annoyed look. 'Doctor, it's so... *unnatural*.'

'Well, of course it is, Jamie! It's the man-made marvel of the century! Each paving stone is set only after months, if not years, of debate by great councils and city-planning commissions. In this city, just a few blocks away from us, are two of the tallest buildings in the world.'

'Aye, that's as maybe,' said Jamie. 'But it's not for me.'

'Oh, Jamie,' snapped the Doctor. 'Will you –'

Victoria placed a hand on the Doctor's shoulder, trying to calm him. 'Perhaps we should be going,' she said. 'We're nearly there, aren't we?'

Edward Grainger's fingers itched. It wasn't a physical itch. It was the itch of *the habit*. No matter how many years passed, it would still nibble at him, especially when he thought about work or was working. And that was exactly the problem. He wasn't working, not as such. This was a personal matter.

An American couple had taken the table next to him at the café. She was a smoker, he was not. Edward wished things were once again as they had been during his mother's time, when such a thing would be deemed unladylike, and he would now be saved these wisps of temptation floating his way. He stared at his untouched Danish pastry and used his fingers to turn its plate round in place once, twice, anything to keep his fingers busy. To stop the itch.

He was finally saved from his frustrations as *another one* stopped by the building on the other side of the street, caught in the web. The boy must be Scottish, unless he was local New Yorker who wore a kilt as some kind of fashion statement. So the question was, would he go in, or would he finally drift away as number of others had these past few days?

Neither; he was with two others, a middle-aged man and his daughter perhaps. Perhaps this was his son. Perhaps she, his sister. Perhaps they were merely strangers asking for directions.

As their unheard conversation progressed, Edward's last thought was dispelled. He saw the same sort of friction he'd been having with John recently. As boys became men, why did it always seem they had to argue with their fathers? So this man with the young girl was the boy's father. Or at least some sort of adult guardian...

'Now, then.' The Doctor looked straight at Jamie, his expression serious and concerned. 'Are you sure you want to go through with this?'

'You asked me to, Doctor,' he said. Jamie had known that the Doctor would worry; he always did about his friends.

'Yes, but I also said that you shouldn't feel like you don't have a choice.'

'I'll be fine.' Jamie looked across the street at the building they'd searched the city to find. 'Besides,' he said, 'I'll have Victoria to help me.'

'Yes, Doctor,' she said. 'We'll be all right.'

The Doctor's smiled. 'Okay, then. As we discussed. If there are any problems – anything at all – you leave, call for help, come and find me. Then, when we've found out what's going on, we can explore the city!'

'One thing at a time, Doctor,' said Victoria.

'There's the United Nations and there you can see representatives of all the nations of the Earth.' The Doctor was trying to change the subject, both Jamie and Victoria could sense that. 'We could go to Yankee Stadium and I could teach you about Newton's laws!'

Jamie was struggling to keep up. 'Newt ton?'

Victoria giggled. 'Sir Isaac Newton! My father was an admirer of his.'

'Yes!' The Doctor was almost dancing about. 'One of the greatest minds of the seventeenth century! Of the many things he deduced was that for every action, there is an equal and opposite reaction! It's quite simple when you think about.'

Jamie's brow furrowed for a moment. 'So, as Victoria and I go undercover into that building, it makes you nervous?'

'I think you're right,' Victoria agreed.

The Doctor snapped back, 'No! No! Not that. It's about physical objects in motion!'

Jamie smiled. 'What? You mean that if I throw a knife, I'll go flying off in the other direction?'

'That's absurd, even for you, Doctor!' Victoria laughed.

The Doctor clenched his fists in frustration, and fought to stop his forearms from shaking. 'No! No! It's much more complicated! It all depends on the mass of the objects. For example, the spin of a baseball as it moves through the air –'

Jamie began laughing too. 'I thought you said it was simple.'

'Oh!' The Doctor felt the need to channel the rage building up in him. '*Fiddlesticks!*'

His exclamation only fuelled the two's laughter.

'Fine!' the Doctor declared as he looked about for something else to attract his attention. 'You go do what you have to do, be gone with you! And I'll...' Indeed something did catch his attention across the street. A face that suddenly looked away as if he didn't want to get caught watching them. '... I'll be over there, at the café.'

Edward winced at himself. In his younger days he would never have been caught observing a subject while at work. He again stared at his pastry, hoping that the subject would think his glance just a random coincidence and stop moving toward him. But another glance confirmed that the figure was still making his way through traffic towards him.

The occasional car blew its horn but it only caused the stranger to stop in the car's way to argue back in a way that Edward would have normally found humorous. But under these circumstances, nothing was humorous. He again stared at his pastry and sipped some more of his tea.

'Excuse me!' The stranger had arrived at his side.

Edward pondered if he should play the fool and pretend not to hear, but concluded it would be more suspicious. Putting on a touristy smile, he looked up to the stranger. 'Yes, may I help you?'

'Yes,' said the stranger, a fellow Englishman by the sound of it. 'I was wondering why you were watching my companions and myself?'

'Was I? No. I was just noticing the street life. It's a strange city. If I happened to glance your way, I meant nothing by it.'

The stranger paused and studied Edward for a moment. He then leaned in closer to talk in a muted, yet more stern voice, 'Now, we can go in circles, chasing each other's tails on this matter for hours. But I suspect that you need my help as much as you might be able to help me. So, shall we drop this pretence?'

If they had been in a back alley or some other secluded location, Edward would have considered a *professional* end to their meeting. Still, in this café, with so many people milling about, he felt he had few civil options open to him. Actually, who was he trying to fool? Perhaps when he was younger – but not now he was in his seventies.

Using his foot, Edward pushed one of the table's chairs out to allow this stranger a seat.

'Welcome! Welcome!' announced the man at the desk with a hollow enthusiasm as he had probably done hundreds, if not thousands, of times before. 'How may I help you?'

225

Victoria discreetly followed Jamie as he walked over. The man was somewhat odd. Bright, light blue suit, a cheery smile of porcelain white teeth, yet empty eyes – like an undertaker working years past his retirement. The shaved temples, with stringy comb-over strands on the top of his head, didn't help. Victoria wasn't sure if she should feel sorry for him or shudder.

Jamie replied simply, 'I'd... ah... like to sign up!'

'For?' the man asked in a manner that was either excited or nervous.

'For... the classes...' Jamie answered with a confused smile.

'Yes, of course, sir. But which class would you like to take?'

Victoria saved Jamie a moment's embarrassment. 'There are more than one? We've only heard of one.'

'Of course, ma'am. We offer a wide range of courses,' he returned with his practised laugh. He must have noticed Jamie's continued blank stare as he indicated a large blackboard hanging on the wall behind him. 'Perhaps this will help?'

Victoria inspected the board with Jamie. It listed evening classes in singing, numerous forms of dancing, French, Latin, Spanish, modern art, sculpture, history, literature and psychology – whatever that was. Victoria could see that Jamie was struggling to choose which course he should pick. 'Perhaps the "martial arts" evening classes, Jamie,' she said.

'A wise choice,' said the man behind the desk. 'Is your fiancée interested too?'

Victoria snorted. 'We aren't together. I'm just helping him sign up.'

'Oh, then you, yourself, wouldn't be joining us?'

'No.'

'Such a shame. Still, we'd be happy to have you, sir.'

'Thank you... sir,' Jamie returned.

'So, from your companion's words, I take it you'd like to sign up today?'

'Aye,' Jamie said, nodding. Victoria gave his elbow a reassuring squeeze.

'Very good, sir.' The clerk reached under the counter and handed Jamie a number of forms. 'Please fill these out.' He smiled. 'There are pens on the table behind you.'

Yet Jamie's enthusiasm seemed to be dissipating as he accepted the forms.

Victoria followed him as he sat down next to a low table – some kind of waiting area – uncertain of his change in attitude. 'What's the matter, Jamie? He doesn't suspect that we're "undercover".'

'I cannae fill out these forms,' Jamie replied, dropping his head. 'I don't know how to write.'

The Doctor stared over the café's table, to the man in his late sixties or perhaps even early seventies. Upon sitting, the two had fallen into a silence, each waiting for the other to break it. Finally, the Doctor spoke.

'So are we just going to sit here and stare at each other? Or are we going to talk?'

Despite his words, the other man continued to eye him up and down, apparently uncertain what to make of him. After a moment he pulled out a photograph and slid it across the table.

The Doctor picked up the photo and looked at it. The sunlight bounced off the café's table and lit the picture from behind giving the subject a slight glow. 'She's very pretty...'

'Do you know her?' the other man rattled off. 'Do you know what happened to her? Do you know where she is?'

'No, no and no. I can give you a guess that her name is Moira, she's in her mid thirties in this picture and she's probably yours, or someone else's, god-daughter.'

'How do you know that?' the man snapped.

'Because it's written on the back of the photo and the light is shining through,' the Doctor said with a bit of a smile. A date was also there – presumably when the photo was taken – but as the Doctor was unsure of the current year he asked, 'When was this taken?'

'Last year.'

'So it's 1982,' the Doctor mumbled. 'And she was born in 1948?'

'Yes.'

'And?'

The other hesitated. 'Her name is Moira Tillyard, and, yes, she's my god-daughter. She's lived in New York City since she was a child. And, since she and her fiancé started evening classes a couple of months ago, no one's seen or heard from them.'

'Evening classes?' the Doctor said.

'Yes. Why?'

'My companion, Jamie, is at that institution at the moment.' The Doctor pointed across the street to the building Jamie and Victoria were in. '*Oh, so you're here watching them! It wasn't us.*'

There was another pause before the man confirmed, 'Yes.'

The Doctor leant in closer to the man. 'Let me guess,' he said. 'Moira left an answerphone message...'

The man reached into his coat pocket and took out a small dictaphone. He pressed play and a crackly recording of a female voice – originally English but with a slight mid-Atlantic twang. 'It's me,' it said. 'Don't worry, but I won't be around for a while. I met some new friends and I'm going to go travelling.' The tape clicked off.

'What do you make of that?'

'It's a fake,' said the Doctor.

Edward was startled by the stranger's quick understanding. While he seemed to be playing dumb at times, it was clear he was highly intelligent. Edward decided to confirm the stranger's conclusion.

'It immediately raised the concerns of the Tillyards as in her message Moira make no mention of her fiancé. And while it *sounds* like Moira, my people –' Edward realised he had just given something away '– determined it was a faked recording just the same.' He hoped the other man hadn't noticed the lapse. 'I've been doing some research into other recent disappearances. I've found five other missing-person cases where the person left an answerphone message... using exactly the same wording and intonation as Moira's.'

'I'm not surprised,' said the stranger. 'The quantisation errors alone show that recording up as a synthesised voice. It may sound like Moira, but I'm willing to wager that it's not her.'

Edward was again surprised by how much this stranger seemed to be aware of such things. 'So you know the sort of device that could have fabricated this recording?'

'Yes! And no.' He frowned. 'Digital editing techniques like this are probably a decade or two off yet. And something to this sophistication... Not in 1982, at any rate.'

Something about those last sentences seemed too familiar to Edward.

Before he could follow it up, the stranger added, 'The questions are: who's doing it and why?'

'Och! You're a saint, Victoria. Thank you.'

Victoria finished up the last couple of touches and checked over the forms. 'So remember, Jamie, you've promised to practise writing once we get back to the TARDIS.'

'Oh, aye. Of course I will.'

'Jamie!' Victoria snapped, understanding his tone. 'All you have to do is match the lettering on this, or any other form... Do I have your promise?'

Jamie smiled and nodded.

Though she still didn't trust him, she smiled back. 'I better have.'

As Victoria gathered the pages for Jamie, she glanced up to notice a twenty-something in thick-rimmed glasses walking up to the counter with a rucksack. It had some kind of badge on it – an emblem for a group called the New York Giants. 'Hello,' he said to the clerk.

The clerk gave a repressed smile as he looked at the twenty-something.

'Is this where I register?' the man said. 'I've already done my forms.' He passed a few sheets of paper to the clerk, who glanced at them before filing them away in a draw.

'I see,' he said. 'Yes, welcome, you're now registered for the introductory class in pottery, which, coincidentally –' he smiled and stood up from his desk '– starts in just a few minutes.'

'Oh, right,' the man responded with another, nervous laugh. 'That's great.'

'Just through here, sir,' said the clerk, opening a door for the twenty-something to go through.

'And are you ready to go?' Victoria asked quietly of Jamie as they waited. He seemed to ponder her question for a moment, then said, 'Yes. I am.'

'Well, good luck to you, Jamie.' She gave him a hug.

He savoured the moment, holding on for a beat. 'Me too.'

Victoria watched as Jamie handed his forms over the clerk. Unsurprisingly, the clerk smiled again – and motioned for Jamie to follow the twenty-something. 'You have very nice handwriting,' he said as Jamie walked past. 'I'm sure you'll fit in here.'

Jamie was on his own now, thought Victoria. But at least their plan was running smoothly.

Edward found himself talking more comfortably with the stranger. A voice in the back of his mind tried to warn him of this. Despite that, he continued. 'When Ronald Tillyard announced his retirement and plans to return to England... Well, having spent the majority of her life in the United States, his daughter Moira decided to stay. She'd got engaged – a nice man called James – and it made sense. She'd lived here since she was a child; she's practically American now.'

'What happened?' asked the stranger.

'They went missing. Both of them. Not a word. Then, a couple of days later, Ronald received that message on his answering machine.'

'So, Ronald asked you to come over here and look into this for him.'

'Ronnie's an old friend of mine. We've often worked together. But he's... he's not too well these days. So, I offered to come over and see if I could find her.'

'And your investigations led you here. To –' the stranger looked across the street at the building they were watching and read its sign '– the New York Supplementary Education Institute. You've done well to track the clues this far.'

Edward paused for a moment as he noticed he was about to give away another bit of himself. He wasn't sure whether he should be trusting this strange man. But, somehow, he knew he could. 'I have alternative means, and some contacts, to look into this.'

'I'm sure you do,' the stranger mumbled. He paused for a moment, then asked, 'And the results of your surveillance?'

'In the past two days, I've noticed that many people go in, but do not come out. I observed the alleyway around the back, but I never saw anyone leave from there either.'

'Have you... *observed* the inside of the building during off-hours?'

Edward smiled as he knew what the stranger meant. 'Being a foreign national, not on *official* business, I've found my chances somewhat limited.'

'Very well, then, we'll have to make some for you!'

'I beg your pardon?'

'Well, I've been investigating the New York Supplementary Education

Institute too. My friends and I became aware of them a few days ago when we first arrived in this year – I mean, this *country*.' He smiled, seemingly embarrassed about something. 'I have, at this very moment, two undercover accomplices inside that building, finding out all they can.' He took a small fob watch from a pocket – it wasn't attached to its chain, Edward noticed – and stood up. 'However, they've been gone for five minutes now. I think we best go and see what's happened to them.'

Edward liked the idea of storming in and slipping through to the back to see what he could find. It occurred to him that he hadn't properly introduced himself. 'By the way, I'm Edward Grainger.'

The stranger shook his hand. 'Pleased to meet you, and I'm the –'

'There you are!' called a young girl sprinting up to them. 'Well, he's in.'

'What?' The stranger was clearly disturbed by this. 'Oh, no! I didn't say to *go in*!' he said and once again dived into traffic as he made his way across to the building across the street.

Edward, understanding the urgency, followed leaving a few dollars on the table to cover the bill.

Jamie heard a muffled yell from behind a door marked 'Private'. Before he could ask about it, the clerk answered automatically, 'Inoculations.'

'Ah.' Jamie hadn't a clue what that might mean, but the clerk's lack of interest assured him it was nothing to worry about. They were in a corridor with a number of doors leading off it and a staircase at the end.

'Third door on the left,' the clerk said, smiling as ever.

Jamie gingerly walked down the corridor. The third door in the left was marked 'Martial Arts' – the subject the Doctor had picked out for him as his 'cover story'. He turned the handle, then paused. Instead of pushing the door open, he turned back to the clerk. 'I, ah, have a few more questions.'

'What a shame!' the clerk said as he pushed Jamie backwards through the door.

The room's walls shimmered with reflected, dancing blue light. As Jamie slowly turned around, he saw the twenty-something's rucksack poking out of the top of a small dustbin. Then he heard a series of high-pitched, ascending whistles from behind and turned to see three huge, glistening aliens, with only concave depressions for faces, confronting him. Jamie reached for his dirk but the clerk snatched it from his hand.

'Now, let's not be difficult,' he said, then pointed to the source of the dancing light.

Jamie looked to the blue column of sparkles giving off a sound like something between a waterfall and frying bacon. There were no other doors in the room for escape. Jamie looked back to the clerk and tried the polite route.

'You know, I think I've changed my mind.'

⋆ ⋆ ⋆

Victoria had chased after the Doctor and his new friend through the traffic and began to catch up with them as they burst into the institute's office. It was empty. The friend scanned the interior carefully, as if looking for some hidden menace, as the Doctor went straight for back door and yanked it open to reveal the clerk.

'I beg your pardon, sir. No one is allowed back here.'

'Where's Jamie?'

'I have no idea who you're referring –'

Victoria, while unsure of the two men's urgency and concern, knew a lie when she heard one. 'Yes, you do!' She turned to the Doctor. 'He's the man Jamie and I dealt with.'

'Out of my way!' demanded the Doctor.

The clerk held up his hands, trying to calm the situation. 'Sir, I don't know what the girl's talking about. But if you'll just move back behind the counter, I'm sure we can figure this all out.'

The Doctor's friend sighed. 'I'll take care of this.' He took the clerk's lapels and pulled him out of the doorway, allowing the Doctor and Victoria to gain entrance.

'How dare you!' the clerk bit back, but a quick knock on the head soon made him quiet.

As Victoria chased the Doctor into the hallway, she could hear Jamie's muffled protests. 'Let go of me!'

The Doctor dashed through the door and then stopped dead in his tracks.

'Virtors,' he said.

At first Victoria didn't know why. Was it some curse word from the Doctor's home planet? Then, as he stepped aside, she saw three... things... monsters surrounding Jamie. At first she had taken them for three piles of wet coal sacks, but now she noticed they were stacked in some approximation of a human shape. Victoria realised two of them, the ones holding Jamie, were facing her direction. These were aliens, it was now clear.

'Unhand him!' At the sound of the Doctor's voice, the three stopped what they were doing to look in his direction; they all began a cacophony of ascending whistles.

Victoria fought off the urge to scream. She slid sideways against the wall to allow the Doctor's friend to enter. He seemed to be stunned by the sight.

The Doctor flew at the group of aliens and began wrestling with the Virtor holding Jamie's bag. He was only partly successful; the monster released its hold, only to take the Doctor's wrist in its thick, elephantine fingers. He was now caught in its unbreakable grip and desperately fumbled in his coat pocket for something.

Victoria noticed the Doctor's friend again scanning the room before deciding to make his way to the pile of bags on the far side of the room.

'Stay clear of the portal!' the Doctor shouted at him, indicating an odd column of blue sparkles.

The man skirted around it, then grabbed a bag with big straps from the top of the pile. As he held it up for his first swing at a Virtor, its side burst open as if hit by some unseen force.

Edward recognised the muffled sound of a silencer as the suitcase split with the impact. He lowered it.

The clerk had entered the room, gun in hand. 'Where's the girl?' he asked, unaware that she was against the wall behind him.

'She fell into the portal!' Edward heard the stranger snarl back, his wrist and hair still held by one of the monsters and his other hand in his coat pocket. Edward saw him wiggle his nose, which the girl seemed to understand.

As the clerk gave a brief laugh of satisfaction, the girl quietly slipped back to the door and escaped out into the corridor. The creatures whistled in her direction, but the clerk took no notice.

Still, to be safe, Edward distracted the clerk's attention. 'Where's my god-daughter?'

'Long dead, I'm sure.'

'The Virtors' home planet has a very peculiar orbit,' said the stranger as he struggled against the creature. 'Time travels rather quickly there. In the time she's been gone, she would have aged many years. And I suspect they would not have been easy years.'

'Quite so,' the clerk confirmed. 'You seem to know a lot about my little friends.'

'We've met on occasion.'

The boy, who Edward assumed was their Jamie, again began to struggle with the aliens holding him. Yet his struggle was in vain. The two Virtors began dragging him to the portal.

Edward thought about making a dash for Jamie to help, even with the clerk covering him, but then movement caught the corner of his eye. 'Wait!' he called out to the girl as she re-emerged from the hallway holding a pen – apparently the only weapon she could find.

'Wait for what?' the clerk asked Edward.

Edward looked to the stranger. He now understood that the two knew what they were doing as the stranger yelled, 'Now, Victoria!'

At his call, the girl stabbed the pen into the clerk's shoulder. He cried out in surprise, but it didn't penetrate. The clerk twirled to face her, gun at the ready. Edward flew into action but was not fast enough; the only thing that saved Victoria was a piercing whistle from the stranger. Edward noticed that the man had taken the chance to pull a penny whistle from his pocket. He had it planted firmly between his lips and was blowing with all his might into the Virtor's bowl-like face. It worked! The Virtor released its grip on him and tried to use its hands to fend off the deafening sound.

The clerk glanced back at the noise too, allowing Edward to grab his gun hand and safely aim it to the ceiling. As Victoria took the chance to kick the clerk in the rear, Edward punched him in the face. He recoiled with the impact. Before he could regain his balance, Edward used the grip on his hand to pull the clerk back and land a more solid blow to the face. This time, definitely, the clerk was unconscious. Edward took the gun from the now limp hand and looked to take aim at one of the aliens.

The Virtor holding Jamie had released his arm and grabbed the dangling cord of the whistle, ripping it from the stranger's mouth. Throwing it to the floor, the Virtor's foot squashed it flat.

Edward aimed the gun at it –

'No!' cried the Doctor, catching Jamie's attention. He looked over to see the Doctor's original Virtor had again taken one arm and it was reaching out to grab the other. The Doctor ignored it and continued talking to the old man holding the gun. 'The bullets won't penetrate their flesh and the ricochet could kill us!'

Jamie's Virtor began dragging him to the column of shimmering lights. He used his free hand to punch the Virtor in the middle of its face – with little effect. Remembering the effect of the Doctor's whistle, Jamie decided to try his best clan yell into the concave head.

It worked! The Virtor released its grip on Jamie and guarded its face with its paws. The man joined him and, with his help, the two pushed the Virtor towards the column of light and into it. There was a loud snap-crackle and the Virtor was gone.

Jamie glimpsed something coming at his head and ducked. The man was not as lucky – a carry bag ploughed into his belly and sent him crashing into a wall. Stunned, he slumped to the floor.

The Virtor who had thrown the bag again seized the Doctor's flailing arm and the two dragged him toward the column of light. Jamie regained his feet and immediately tried to prise a Virtor away from the Doctor, but alone he was little more than an annoyance. He turned to Victoria to call for her help. Before he could, the Doctor called to him calmly, 'Jamie?'

Jamie turned back. The Doctor was almost in the column, with a Virtor to either side. Yet he did not look worried. He raised one foot and placed its sole on Jamie's chest. Jamie looked at it in confusion, and watched as the Doctor's other foot joined it. Jamie looked back to the Doctor for an explanation, but the Doctor only said, solemnly, 'Goodbye, Jamie.'

Thrusting with both of his legs against Jamie's chest, the Doctor succeeded in throwing the two Virtors off balance and all three tipped into the column of light. They were consumed with a loud flash.

Jamie found himself thrown to the floor as he realised what was happening. 'Nooooo!'

Victoria screamed.

★ ★ ★

233

The high-pitched scream brought Edward out of his winded, semi-conscious stupor, and he pushed the rucksack from his lap. He looked around as he carefully got up. The room was empty of monsters; only Jamie, Victoria and the unconscious clerk remained.

The two looked frantic. Jamie tried to comfort Victoria as she continuously asked, 'What should we do? What should we do?'

'I... I don't know,' replied Jamie as he looked around for something, *anything.*

Edward guessed the stranger had gone into the column with the last of the Virtors, and began to understand their loss. He too looked around the room for lack of any better idea what to do. If only the girl had used that piercing scream of hers, it might have changed the outcome of the fight. But he was also to blame, as he could have removed the silencing muzzle from the gun and shot it overhead; surely the silencer had been used more for the Virtor's needs, not the clerk's. 'I'm sorry,' he said to the two.

'Sorry?' Jamie was having none of it. 'Sorry's not going to help! How are we going to get the Doctor back?'

Edward stiffened upon hearing the name 'Doctor'. It couldn't be! Was he another one of *them?*

'We'll have to go after him!' Victoria said and sprinted for the column of light.

Jamie caught her arm and stopped her. 'Don't be daft! We don't even know if those sparkles lead anywhere.'

The boy was right, thought Edward. The column might have simply been some means of disposing of rubbish. Yet the more he thought about it, the more it seemed unlikely, and his eyes returned to the dustbin full of suitcases. Surely the aliens hadn't set up this entire scheme just to collect a random assortment of used clothing.

'We've got to do something!' Victoria bit back between tears as she tried to free her arm from Jamie's grip. 'Let go! We've got to do something!'

Edward bent down over the clerk. Perhaps he could revive him and ask questions. But the clerk was clearly going to be out for quite some time.

'No, you cannae!'

'Jamie, don't you understand. The Doctor said time is different there. Every moment we wait could be days without help!'

Jamie seemed to reflect for a moment, then said, 'I'll go. Alone.'

'What?' Victoria was now caught off-guard.

'You stay here with the old man. I'll go.' He released his grip of Victoria and prepared to run into the column of light.

'No!' Edward shouted.

Perhaps it was because of his age and the good life he'd led, that he decided it might be time to make a sacrifice. Or perhaps it was the touch of insult at being counted out because of his age. Either way, his decision was made. Edward closed his eyes and ran toward the column of light before second thoughts got the better of him.

There was a loud crackle and Edward felt an impact to his chest, causing him to fall back onto the floor. He opened his eyes to see the Doctor beaming back at him.

'Oh! Excuse me!'

As the Doctor got to his feet, Edward found he was still in the room.

There was another crackle and an elderly man, of perhaps seventy, emerged from the column of light and walked into the room. Then another, a woman in her forties, and another in her sixties, all wearing tattered rags. Each shielded their eyes from the light of the room.

Edward returned to his feet as he watched the parade of people emerging from the unknown. One, perhaps in his early thirties, appeared, wearing a pair of thick glasses, one of the lenses cracked. After a moment looking around, he spied the New York Giants rucksack. He made his way over to it and, as he picked it up, began to cry.

'Some of them might be able to continue their lives,' the Doctor said into Edward's ear. 'But, for others, they would have aged too much. They'll likely need new identities. I believe *your people* can help with that? Oh, and I suspect this wasn't the only location they were taking people from. Can you look into that for me? I'll permanently close this portal once the last of the victims has returned.'

With a curt smile, the Doctor made his way to Jamie and Victoria, who were overjoyed by his return. He gave Victoria a hug as she settled her head against his chest. He told them of his little insurrection of the slaves on the planet Virtus. The three shared a moment of laughter as Edward watched. Victoria looked up and picked out a hair on the top of the Doctor's head, asking if he had gained a few grey hairs while he was gone. The Doctor brushed her hand aside in false indignation and the three again shared a laugh.

An elderly woman, perhaps in her late eighties or early nineties, tugged at Edward's sleeve and he looked to see her aged, yet still tender eyes looking back up at him. 'Do... do I know you?' she asked in what was now a craggy voice.

Moira, Edward realised.

The last of the survivors had returned and they had all filtered into the front room. True to his word, the Doctor had made the column of sparks go away. Jamie watched as the 'Grainger' fellow finished with the shop's telephone and set it back on its base.

'It won't be long now until the authorities arrive,' the Doctor noted. 'I'd better check on him, make sure he'll be all right.' With that, the Doctor drifted away.

'You didn't tell me the Doctor had simply told you to find out what the office looked like,' said Victoria with another quick glance at the elderly woman Grainger had called Moira. 'He didn't tell you to go through with the charade of applying for the class.'

Jamie mulled over his answer for a moment before he said, 'Aye, well... it seemed more productive than just having a quick look in the first room. Where would that have got us, eh? Anyway, the Doctor would only have worried if I'd told him beforehand, wouldn't he? It's best that he was... left in the dark.'

The two laughed as the Doctor returned.

'What's so funny?' he asked.

'We were sharing our deepest gratitudes for you,' answered Jamie. 'Amongst ourselves.'

'I somehow doubt that. Very well, keep your secrets,' he said with a raised nose and a sniff.

A black van pulled up and parked outside the window. 'We'd better get going,' the Doctor mumbled as he pointed it out to his two companions. The three moved to the front door and the Doctor opened it, standing aside.

Grainger called out over the heads of the others. 'Wait, Doctor! I need you to explain –'

'Yes, thank you for the directions! Great seeing you too!' the Doctor called back, cutting him off, as he held the door open for the black-suited men to enter. With the last of them in, the three slipped out before Grainger had another chance to stop them.

They made their way casually down the pavement, glancing back over their shoulders. By now, more black vans had arrived, and this time the men within wore white coats and pulled out stretchers.

'Doctor?' asked Jamie after a while. 'What was it like?'

'What was what like, Jamie?'

'Inside that... light.'

The Doctor stopped walking, suddenly looking sad. 'I won't lie to you, Jamie. It wasn't pleasant. The Virtors' home planet is an odd place – and not just because of the time shift.'

'Time shift?' asked Victoria. 'You said it moves faster there.'

'Yes,' said the Doctor. 'From my point of view, I was away for a few weeks.'

'A few weeks...' Jamie couldn't believe it. The Doctor had only been gone a few minutes.

'The Virtors run what is essentially a planet-wide labour camp,' he continued. 'The prisoners are people from all over the galaxy – different species from thousands of different worlds. The Virtors hand-pick people. They don't just want labourers; they want enquiring minds, intelligence and men and women with a thirst for knowledge. I suppose that's what the charade of the education institute was all about – they thought they could attract a certain type of citizen.' His face flushed angrily. 'The fools.'

'Did you manage to bring everyone back, Doctor?' asked Victoria.

The Doctor smiled softly. 'Most of them.'

There was a moment's pause, a silence between the friends, before they started walking again.

'Come on,' said Victoria, moving in between the Doctor and Jamie and putting her arms through theirs. 'Back to the TARDIS.'

Old Boys

James Parsons & Andrew Stirling-Brown

An Adventure of the Sixth Doctor,
with Peri Brown, Melanie Bush and Evelyn Smythe

86 Hobb's Lane,
Knightsbridge, SW7

27 September 1986

My dearest Sam,

I hope that this finds you well. I know it's been many years since we spoke and I am sorry I haven't found the courage to write before. I've often picked up a pen and contemplated how I would start a letter but I never found the right way and the letter remained unwritten.

However, something happened recently which gave me the excuse I needed. You'll have to bear with me but it will finally answer questions which go back nearly 25 years.

Post-retirement, life had been less fraught than it was, but not all that different. It was Eleanor's death which really changed things. I hadn't appreciated that my social life had grown so dependent on her friends. The office was never particularly sociable but Eleanor more than compensated for that and we had a wide circle of friends.

But they were her friends, and her death meant that we started to drift apart. I'm a solitary creature by nature but I miss a good chat.

Which is why the invitation I received two weeks ago came as a nice surprise. It was unsigned but asked me to join three of our former colleagues for dinner at the Connaught to mark the fiftieth anniversary of our first working together.

Odd choice of event to celebrate, I thought. I even checked the dates to confirm. It seemed a contrivance; we could have met up for a drink without an excuse. Not that it would have stopped me going. Once my curiosity was piqued there was never any doubt about that.

But when the time came I found myself pocketing the miniature tape recorder that John bought me for my birthday a few years ago. As I dropped it into my pocket it struck me that it wasn't just my curiosity which had been aroused but also my suspicions.

I arrived to find two of them already waiting for me: Angus McCloud – whom you'll remember for his chain smoking – and Warwick Montfort. In fact he's Sir Warwick now. I can't imagine what for, though. Services to the paper industry probably, given the amount he used up endlessly rewriting reports – that, or all his sucking up finally paid off. Angus is as dour as ever, so dry he's arid. The table was already wreathed in its own little fog of smoke, courtesy of Angus. I wasn't sure whether I was glad I had given up or about to regret it and lapse. Both of them asked if I had heard from you. I said no.

After a few minutes, Guy Oliver, from naval intelligence, joined us. He's in a wheelchair now, poor devil, chronic osteoporosis, but he still looks like you wouldn't want to meet him in a dark alley. And his temperament hasn't changed either, still the most down-to-earth man I've ever known, no self-pity, nothing. His driver brought him to the table, then retired to another and sat down.

I only mention the driver because, inadvertently, he sparked the conversation for the evening. We'd just ordered our meal when I spotted him using a portable telephone. Personally, I think it's damned rude to use one in a restaurant but, this being the Connaught, they were wonderfully discreet and no one said a word.

It provoked an interesting set of responses from my companions.

McCloud and Montfort thought it was nothing more than a toy for rich, city types. In today, out next week.

Oliver, on the other hand, was almost paranoid about them. I wouldn't have imagined him as a technophobe. But he expressed his dislike of them in his, let's say, typically expansive manner.

I can see how useful they could be, especially in our line of work. Although I'm not sure I could ever see them becoming as ubiquitous as the people on *Tomorrow's World* seem to think. Mind you, they promised us paper clothing by the 1980s, so what do they know.

Our conversation turned to the rash of new gadgets and gizmos which have appeared recently. Things which will 'fundamentally change our way of life' according to my technology-mad son. I think he's probably got a point but my friends disagreed, vehemently. In fact, Oliver began to relate a story which, he said, 'only serves to highlight the dangers of believing that all that glisters technologically is gold.' Pompous twit!

This is where my tape recorder comes into its own. For once, my memory being as rangy as it is, I can quote with accuracy. Oliver set the scene: 'December '75, height of the Cold War. I was stationed in Hong Kong, running surveillance on what our American friends charmlessly called gooks. I'd been buried in a basement for weeks, monitoring communications. Routine stuff, mainly. All the latest whiz-bang American technology. Boring. Boring. Boring.

'At least until one night. On my own in the computer room, about 3am. Sitting there, flicking through the day's surveillance data and wondering what I'd done to deserve this posting, when in walked this woman. Short. Redhead. The most bizarre outfit you can imagine – and remember we're talking about the seventies here – like something out of a pantomime. Anyway, she walks straight in, tosses a "hello" at me, sits down at the desk, pulls a black box out of her bag and starts wiring it into the mainframe.

'I'd never seen anything like it. Utterly brazen. I just sat there like a monkey. Took me a few seconds to recover, get up, pull my gun, and ask just what the devil it was she thought she was doing.

'She looked at me as if I had just asked the most absurd question imaginable. Then her whole face just sort of crumpled in pain. Then, to my astonishment, a hand smacked down on my wrist, my gun was snatched away and chucked into the wastebasket, and I was spun around.

'Well, the man facing me made the girl look tasteful: 40s, heavy-set, curly hair and in an outfit which I couldn't even begin to describe. Ghastly riot of colour. Looked like he'd got dressed in the dark. Extraordinary.

'What I found hardest to grasp was that I'd been taken by surprise. First time ever. I was about to ask what the hell was going on when the man gestured for me to sit down. And I sat. Too stunned to do much else.'

Oliver paused here and stared, as if he were looking right through me. 'Odd thing is it never occurred to me to retrieve the gun. Shock, probably. Anyway, this chap explained, as though talking to an idiot, that his friend, Mel, needed to use our satellite uplink for a few minutes. Otherwise life on Earth as we knew it would cease to exist.

'Perfect, I thought, I've been shanghaied in one of the most secure locations in the whole of Hong Kong by a lunatic and his pantomime pal.

'I managed to angle myself round so I could see what they were doing. She was tapping away at a keyboard and he was watching intently. They didn't say a word to each other. But for some reason I began to realise that they were deadly serious. I'd been in this game a long time and I know when I'm dealing with fantasists and when I'm facing people who, rightly or wrongly, believe absolutely in what they are doing.

'The man noticed me watching and started to explain what they were up to. I suppose he thought he was being helpful. Most of it was technical jargon but the gist seemed to be that whatever they were using was way ahead of anything we might have. I don't mean cutting-edge. I mean beyond cutting-edge. Years ahead.

'He said that in order to prevent what was going to happen – I'll come to that – they had had to, quote, bend the rules. Mel seemed to think that this was somehow cheating. I suggested that if one is trying to prevent the end of life on Earth as one knows it, then one shouldn't worry oneself too much about being fair. She muttered something about "so much for the British spirit of fair play". Then her box beeped and she said, "Okay, I'm in. What do I do now?"

'Never forgotten what her friend said next: "While the opposition are looking for you 26 years from now, you have to have crossed the four extant bridges to Vrahn, raise the portcullis at gate six and kill the Cell-Core. Once that's done, the secondary function sequence of the plug-in can activate and do its job." That was it. Word for word. Pure gibberish. But she seemed to understand what he meant.

'As Mel started typing furiously away, peering at a tiny screen built into the box, I spotted the bronze bracelet on her wrist. It had an intricate entwined leaf pattern on it, like ivy, except the vine seemed to wind from the bracelet up onto her arm and then actually into her skin. I asked what it was. The man explained that Mel was playing a game against something called The Rainbow. He described them as, quote, a vicious, amoral, intergalactic gaming cartel, and the bracelet was the reason she had to go on playing. She'd been tricked into wearing it and every time she made a mistake it administered a punishment.

'"What exactly are the stakes?" I said. Because, despite myself, I believed him. It was all quite bonkers, but I believed him. Still do in fact.

'"The twentieth century," he said, in such an off-hand manner I almost laughed.

'"No, seriously," I said.

'"I am perfectly serious," he replied. "If Mel wins then all stays as it was; if she loses then the cartel takes twentieth-century Earth out of time, carves it up into neat little packages of technological development and sells them off to the highest bidder. It doesn't," he observed as he turned back to her, "get much more serious than that."

'Then Mel gave a little whoop of joy. Whatever she had done she was delighted with herself. The next second, though, she was crying out with pain and I could actually see the tendrils growing, climbing up her arm, digging deep into her skin. In a few moments they'd reached her face.

'"You've got to fight back, Mel,' the man said. "They've found you. You've only got seconds now." There was more gibberish, about opening boxes, and then about how he couldn't do it for her because the keypad was locked to her "bioprint". The pain on her face was terrible, but she still kept stabbing away at the keys, but you could really see it was a struggle now. I could see some sort of clock on the screen ticking down to nothing.

"I swear that clock speeded up as it went on. Anyway, just as I thought she couldn't possibly hit the keys any faster, faces started popping up all over the screen.

'"That's it," the man cried. "Name and shame them all, Mel. Now!" She hit a key and the faces disappeared. Then it started flashing "GAME OVER". The bracelet dropped from her wrist and the tendrils just crumbled away.

'She collapsed back in her seat and the man looked triumphant. They had won, he said, and in addition, sent details of the identities of the cartel to the authorities. One bad business busted.

'At last, the old brain kicked into gear and I dived over to the bin, grabbed my gun and turned it on them.

'"And what are you planning to do with that?" the man said, as though I'd just pointed a pork chop at him. I explained that the plan was to keep them prisoner until I could find out who the hell they were and how they had managed to breach security. He told me, equally calmly, not to be so silly and that they were, in fact, leaving. So I had a choice: I could shoot them and then have to try to explain the presence of their bodies or I could let them go.

'And, damn me, I did. I have never met anyone so cool and calm. So I just let them walk out. Never saw either of them again. To this day, I don't know what really happened. Gave up trying to make sense of it years ago.'

At this point, McCloud chipped in to the conversation: 'What was the fellow's name?' he said.

'Not a clue,' Oliver admitted. 'I never found out. Never even asked. It all happened rather fast,' he added a bit sheepishly.

'The reason I ask,' McCloud said, 'is that I think I met him myself. Well, when I say think, am absolutely damn sure. You don't forget someone who looked like him, however hard you try.'

McCloud's story was more recent. In fact, he didn't want to talk about it at first, given that the investigation was still ongoing or at least unresolved. However a few more glasses of wine loosened his tongue. It's reassuring that some things never change!

I've cleaned it up a bit, otherwise it would just be a stream of expletives.

'Toby, my eldest grandson, works in the video industry. Something called the sell-through market. Says it is going to be huge. Always been very fond of the little beggar and when he invited me along to watch the recording of one of their fitness videos I thought it might pass an amusing few hours. And the promised presence of half a dozen Lycra-clad ladies provided an additional incentive. Toby knows how to get me out of my armchair.

'The video was being produced to promote some new weight-loss thing called Sure-to-Slim – describes itself as a "low-calorie meal bar"; sounds revolting – which was due to launch earlier this year. It never happened. The official reason was that there was a fire at the factory, but that's a load of nonsense – or at any rate it's certainly not the real reason.

'So one morning, about a year ago, I was sitting just behind the cameras, enjoying the view – not to mention the confusion, which Toby says is perfectly normal in a studio. Five nubile young lovelies and some hunk of a black guy were milling around, apparently waiting for the sixth girl to arrive. She was already an hour late and impatience was rapidly turning to panic. Much telephoning and cursing there was.

'In the midst of all this hoo-ha, I spotted a young woman in an orange Lycra top and shorts standing over by the door. At first I thought she was the missing girl but she was making no effort to alert anyone to her presence. I called Toby over and pointed her out. His eyes lit up and he made a beeline for her.

'Toby had assumed that she was the missing girl – but from her reaction I was pretty sure that she wasn't. Toby probably realised it too, but she was just what he needed. Using bags of his charm – he is a very charming young man and he knows it – he soon persuaded her to take part in the routine. She removed her shorts and walked over to the other girls looking, in equal parts, bemused and amused.

'Turns out her name was Perry, and she was soon in the middle of the troupe, learning the moves, so I sat back to enjoy the rehearsal.

'About two hours later they started shooting the video: lots of cameras moving around, some of them shoved right up the noses of the girls or down their cleavages. And all the time I can see this Perry person sneaking glances at her watch and then looking over at the door. Clearly waiting for something, or someone.

'After they had finished the first routine she came and sat down, rather heavily, next to me. She tried to strike up a conversation. There was an American twang to her voice, but like she hadn't lived there for a while. She wasn't really fit enough for this sort of thing, she said.

'And still she kept glancing from her watch to the door and back. Despite the chattiness, she seemed really wary of me. Kept on peering at my eyes. I turned to look straight at her – if she wanted to see my eyes then I'd let her and see what happened.

'She looked deeply into them and then said, with some relief, "You're okay." I asked what she meant and she said it didn't matter. Blatant tosh, as it obviously did matter.

'For the next part the girls were each given one of the rabbit-food bars. They were told they had to unwrap them and take a bite while still doing their aerobic routines. All sounded a bit clumsy to me. The effect on Perry, though, was astonishing. She seemed terrified of this idea. Really, genuinely quite terrified. I couldn't quite work out why to start with – seemed a bit of an extreme reaction to the risk of indigestion, then I clocked that it was eating the bar itself which scared her so much.

'Then some company rep – thin, pallid, weaselly looking specimen – grabbed her, quite roughly, by the arm and thrust one of the unwrapped bars under her nose and said, "Don't worry, it won't bite."

'Three things struck me as odd. Firstly, the phrase itself. Secondly, his voice, which sounded flat and unnatural. Thirdly, the way her mood changed almost instantly from near hysteria to total calm when he placed the unwrapped bar in her hand.

'So, they lined up the shot, all the girls holding their bars. The company rep says he doesn't want the girls to unwrap the bars in the shot, he wants them to do it beforehand. So they all do. And the same, blank, peculiar expression spreads across their faces too. Except I can see that Perry is sweating furiously; it's pouring off her. As though she's trying to fight the urge to take a bite.

'Toby yells "action". The girls start the routine and raise their arms to take a bite. As Perry lifts hers, I can see that her arm is shaking, violently.

'Then the doors burst open and we're knee-deep in armed police, military types, and heaven alone knows what else. Utter confusion. And leading the charge is a chap who sounds like the spit of your fellow, Oliver.

'The man just exudes authority. He's shouting orders, controlling the whole shebang. Taking in everything at once. Amazingly powerful presence. Then, and this is the really damnable thing, everyone is handed a small green pill and told to take it. It is made clear that this is neither a request nor an option: you take the pill voluntarily or you'll be force-fed it.

'I swallowed it before I even realised what I was doing. Had no effect whatsoever as far as I could tell. At least that's what I thought until I looked at the girls. Each of them looked as though they had just woken up and hadn't actually seen the police arrive. Utter shock and bemusement. Perry was the most affected and ended up holding onto the blond fellow for support and sobbing. She asked why it had taken him so long to find her. He said the answer machine message hadn't recorded properly.

'I decided to ask what the hell was going on. The blond fellow looked at me with the smuggest expression you've ever seen. Said he would show me; in fact, he would show all of us. He took the rabbit bar from Perry, dropped it on the floor, pulled a torch from his pocket and shone it over the bar. Wasn't a normal torch – it produced an odd purple sort of light. And the bar melted. And from inside it emerged a small, blue-speckled worm-like thing, like a tapeworm. It was nauseating! Then the damned thing reared up and hissed! The blond chap promptly popped a mug over it, seemingly utterly unperturbed by what had just happened.

'It was, he explained, a segment of a highly intelligent, telepathic alien creature and the pill we'd taken was an inhibitor. The whole thing was an elaborate invasion plan with millions of worms ready to infest the Earth.

'You can imagine I wasn't entirely convinced and said so. Without a pause, our blond friend strode over to the company rep and whipped off his sunglasses.

'We all just stared, horrified. His eyes were like swollen, transparent marbles. And inside them – makes me ill just thinking about it – there were worms. Writhing and wriggling. Like his head was full of them. Like his whole body was. "Eat one of those bars," the man said, "and that's what would end up happening to you." It was the most disgusting and disturbing thing I ever saw. After that everyone was bundled away. I was hauled off to the local police station and questioned by some young whelp of a detective. I told him who I was and was swiftly, and apologetically, released. But by then Mr Colourful had long since gone. I saw nothing more of any of them except for Toby who was as bemused as I was. But I'm certain that was your chap, Oliver.'

Oliver nodded. The conversation meandered along for a while; post-department life, et cetera – not much to relate, to be honest. We all seem to have sunk into slippered retirement. Then, out of the blue, Montfort said, 'You say this chap was in his forties?'

More nodding.

'I've met him too,' he said. 'Briefly, but I'm sure it was him. Problem is that it was in 1957!'

I'm sorry, Sam, there's no easy way to tell you this. So I'll be blunt. It was Monty who organised the evening, because he has cancer. It's terminal, and he wanted to get a few things off his chest while he still could. A confessional. The story he was about to tell us was, it turns out, the reason he had got us together.

He started off by apologising. He had, he said, been 'ruthless in my ambition' and had frequently 'clambered over the backs of colleagues', lying, using and manipulating us.

No one was surprised by the admission. We'd always suspected his advancement had been at our expense. The apology, though, was unexpected, as was its long and rambling nature. I'll spare you the maudlin and sentimental details. He then came to the story he wanted to tell us.

'I was called into the head's office at some ungodly hour one morning and told they suspected we had a mole. The usual kerfuffle and fuss, no idea who, vague evidence, and yours truly assigned to find him, blah, blah.

'I was never convinced, mind you. Seemed like a whole fuss and panic on the basis of scant to non-existent evidence. Far more likely, I thought, to be coincidence and cock-up rather than conspiracy. But they were certain and determined to find him. Or rather that I should find him.

'For weeks, I dug and searched and snooped and found sweet Fanny Adams. Whoever it was, was clever and thorough, if he existed at all. But the pressure was on me to find him and that pressure got worse as the weeks dragged on. I was more or less being held to ransom over it – my career on the line for something that might not even be happening. But I needed a result. Soon I was getting desperate, grabbing at any hint of evidence.

'Then I got my lucky break. I was in the cipher room when a message started coming in. It was only a partial message, some of it had got lost in transmission, but what there was suggested to me that it was meant for my mole. So I cleared the room and finished the decryption myself. I wasn't really qualified on the new system but I needed his scalp. So I did it anyway.

'And I was pretty sure by the end of it that I had my man and, better still, I knew where he was going to be. Well, after the failure of the last few months I decided I needed to bag him personally. If I was going to redeem myself I needed to present the head with one firmly closed case. Complete with body.

'So, two days later, I was aboard a cruise liner heading out from port with my man in my sights. I just needed to take my time and pick my moment. Quick, clean, simple. A sitting duck.

'Well, nothing's ever easy, is it? I soon realised that I was being watched. And not very subtly either. Some old biddy was trailing me! No subtlety at all, mind you – just brazenly watching me – and not just me, every man of my age. Wherever I was, she was, and any time I got near my target she was there too. I began to get irritated with this. And I mean really very irritated.

'So, after two days of this, I collared her and asked what the hell she thought she was playing at. I don't know what reactions I was expecting, but relief was not one of them. She was actually pleased to talk to me. Wary, but pleased. Yes, she was looking for someone, problem was she wasn't sure what he looked like. She only had a vague description from some friend of hers who had left her there with some important message and then dashed off to do something else. She was evidently less than pleased. I kept prodding her for more details but she was very good at being evasive – her message, she said, had to be delivered to the right person.

'Eventually, she introduced herself as something Smythe so I, automatically, introduced myself, even used my own name. And instantly her wariness vanished.

'She took me firmly by the arm, marched me off to the bar, steered me towards a table, sat me down and said I was just the man she had been looking for and her message was for me. She couldn't, she said apologetically, explain where it came from, just that she had been looking through some papers and had come across it. Then she handed me the full text of the message I had tried to decipher. As I read it, the expression on my face must have been priceless because when I looked up she was laughing. I was flabbergasted, as much because it was clear I had got the decryption horribly wrong as because she had the thing in the first place.

'I tried to get her to tell me where she had got it from. What she said made no sense at all. She claimed she had read my diary in amongst some papers she had got hold of for some research paper she was writing and had come back – she used the word 'back', I remember it distinctly – to prevent me from making a terrible mistake. It was such a stupid story I couldn't work out why she was even bothering with it.

'I tried to get her to tell me more, but then her friend turned up. And guess what... it was the man in the technicolour dreamcoat. Exactly the same man. I'd lay money on it. He firmly ended our conversation, asked her if she was satisfied now that she had "fulfilled her historical role". Didn't wait for a reply, just said he was sorry to have to drag her away but that they had to be somewhere. And with that, they were gone. Didn't see them for the rest of the voyage. Vanished. The pair of them. I lay low until we got to New York then took a flight back to London and closed the case on the mole. My one and only failure.

'I'm just glad she got to me before I could act on my half-baked evidence. If I had you wouldn't be sitting here now.'

This last remark was directed at me. Oliver and Angus looked stunned. There was a very long silence. Then Warwick started apologising. Over and over again. I was squirming with embarrassment, and Oliver and

Angus were right there with me. We parted soon afterwards with Monty still saying how sorry he was and how glad he was he hadn't gone through with it as I walked out to my taxi.

Except, of course, Sam, that you and I both know that that wasn't entirely true. He had tried to carry out his self-appointed mission. You remember the night you woke me up and said there had been someone in our cabin with a gun, and you thought it was Warwick Montfort and I didn't believe you? Now I know you were telling the truth.

All this time and he never breathed a word. From the way he looked at me over that table I guessed he knew it was you with me that night, not Eleanor. Perhaps not saying anything all these years was his way of making up for attempting to kill me.

I should have believed you. What was meant to have been our time together, alone on a romantic cruise, became the moment at which it all started to go wrong. Trust is such a delicate thing in our business and the moment my trust in you was shaken it all started to fall apart.

I have always regretted what happened between us, Samantha. Always regretted the distance, which became a chasm. I know it's far too late to repair it, but it's not too late for me to say that I was wrong and that I'm sorry.

Yours always,
Edward

Testament

Stephen Hatcher

An Adventure of the Seventh Doctor

It had taken some moments for the Doctor to realise that there was something wrong. At first glance, the residential street in which the TARDIS had materialised seemed exactly as it should have done in the London of the mid 1990s. The litter, which lined the gutter, had been turned to pulp by a recent downpour. A cat, disturbed by the emergence of the Doctor, took shelter under a parked car.

Not knowing why or what in particular he was looking for, the Doctor inspected the nearest car, a maroon Ford Fiesta. It had clearly been abandoned. Three of its tyres were completely flat, a window had been smashed in and the whole thing was covered in a carpet of decaying leaves. The Doctor took in the other cars in the street. At least two seemed to be in a similar state. Pushing back his straw hat, he sniffed the air. Nothing particularly unusual, perhaps a little less carbon monoxide than might be expected, but not too much to worry about. Everything seemed pretty much typical of London in the mid 1990s. Then it hit him. This wasn't supposed to be the mid 1990s. According to the TARDIS chronometer, the date was 19 June 2025.

'How very odd,' the Doctor commented aloud to himself. 'It's not like the old girl to get something like that wrong.' Feeling a little guilty for doubting his ship, the Doctor turned to another of the cars and examined the date on its tax disc, hoping to find conclusive evidence. 'Expires end of July 2025. How very odd,' the Doctor repeated.

It was then that he realised that he hadn't yet seen any people. This couldn't be right, could it? The Doctor's mind raced through the possibilities: the human race wiped out by nuclear war, plague, alien invasion, famine? Just as he was starting to become concerned, a young boy came running out of one of the neat, comfortable-looking houses, screaming with laughter. Oblivious to the Doctor's presence, he cannoned into him, knocking him to the pavement. The Doctor looked up at the child in astonishment.

'Hello,' he asked in a friendly tone. 'Who are you?' The boy adjusted his improbably long striped scarf, tipped back his floppy felt hat and in an attempt at a deep booming voice, intoned, 'I am the Doctor. I'm going to save the world.' He then seemed to take in the Doctor's chocolate brown jacket, straw hat and strangely shaped umbrella. 'Oh, are you playing Doctors too?'

The idea of writing the book had always been there somewhere in the back of his mind. When he was younger, whenever he talked about the future, he had always joked about it – with Eleanor, with his colleagues, with Sam. Whilst he was in the service it was out of the question. Apart from the fact that he would never have had the time, it was too dangerous. Too many lives would be put at risk, too many reputations. There was also the little matter of the Official Secrets Act. Edward really didn't like the idea of ending up in prison. For that matter he had signed the act of his own free will. He had known what he was getting into. He had considered himself honour bound.

Edward couldn't have pointed to a moment when things had changed for him. It had happened slowly, over the course of a number of increasingly troubled years.

In his younger days, he would never have believed himself to be the sort of person who would allow things to get on top of him, but then Eleanor died. As he got older, as he began to see less and less of his family, and as there became less and less for him to do to fill his days, he began to brood. His memories started to weigh him down.

He would spend hours alone, staring into space, reliving the past – a past that marked him out as a man alone. His father's generation, the generation that had been blighted by the trenches, by barbed wire and by mustard gas, would have called it shell shock, but in many ways it was worse than that. To Edward, it often seemed as if his head were bursting, all those strange memories were screaming to be let out.

The nights were the worst. He would often lie for hours, unable to sleep, pondering on the meaning of everything that he had seen. When he did manage to escape into unconsciousness, his sleep would be troubled and broken by terrifying nightmares.

He had seen so many things, witnessed so many unexplained events. Aliens, supernatural manifestations, he had seen the lot. Running through it all, a constant thread, like the name of some seaside town through a stick of rock, were the Doctors, that strange group of men who always seemed to be there at times of crisis. Looking back over his life, Edward discovered more and more occasions when he had met one of these men.

There had been a man in his childhood with white hair, eyes that sparkled and a confident manner. There was something about those eyes that brought to mind a man whom he had met years later, a fair-haired young chap back in China, who had also called himself the Doctor. Down the years, he'd wondered whether the two might be connected, but he had soon dismissed the idea. In so many ways they were similar, but in just as many they were very different. But, over time, there had been others. Other Doctors.

He revived long-forgotten thoughts of a third, the one with the two young friends who had turned up unannounced at his fiftieth birthday party. There was also that strange little man, the one whom he had met in New York, while he was looking for Moira. He too had called himself the

Doctor. Then there was that chap at the White Rabbit during the War; he was another one. Could it all just have been a coincidence? At first Edward had been inclined to think so, but the more he thought about it the more he became convinced that there had to be a connection between these men. Things came to a head back in '86, on a night out with some old friends. From the stories that McCloud, Montfort and Oliver had told him, it was clear that they too had met an odd man called the Doctor, and that Edward owed him his life.

He began to look deeper into it and although he found out little more than he already knew, his conviction grew. Then one day he found something extraordinary. It was in a bundle of papers that had belonged to his mother, papers that had been in his possession ever since her death but he'd never got round to reading. It was a letter, written by his mother to Lady Louisa Pollard and probably returned to her after Lady Louisa's death. It discussed the strange events that they had both witnessed when Edward had been born. In astonishment he read his mother's description of the white-haired old man and his young friend, and the role they played that day. His mother had known the name of only one of these men – the Doctor.

Edward was convinced. These 'Doctors' had been dogging him and his family from a time even before he was born. He had no idea exactly what, but something had been going on. He had a story: he was going to follow it and he was going to tell it.

This wasn't a case of some crusading need to reveal the truth to the world. If he was honest with himself, he had no particular regard for the great, unwashed masses. He didn't see that it particularly mattered whether or not Joe or Jenny Sun-reader knew what was really going on. That wasn't the point. It was more a matter of just getting it off his chest and seeing if the fact of telling his story might flush out more information. Perhaps others had had similar experiences.

There was another factor too, one which he scarcely admitted to himself. The fact that his retirement from the service had come neither at a time nor in a manner of his choosing had certainly helped make up his mind. Then there was the matter of the knighthood. As a senior civil servant he could have expected to be awarded that particular honour on retirement – it had taken almost 18 years. Eighteen years, if not of resentment, then at least of a growing feeling of grievance.

There was still the Official Secrets Act, of course, but in the three years since Peter Wright had published his book and that fool of a woman had tried unsuccessfully to stop him, the climate had changed. Things should be a little easier now. In any case, with Eleanor long dead and only John and Linda of his immediate family still around, he had ceased to care. More importantly, Edward knew that it had to be now, before it was too late.

He was already of a great age to be writing his memoirs. The strain of his 84 eventful years was beginning to take its toll. Although the memories were still sharp, there were times when he scarcely had the energy to remember, let alone to go through the mechanics of writing it all down. That was why he had engaged Smith.

He didn't remember where he had found him – he may have been the grandson of an old acquaintance, but Edward wasn't sure. In any case, even with the help of the little Scot, he had to write the book now, while he still could. From the moment the decision was taken, the nightmares seemed to ease a little and the daytime brooding was replaced by work and a new sense of purpose.

The boy ran off before the Doctor could answer. He shouted after him, but the child was too caught up in his game to hear the call. Something was not quite right. Not a great deal should have changed in the last thirty years; people were still due to be people. It wasn't as if some sort of golden age should have started. The world should be facing the same problems that it had faced since the beginning of civilisation and even before. Nonetheless, there should have been some changes. Another small step or two should have been taken along the long road that would lead mankind to their destiny in the stars.

'Like that, for example,' the Doctor said aloud, noticing the red pillar box. 'The last one of those was supposed to have disappeared at least ten years ago. And come to think of it, these all appear to be old-style petrol-driven cars.'

At that moment, he became aware of a commotion around the corner at the end of the street, the sound of a sizeable crowd cheering and shouting. At the same instant, an insistent humming filled the air. The Doctor's gaze was drawn upwards.

It was a spaceship. About the size of a double-decker bus, which would have been just as anachronistic, the spaceship was probably a cargo shuttle of some kind. It was metallic blue in colour, though tarnished with age and use, and sported white racing stripes. In its day it would probably have been admired as rather sleek and stylish. Clearly, however, that day had long passed. Coming in low over the rooftops, it landed in the direction of the cheering.

Hurrying to the corner, the Doctor kept out of sight as he observed the scene in the square where the spaceship had landed. A large hatch opened in the rear of the shuttle and two alien figures emerged. They were humanoid, no more than four feet tall and covered from head to foot in what appeared to be brown wool or fur. As the Doctor watched, the crowd began to cheer and applaud even louder.

The aliens then began to hand out some sort of parcels. There was no sign of impatience among the crowd, no pushing or shouting, just happy chatter and laughter. The Doctor considered it to be one of the best-behaved crowds that he had ever seen, particularly on Earth. When everyone had received a package, he or she began to move away, still smiling and laughing. A group of three young women came in the direction of the Doctor. He raised his hat and greeted them. 'Hello, I'm the...'

'The Doctor, yes, of course you are,' interrupted one of the girls, giggling.

'The Doctor, yes,' the Doctor continued. 'What have you got there?'

Another of the women gave him an odd look, almost like he'd just asked as stupid a question as might be imagined. 'Food, of course,' she said. 'It's our rations for the week. Very generous too, if you ask me. I don't know where we would be if it weren't for the Benanki. They always make sure we have plenty to eat.'

'Of course, yes,' said the Doctor. 'The Benanki. I'm afraid I've been away. Tell me about the Benanki? Who are they?'

'Where have you been, then? The Benanki are our masters – and jolly good ones too, I should say. You must have been a long way away not to know that. Have you been off in that TARDIST of yours?' The women giggled pityingly again and began to walk off.

The Doctor called after them. 'How do you know who I...' But the women had already left, the sound of their laughter fading into the distance.

Sir Edward Grainger was starting to become frustrated – a condition with which he was increasingly familiar in recent years. It seemed that every time he settled himself down to begin writing his memoirs, he was disturbed. Initially it had been Smith who had not understood what was expected of him. Edward would begin discussing a particular episode in his life, intending to clarify his thoughts prior to drafting the relevant chapter, but the dratted man would begin talking about other things altogether. Often he would pick upon some minor point that Edward mentioned in passing and begin asking him interminable questions about it. Days would pass with very little being achieved.

It was at the end of one particularly unproductive week that Edward's patience snapped. 'Smith, let me make it clear to you, we are here to do a job. Do you understand that?'

His assistant looked up in alarm. 'Of course, Sir Edward. My only purpose in being here is to help with your memoirs.'

'Well, exactly, Smith. All of this idle chit-chat is not helping at all. In fact, it's stopping me from working. I'm afraid that unless you can become more focused upon the task in hand, I will have no option but to dismiss you.'

Smith apologised immediately, but the penetrating stare was anything but apologetic.

From then on, Edward found the man easier to work with. Unfortunately, this was when all of the other interruptions began.

At first it was the butler, Norris, who kept making unscheduled appearances – he was soon put in his place. Then Linda began visiting more frequently than ever before. The problem of the mystery telephone calls was easily solved by leaving the wretched thing off the hook.

Hobb's Lane was usually one of the quieter parts of London, so it came as something of a surprise when the neighbours on both sides found it necessary to have builders in. The resulting disturbances delayed work on chapter two by three weeks. No sooner had that problem passed than the council began digging up the road directly outside Edward's window – which was curious, because no one in the lane could remember that ever happening before. When one of the neighbours complained, the council denied all knowledge of it. The workmen disappeared overnight, to be replaced in short order by the electricity company, the gas company, a cable-television company and the telephone engineers, all of whom found it necessary to excavate the road, using the noisiest pneumatic drills on the market.

Through all of these interruptions, Smith tutted sympathetically, although Edward couldn't help thinking that on more than one occasion he detected a look of satisfied amusement on his face.

'It's no use, Smith,' announced Edward finally. 'I'm going to have to admit defeat.' At this Smith smiled broadly.

'Oh, Sir Edward. I'm so sorry,' he said. 'It's such a shame that your memoirs won't now be written. Although, I'm sure that it will turn out for the best this way.'

'Oh, no, Smith, you don't understand. I'm still going to write my memoirs. However, I am not going to be able to carry on writing them here. I need to find somewhere where I can concentrate on the job. And I know just the place.'

The Doctor considered his options. Clearly things were not as they should have been. History had not gone according to plan. Earth should have been on the road to establishing its own first empire, not languishing as subjects of the Benanki. A quick check in the TARDIS databanks revealed them to be a minor trading power – certainly not the type to invade Earth.

He was concerned too about the behaviour of the people he had spoken to. They were well fed, and cared for – happy even – but they should have been out there getting ready to take to the stars, rather than being content with living on charity. And then there was the matter of the boy who had been wearing a very familiar-looking ensemble, and the women who had recognised him – or at least sort of recognised him – and had heard of the TARDIS.

The Doctor felt distinctly uneasy about the whole thing. He decided to go ahead with his original plan. He had come here to London in 2025 intending to drop in on some old friends – in particular Linda Grainger. If he paid a visit to Linda, then he might be able to pick up some clues as to what had happened to cause such a disastrous change in the course of events.

The two men were to spend the next three months in the library of Edward's club. Each day they would arrive at around 9.30, and settle down quickly to work. At first, Edward would use an old portable typewriter, but this soon developed a mysterious fault that was impossible to find, let alone cure. Smith said he would find a replacement, but was unable to do so. Edward continued in longhand.

The first weeks were a happy period for Edward, writing about and reliving his childhood. As they worked together, he and Smith developed a close relationship which, Edward reflected while travelling home late one night, might even become a friendship. However, despite this relative contentment, his mother's letter to Lady Louisa kept nagging at the back of his mind.

Edward studied the letter in silence, brooding on what appeared to be the first time that his path had been crossed by the mysterious Doctors. His assistant was sitting across the table, sorting some papers. Finally Edward looked up. 'This is where it all began, Smith, the very day that I was born. Have I ever told you about that?'

Smith regarded his employer with keen interest. 'No, Sir Edward, I don't believe you have. What happened?'

'Well, according to my mother there were strange goings on in the house that day, weird manifestations. Things happened that no one could explain. And wouldn't you know it, Smith, one of those Doctors was there that day too.'

This seemed to alarm Smith. 'The Doctor? When you were born? Sir Edward, no! Don't tell me! I mustn't know.' As he became agitated, his Scottish accent became more pronounced. He hurriedly gathered his papers together and left the room, muttering something under his breath that the bemused Edward didn't quite catch.

The imposing front door was opened by a man of about fifty in a frock coat, whom the Doctor took for the butler. 'Good morning. I've come to see Miss Grainger. Please tell her it's –'

'The Doctor, certainly, sir,' the man interrupted. 'If you come this way, I will let Mr Grainger know that you are here.'

The Doctor raised a curious eyebrow at the correction and was ushered by the butler into an airy room lined with bookcases. After a moment he was joined by an elderly man, who greeted him.

'Doctor, it really is you.'

Momentarily confused, the Doctor paused before removing his hat and proffering his hand. 'Hello, Grainger.' The two men shook hands. 'I had been expecting to see Linda.'

'Linda? No she moved to the country some years ago. She rarely comes up to town these days and I can't get around as well as I used to, so we don't see much of each other.' A look of sadness came briefly into Grainger's eyes. He motioned the Doctor towards a chair and sat down himself. He rubbed his left knee as he spoke, as if to ease some ancient injury. 'You seem surprised to find me here. Where else would I be?'

The Doctor didn't answer the question, but came straight to the point. 'London seems a very different place to when I was last here. I was hoping you might be able to fill me in on some of the details about what has been happening. Tell me about the Benanki.'

'The Benanki?' The old man raised an amused eyebrow. 'So, you've come across them, have you? Let me tell you, Doctor, the Benanki are the very least of our worries. They're a nice bunch, really. In fact, we would be lost without them. No, what worries me is rather more fundamental. This society is dying. Not just London or England, the whole world. We've had it. Culturally and spiritually, the human race is finished.'

It was about six weeks since they had first come to work in the club. Smith was busy going over some of Grainger's papers. Edward was taking a moment to marshal his thoughts. He noticed that as Smith read he seemed to be becoming more and more preoccupied.

'What is it, Smith?' he finally asked, being quite unable to concentrate while his assistant tutted and sighed so. The man looked up from what he was reading.

'It's just this story of yours about your time in China. Those smugglers, Sir Edward. It just occurred to me that perhaps this might be best left out of the book. After all, it was a long time ago and I'm not sure anyone would be very interested in that sort of thing.'

'Nonsense. It was all rather exciting. Just what we need. Besides, that was the first time that I met one of the Doctors – since I was a boy, anyway. I have told you about the Doctors, haven't I?'

Smith mumbled, 'Yes'.

Edward continued. 'This one was a young blond chap. A nice enough sort of fellow. I met the same chap again some eight years later during that Cup final business that I was telling you about. Anyway, back in '28 he seemed to be with a young couple, always arguing. She was Australian, I think; don't know where he was from. You know, Smith, it's the strangest thing. I'm quite sure I saw that young woman again years later, in the hospital, when my son was born. She was a nurse. Let me see, that must have been 22 years later but she didn't seem to have aged a day. I didn't think anything about it at the time. It was a day or two later that I made the connection. When I asked at the hospital no one knew anything about her. But, from something the ward sister said to me, I am sure that the same blond Doctor chap, or at least someone very like him, had been there too.'

Smith didn't answer and returned his attention to the sheaf of papers.

Edward began writing again until, after a few minutes, his favourite fountain pen, which he'd used throughout his career in the service, began to spill ink over most of the pages that had been written that morning. They were irretrievably damaged.

Edward sent Smith to buy some ball-point pens – the old man hated the things, but it was either that or abandon the day's work altogether. When, after an interminably long time, Smith returned, Edward was dismayed to discover that not one of the pens in the pack that he brought with him actually worked. It was decided to finish early for the day.

The Doctor held the old man's gaze. 'Tell me more. What's been going on?'

Grainger paused a moment and then continued. 'In truth, Doctor, there hasn't been anything dramatic – apart from the arrival of the Benanki, of course. It's more a question of what has not happened. Some of us have come to believe that in the last 25 years human society has stagnated. All the technological and scientific progress that we witnessed in the last century has just ground to a halt. There have been no major developments in the field of medicine – in fact, most of the research establishments have shut down, ostensibly for lack of funding, but the real reason was just lack of interest.

'There hasn't been a single important invention, at least not that I'm aware of, since the turn of the century. Pure scientific research too seems to have ground to a halt. But then since most of the universities closed down there wouldn't have been anywhere to do the research, anyway. Of course, the up side of this is that war has become a thing of the past too. No one seems to consider anything worth fighting for any more. So when the Benanki arrived, claiming the planet as part of their empire, we were rather a pushover. They met no resistance. There were plenty who welcomed them, in fact. Those that didn't tended to think that we wouldn't have to worry about it. They put their trust in a higher power.'

The Doctor raised an eyebrow.

'It's been a similar story in so many fields: the arts, literature, film, theatre, music, even sport. Nobody seems interested anymore. I cannot remember the last time I heard a new piece of music – not just another version of an old piece, but something really new. The same goes for painting, sculpture, the lot. I was there at the last ever Test match, at the Oval in 2005. England lost by six wickets and Australia retained the Ashes. Shame, that. The publishing industry has all but given up too. Yes, you can still buy reprints of old classics but there is nothing new and there hasn't been for over a quarter of a century. It's as if humanity has simply lost the will to excel.'

The Doctor shook his head sadly. 'But it just shouldn't be like this. The human race is one of the most vibrant, creative forces in the universe. Right from the moment that the first man and woman climbed down from the trees and stood upright, they have seen mystery and excitement in the

257

shadows. The terrible struggles to survive have been the inspiration for the most fertile imaginations, spawning great painting, literature, music and all the rest – the art that comes from living your lives in a beautiful but dangerous world. How can the species that produced Michelangelo, Rembrandt, Mozart, Beethoven, the Beatles, Shakespeare, Schiller, Pushkin, Brunel, Newton, Einstein, George Best, Shane Warne and so many, many more simply give up? What caused this, John? Whatever happened?'

John Grainger listened to the Doctor's tirade in silence, not taking his eyes from his guest. 'What happened? Oh, that's easy. When it comes down to it, Doctor. It was your fault – yours and my father's.'

'It was in 1932 that I met the man who was to recruit me to work for the service and who taught me so much. I never knew his name. We always called him just "Professor", but the more I have thought about it over the years, the more I have come to believe he was another of those strange men whom I have met again and again during the course of my life, who were each known as the Doctor.'

Edward's mind went back to that odd little man, whom he had known so long ago and who had meant so much to him during his early days in the service. As he thought about his friend, whom he had not seen for the best part of sixty years, something gnawed at his consciousness. He looked over to where Smith was redrafting the pages he had written the day before. In a flash he understood; he knew for certain that Smith...

But, then again, what did he know? Almost as soon as the thought came to him, he lost it. What was he thinking about? He struggled to remember, but the memory had gone. It was something about Smith, but he couldn't think what.

There was some connection between the events of 1932 and his assistant. Edward struggled to recapture the thought for a moment, but then abandoned the fight. His mind wandered, perusing the vast bank of memories that made up his life.

Travelling forward in time, he came to 1940 and the strange business at the White Rabbit. That was when he became absolutely sure that aliens not only existed, but were visiting the Earth. There was that strange, suspicious-looking man. At first, Edward had taken him for a Nazi spy, but later he knew. The man was a traveller from another world.

The Doctor... a Doctor had been there too – big, curly haired, blond chap in a ridiculous coat.

'Wait a moment!' Edward said aloud. In his mind some of the pieces began to fall into place. 'Smith, find me those notes that I wrote about my meeting with McCloud, Montfort and Oliver back in '86.'

Smith took a moment to find the papers, then passed them to Edward. He scanned them quickly, becoming more and more agitated as he did so.

'That's it!' he exclaimed excitedly. 'It was the same man. The same man! They all met him: Oliver in Hong Kong in '75, McCloud here in London in

'85, and Montfort halfway across the Atlantic in '57. Big blond, curly headed chap with no dress sense. The same man! And I'll tell you what, Smith. I met him too – during an air raid here in London in 1940. And if you believe the descriptions, on all four of those occasions, over 45 years, he never seemed to age a day.'

Smith listened quietly, smiling slightly, then attempted to calm the old man down. 'Sir Edward, how can that possibly be? From their descriptions, these three men could have been anyone. There's nothing to link them to this Doctor you met in 1940. Perhaps your memory is playing tricks on you. Maybe having heard your friends' stories, you transposed their rather vague descriptions of a man onto the Doctor you met all those years ago.'

'No!' exclaimed Edward vehemently. 'Definitely not. It was the same man, I tell you. And now I think about it, how about the blond chap, that other Doctor? Didn't I say, that description from that ward sister... It was him in 1950, looking just as he had when I met him in 1928 and then again in 1936. And there was that Australian girl too. There's another thing, that blond Doctor had a girl with him in '36. Let me see.'

Edward studied the notes again.

'A-ha! There we have it. There she is again, but with the other one this time. McCloud saw her in '85. Let me think, let me think!' Edward was becoming more and more agitated. 'Two possibilities! Either these Doctor chaps don't age, which is crazy. Or something even more crazy – these Doctors who seem to have been following me about all of my life are time travellers!'

'My fault? How do you mean? How can it be my fault?' The Doctor looked at John Grainger in alarm.

'It all goes back to the book.' Grainger rose unsteadily to his feet and walked over to one of the bookcases. Taking a thick, brightly coloured paperback from one of the shelves, he passed it to the Doctor, who examined the cover in horror. The illustration depicted a tall, middle-aged man, his rugged features topped with white bouffant hair. He was wearing a frilly shirt, smoking jacket and black cape. In all respects apart from the face, which was quite wrong, it was clearly intended to depict one of his early incarnations.

'That damned book. I wish it had never been written.' Grainger eased himself back into his seat. 'What you are holding, Doctor, is probably the most important book written in the last thousand years – and the most damaging. It was a publishing phenomenon. Of course, there had been any number of books published over the years claiming to be eyewitness accounts of meetings with aliens. Who knows, perhaps some of them were even true. But this one was different. The memoirs of a respected, retired civil servant, a member of the Establishment, a knight of the realm, containing detailed, first-hand accounts of aliens on the Earth. It was much more credible, conclusive proof. And, of course, it featured you, Doctor, in all of your various guises. A benevolent, time-travelling outsider who was always there at the hour of humanity's greatest need. Always ready to ride to the rescue. As a character, Doctor, you have great popular appeal.

'The book was first published to no great attention in early '91, but then the Government noticed it and made a dreadful mistake. They tried to ban it. There was a huge fuss, the upshot of which was that not only did they fail to suppress it but millions heard of the book who otherwise would never have done so. It was soon picked up by one of the popular publishers, serialised in a daily newspaper and became a worldwide bestseller. You became very popular, Doctor.'

'Ah, yes, I've seen some of the results of that.'

'The reaction was very strange. At first it all seemed fine. People seemed rather excited to know that we weren't alone in the universe and that we were being looked after, so to speak. Then, subtly and slowly, it changed. I suppose that, despite everything, the prevailing view was that all in all the human race was sort of doing all right. We were getting along reasonably nicely; managing quite well. The revelation that we owed our survival as a species to an alien hit some people very badly. It was... complicated. Some became very complacent, adopting the attitude that in the end it doesn't matter what we do, the Doctor will always save us. There may also have been an element of end-of-millennium fever, I don't know. People became decadent and lethargic. Crime rates rocketed. Others reacted with abject fear to the knowledge that aliens existed. They became inward looking and isolationist. Some even locked themselves away and refused to come out. Suicides went up alarmingly.

'If only you had not kept interfering, Doctor. If you hadn't kept coming back time after time, that damned book would never have been written. I don't think I can forgive you for that, Doctor.'

The Doctor looked at John Grainger and shook his head sadly as if unsure what to say. He glanced down at the book and read the title again. *My Life With The Doctor* by Edward Grainger.

'Time travel, it's the only logical explanation.' Edward had brought Smith back to his house and the pair had sat up long into the night arguing. Despite all of Smith's protestations, Edward had made his mind up that he had solved the mystery of the Doctors. 'I don't know, there are maybe five or six of them – members of who knows what organisation – who travel in time, saving the world and heaven knows what else.'

'But, Sir Edward, really! Time travel. Do you really believe that?'

'It's the only explanation. Think, Smith. That business I told you about in New York, back in '82. Those creatures took that little Doctor chap through their teleport machine or whatever it was. When he came back, he was unchanged. Yet everyone else who went through it had aged horribly, my own god-daughter Moira included. But he wasn't a day older. I tell you, time works differently for these chaps.'

Smith had no answer.

'I never intended to keep coming back, it just sort of happened. After the first few times I became curious as to why, in the whole of time and space, I kept on coming across this one man. I started to seek him out – to get to know him, to try to find out what was special about him. And your father was a very special man, John.'

'Yes, he was, Doctor. But you killed him.'

Edward put the final touches to his manuscript. It had taken longer than it should have done. As the work had gone on, Smith had become more and more argumentative and obstructive. He seemed to be doing all he could to prevent Edward finishing the book. He had spent hours trying to persuade his employer to abandon the project, using all the arguments that Edward had heard before. If Edward hadn't grown to like the man immensely, he would certainly have dismissed him, but as it was he tolerated his assistant's objections with some amusement – and ignored them. The book was finished. A publisher had already expressed some interest. Sir Edward Grainger, pillar of the Establishment, was going to have his say. People would read his testament.

There was still work to do, of course. The manuscript needed to be checked over. There was the question of the bibliography and the index to sort out. But in essence it was over. He looked up at his assistant.

'You go, Smith. I can finish tidying up here on my own.'

'Well, if you're sure, Sir Edward. Thank you.' The man gathered his things together and opened the door. 'See you tomorrow, then.'

Edward didn't look up from his papers as he answered absent-mindedly. 'Good night then, Doctor.'

He didn't know from what part of his subconscious that had come. But, the moment he said it, he knew for certain. He looked up at the man he had known as Smith. Without saying a word, the Doctor stepped back into the room, closing the door silently behind him.

John Grainger thought better of the accusation as soon as it was made. 'No, that's not fair, his death wasn't your fault. All the initial fuss over the book, the court case, the press, television and everything, that took a lot out of him – he was a very old man, after all. In the end, when he saw the way it was going, how his book had changed things, he seemed to lose interest in going on. He died in 1992, just short of his eighty-sixth birthday. At one time, he had his heart set on reaching a hundred, but by the end that didn't seem to matter any more.'

'John, I'm so very, very sorry.'

* * *

'It is you, isn't it?' Edward asked softly.

The Doctor looked steadily at the old man. 'Yes, Edward. It's me.' He sat down opposite him.

'It is the same you I knew back in 1932. Why haven't I been able to see that? Now I say it, it seems obvious.'

'It is me, Edward, the same me. You'll have to forgive me, I'm afraid I've been manipulating your memories a little. I needed you not to remember me.'

Edward shook his head in astonishment. 'And you are a time traveller?'

'A time traveller? Oh, yes, and so much more.'

Edward looked at his old friend. As he did so, the final part of the jigsaw fell into place in his mind. He could see all that until now he had only suspected – and what he hadn't even begun to suspect. He knew the truth.

'They were all you, weren't they?' Edward said. 'All the Doctors? I can't pretend to understand it or even to understand how I know it, but I do know. All those men over all the years, all called the Doctor... you're all the same person. They're all you.'

The Doctor looked directly into his friend's eyes. 'All me, yes. They... we are, or were, or will be. But then I think, deep down, you've known that all along. Haven't you, Edward?'

Edward didn't contradict him. 'Why are you here? Is it something to do with my book?'

The Doctor hurried away from the house as the butler closed the door behind him and set off back towards the TARDIS.

This future was all wrong and it was his fault – his and Edward's, but mostly his. He had to put it right. Edward had to be stopped. The book must never be published. History had to be put back on course, then the human race would reach the stars, Edward would live to reach his century and John.... Ah yes, John. John wouldn't live to see this future or any other.

'There always has to be a price,' the Doctor reflected grimly.

The two friends sat in silence for several minutes, Sir Edward thinking over the implications of what his friend had just told him, the Doctor waiting patiently for a decision. Finally Edward spoke. 'If what you've said is true, then... my book can't be published. I can't take the responsibility for endangering the future of the entire human race.'

'Thank you, Edward. That is the right decision.'

'But there is something I want you to promise me in return, Doctor.'

The Doctor nodded.

'Look after my manuscript. If it ever becomes safe for the world to know about it, then perhaps it could be published.'

'Of course.'

Edward hesitated before continuing. 'And there is one other thing, Doctor. All this... knowledge that I have, all these memories. They've been a burden. Sometimes, it's felt as if my head were about to burst; there is so much in there. I don't think I can go back to the sleepless nights, to the nightmares.'

The Doctor regarded his friend sadly, saying nothing.

'I want you to take all this knowledge from me. I know you can do that. I have no use for it now anyway. I'm an old man, Doctor. They are the memories of another life – they're no good to me any more. Can you do that?'

The Doctor shook his head vehemently. 'No, Edward. It would be too dangerous. I have already interfered with your memories too much. If I attempt to do what you want, it could damage your mind beyond repair.'

'Please, do this one last thing for me. Whatever the risk, I would rather take it than carry the burden of all this knowledge. I am very old. I'm becoming very... forgetful anyway. Please do it, Doctor.'

The Doctor sighed. 'Very well. I'll try.' He paused. 'When it's done, it is possible that you might not remember who I am. Just in case, I want to say that to have known you, Edward Grainger, has been an honour and a pleasure.'

Edward stood up. The Doctor took his hand and shook it warmly. As he did so, Edward felt the Doctor's presence enter his mind, probing and pushing gently. He felt overwhelmingly tired; his eyes closed, but he did not sleep. In a rush, memories seemed to pass before him – his childhood, Australia, joining the Service, the War, Eleanor, Berlin, John's birth, New York, everything. All his memories of the Doctor, of aliens and all the rest, seemed to swirl around in his mind at such speed that he couldn't follow them. Then there was calm.

Edward opened his eyes and blinked. He saw Smith. He was shaking his hand. Edward released himself from the man's gentle grip and sat down. Now, what was he thinking? He couldn't remember. Where was he? Oh, yes, his club. His memoirs. He really ought to get down to writing them one day. But, then again, what was there for him to write about? Besides, he was getting old. Edward was aware that his mind wasn't what it used to be. He was tired. It must be nearly teatime.

Edward watched Smith pick up a large bundle of papers and tuck them into his jacket pocket. Making to leave, Smith turned to the old man and spoke. 'Well, goodbye, Sir Edward. I promise you, we will meet again.' He left.

Edward spoke, almost too quietly to be heard. 'Goodbye... Smith.'

Forgotten

Joseph Lidster

An Adventure of the Eighth Doctor

Saturday 24 June 2006

'I have to marry Shayne Ward!'

Linda Grainger looked over at her daughter. 'What's that?'

'Look!' Ellie slid her copy of *Heat* across the table. 'He's fit, famous and loaded.'

Linda shrugged and sipped her smoothie. 'Money isn't everything.'

'Yeah, right, Mum. You tell yourself that.' Ellie paused. 'You don't even know who he is, do you?'

'Of course I do! He's... isn't he the one going out with that girl from *Big Brother*... Chantelle?'

Ellie let out a long, dramatic sigh. 'No, Mum, that's Preston. From the Ordinary Boys.'

'They're all ordinary to me.' Sneaking a glance at her watch, Linda stood up. 'Anyway, finish your breakfast. Your dad'll be here soon.'

'Do I have to like spend the entire weekend at his?'

'You make it sound like forever.'

'It is forever.' Ellie bit into her toast and grumbled. 'And I wanted to see my mates.'

'You can see them on Monday. At school.' Grabbing a cloth, Linda started to wipe the breakfast bar. 'And, I told you. I've things to do today.'

Smirking, Ellie stood up. 'Got a new bloke, have you?'

'No! It's nothing like that. Now, come on.'

'What then?' Ellie asked, swinging a rucksack over her shoulder. 'You can tell me. I won't tell Dad.'

'It's nothing,' Linda repeated without looking up. 'It's just a doctor's appointment.'

'And it's the first match in the second round of the 2006 World Cup! You join us live, here in Munich...'

'Yes, love. What can I get you?'

Linda turned away from the television set and considered her options. 'Well... a red wine. Please. Just a small one. I'm not stopping long.'

As the barmaid went to get a glass, Linda looked around the White Rabbit. Sixteen years. Sixteen years since she'd been here and nothing had changed. Same purple floor. Same purple walls. In fact, it didn't look as if it had changed since whenever it'd been built. She remembered her granddad saying how it had once survived a direct hit from a German bomb. Then again, so many years later, it had survived her mates and their tequilas and karaoke so, yeah, it was probably indestructible.

'How can it be 2006?' she murmured.

'What's that?' asked the barmaid as she poured the wine.

'Sorry. It's just... I was here. A long time ago and... it hasn't changed.' She looked up at the barmaid and smiled. 'Same can't be said for me, though.'

'Oh, I don't know.' A voice sounded in her ear. 'I like the dress!'

For a moment, she froze. His voice was different but, somehow, she knew. She turned to face him. His old-fashioned clothes and long hair fitted in perfectly with the retro look of the bar. All very Jules Verne. All a bit mental. He grinned, then, looking over her shoulder, spoke to the barmaid.

'I'll get this, Michelle.' He turned back to face Linda. 'Well? Don't I even get a hello?'

'Hello, I'm the Doctor and this isn't a taxi rank.' She crouches down and turns the man onto his back. His eyes flash open and she flinches...

She gripped the bar to steady herself as memories bolted through her mind. Christmas, 1990.*

The taxi driver's skin completely melted away, his entire body covered in the same dull, grey scales. She looks back down at the Doctor. 'Can you help us?'

He smiled and gently took her hand. 'Why don't we sit down?'

Fighting back the memories, she allowed him to lead her to a secluded booth.

'You saved them, Linda,' he says, squeezing her hand. 'Happy Christmas.'

'You too, Doctor.' She closes her eyes as she feels the hot breath of the two Festulasions bearing down on them...'

They sat down on either side of an ancient wooden table and she looked him in the eye.

'Doctor?' she asked, her voice breaking.

He smiled reassuringly at her. 'That's right.'

'You've changed.'

He nodded. 'How are you, Linda Grainger?'

She didn't know what to say. Ever since the note had been thrust into her hand at Serena's post-PTA party, she'd been preparing for this. *Meet me on Saturday, 4pm. The White Rabbit.* Somehow, she'd known it was from him. She tried to say something, anything, but couldn't. So they sat in silence, waiting for the barmaid to bring over their drinks.

Trying to ignore the cigarette smoke drifting over from another table,

---

* – See *She Won't Be Home* in *Short Trips: The History of Christmas* (2005)

she fiddled with the clasp on her handbag. Uncomfortable silences, the ex-smoker's worst enemy.

'I... I can't wait for the ban to come in,' she muttered.

He tilted his head. 'The ban?'

'The smoking ban. I mean, it'll be weird. You know, odd. No smoking in the pub? That's just... but, I gave up. Not long after I met you. And so it'll be easier because I still get cravings, you know. Sometimes, it's all I want. Ellie will be going on about... sorry, that's my daughter. What am I saying? You probably know that anyway. But, yeah, I still sometimes get the craving for... you know.' She paused. 'I'm babbling, aren't I? Am I babbling?'

He grinned. 'Yeah.'

'Sorry.'

'There's no need to apologise.' He reached over and took her hand. 'Linda?'

'Yes?'

'I was so sorry to hear about your father.'

She pulled her hand away as the barmaid came over with the drinks. 'Accidents happen.'

'John was a good friend.' He paused. 'And your grandfather? How's Edward?'

She forced the tears back. She wasn't going to cry. She didn't know what this man, this alien, wanted but she was not going to cry.

'He's... old. Confused. Living in the past.'

The Doctor looked up through his long eyelashes, like a puppy seeking reassurance from its master. 'I'm sorry.'

'Don't do that,' she muttered.

'What?' he asked, looking confused.

'Don't pretend to be something you're not. Don't try and look so... innocent. I know what you did.' She paused. 'Dad told me.'

His face hardened. 'I had to do it. If Edward's book had been published then everything would have been destroyed. You've seen what I have to deal with. You know, more than anyone.'

She thought back to lizard monsters in a dingy cab office. She remembered his offer of a life in the stars. And she thought of her subsequent life. Marriage, Ellie, divorce, the cul-de-sac. If it hadn't been for him, she wouldn't have had that. If he hadn't taken her home that Christmas...

'Yeah, you had to do it.' She downed the wine in one and reached for her handbag. 'Thanks for letting me know. See you around.' She stood up.

'Wait!'

She looked down at him. Suddenly, he seemed genuinely lost. Even lonely.

'Well? What do you want? Why did you want to see me, Doctor?'

He looked down at the table and ran a fingernail through a groove in the wood. Then, quietly, he answered her. 'I want you to take me to him. I want to... I want to say goodbye to Edward.'

Shielding her face, she looked across the Thames. Over on the South Bank, the London Eye gleamed in the sunlight. Another reminder of how much time had passed since she'd last stood here. She heard the pub door clatter open behind her, but didn't turn around.

'Why did you run out like that?'

She felt him take her arm. As he turned her to face him, she kept her voice steady. 'Please. Just go.'

'Linda?'

Then, her head spinning, she started to cry.

'I'm... I'm so old, Doctor. Everything's just... what happened?'

He held her in his arms and spoke softly. 'You're not old. You're only... what, 38?'

'I feel old.' Suddenly, she found herself laughing. 'You see that drain over there? When I was last here, I was throwing up into it. You know, the end of another mad night out. I was so drunk and... young. And now? Now I don't even know who Shayne Ward is!'

He started to laugh. 'It doesn't matter.'

'It does! It's different for you. It isn't... it isn't a one-way journey. You keep coming back and... we can't do that. I can never see Dad again. I can never be a kid going on day trips. I'm stuck like this. Getting older. Going grey. Doing nothing.'

'Doing nothing? What about Ellie?'

Linda sniffed and rubbed the tears out of her eyes. 'She thinks I'm boring and old.'

'Well, I don't! And, in case you didn't know, I'm the most important man in the universe.'

She laughed. 'The most arrogant, maybe.'

'Yeah,' he said with a shrug. Then he took her face in his hands. 'Please. Take me to see Edward. It really is time to say goodbye.'

He stared at the wallpaper, willing the faces to appear again. He'd found that by tilting his head to a certain angle, he could see the little smiling faces trapped in the gaudy floral design. He hadn't told anyone about his discovery. Not that they didn't think he was mad already. He liked to believe that the faces were his old friends and family. That they were waiting for him. One day, he'd join them. He mouthed a 'hello' at his mother's face, then began the slow bend down to reach his slippers. *Deal Or No Deal* was due to start in twenty minutes and one of the contestants on it reminded him of someone. He was trying to remember who it was when he realised he was stuck.

'Come on, back. Move!' he grunted. His spine seemed to take great pleasure in locking at the most inopportune moments. Usually when he needed the toilet or when there was a rush for that extra portion of dessert. Of course, that only happened when one of his fellow inmates popped their clogs. It'd been Mrs Barrett's turn last night. One minute, she'd been drooling into her soup, the next she'd collapsed. He had tried not to laugh as the thick orange goo had splattered across the tablecloth. Stupid old woman. He wondered if she'd had a heart attack or whether she'd drowned in the soup. It had taken five minutes for any of them to react so the poor cow could've been gurgling her last for ages. Funny thing was she'd once said she knew him from somewhere. Well, she had thought it was funny. He'd just thought she was mad. A mad old biddy, he'd told his god-daughter in the wallpaper. Choking on a bitter laugh, he wondered what he was doing.

'Why the hell am I crouched down like this?' he muttered. He looked over at a stuffed toy sitting on top of a pile of books. 'It's all right for you,' he said to the bear. 'Sitting there with that stupid grin on your face. Still can't tell me why I'm like this, eh?'

Then, he remembered *Deal Or No Deal* and his slippers and he stopped laughing. Perhaps, if he was lucky, it'd be his turn tonight. An Australian voice sounded in his ear, muttering on about turtles. He was so sick of being the one fighting on.

Perhaps, if he stayed quiet and still for long enough, he'd just stop breathing. He could be eaten by the shark.

A loud crash suddenly interrupted his silence *and he tried to duck from the Germans' shell.*

'Get down!' he hollered as he collapsed onto the carpet.

'Edward,' said a voice. He opened his eyes and... *somehow, the pub was still standing!* Then, he saw a pair of shoes. Slowly, he lifted his head to look up at... him. Stood in the doorway, grinning like a madman.

'I know you!'

The young man reached down and, struggling under the weight, managed to manoeuvre him back onto the bed.

'I know you...' he muttered. Then, he looked across at the woman who'd also entered. Her face stood out against the wallpaper. She always stood out.

'Eleanor?' He started to whistle a long-forgotten tune. *Funny and sad at the same time...*

'No, Granddad. It's me. Linda.'

'Hello, Linda,' he said, politely pretending to know who she was. He turned to the man who'd helped him. 'And you must be... erm...'

Carefully, the man cleared his throat before replying.

'I really don't think a doctor is necessary.' The visitor's voice was muffled through the bloody handkerchief.

'Well,' replied Mrs Price, Oak Hill Residential Home's ever-calm manager. 'If you're sure?'

'Edward was just a bit confused.' The man winced as he tried to smile. 'Got a great punch for an old bloke though!'

'I know. We've warned him about it before.' Mrs Price stood up and moved to the doorway. 'This is your final warning, Edward. No more fighting, please.'

She closed Mr Grainger's door and returned to the other oblivious residents. They'd been too engrossed in Noel Edmonds to hear the eruption of shouting, screaming and breaking furniture from room three.

Looking over at Edward, the Doctor pulled the handkerchief away and gingerly touched his nose.

'You remember me, then?' he asked.

Edward's response made Linda blush. She sat down on the bed and took his hand.

'Well, Granddad? Do you remember the Doctor?'

'Of course!' Edward pulled his hand away from hers. 'But, who the hell are you?'

'It's me, Granddad. It's Linda.'

'Nonsense!' He looked over at the wall and spoke to the faces. 'I don't have any grandchildren, do I? Not since John died. He was my son. My little boy. But he died.' Suddenly, he turned back to Linda and grabbed her arm. 'When did he die? He'd know, you know. He was always good with dates and numbers. The last Grainger.'

The Doctor walked over and put an arm around Linda's shoulders. 'I can help him,' he whispered into her ear.

'How?' she shouted, her eyes filling with tears.

The Doctor put a finger to his lips. 'Trust me. I'll make sure he knows everything. I'll make sure he remembers you. I'll make sure he's happy.'

For a second, she looked confused. 'Are you... are you taking him away?'

The Doctor looked down at the old man. 'It's up to you, Linda. He can stay here and wither away or... or I can give him one last great adventure.'

She didn't speak. She stood up, bent down and kissed her granddad on the forehead.

'You could always come with us?'

'No.' She shook her head. 'It's a one-way journey. That's how it is.'

Then, without looking back, she walked out of the room.

'Edward,' muttered the Doctor. 'Edward, can you hear me?'

The old man's eyes opened. 'What do you want?' he snarled.

'To say sorry.'

The man's eyes once again tried to focus on the wallpaper pattern. 'I remember... a book. There was a book and it was about a boy and his teddy bear. And there was a tiger and a donkey... no, wait! It was about a man and what... the thing's he'd done and the people he'd known... I knew a lot of people, you know? Sometimes, I can see them. I don't know their names but they're there. In the wallpaper.'

The Doctor sat down. 'Would you like to know their names again?'

The old man's eyes filled with tears as he nodded.

'Well, then, Edward Grainger.' The Doctor leant forward and whispered in his ear. 'We're going to have to get you out of here.'

Edward smiled.

The doors to the magical box opened as the Doctor led him inside. He staggered, trying to take it all in. A huge cavern of books and alleyways, with flickering candles lighting up secret passageways. In the middle of it all, seemingly carved out of a single great tree, stood what appeared to be some kind of control area. A haunting blue light suddenly shot up to the impossibly high ceiling as the Doctor played with the controls. He danced around the console, flicking switches and turning dials, a whirlwind of energy in a place that time seemed to have forgotten. Then, the Doctor stopped and looked across at him. 'You okay?'

Edward leaned back against one of the walls. 'No... not really. It's... it was real?'

The Doctor bounded over to him and gripped his arms. 'It's all real, Edward. Every word, every action... Edward?'

The old man started to smile at the Doctor's unending enthusiasm. 'Yes, Tigger?'

'Happy birthday!'

Edward just shook his head as the Doctor led him over to an old chaise longue.

'Take a seat!'

As Edward eased himself down, the Doctor ran over to the console. Again, he played the dials and switches and then, turning back to Edward, he pointed up. The old man lay back and watched as the ceiling... vanished. Suddenly, he could see stars and galaxies and planets and... He gripped the back of the chaise longue and gasped.

'Are you ready, Edward Grainger?'

He smiled. 'For what?'

'Your memories are still there. They're just locked away.' He patted the console. 'The TARDIS is going to find them. Refine them. Then, it's going to show them to us... up there!' He pointed towards the ceiling before rushing over and kneeling in front of his friend. 'Everyone you ever loved. Every adventure you ever had. You'll remember it all.'

Edward nodded dumbly as the panorama changed once more.

'Remember it all, Edward.' The Doctor shouted. 'It's the trip of a lifetime!'

And as the languid smoke dissipates, he sees his mother. She looks sad as she takes the photograph out of his hands and says, 'Sometimes, Teddy, God needs special people up in Heaven,' but then he keeps on punching, even when the bigger boy falls to his knees, even when the bigger boy pleads for mercy, even when the bigger boy loses consciousness and his mother is telling him his father is drunk, dead drunk, dead as three gunshots ring out 'Mai Ling!' The blue marble smashes and he's blind, reaching out 'This is my job, Doctor,' he shouts over the sound of the bombardment from above but the bomb smacks squarely down on the pub and he looks into the eyes of his exhausted wife as she clutches their precious offspring and the pub's still standing and 'life fights on' he thinks as the tears catch him again and the wind drops as he and his son rush towards each other and Eleanor, freed from whatever's holding her back collapses onto the bed and the decision is made as he closes his eyes and runs towards the column of light before he, or the others, can have a second thought, but then, McCloud's languid smoke slowly dissipates, and he realises that Montfort's been sent to kill him and stop his autobiography being published and they don't believe his stories except for little Linda who brings the man, the one man who's been there throughout his life, the man who's there when he meets Eleanor, when Tremayne dies, when John is born, the man who's in the White Rabbit and the man who's in the magic blue box.

And he's in the TARDIS and then it stops.

And the smoke has cleared.

And he remembers it all.

And he sleeps.

He woke up.

'Doctor?' he called, shuddering at how weak his voice sounded.

The room was in near-darkness and all was silent.

Edward…

He moved suddenly, knocking a blanket onto the floor. 'Doctor?'

Edward… Come to me, Edward Grainger…

He placed his feet onto the cold floor and slowly eased himself up.

Quickly, Edward… come to me.

'John?' he called. 'Is that you?'

It's me…

He stumbled across the room to a set of doors. After a while, he realised that they weren't the doors he'd come in through. He pushed at them and with a tremendous creak they opened. He paused then stepped through into a long, narrow corridor. Leaning against the stone wall, he began to ease himself along to another set of doors he could just about make out at the far end.

Edward Grainger!

The voice was getting louder, clearer. He continued to ease himself along, already breathless at the exertion. He grimaced as he remembered how once he could have run the length of the corridor without breaking into a sweat.

'I'm coming,' he called out.

He passed another few doors, heading closer and closer to the end of the corridor. Then, stopping, he put his head up against them and listened.

Open the doors... Edward...

Struggling in the darkness, his hands fumbled at the solid metal ring bolted into the wood. He turned it and the doors opened. He looked into the room, his eyes adjusting to yet more darkness. It was about the same size as the control room. A huge stone staircase led to high-up gantries and, there, in the middle of it all, carved out of the ground, was a great stone... thing. He stared at it, his mind desperately trying to give it a name. A tomb. He hobbled towards it, his feet cold on the stone floor. The voice screamed in his mind.

TEDDY!

'I'm coming!'

Gasping for breath, he clambered up a ramp and practically fell onto what he could now see looked like a giant, closed eye. He gripped a nearby stone staff to support himself. His breathing slowed back down and there was silence. Then –

The staff exploded as a huge shaft of icy-blue light shot out and *made a break out of the sand. Straight into a shark's mouth!*

He collapsed back and tumbled down the ramp, screaming out for the Doctor as the Devil itself shot up towards him. Shrieking, it flew past his head and out into the corridor.

'Doctor!' screamed Edward, his body breaking and his mind nearly gone. Suddenly, the ramp buckled as *the bomb smacks down squarely on to the pub* and he heard the all-too-familiar sound of distant explosions. He crawled across the floor, his thin skin tearing like paper on the stone.

'Doctor!' he screamed again, as the floor shook once more and he was flung back out into the corridor. His head bounced off the wall *'The nature of the fetal heart rate is making our decision difficult'* and darkness began to engulf everything and *with the entity's words still resounding in his ears, Edward races through the house. He reaches his son's room in a matter of minutes and his blood turns to ice at the sight that greets him* and then he saw the shoes and he looked up into the Doctor's face and...

He woke up.

'Doctor?' he called, shuddering at how weak his voice sounded.

He was on the chaise longue. His eyes adjusted to the blue light emanating from the column in the centre of the room.

'Did I dream... was that real?'

The Doctor crouched down beside him and looked him in the eye.

'Oh, Edward. Do you know what you've done?'

Edward struggled to sit up. 'What I've done? You brought me in here!'

Angrily, the Doctor stood up and walked away. 'I shouldn't have bothered! You stupid, stupid old...' He trailed off as he turned back. 'I'm sorry. It wasn't your fault.'

For a moment there was silence.

'Another column of light,' Edward muttered. 'What was it?'

The Doctor put his hands on the central console and sighed. 'That...' He paused. 'That was the Master.'

Edward eased himself to his feet and walked over to join the Doctor. 'The Master?'

'Yes, he's a... well he was a Time Lord. Like me.'

The Doctor turned abruptly as Edward started to laugh. 'What's so funny?'

'Yet again, I'm caught up in the middle of one of your... adventures and, yet again, I've haven't a flaming clue what you're talking about. Even now.' He stopped laughing. 'You couldn't just let me die, could you?'

The Doctor smiled sadly. 'I could never just let you die. Not after everything you've done.'

Edward, feeling an energy he hadn't felt in years, put an arm protectively around the other man's shoulder. 'So, what's the situation? Where's he gone?'

'He's left the TARDIS. We'd better see where and when we are.' He turned a dial and they both looked up.

A bustling city. Horse-drawn carriages moving through the streets as the sun sets. The sound of Big Ben ringing throughout the TARDIS...

'London. And the date?' asked Edward.

The Doctor looked at the controls in front of him and pointed.

Sunday 24 June 1906

'I need a drink,' muttered Lawrence Grainger as he lurched through the doors and into the sunlight.

He looked up at the never-changing Houses of Parliament, took a deep breath, then viciously punched the wall. Yet again, he'd been bawled out by Bellamy. Yet again, he'd been ridiculed in front of his colleagues. And, yet again, he'd found himself utterly bewildered at what was happening to the world. Russia with its unions and its Duma. Transvaal's independence. And here, here in Great Britain... a Liberal Government. It was sickening. Then, as he massaged his bleeding knuckles, the voice he despised the most sounded in his ear.

'Afternoon, Mr Grainger.'

He turned around. 'Mr Hardie, sir. Working on a Sunday?'

'I know,' Keir Hardie replied with his oh-so-charming smile. 'What is the world coming to?'

Lawrence fought back the urge to give him a bloody nose. 'Indeed. If you'll excuse me.'

'Of course.' Hardie stepped past him. 'Oh, please give my regards to your wife. I believe she was seen at one of Mrs Pankhurst's meetings.'

Lawrence forced a smile and walked away. When the smirking Hardie was out of sight, he took a hip flask out of his pocket and quickly gulped down a mouthful of whisky. Suffrage for women? His own Mary?

'What is happening to us?' Then, taking another swig to try and calm his nerves, he went to hail a cab.

Across the street, two men watched him climb into a horse-drawn carriage.

'Terrible creature,' muttered Edward Grainger, leaning on a walking stick the Doctor had given him.

'I seem to remember that you weren't the most pleasant of young men,' said the Doctor, raising an eyebrow.

'With a father like that? What did you expect?'

Smiling sadly, the Doctor put an arm across the old man's shoulders. 'The world is changing all the time, Edward. People sometimes find the journey difficult.'

Suddenly, Edward snarled. 'Don't patronise me.'

The Doctor shrugged. He crouched down and picked up an abandoned copy of the *Evening Standard*.

'There's a coincidence.' He pointed to a headline. 'San Francisco.'

Edward turned to face him. 'What?'

'That's where I last fought the Master. He'd changed. Used to be a normal Time Lord like me, but he'd... well, he always was afraid of dying.'

Edward didn't respond.

'Anyway, to cut a long story short, he turned himself into this energy creature thing, possessed a man and tried to destroy me. For some reason, he really does seem to have it in for me.'

'That's a feeling I can sympathise with.' Edward smiled.

'Thank you!' The Doctor smiled back. 'Anyway, we had a bit of a scrap and I ended up locking him away in the TARDIS.' His face darkened. 'I always thought he'd been destroyed by what's in there.'

'And now I've released him?'

'Looks like it.'

'And we're going to have to sort him out? Like the old days? Shoulder to shoulder?'

The Doctor carefully folded the newspaper and looked down at his feet.

'What is it?' asked Edward. 'What aren't you telling me?'

The Doctor took him by the arm and they started to walk. 'Our lives, you and me, we've become somewhat... intertwined.'

'You mean you couldn't keep your nose out of my business!'

The Doctor shook his head. 'What date is it? Today, I mean.'

'According to your machine, it's the day I was born,' replied Edward.

'You think that's a coincidence?'

Sir George Steer straightened his tie and pulled on his jacket. He was in the mood for a good party. Then, he noticed something reflected in the mirror...

* * *

They stopped walking and Edward turned to face the Doctor. 'What do you mean?'

'The Master existed inside the TARDIS. He would have seen your memories,' said the Doctor calmly. 'He knows about all the times we've met.'

Sir George screamed as the serpent forced its way into him and swallowed his soul.

There was a pause then, suddenly, Edward staggered. 'So, if he... if he kills me. If I die now then none of it will happen. My wife. My son. Linda.'

'Let me take your coat and escort you to the drawing room.'

Sir George smiled. 'Thank you. I presume your master hasn't arrived home yet?'

Peake turned from the coat hooks. 'Not yet, sir, no.'

'Moira. Mai Ling. Me.' The Doctor stumbled as he tried to hold Edward upright. 'By destroying you, he destroys me. My life. My history. Everything.'

'Well.' Edward cleared his throat. 'We'd better stop him then.'

'George! I'm so glad you could make it!'

Sir George took Mary Grainger's hand and kissed it. 'Oh, I wouldn't have missed this for the world.'

Then one day Edward found something extraordinary. It was in a bundle of papers that had belonged to his mother, papers that had been in his possession ever since her death but he'd never got round to reading. It was a letter, written by his mother to Lady Louisa Pollard and probably returned to her after Lady Louisa's death. It discussed the strange events that they had both witnessed when Edward had been born. In astonishment he read his mother's description of the white-haired old man and his young friend, and the role they played that day. His mother had known the name of only one of these men – the Doctor.

'I'm the Doctor and this is my friend, Edward.'

Mrs Best stared at the two men. 'What are you doing in my kitchen?'

'We're here to see your master.'

Mrs Best snorted. 'And you came in through the tradesmen's entrance?'

'Let us past, you stupid old woman!' shouted Edward, raising his stick into the air.

'Old?' Mrs Best picked up the rolling pin and brandished it in his face. 'How dare you!'

'Ever the diplomat, Edward.' The Doctor sighed. 'It might be best if I dealt with... oh, we've got company. Hello.'

The three turned to look at the young maid. Edward felt a chill inside.

'Girl,' he called. 'Is this 86 Hobb's Lane?'

The maid nodded.

'And are my... are Mr and Mrs Grainger upstairs?'

The maid nodded.

'Don't just stand there, Violet!' Mrs Best turned back to face the two strangers. 'Go and tell Mr Peake that we've got intruders!'

Violet ran out of the room and into history...

Richard stood up and moved to sit next to Violet.

'Don't cry, my dear,' he said, putting an arm across her shoulders.

She looked up, the fire, the revellers, her fiancé, everything just a blur through the tears.

'I was so scared, Richard. I was so scared.'

'Would you like another drink? A brandy?'

She took out a handkerchief and dabbed at her eyes. Then, forcing a smile, she shook her head.

'No. No, thank you. I want to tell you the rest of the story.'

'It's a boy, Violet. I've got a son!'

Lawrence Grainger took the baby from his exhausted wife and held it to his chest. Violet crawled past Sir George's unconscious body and over to her master and mistress.

'Pardon me for asking, sir, but what will you call him?'

Mary Grainger turned to her husband. 'Well, dear?' she asked. 'The King?'

Lawrence's face broke into the biggest grin. 'His Majesty!'

Edward looked down on his parents as they hugged the child tightly. He felt someone squeeze his hand.

'You all right?' whispered the Doctor.

'Edward Grainger...'

Edward watched as his father, the man he'd always hated, cried with joy. He watched as his mother hugged her husband and cried with him. He watched as the maid gently stroked the baby's face.

Then, suddenly, came the sound of angry men – Lord Greystone, Mr Pollard and the others – bursting in through the door, led by a pistol-brandishing Mrs Best. The two strangers gave one last look at the baby before swiftly striding out of the back door. I stroked the infant's face and ran out into the road. They were just standing there, looking up at the house.

They stood in the road and looked up at 86 Hobb's Lane.

'That's it, Edward. That's where the journey starts.'

'My mother.' Edward Grainger wiped his eyes. 'My father. I don't remember him being like that. I... I want to...'

The Doctor shook his head. 'Everything ends.'

'They don't know... don't know what's coming.' Edward took a deep breath and continued to look at the house. 'What about the other guests?'

'There'll be a few sore heads but nothing they can't blame on the wine.'

'And the Master?'

'He's on his last legs. I don't think he'll be a problem any more.' He laughed. 'The most evil man in the universe, beaten by a maid.'

And then, as they stood there, the maid came running over to them.

'You're leaving?'

'We have to. We've done what we came to do.' Edward suddenly felt cold.

'Pardon me for asking, sir.' She pointed to the kitchen window. 'But what happened in there?'

'Sir George was possessed,' explained the Doctor. 'He doesn't know what he tried to do. Make sure he's okay.'

Violet nodded then turned and looked up at Edward.

He wanted to grab her, take her with them. Keep her safe.

'Are you... ill?' she asked.

He looked at the Doctor, who was gently shaking his head. He sniffed and turned back to her, forcing a smile.

'What? I'm... I'm fine. A tiring business all this, yes?'

The girl nodded.

Suddenly, the Doctor leaned forward and kissed her on the cheek. 'You were very brave in there, Violet.' He leant back and grinned. 'You've just saved the world!'

The girl, blushing looked down at the ground as the Doctor and Edward started to walk away. Then, Edward turned to look at her one last time.

'You won't be forgotten,' he called. 'Trust me.'

She looked up as they disappeared into the mist. Standing alone, she shivered. Then, without another word, she went back into the house to resume her duties.

'What made you say that?'

The Doctor was now supporting most of Edward's weight as they walked through the fog and back to the TARDIS. The old man grunted.

'Edward?'

He turned to look at the Doctor. 'She's dead.'

The Doctor paused, allowing Edward to get his breath back. 'They're all dead. I'm sorry.'

The old man shook his head, coughing as his breaths became shorter and harsher. 'You don't understand.'

The Doctor shifted, uncomfortable under the other man's weight. 'Don't you think it's... well, I think it's quite funny.'

Edward's eyes suddenly flashed with anger. 'Funny?'

'Yeah! Your life, well mine too, we were saved by a maid with a well-aimed rolling pin! You know, sometimes direct action is the best approach. I once knew a man who...'

Edward wasn't listening any more.

'Edward! I thought I told you to go to bed!'

'Sorry, Mummy.' He turned back to face his mother.

'What is it now?'

'Mummy, who's that?' He pointed at the small black-and-white photograph on the mantelpiece.

Mary Grainger looked up and her leg started to shake. 'That's... that was Violet. She was our maid.'

'A maid?' he laughed. 'Why have you got a picture of a maid?'

Mary stood up. 'She was very special to us.'

She walked over to her son and took his hand. She led him across the room, took the photograph down and passed it to him.

'Violet, she... she helped me when you were being born.'

'How?' He looked at the girl's face. 'She's pretty.'

'Yes, she was.' She tried to hide her tears.

'What happened to her?'

His mother took the photograph out of his hands and led him back to her chair. She sat down and pulled him onto her knee.

'Sometimes, Teddy, God needs special people up in Heaven. He takes them even when we would rather they stayed with us.'

'Was she special?'

His mother gripped him tightly. 'Oh, yes. She was so special but... on the day after you were born, God made her one of his angels.' She stroked his hair. 'Your daddy and I will never forget her.'

The Doctor flung himself onto the console, pressing buttons and pulling levers seemingly at random as Edward eased himself down onto the chaise longue. He heard his bones creaking... or was it the chair? He wasn't sure about anything any more. After what could have been minutes or hours, he heard the Doctor speak.

'Well, the TARDIS can't seem to find the Master anywhere. Perhaps he's really gone this time.'

He paused before turning to face Edward. 'Anyway, we can't hang around here all day. Present company excluded, 1906 really isn't all that!'

The blue column began to rise up and down as lights flashed and machines thundered into action and the Doctor continued to fly around the room, the tails of his coat flapping behind him.

'Where shall I take you next?' He laughed. 'We can go anywhere!'

The Doctor's voice, still so young and vibrant, somehow sounded muffled. The lights, still so bright and blue, somehow seemed diffused. Edward felt himself being drawn back. Drawn away from the Doctor and his life.

Suddenly, the Doctor stopped spinning and turned to look at him.

'Edward?'

'Hmm?' murmured the old man.

Slowly, the Doctor walked towards him.

'How are you feeling?'

Edward could hardly hear the question. The room was growing darker and colder and yet, he felt calm. Comfortable. The arthritic pain in his legs was fading away. Everything was drifting. He was vaguely aware that someone was kneeling at his feet and holding his hand. The man's face was blurring. His mother's face. Eleanor. John. Staring out of the wallpaper.

'Edward?'

He heard himself mutter. 'I'm fine.'

And then, his eyes closed.

And Edward Grainger gave a final breath before becoming silent.

Sunday 25 June 2006

Linda Grainger looked down the Victoria Embankment as London shivered in the cold, grey drizzle. She took a deep breath before pushing open the door and stepping into the White Rabbit.

The pub was practically empty so it wasn't hard to spot him. Slouched in his booth, mournfully nursing a pint. She walked over to him.

'Doctor?' She touched his arm. 'Is he...?'

He looked up at her. 'At peace.'

She didn't cry. She didn't want to. She actually felt relieved. The Doctor stood and looked unsure as to what to do next. So she hugged him.

'Thanks,' she whispered. 'Again!'

Hours passed as they talked. Remembering, celebrating Edward's life. The Doctor told her about his travels, his friends, his adventures. She told him that she'd never regretted turning him down those many years ago. He knew she was lying but let it go. They talked about how the world was changing, how she was scared by it all.

'But I was thinking about it,' said Linda. 'About what I said yesterday. Me getting older and... you know, not doing anything.'

The Doctor smiled. 'Yes?'

'Things here. They're not... not great. There's these new laws... anti-immigration and all that. Granddad fought against stuff like that.'

'The more things change, the more they stay the same.'

'You reckon? Well, perhaps I can make a difference.' She paused then, smiling, continued. 'You know, stand up and be counted and all that jazz.'

'You're Edward's granddaughter all right.' The Doctor's face broke into a grin. 'That's what I love about you lot. You never give in. Not really. So, you're going to start organising marches and protests and that?'

'We're not allowed to.' Linda shrugged. 'But I'm sure I'll think of something.'

The Doctor laughed. 'Well, that's a start.'

And eventually, it was time to leave. She had to collect Ellie from her ex-husband and he had... places to go.

'It's funny,' she smiled as she pulled on her coat. 'This is where it all started.'

The Doctor looked at her, confused. 'What? Here?'

'Yeah, this is the pub I was in just before I met you. You know, in 1990.'

He suddenly felt very cold. 'This pub? The White Rabbit? Here?'

'Yeah. So? It's just a pub, yeah?'

He looked around the old bar, running his thumb through the same groove in the same table as– *bombs fall, nurses enjoy birthday parties and a maid talks to her fiancé, UNIT soldiers playing darts as London explodes and a drunken professor sings on the karaoke while an old man whispers stories to frightened children, more bombs exploding as Cromwell's men arrest a twentieth-century sailor, the London skyline rising and falling while plague victims hammer on the door as the city burns and office workers drink to forget the million chimes from Big Ben resonating through the wooden walls as the windows smash and the people scream and laugh and dance and drink and time suddenly–*

He pulled his thumbnail from out of the groove and looked across at Linda.

'Yeah,' he grinned. 'It's just a pub. Come on, let's go.'

They stood up, walked over to the door, pushed it open –

Monday 25 June 1906

And stepped out, into the fog.

Violet's fiancé placed a protective arm over her shoulder as the door closed behind them.

'It's cold,' she muttered, shivering. Then, as they began to walk, she whispered to herself. 'I do wonder what will become of him.'

'The child?' asked her companion, as he led her along the darkening river. She struggled to keep up with his long strides.

'Edward,' she gasped, breathless. 'His name is Edward. Richard, please slow down.'

He stopped and held her arms. 'I'm sorry, my dear. Sometimes, I forget how slow you can be.'

She looked indignant. 'I am not slow!'

'Oh, of course you're not.' He looked into her eyes and something changed. For a second, as the wind coursed through her hair, she felt a chill as if... as if they were the only two people left in the world. Then, the chimes of Big Ben echoed out once more across the sleeping city and she laughed. She pulled free from his tight embrace and skipped down towards the bridge before stopping and turning.

'Come on, Richard! It's nearly dark!'

He looked down into the black water and, for the briefest of moments, an unearthly green glow seemed to shimmer across his eyes...

About the Authors

BENJAMIN ADAMS was nominated for a 2002 Bram Stoker Award for the anthology *The Children of Cthulhu*, which he co-edited with John Pelan. His short fiction has appeared in the 1998 Bram Stoker Award-winning anthology *Horrors! 365 Scary Stories*, and in anthologies such as *100 Wicked Little Witch Stories*, *100 Vicious Little Vampire Stories*, *Miskatonic University*, *Blood Muse* and *Delta Green: Dark Theatres*. While most of his professional work has appeared in horror and dark fiction collections, he has always dreamed of coming back to his first love as a fanzine editor in the 1980s: *Doctor Who*. Who says dreams can't come true?

SAMANTHA BAKER has now written four stories for Big Finish's *Short Trips* range, having previously contributed to *Past Tense*, *Monsters* and *The History of Christmas*. She has also written for fanzines and websites, but, unlike her namesake, has never been the editor of *Cosmopolitan*.

JOHN DAVIES has always been a keen writer. However, whilst he is known to post fiction on *Doctor Who* website Outpost Gallifrey, *The Centenarian* is his first professional commission. He is still calming down from being quoted in *Doctor Who Magazine*'s season survey in 1990. Rumours that his final dissertation at university was based on continuity problems within *Doctor Who* are totally founded.

IAN FARRINGTON (editor) has compiled three previous *Short Trips* collections – *Past Tense*, *Monsters* and *A Day in the Life* – and is the range editor of the series. He has also written stories for *A Day in the Life*, *Short Trips: Life Science* and two anthologies in the *Professor Bernice Summerfield* range, and edited numerous novels, short-story collections, script books and factual titles. Ian co-produced Big Finish's UNIT audio series and was the assistant producer of the company's *Doctor Who* range between 2002 and 2006. He has also contributed to *Doctor Who Magazine*.

SIMON GUERRIER has written five audio plays for Big Finish – UNIT: *The Coup*, *Professor Bernice Summerfield and The Lost Museum*, *Doctor Who: The Settling*, *Sapphire & Steel: The School* and *Bernice Summerfield and the Summer of Love*. He has edited four short-story anthologies, including *Short Trips: The History of Christmas*. *Incongruous Details* is his tenth *Doctor Who* short story. His novel, *The Time Travellers*, also involves the bombing of London.

STEPHEN HATCHER is Head of Modern Languages for a secondary school in Stoke-on-Trent. He is the coordinator of the Whoovers, Derby's *Doctor Who* local group, and a regular contributor to a number of fanzines, including *Shockeye's Kitchen, Enlightenment, Myth Makers* and *TSV*. Steve is the author of two stories published in previous *Short Trips* collections: *Ante Bellum* in *Past Tense* and *The Touch of the Nurazh* in *Monsters*.

LIZZIE HOPLEY is a writer and RADA-trained actress. Her radio plays include *The Elizabethan Beauty Law* (starring Annette Badland as Elizabeth I) and *The Cenci Family* (which was nominated for a Sony Award and a First Play Award) for BBC Radio 4, and *Salome* for BBC Radio 3. For the theatre, Lizzie has written *Perseus* (which has toured Canada and New Zealand) and *Oscaria* (which was shortlisted for a Verity Bargate Award). Recent acting work for Big Finish includes roles in *Doctor Who: Night Thoughts, The Tomorrow People: A Plague of Dreams* and Nicholas Briggs's *Cyberman* miniseries. In her Big Finish debut, she played Gemma Griffin, the Doctor's companion, in Joseph Lidster's *Doctor Who: Terror Firma*. Notable TV and film work includes *Pierrepoint* with Timothy Spall (Granada) and *Randall & Hopkirk (Deceased): Whatever Possessed You?* (BBC).

JOSEPH LIDSTER has written extensively for Big Finish's series of *Doctor Who* audio dramas, with his second play, Master, being described by *Doctor Who Magazine* as 'the most moving *Doctor Who* story ever.' His third play, *Terror Firma*, won the *Doctor Who Magazine* poll for best audio play of 2005. He's written five *Doctor Who* plays as well as scripts for Big Finish's *Sapphire & Steel, Professor Bernice Summerfield, UNIT* and *Tomorrow People* ranges. He's also written 11 short stories and a novella for the same company. In 2006, Joseph created an online gaming world for the BBC's *Doctor Who* spin-off websites.

GLEN McCOY wrote *Timelash* for the 1985 season of *Doctor Who*. He has written several short stories, and his other television credits include episodes of *Angels, Emmerdale Farm, EastEnders* and *Eldorado*.

IAN MOND has been scribbling *Doctor Who* stories since he was ten years old. It's only recently that they've started being published in anthologies such as the *Short Trips* collections *Past Tense, Monsters* (both co-written with Danny Oz) and *A Day in The Life*, and *Myth Makers*. Ian has written for the Doctor's former companion Bernice Summerfield in three short-story collections – *A Life During Wartime, A Life Worth Living* and *Something Changed*. He lives in Melbourne, Australia, and recommends people read Les Carlyon's book *Gallipoli* if they want to know more about that tragic campaign.

JAMES PARSONS is an actor, writer and designer. His recent stage roles have included appearances in *Stephen King's Misery, Five Eleven, The Servant of Two Masters, The Gamblers, Othello, The Cripple Of Inishmaan, The Importance Of Being Earnest, Twelfth Night* and *To Kill A Mockingbird*. On film, he has appeared in *Love In A Lecture Theatre*, *Because I Can*, *Fruit Graffiti* and *Zero Option*. He also appeared in the Big Finish *Doctor Who* CD *Thicker Than Water* and played Brint in the *I, Davros* miniseries. He co-wrote *Doctor Who: LIVE 34* with Andrew Stirling-Brown for Big Finish's range of audio dramas and they are currently working on an idea for a radio play.

STEL PAVLOU makes things up for a living. So far he's made up a movie, *The 51st State* starring Samuel L. Jackson and Robert Carlyle, and two best-selling novels, *Decipher* and *Gene*. His first published short story came out in 2005 in the collection *Elemental*, which was published to raise money for Tsunami Relief. Stel has travelled widely, lived in America and Cyprus, and been a soldier, a shopkeeper and a fake land-mine dongle riveter (seriously). He is of mixed Anglo-Greek descent and therefore only fifty per cent of his gift-giving should be treated with any suspicion. Read more at www.stelpavlou.com.

GARY RUSSELL has worked widely in media, as a television actor, script consultant, magazine editor, reviewer, novelist and audio producer. His non-fiction publications include books on *Frasier*, *The Simpsons*, *Doctor Who* and *The Lord of the Rings*. He has written many *Doctor Who* novels and was the editor of two *Short Trips* collections – *Repercussions* and *The Solar System*. From 1999 to 2006, he was the producer of Big Finish's range of *Doctor Who* audio dramas.

RICHARD SALTER has had a number of short stories published. His first, for Virgin Publishing's *Decalog 4*, was in 1997 and this has been followed by six for Big Finish, most recently in *Short Trips: The History of Christmas*. He also co-edits a popular, award-winning fiction fanzine called *Myth Makers* for the Doctor Who Information Network (www.dwin.org). He's an ex-Brit, now living near Toronto, Canada, with his wife Jennifer and working as a software development manager – though he'd rather be writing.

STEVEN SAVILE has edited a number of critically acclaimed anthologies and collections, including *Redbrick Eden* and most recently *Elemental* for Tor Books in the US, as well as *Smoke Ghost & Other Apparitions* and *Black Gondolier and Other Stories*, the collected horror stories of Fritz Leiber. Steven is also the author of the *Von Carstein Vampire* trilogy, *Inheritance*, *Dominion* and *Retribution*, set in Games Workshop's popular *Warhammer* world, and has re-imagined the blood-thirsty celtic barbarian Slaine from *2000 AD* in a new trilogy of novels for Black Flame. Steven has written for *Star Wars* and *Jurassic Park* as well as his own novels and short stories, including *Houdini's Last Illusion* (Telos) and *Angel Road* (Elastic Press). In his copious spare time, Steven... erm... writes... He was a runner up in the British Fantasy Awards, and a winner of a Writers of the Future Award in 2002.

L. J. SCOTT created the DreamZone in 1983, one of the first online fiction sites. She co-founded DWIS (the Doctor Who Information Society) and was an editor and contributor to its newsletter. She provided film stock for the completion of *Hick Trek*, and did some tentative work in television and radio during the late 1980s. While heading the Science Fiction Association of Colorado Springs into the 1990s, she wrote the original draft of what became the *Star Trek: The Next Generation* episode *The Quality Of Life*. Taking a decade off to help fuel the telecommunications boom, she has since returned to writing.

ANDREW STIRLING-BROWN is an armourer and writer. Notable armour commissions have included suits for the Royal Armouries and Hampton Court Palace, seen on Channel 4 shows such as *Time Team*. He has provided pieces for Shakespeare's Globe's period-style recreations of the Bard's plays, including *Richard II* (broadcast live on BBC 4) and *Twelfth Night*, which won that year's Olivier Award for Best Costume Design. As writer, Andrew has specialised in Herefordshire medieval history, culminating in the book *Pembridge Past*, published in 2005. That same year, his first Big Finish commission, the audio play *LIVE 34*, co-written with James Parsons, was released.

BRIAN WILLIS was born in South Wales and still lives there, much to the annoyance of the residents of Swansea. He has written numerous stories, occasional reviews for *SFX* magazine and a novel – *Scorpion*, co-written with Chris Poote. Brian won the British Fantasy Award in 2001 for editing the anthology *Hideous Progeny* for Razorblade Press.

Read more from the authors of *Doctor Who: Short Trips – The Centenarian* online at <u>thecentenarian.blogspot.com</u>

Coming soon...

SHORT TRIPS:
TIME SIGNATURE

A short-story collection edited by
SIMON GUERRIER

ISBN 1–84435–235–8

A city destroyed by time itself. A country torn apart by revolution.
A man in a boat with a biscuit tin...

The Doctor doesn't just change the lives of those around him, his
actions echo through history. Shaping the universe, changing it,
rewriting in his own hand.

But making it better? It's a good job he never sticks around
for long afterwards.

And yet, for all that the universe may be infinite, for all he keeps
moving, the Doctor can't outrun the consequences forever.

*Featuring stories by Ben Aaronovitch, Andrew Cartmel, Joseph Lidster,
Marc Platt, Matthew Sweet and many more*

An extract from Doctor Who: Short Trips – Time Signature (edited by Simon Guerrier)

The Twilight City
Philip Purser-Hallard

'What colour would you like to be, Ian?' Susan asked, proffering a handful of the wooden counters.

Ian considered. 'I suppose I'll be silvery-grey. But you'll have to explain to me how all this works.'

'Oh, but it's easy,' the girl said at once. She launched into a tortuous explanation, as Ian gazed in bafflement at the landscaped board.

Barbara smiled to herself. Ian was both too kind and too stubborn to admit to their young friend that this game of hers was beyond him. 'Won't we be arriving quite soon, Susan?' she asked.

'I don't know.' Susan looked over at the Doctor, fussing away at his controls as usual. 'Once the ship's in flight, I don't think even Grandfather can tell. But it's very simple really, Ian. This house is yours – it's the same colour as your counters, you see – and you're trying to get home.'

Now Ian glanced over at the Doctor. 'Isn't that the truth,' he said ruefully. Susan gasped, dismayed at her own tactlessness.

'Have you had the game long?' Barbara asked quickly, wondering which planet – and which century – had produced the ornate box-board, with its wooden dice and counters.

'Oh, yes,' Susan replied. 'This set's been in Grandfather's family for thousands of years.'

'Thousands?' Ian stared at her. 'Surely you mean "hundreds"?'

Susan gave him a mischievous smile. 'Well,' she admitted, 'it's hundreds of thousands really. But I didn't want to shock you.'

A once-grand piazza, unchanging beneath a grey sky. Its fountains dry, its buildings and its paving-stones empty of life.

A walkway, arching gracefully overhead. The sky above, drab twilight, scant of stars.

There was no movement here. No breeze perturbed the scraps of dust and rubbish. No rats scampered from the darkened doorways, and the sky was bereft of birds. Not a sound escaped from the surrounding city.

Where previously had been a vacant flagstone, now stood a squat and foreign presence – an English police box. Its beacon flashed sharp white, tearing apart the glowering dusk.

The four companions wandered down a broad and empty boulevard. Skeletal trees accused the grizzled sky.

Ian was carrying the box containing Susan's game board and pieces. He'd just been getting to grips with the rules when the ship had landed. Susan was hoping they could set it up again somewhere.

The women were instinctively whispering, but the Doctor insisted on breaking the museum silence. 'Oh, I shouldn't think there's any reason to worry. This city's been deserted for some time, I should say. Besides,' he added sagely, 'there's nobody about.'

Ian was unconvinced.

The Doctor had been mistaken before, to say the least. And, if any locals were still lurking in the desolation, they'd hear him streets away.

'It must have been beautiful once,' Barbara mused, 'when there were people living here. It feels desolate without them. Why do you suppose they left?'

'My dear Miss Wright, every civilisation comes to an end eventually,' the Doctor said. 'I should have thought a history teacher would know that.'

He scraped at the dust beneath their feet with his walking cane, revealing the intricate mosaic that formed the pavement here. In daylight it might have been colourful, but this dim undifferentiated twilight rendered it in shades of dark and paler grey. 'Some day your own city, London, will be deserted just like this one.'

A shriek cut through the silence. Susan stood some way ahead of them, hands to her mouth.

Ian was at her side instantly. 'What's the matter, Susan? What did you see?'

Cross at being startled, her grandfather snapped, 'What is it now, child?'

'A man!' the girl gasped. 'Over at that window. Standing there completely still, just watching us.'

Her shaking finger pointed across the street to a dark aperture near the base of a tapering tower. 'Ian, he's still there!'

He put a hand on her shoulder. 'I'll go and look,' he said. 'I'm sure it's nothing, though. You stay here with the others.'

Susan's horror did not dissipate over the next hour, as the travellers found more of the immobile figures. Once they knew what to look for, the natives were everywhere: standing at windows, slumped on floors, propped awkwardly amidst the dusty furniture. Not sleeping, and apparently not dead; but not alive.

They looked like human beings, more or less... but so had people on so many of the worlds Susan had seen. Horrifying though they were, now she was more used to them they seemed terribly sad as well, like faded photographs.

'So many of them,' said Barbara as they entered a pillared hall where dozens of pathetic figures huddled motionless. 'Doesn't it remind you of Pompeii, Ian?'

'Pompeii? What's she talking about now?' Grandfather muttered. He was agitated, and Susan could easily understand why.

'What do you think happened to them, Doctor?' asked Ian.

'They're frozen, aren't they, Grandfather?' said Susan. 'Not in temperature, I mean. In time.'

'Yes, well. I thought I'd taught you not to jump to such absurd conclusions, child.'

'But, Grandfather, haven't you noticed? The light.' She pointed through a shattered skylight at the toneless sky. 'Since we arrived it hasn't changed a bit.'

'There must be... there could be all kinds of reasons for that,' the old man blustered. 'Perhaps this world just moves too slowly around its axis for us to see the change in the light. Or we may be in one of the polar regions. Yes, I dare say that's it. We're simply beyond the region of this planet's day and night.'

'*Ian!*'

Now it was Barbara who cried out. From a shadowed corner, one of the stiff figures stepped towards them.

As it moved forward between the pillars, a pale face came into the light. Marred by a scar across one cheek, it remained strangely beautiful.

Calmly, it said, 'I wish that was the case.'

'Thank you so much for your hospitality, Vedirioi,' Barbara said.

Smiling wryly, the alien – the Torcaldian – inclined his head. 'It isn't much to offer you, I know.'

The village of Cantosi, Vedirioi's home, was built in what had once been a city park. Tents and ramshackle sheds were set amongst low ornamental walls and hedges, with row on row of crops planted in what had been flowerbeds. A paved convergence of paths had been cleared of its statues and now-useless sundial to form a rudimentary village square, where the Cantosians sat at wooden trestles with the strangers. In all directions, graceful, lifeless buildings buttressed the skyline.

'We don't see many visitors,' Vedirioi went on. 'Not friendly ones, at least.'

'Oh, don't worry about that, my friend,' the Doctor replied generously. 'Your food may be basic, but it's most adequate. Most adequate, I can assure you!'

Ian frowned – troubled, Barbara supposed, by this scarcely appropriate reaction to the villagers' selfless hospitality. 'You've really been extremely kind, Vedirioi,' he said. 'You've more than made up for the fright you gave us out there in the city.'

'It's the least I can do,' Vedirioi said. 'And I'm sorry for not announcing myself to you sooner. We've been having trouble recently with bandits from the other cities.'

'Bandits?' Susan's eyes were wide.

'I'm afraid so. Our world's resources are scarce. Not everybody chooses to come by them peacefully.'

Barbara traded a glance with Ian. The question had to be asked.

'What happened here, Vedirioi?' she said. 'Was there some terrible disaster?'

The Torcaldian gazed gravely at her. 'No,' he said. 'Not really.'

'What happened, then?' asked Susan eagerly.

Barbara saw Ian wince at her poor manners.

Vedirioi considered the question.

'Nothing,' he said. 'Nothing happened. There was a city, and noise and hurry and change. And then it all gave way to... nothing.'

'What can it have been?' asked Susan. 'Do you know, Grandfather?'

'I don't, my dear,' he said. His eyes were focused on the distant buildings. 'I simply don't have any inkling.'

But he refused to return her questioning gaze.

Next Episode: The Dying World

Available now...

SHORT TRIPS:
FAREWELLS

A short-story collection edited by
JACQUELINE RAYNER

ISBN 1–84435-151-3

'After all, who knows, if I go down well, I might
even make it my farewell performance.'

Sometimes it's easy to say goodbye – to a friend, to a way of life,
to a lover. Sometimes it's heartbreaking. And sometimes they just
won't take the hint.

Say hello to 14 stories of goodbyes, as the Fourth Doctor contemplates
his mortality after a funeral; a young man goes to murderous lengths to
stop Jo Grant from leaving him; the First Doctor considers his flight
from Gallifrey; the Fifth Doctor desperately tries to get rid of an
unwanted companion – and more.

*Featuring stories by Paul Magrs, Steve Lyons,
Steven A. Roman, Joseph Lidster and many more.*

Available now...

SHORT TRIPS:
THE HISTORY OF CHRISTMAS

A short-story collection edited by
SIMON GUERRIER

ISBN 1–84435-149-1

Christmas is a time for many things. For family and old acquaintances.
For giving, for receiving, for feasts and celebration. For huddling round
the warmth of the fire, sheltered from the dark and the cold outside.

And the monsters.

It's also the busiest time of year for the mysterious Doctor, whether he's
caught up in the violence of ancient Rome, taking Leonardo da Vinci on
a day trip to the stars, or popping in on the very first Christmas
on the Moon.

Spend Christmas with the Doctor. If you dare.

*Featuring stories by Marc Platt, Jonathan Clements,
Eddie Robson, Joseph Lidster and many more!*

DOCTOR™ WHO

SHORT TRIPS

A series of short-story anthologies featuring contributions from many of Doctor Who's most popular authors from the worlds of television, print, comics and audio, as well as new talent and fresh voices – including Robert Shearman, Paul Cornell, Gareth Roberts, Gary Russell, Eric Saward, Marc Platt, Ben Aaronovitch, Andrew Cartmel, Terrance Dicks, Glen McCoy, Justin Richards, Stephen Cole, Jacqueline Rayner, Steve Lyons, Nicholas Briggs, Steven Savile, Steven A. Roman, Paul Magrs, Dan Abnett, Matthew Sweet, Stel Pavlou, Rebecca Levene, Nev Fountain, Lawrence Miles, Juliet E. McKenna, Simon Guerrier, Joseph Lidster, Lizzie Hopley, L. J. Scott, James Swallow and many, many more...

ALSO AVAILABLE...

Zodiac
edited by Jacqueline Rayner
(ISBN 1-84435-006-1)
Companions
edited by Jacqueline Rayner
(ISBN 1-84435-007-X)
A Universe of Terrors
edited by John Binns
(ISBN 1-84435-008-8)
The Muses
edited by Jacqueline Rayner
(ISBN 1-84435-009-6)
Steel Skies
edited by John Binns
(ISBN 1-84435-045-2)
Past Tense
edited by Ian Farrington
(ISBN 1-84435-046-0)
Life Science
edited by John Binns
(ISBN 1-84435-047-9)

Repercussions
edited by Gary Russell
(ISBN 1-84435-048-7)
Monsters
edited by Ian Farrington
(ISBN 1-84435-110-6)
2040
edited by John Binns
(ISBN 1-84435-111-4)
A Christmas Treasury
edited by Paul Cornell
(ISBN 1-84435-112-2)
Seven Deadly Sins
edited by David Bailey
(ISBN 1-84435-146-7)
A Day in the Life
edited by Ian Farrington
(ISBN 1-84435-147-5)
The Solar System
edited by Gary Russell
(ISBN 1-84435-148-3)